I0639554

Bedeviled

BOOK FOUR OF THE GWEN ST. JAMES AFFAIR

NICOLE MCKEON

TOWER ROOM PUBLISHING

Copyright © 2023 by Nicole McKeon

All rights reserved. Published in the United States by Tower Room Publishing.

Book Cover Copyright © 2023 by Elena Nedeleva

This is a work of fiction. Names, characters, businesses, places, events, locales, and inci-
dents are either the products of the author's imagination or used in a fictitious manner.
Any resemblance to actual persons, living or dead, or actual events is purely coincidental.
No portion of this book may be reproduced in any form without written permission
from the publisher or author, except as permitted by U.S. copyright law.

www.towerroompublishing.com

Contents

Content Notice

MAY CONTAIN MILD SPOILERS

B edeviled was written for adults and contains themes, language, and content not suitable for every reader. Please read the content warnings below and protect your mental and emotional health. These warnings are not exhaustive and may not cover all triggering content.

- Violence including:

  - Gun violence

  - Decapitation

  - Torture

  - Fire injury and death

- Death, including implied vehicle death

- Animal injury

- Graphic sexual content

    - If you'd like to avoid these scenes, please see the content warning with chapter list at https://nicoleyork.com/bedeviled

- Fire injuries

- Swearing

- Grief and dissociation

Pronunciation Guide

BOLDED SECTIONS INDICATE WHICH SYLLABLE IS EMPHASIZED

1. <u>Aris:</u> **Ah**-riss

2. <u>Ophelia:</u> Oh-**feel**-leah

3. <u>Delilah:</u> Duh-**lie**-luh

4. <u>Fleur:</u> Fl-uh-r

5. <u>Obyrron:</u> **Oh**-buh-rohn

6. <u>Geis:</u> **geh**-sh

7. <u>Cyrus:</u> Sigh-russ

8. <u>Aes Sidhe:</u> Ay-s Shee

9. <u>Grimoire:</u> Grim-**wahr**

To Mr. Stan Smith
You made me fall in love with writing as an art form. Every student deserves an English Teacher like you.
Your influence lives in every word I write.

Room 212 for life.

And to Frank Booker
Every author, every person, deserves a friend and cheerleader like you.

1

Playing Hero

ARIS

A ris perched on the chimney and watched the light fade
from the rooftops and spires of New London, waiting
for his prey to creep through the darkening streets. The last
rays of the setting sun turned the forest of chimney smoke and
industrial steam into golden pillars that held up the sky.

When the sun winked out beneath the skyline, he spotted
her, weaving through the labyrinthine streets like a ferret in a
warren. Aris flexed his claws, then launched himself into the air,
tucked his wings in tight, and plummeted below the rooftops
like a falling stone.

It was time to hunt.

His wings snapped open and he twisted, banking around the
side of a brick building as the updraft lifted him above the bottom
row of windows. She shot across the side street in front of him,

the brass rim of her goggles reflecting the electric lamplight just coming to life on the main thoroughfare.

With a few pumps of his wings, Aris rose high enough to follow as she took a sharp right turn to parallel Main Street, keeping to the shadows to hide the wheeled boots that powered her down the alley. Candles and lamps flickered to life in the windows below him as the twilight glow of the clouds faded into night.

She slowed, cutting the power to her wheels, which retracted far enough to let her heels hit the ground with a soft thud. That meant she wasn't going much farther, so he could catch up if he cut her off at the next intersection. Flexing his claws in antici-pation, Aris sailed into the next alley, dropped to about six feet from the dirty cobbles, and shimmered into his human glamour.

He hit the stone silently just before the intersection of the alley and cross-street, next to the dented door of a boarding house. With a quick snap, he straightened the lapel of his black jacket, grinned, and turned the corner.

She nearly ran into him, squeaked in surprise, and leveled a pistol at his chest before he could blink. With the huge goggles obscuring half of her face and her hair wild from the speed of her wheeled boots, she looked absolutely adorable.

What this situation called for was an expression of shocked dismay that was one or two degrees too ridiculous to be serious.

He raised both hands and said in a low voice, "Why, Lady St. James! Threats of violence against someone who is only here to help? I'm shocked at you. Shocked. What would your mother say?"

Growling, she dropped the pistol, pushed her goggles onto her forehead, and glared at him. "She would say that I am well within my rights to shoot you, you interfering corvid. The prospect gets more tempting the longer you stand before me."

He tsked. "Manners, my lady, manners."

"Why must you sneak up on me at every opportunity?"

The woman did not know her appeal when she was a disheveled, irritated mess. He closed the distance between them with one smooth step, bringing his chest nearly into contact with hers, and stared down at her, knowing she'd rather die than retreat an inch. It made teasing her so unfairly easy.

With one finger, he touched the space between her brows where the wrinkle from her scowl was deepest. "For this expression, right here. It is unbearably adorable."

His proximity made her react as it always did: her pupils dilated and her breath caught, heart speeding audibly. But she got the better of that reaction, letting her instinctive passion morph into anger.

Gwenevere St. James had a temper she rarely showed the people who loved her, but Aris was particularly good at kindling it. He ought to be, having known her so long. Pretending to be a pet raven for years had given him unique insights into her life, and an honest understanding of her character that not even a partner could match...which meant he knew every button to push.

And if triggering her temper kept her from deteriorating into the maudlin mess she had been for the past several months, he was more than happy to be on the receiving end of her ire.

Moving faster than any mere human, she grabbed his finger, executed a move he was unfamiliar with, and turned his wrist into something she called a joint lock.

"Gwen," he said, reasonably. "That hurts."

"Do all faeries lie as prettily as you?" she asked, letting go of him to stuff her goggles into the leather satchel she wore across her torso. They left red marks around her eyes. Rather like a raccoon. "Or have you cultivated that skill on your own?"

"Faeries cannot lie, you know that."

"I wonder. Perhaps you have lived too long among humans."

"There is no question of that. You have thoroughly corrupted me."

With a few deft motions, Gwen tucked her brown curls into something resembling an acceptable hairstyle and made herself presentable. Or as presentable as she could be after motoring around the New London streets on a piece of wheeled artifice. He plucked a stray leaf from the top of her head.

She waved him off and bent to secure the wheels of the foot rig to the clamps on her calves. It was an ingenious bit of artifice that stored the kinetic energy of her every motion in the runes engraved along the sides and used the stored power to turn the wheels. Leaning forward released more power, and leaning backward slowed the wheels.

Using the wheels required a surprising amount of skill and often resulted in the rider landing on their arse. Watching Gwen master the tricky device had been one of the more enjoyable experiences of his life.

The contraption was built to fit over her boots and hid nicely beneath the hem of her enchanted coat. So aside from the lack of hat and gloves, she was, at least, moderately presentable. Not that it would make much of a difference to the person they were about to ambush.

"Corrupt or not," Gwen said, glaring at him from the corner of her eye, "you will behave yourself. If you intimidate her into hiding, I will not forgive you."

Aris held up both hands to show his innocent intentions, plucked a pigeon feather from her hair when she wasn't looking, and followed Gwen to the middle of the next street. They stopped in front of a door that was rather nice for the neighborhood and knocked three times.

When it opened, a small elf woman peeked out. A pair of wide eyes peered at them from a round-cheeked face, and her dimpled chin waggled uncertainly as she tried to decide whether to ask them what they wanted or slam the door in their faces.

"You must be Miss Heatherbloom," Gwen said. Her voice was gentle and disarming, which had an immediate effect on the smaller woman.

"I am. What can I do for you?"

"My name is Lady St. James, and this is my friend, Mr. Crow. Our mutual friend, Mr. Bywater, suggested we might visit you. He said you are the finest taxidermist in the city, and that the birds you provide always look the most lifelike on ladies' hats."

Miss Heatherbloom's tan cheeks turned a dusky rose color with pleasure, and she tucked a stray lock of hair behind one pointed ear. "It's very kind of him to say so. He is the most talented milliner

in the city, so it is an honor to work with him. But it is getting
a bit late and, well"—she searched the street behind them with
worried eyes—"given the state of things, I'm sure you'll understand that accepting visitors—"

"Of course, we understand. These are frightening times. But
if we might leave you with this?" Gwen held out a pamphlet for
S&P Investigations, Inc.

Miss Heatherbloom took it carefully, glanced at the cover,
and said, "I'm afraid I don't need any help solving magical
mysteries, thank you."

Gwen was not put off so easily. These conversations always
got tricky at this point. Aris prepared himself for a quick
demonstration.

"Given your circumstances, I understand you may not feel
safe trusting anyone. But please know that we are here to help,
should you find you need it. Refugees from the Sunset Lands
are always welcome."

Miss Heatherbloom's mouth popped open. Her fingers
tightened on the pamphlet until it crumpled, and she went as
still as a hare hiding from foxes. Poor thing.

With a shaking voice, she said, "I'm sure I have no idea what
you are—"

Aris interrupted her by shifting into his raven form. It took
no more than an act of will, and his human glamour disappeared. He landed on Gwen's shoulder in his raven form to give
the woman a friendly croak. She blinked, all the color drained
from her face, and Gwen leaped forward to catch her before she
fainted.

"Was that really necessary?" she demanded as she lowered the limp woman into a sitting position on the floor of her foyer. He leaped off Gwen's shoulder and shifted back to his human glamour to help. Miss Heatherbloom was a solid little thing, heavier than she looked, which meant she was also likely larger in her true form.

While she was unconscious, her glamour slipped, revealing traces of the faerie beneath. Maintaining a glamour took an act of will, and while only those with years of experience could create a glamour that lasted through even a few hours of sleep, fainting was a different story.

"She's relatively young," Aris said as he began fanning her. "Wake her quickly, or the glamour will fade and she'll be even more terrified than she already is."

Gwen pulled smelling salts from her satchel and swiped them beneath the woman's nose. She snorted, her body spasmed, and her eyes popped open. With a squeak, her glamour solidified, and she tried to scoot away.

Gwen let the woman go and held up her hands. "I am so sorry we frightened you. It was not my intention. I simply wanted you to know that we understand, and you have a safe place, should you need it."

Miss Heatherbloom scrambled to her feet, regained her bearing, cleared her throat, and said, "Your visit was most appreciated but I have quite a lot of work to do so, if you don't mind, I'll have to ask you to leave." She bravely shoved them into the night before slamming the door in their faces.

They stood there for a moment, listening to several locks click into place.

Aris said, "Mr. Crow? Really?"

"You are the one who insists on coming along for these little visits. If you'd like a better pseudonym, you are free to make one up yourself."

"Perhaps I shall. We couldn't do much worse. Though she still had the pamphlet in her hand."

The last fae refugee they visited had thrown the crumpled paper in his face.

Gwen sighed. "I doubt she will be able to read it after crushing it so."

"She knows she is not alone now. That is the important part."

And they would be able to warn her when King Obyrron eventually invaded with fae armies at his back. Whenever that might be. It had been over six months since he and Gwen escaped the Sunset Lands after stealing Gwen's sister, Ophelia, back from the fae king. Which meant likely only two weeks had passed in faerie time, as mortals reckoned it.

That wasn't long enough for the faeries to adjust their invasion plans after losing their general. At least, they could hope so. But Ophelia, the general in question, still would not speak to her sister, so they could not be certain. Whether they could call on the hidden fae to fight when the king invaded was another story.

She glanced at the door one last time and squared her shoulders. "Perhaps she would have given us a warmer welcome if you had not gone avian on the poor woman."

"We've had little luck either way. Best to make things clear quickly. At least then you have the rest of the night to run about being a hero."

"If you do not like it," Gwen said as she hopped down the stairs, "you can fly home and play chess with Samuel."

"He beats me too often, these days. I do have my pride, you know. Besides, who will be here to rescue you if I leave?"

She sniffed. "I do not need rescuing."

"If you keep fighting monsters, you will."

"No one else is protecting these people," she snarled, suddenly angry. "Scotland Yard has neither the knowledge or the manpower to make a difference, and they refuse to consult me despite the obviously supernatural nature of the murders and disappearances. They are convinced Jack the Ripper has resurfaced, the fools.

"Tony's agency is the only one that can recognize the truth of the situation, but he is still so understaffed that he cannot do much good. The witches refuse to tell me what they are doing to help, and the government turns a blind eye despite all my warnings.

"Aside from all that, this is the only—" She swallowed the last words, took a deep breath, and shook her head.

"And it is the only thing that makes you feel alive," he finished.

Gwen made a sound that meant *I hate it that you know that about me*, then bent to unstrap her wheels and lock them in the down position. Once she settled the goggles back over her eyes, she said, "If you want to help, float about and signal me if you see any ne'er-do-wells. If you'd rather irritate me with that clever tongue of yours, you can fly home."

"I could think of a few other things to do with my tongue if you'd like," he said before he could stop himself.

A vision of Gwen as he had seen her in faerie, stretched out beneath him with her dark hair spread on the moss around their naked bodies, flashed across his memory, making him hard in a rush. Luckily, his glamour could easily hide that, but he doubted she'd missed it.

Gwenevere St. James did not miss much.

She leaned toward him, bathing him in her scent, and said, in a low voice, "What I would really like you to do with your tongue is bite it off."

Then she rocked onto the wheels and rolled into the darkness at unsafe speeds. Aris swore and leaped, shimmering to his raven form at the height of his jump, and pumped his wings until he was high enough to spot her. He could not smile as a raven, but his amusement bubbled up into a series of caws that made Gwen shake her head.

He would take her angry, frustrated, cutting, or sarcastic, so long as she was passionate and alive. But Ophelia had not forgiven Gwen for dragging her back to the mortal world. Adjusting to the change hadn't been easy for Lia, and the joyful reunion Gwen dreamed about for a dozen years had turned into a source of constant pain. For weeks she had put on a brave face, smiling and laughing for the benefit of Sam and Sally...but then she would do almost anything to protect her young wards.

In the quiet hours of the evening, however, when she was alone, she sat unblinking before the fire, lifeless as the mannequins in Percy's shop. Now and then he found her curled on the floor, unresponsive.

When he'd been trapped in his raven form as Aristotle, he wanted nothing more than to carry her to her bed on the nights she worked herself to sleep in the study. Now that she knew what he truly was, he could finally carry her safely to her room, but that did not stop the gut-deep sensation of falling he felt every time he saw her suffer. It was the same sensation he felt when the air went flat beneath his wings and he dropped without warning.

Watching the woman who had always seemed more alive than anyone else fade like the pages of the old books she read was something worse than heartbreaking.

Then Tony Hardwicke, the former inspector for Scotland Yard, had started his agency. He called upon her to consult on a case and a little life returned. But those cases had been few and far between in the first couple of months. She hadn't come fully back to life until the monsters invaded New London.

Movement caught his eye, cutting off that thought. It was just a simple shift in the shadows between a bakery and a rundown public house, but to the eyes of a fae raven, it was enough.

Aris shifted his wings, gliding above the shape that slunk across the alley and croaked three times. Gwen slowed, oriented on him, and raised a hand. He shifted his wings twice, and she pulled the pistol with silver bullets from her pocket. She was two streets over to the south, but the werewolf raised its head and scented the air, picking up the smell of her fear. The creature shivered as if the scent was a physical pleasure.

Then it began stalking her.

Aris stayed above it, giving Gwen a marker to follow, keeping his eyes on both predator and prey. She disengaged the wheels, produced a silver knife in her free hand, and crept toward the cross street on silent feet. If she was careful, she could cut the wolf off and shoot it before it attacked.

Of course, he would have to carry the body out of town under a glamour, which was both tiring and irritating. But better than leaving what would appear to be a dead mortal on the street.

If the creatures remained in their wolf shape after death, his role would be much easier. But it had been so long since monsters were common in large cities that the old method of identifying magical creatures, like tying wolfsbane around the wrist or ankle of the dead werewolf, would mean nothing to the citizens or constables.

Instead of being heroes for ridding the city of a dangerous monster, they would be considered murderers.

The wolf stopped, raised its head with ears erect, and turned its muzzle east. Aris did not hear as well when in raven form, but he saw clearly. A dwarven man plodded down the main street in his soot-stained overalls, likely returning from his shift at the ironworks. Light reflected from the steel toes of his boots, and the rhythmic thud of his steps echoed off the buildings. He did not know what danger waited nearby.

The beast growled a low warning rumble meant to protect his hunt from other predators, but it made the dwarven man freeze. It wasn't the growl of a stray dog anyone might hear on any given night; it was the vicious hunger of something unnatural, something that enjoyed the scent and taste of fear almost as much as the kill itself.

Damn.

Aris cawed and dropped his head in warning, but it was too late.

The dwarven man spun in a slow circle, searching the shadows for danger as he pulled a heavy mallet off his shoulder. At least he was armed. Gwen's fear wasn't strong enough to keep the wolf on the hunt, not when the scent and sound of more terrified prey leached through the air.

Aris had a split-second to decide whether to stay aloft so he could monitor everything, or drop to the ground to put himself between the beast and its victim. The wolf sprang into a run. Gwen rounded the corner with her pistol raised, and Aris dropped from the sky, shimmering as he fell.

He hit the ground as she fired the first shot and spun to see the werewolf's tail disappear around the corner; her shot sent chunks of brick flying from the building across from them.

Gwen swore, kicked her wheels down, and leaped forward.

"Two streets to the south!" Aris yelled as he sprinted after her.

Gwen's wheeled boots were fast, but the werewolf had a head start. By the time they reached the street, the beast was already circling the dwarven man, snarling and frothing in a display meant to heighten the fear to a fever pitch. The bulky man held his mallet at the ready, prepared to swing, his arm muscles bulging. And while his hands did not shake, even Aris scented the fear and adrenaline polluting the air.

"Get me a clean shot," Gwen said, leveling her pistol.

The wolf was relatively small for its kind, but still nearly reached Aris's waist at the shoulder, making the burly dwarf look childlike by comparison. It was smart enough to keep the dwarven man between them, pacing back and forth so that Gwen would not have a clear shot. But the smell of fear must have been driving it mad because it quivered with anticipation and great gobbets of slobber dropped to the ground with audible splats.

He needed to move before the wolf sprang, or the dwarf would likely be dead even if Gwen managed to squeeze off a shot. So, Aris edged closer, not even pausing when the werewolf turned toward him and snapped.

"Brace yourself," he warned the man, then coiled and leaped in a smooth motion.

He hit the dwarven man, wrapped his arms around his barrel chest, and turned as he fell, taking the impact on his back and shoulders. The weight of the dwarf drove the air from his lungs as they hit the street.

Gwen opened fire, but the wolf had already leaped, and rock chips skipped off the cobbles where the beast had been. It landed and sprang forward at an angle, aiming at the dwarf's exposed back. Aris raised his legs, planted his feet on the monster's massive chest, and pushed. The creature sailed over his head, the gun barked again, and the werewolf yelped in pain before it hit the ground.

Long claws scrabbled against the cobbles as the beast righted itself, filling the air with scraping and deep-throated growls tinged with a sharp edge of pain. It didn't wait for Gwen to fire another shot, it simply attacked.

Fear squeezed an iron fist around his heart as the beast tore toward her, but Gwen did not flinch. She sighted down the barrel and pulled the trigger once, twice more, aiming as cooly as a veteran soldier. But the monster did not stop.

Gwen tried to leap aside, but the beast hit her in mid-air. The two of them spun sideways, going down in a tangle of limbs and fur, claws, and teeth.

2

Office Work

GWEN

If there were any valuable lessons to be learned while slaying magical monsters, the most important was this: if one must stroll through town covered in blood, viscera, and werewolf hair, one should always do so at night. Had I any reputation worth maintaining, one sight of me would have ruined it. As the situation stood, however, I wheeled my sweat-soaked, wolf-pelt-smelling, tangle-haired, cracked-goggled self toward the agency under the cover of darkness in relative peace and quiet.

At least, if doing anything with Aristotle could be considered peaceful. Or quiet.

"You could have helped me dispose of the body," he said reproachfully after flying to my side as a raven and shimmering into his human form. Of course, Aristotle, or Aris, as I had begun to think of him, was not human; he was Aos Sidhe, one of the most powerful orders of faeries from the Sunset Lands.

His ability to become a raven allowed him to live in my household in secret for the last several years, but when we were pulled into the Sunset Lands through a badly mishandled spell, he revealed his true nature.

For which I still had not fully forgiven him.

"I could have," I agreed, "but you were doing so well on your own."

He snorted.

Killing a slavering werewolf who hunted innocent mortals was one thing, but werewolves shifted back to their mortal forms after death, and carrying off the body of a dead human was another matter entirely. Particularly when that body belonged to someone so young. It had taken all of my self-control not to vomit.

"You know," Aris began, "we don't have to go to the agency and wake Tony. We could simply go home, and I could help you clean off"—he waved his hand in my direction—"all of that."

"The agency is closer. I keep a change of clothes there, and I promised to notify Tony of any kills as soon as possible."

"I doubt he intended you to wake him at midnight to do so."

"That's part of the fun, my dear raven."

"I could carry you home, anyway," he threatened.

"Only if you'd like a black eye. You cannot avoid Tony forever, you coward."

"Cowardice has no part in it. I simply dislike the man. He is far too sanctimonious for my taste."

"And you are too much a scoundrel for his."

"A scoundrel?" he asked, one hand pressed to his chest in mock outrage.

"As if you do not do your best to convince him of it every time the two of you are in company."

"There are several things I would like to convince him of," he muttered.

"So long as you keep your hands to yourself, you are welcome to try."

"I have given up the effort. The man is nearly as pigheaded as you are, my lady."

"I shall remember that statement the next time you try to slip into my bed."

"I take it all back. I spoke in haste. He is a charming fellow and you are the very soul of reasonable, well-bred gentility."

"Your compliments are more unpleasant than your insults."

"There is no winning with you."

I grinned and picked up the pace as we rounded the corner to see the sign for Supernatural and Paranormal Investigations, Incorporated rocking in the breeze. Tony had given me a key shortly after opening the agency, so I dug it out of an interior pocket that was blessedly free of werewolf goo and let us in through the front door.

SPI was founded early this year when my mother, the Duchess of Wainwright, hired Tony to find my sister and I. Little did she know when offering to bankroll the project that Aris, Lia, and I were already running for the rift that would let us through the magical barrier separating the Sunset Lands from the mortal world.

We had as much as appeared in Tony's lap while he searched the forest. SPI's first successful case. And since Scotland Yard fired him for helping me, this seemed suitable compensation. Aside from that, he was the only investigator in town who knew anything useful about magic.

Once most major cities outlawed witches, and the Industrial Revolution made powerful weapons available to mortals, magic and monsters retreated to remote areas. Modern people trusted artificery and chemistry and biology, but not alchemy.

They believed in unicorns because one might see them in a zoo, but not werewolves or vampires, let alone faeries. They considered those creatures nothing more than rustic superstition, which made our current situation rather difficult, and explained why I was out hunting monsters when I should probably have been in bed...and *not* in bed with Aris.

His hand curled around my arm just before a low, dangerous voice said out of the darkness, "Don't move."

"It's me, Tony," I said.

A moment later, a light flickered on and the room sprang into view. Tony stood at the foot of the stairs with a pistol in one hand and an oil lamp in the other. The light threw interesting shadows across his bare, rather impressively muscled torso.

"Gwen? What happened to your—never mind. Tell me after you get cleaned up."

"I will do that. As soon as you lower your pistol."

He looked at his hand, surprised to find the gun still in it. "Sorry. If you'd bother ringing the doorbellime, maybe I won't wake up thinking the place is being robbed."

"And announce my presence to everyone in the neighborhood? I think not."

"Suit yourself. If you enjoy being held at gunpoint, that is your prerogative, I suppose."

I scowled at him, then transferred the scowl to Aris. "I am going to clean up. Don't kill each other."

"I make no such promise," Aris said, raising his nose in disdain.

The agency had been an apartment building in its past life, so the downstairs water closet was more than suitable for washing up and changing clothes. I kept a spare set in the cabinet, and it didn't take me long to achieve a marginally presentable state. More importantly, my skin stopped crawling at the feeling of that boy's blood drying on my arms and shoulders.

He had been no older than Sally.

I promised myself I would take a full bath at home, no matter how late I returned, and dropped my bloodied clothing into a burlap sack. Mrs. Chapman, my housekeeper, had gotten incredibly good at removing blood stains over the last three weeks.

After braiding my hair, I returned to the front office to find Tony and Aris glaring daggers at one another. Tension electrified the air, as if every flammable substance in the room might burst into flame at any moment.

The idea of them fighting was more than a little intimidating. Tony was a dangerous man on nearly all counts: smart, fast, and a trained pugilist. He was broader across the shoulders than Aris and heavy with muscle.

But Aris was a fae assassin, and dangerous in a way I rarely encountered. Not only were faeries faster and stronger than humans, but distinctly more ruthless. Tony had scruples and the restraint to follow them.

Aris did not.

The only way to break the face-off safely was melodrama of the grandest variety. That would make both men feel ridiculous, diffuse the situation, and appease my sense of humor at the same time.

So, in the grand tradition of the theatre, I clutched my chest as if my heart were about to give out and cried, "Did I miss the ego-measuring contest?"

To my great satisfaction, my voice carried such exaggerated disappointment it could have choked the entire cast of an American Vaudeville show. "Wait, do it again and I promise to be impressed." I sat on a rolling chair, folded my hands in my lap, and stared at the two of them with wide, disingenuous eyes.

The effect was something like letting the air out of a balloon.

Tony broke eye contact, set the lantern on the desk, and chose a chair to flop into. A year ago, he would have considered being bare-chested in my presence scandalous, but the man had been thoroughly corrupted. Or, more likely, my preference for familiarity had worn down his sense of propriety like waves breaking against the seashore.

He ignored Aris, who muttered something about putting a shirt on, and said, "I assume you woke me in the middle of the night to explain why you were covered in blood?"

"After passing out yet another unsuccessful leaflet to a faerie refugee, we spotted a werewolf. It attacked. I shot it, but not before it landed on me. Aris discarded the body outside the city."

Tony gestured to a stack of paper on the table. "Write a description of the body and where you hid it."

"I take it the Yard will receive another anonymous tip?"

Tony shrugged one shoulder. "It's the best we can do for now. Bloody hell, I'm so tired. Mortals won't believe they are in danger from the supernatural, and the supernatural refuses to believe us because we are mortals."

"It is a conundrum," I sighed.

After learning of King Obyrron's plan to invade, I made it my job to warn fae refugees hiding in the city. We tracked them home, waited till it was safe, and approached them in as unthreatening a manner as possible. But their positions were too precarious for easy trust. Most either ignored us or pretended they didn't understand. It was disheartening in the extreme.

Tony sighed and rubbed a hand over his face. "They will never believe us, will they?"

"Not without proof," Aris put in as his pen scratched across the paper. "Most of them have been living here as mortals for so many years they've grown comfortable. Frankly, they have more to lose by believing us than they do by ignoring us."

"Until the fae invade," Tony said.

"At least then, they'll know where to go," I reminded him.

"As long as they're still alive."

"What does that mean? Their glamour protects them from other fae just as well as it does from humans. That's why these are so handy," I said, lifting my goggles. Nearly a year ago I found a hag stone while searching for a lost fae housekeeper. A wise woman told me it would show me the truth, but I had not expected the hole in the middle of the stone to allow me to see through faerie glamour.

Delilah fitted the stone into a pair of goggles that had helped me find, and warn, faeries hiding in the city. Of course, I was very careful not to look at Aris too long while wearing them, because the glamour he used, while much more subtle, protected those around him from his power to influence mortals.

When we were trapped in the Sunset Lands, he let me see him without his glamour to warn me of the danger faeries presented to humans. His presence had been so overwhelming I'd nearly thrown myself at him out of pure desire.

Tony said, "Their glamour doesn't appear to protect them from the monsters hunting the city. Nearly a third of the missing victims so far have been fae."

I sat up straighter in my chair. We had been warning faerie refugees about the potential invasion for at least two months, and Tony kept records of each one I visited in a safe only he could open. But monsters had only been terrorizing the city for three weeks, and I was certain there were still far more refugees in the city than I knew of. "You know this from our records?"

"We only realized the correlation this morning, and only because the name of the missing person was so distinctive."

My stomach dropped. "Not Mr. Rumstumbler?"

"We checked the report in the paper this morning against the files. At least thirty percent of all the reported missing and dead match names from our list."

"That is statistically improbable," I said.

"It's true, nonetheless. The only conclusion I can draw is that the monsters are hunting faeries specifically."

I sat back, mind spinning. "Werewolves don't have preferences. They hunt fear. It is almost like an aphrodisiac. Unless they are defending themselves, they will always hunt the strongest smell of fear."

"Werewolves aren't the only monsters in the city," Aris reminded me. "They're simply the ones most likely to leave bodies behind."

"What about vampires?" Tony asked.

"They are as conscious as you or I which, I suppose, means they might have preferences. But I have read nothing to verify it in my studies. I'll ring Alix tomorrow and ask her, or Doctor Hesselius."

"It is handy having a half-vampire on retainer," Aris said.

"It's expensive, too."

"Do faeries lose their glamour when they die?" Tony asked.

Aris sent me a glance that reminded me of a small child asking *do I have to?* before saying, "Glamour requires the will, so yes, it fades over time without a will to sustain it. How long depends upon the age and strength of the will behind it."

"Then it is safe to say Scotland Yard must have their hands on at least a few corpses they cannot account for."

"Only if the dead fae do not appear similar to mortal races. If I die, I won't look much different from a human. But if there are selkies or nymphs?"

The three of us sat in silence as we thought over the implications of the Metropolitan Police knowing that humans, elves, and dwarves were not the only races living in New London.

The fae had been gone from the mortal world for so long that, as far as anyone was concerned, they were mere legends. Pixies still inhabited forests and thriving gardens, but they were nature spirits, not creatures of magic.

If the general population knew the fae still lived among us, albeit in extremely small numbers, how would they respond? And what would the police force do with such knowledge?

"What is to be done, then?" Tony asked the room at large.

"Personally," Aris said, "I would like a nap and something to eat. A couple of fingers of whisky would not be amiss, either."

Tony glared at him.

"I don't know that there is much to do until we have more information," I said. "We need to know which monsters are in the city, and how they hunt. Hopefully, Alix will have some insight. I have more theoretical than practical knowledge, and no one has killed as many monsters as she and Cyrus."

"What about our meeting?" Tony asked.

"We can hope, but to be honest, I don't know what to expect."

Aris raised one black brow. "From a bunch of politicians? You can expect whatever is most convenient to them remaining in power, not what is best or safest for the people of New London. Especially now that the legislation for equal representation has passed. Everyone will scramble to secure their positions and consolidate power."

The three of us exchanged glances, and I could not ignore a sense of helplessness. Fifteen people found dead in three weeks, and we had not a single accurate lead on why monsters were suddenly converging on New London. Scotland Yard was flummoxed, we were understaffed, and the threat of invasion from a source most people did not believe existed loomed in the background.

"Well, there is nothing to be done about it tonight," Tony said, standing up. "Best to get home and sleep."

The subtle emphasis on the word *sleep* almost made me blush, but not quite. It was no secret amongst our intimate acquaintance that Aris lived with Sam, Sally, and myself, and though we did not share a bedroom, that did not mean we had never shared a bed.

I turned to Aris for comfort when were trapped in the Sunset Lands, and while we were together only once, the experience was burned into my very bones. It was best not to think about it overmuch or I would be tempted to repeat the performance.

I had no intention of knocking on his door in the middle of the night and complicating our already labyrinthine relationship. And Tony never missed an opportunity to caution me against such escapades.

Aris shifted his weight to one leg and folded his arms over his chest, letting his glamour slip and turning his gaze on Tony. Not even the staid former inspector was immune to the ridiculous draw of his influence, or the sheer beauty of form he enjoyed.

Like all fae, he was something more perfect, more proportional, more elegant, and purposeful than any mere mortal. So, when he did not bother hiding behind a glamour to appear human, it was nearly impossible not to desire doing anything in one's power to make him happy, make him proud...make him want you.

Tony stiffened in resistance, glaring furiously. While Aris would never use the advantage of his fae form, it amused him to let Tony think he would.

"Yes, Gwen," he said in a lazy voice, "best we get home and get you into bed."

I pointed a finger at Aris. "Stop it. That's cheating, and it's beneath you."

He raised both hands in feigned innocence. "What did I say?"

I pushed him down the aisle of desks and out the front door, Tony at my heels.

He stepped into the moonlight and sighed. "Very well. I can see where I'm not wanted. I'll just—" He jumped, shimmered, and took flight, cawing with mirth.

"I don't think I shall ever get used to that," Tony said, watching Aris circle overhead.

"It is rather unnerving," I agreed.

He put one warm hand on my shoulder. "What is unnerving is seeing you at midnight covered in blood and other assorted viscera. You are taking too many chances, Gwen."

Why did people keep saying that to me?

"Who else can take them? Besides"—I held up my bag—"I have all these gadgets and contraptions to keep me safe."

He grabbed my chin and turned my head sideways, eyeing my face in the dim lantern light. "They didn't protect you from this." He ran a thumb gently over my cheek where it had scraped against the cobbles.

I took his hand, pressed it, and gave him what smile I could manage. "I'll heal."

"This time."

"What would you have me do? Ignore the danger and allow monsters to roam the streets?"

He let go of my hand and took a deep breath. "Just be more careful. You didn't see...Sam and Sally..." He looked down, hands clenched at his sides. "You didn't see their faces when they thought you were gone. I can't do that to them again."

I took his face between my hands, trying to let my affection for him show without promising anything more. Our past was complicated, and the last six months had not made it any less challenging to navigate. How does one treat a person they love but cannot, or will not, commit to?

So I simply said, "You won't have to. I promise," then headed off into the dark with Aris sailing overhead.

After a block, he flew down to land on my shoulder, and the contact was so familiar that my eyes stung. When Aristotle revealed himself as fae and not just a raven, I lost my closest friend. What we were to one another now was a subject even more confusing than my relationship with Tony.

Were we still friends? Something more, or less than that?

"You had better hope we do not run into any more monsters, my lady," Aris said. His voice was strangely modulated as a raven. "You are not wearing your magic coat."

He was right, yet I could not regret it. My jacket was thick and warm and, thanks to the runes embroidered on it, provided as much protection as a suit of plate armor. But it was stifling. The thin blouse was much more suited to the humid air of a summer evening. If the city was not infested with monsters, it would have been a lovely time for a walk. Even the scent of the Thames had died down and the air only smelled of coal smoke and yeast, thanks to a gentle breeze that dragged clouds away from the moon.

It glowed down with a beneficent face that, despite the beauty of it, made me freeze.

"God's breath, Aris, I have been so stupid. How could we have overlooked this?"

He leaped off my shoulder and shimmered into his human form. "What do you mean?"

I pointed at the sky. The moon was waxing, a couple of days short of being full, lighting the clouds around it with cool silvery light.

"Dealing with werewolves is a dangerous business at any time. But during a full moon? It's going to be murder."

3

Getting Burned

GWEN

Artificer's Row crouched on the edge of the industrial district near the East End, covered in a perpetual cloud of colored smoke that smelled of burnt oranges. Rust and other chemicals stained the exterior of every workshop in reddish streaks trailing from the windows. The buildings looked like old, crying women wearing too much eye makeup.

I pulled back the lever to slow my auto, creeping down the much narrower streets. One never knew when a piece of artifice might get feisty and–a workshop door blew off a building two blocks down and tumbled across the street.

It crashed into the front of the opposite building with a metallic screech. Billowing clouds of green smoke poured from the open door as a dwarven man stumbled into the road, coughing and waving his hands.

"Alright?" I yelled, raising a hand.

He waved me off as he shoved his goggles up and wiped a sleeve across his soot-stained face. Workshops did not have windows along the street-side for that very reason; artificery was a hazardous job, and peppering unsuspecting clients with flying glass was a wonderful way to go out of business. At least doors could be reinforced. Most of the time.

I parked in front of the Iron Rose, stowed my driving goggles and gloves, and let myself in. Delilah Irons, the most talented artificer in New London and my longtime friend, was busy chastising one of her apprentices.

She pointed, stomped, and pointed some more as she said, "Never, under any circumstances, inscribe the symbol to activate a sentence before you've written in your release rune. What do you think will happen when all that energy flows into your kettle and has nowhere to go? Where's your head, Rolf? Did the slagging academy teach you nothing? Stow your tools. You'll be assisting Chen until you can prove you won't blow up my shop."

The apprentice in question hung their tool belt on a bolt in the wall and slunk to the back of the shop.

"A bit hard on him, weren't you?"

Delilah turned to me, her curls seeming to bristle with ire, like an irritated hedgehog. "That's the least the little fool deserved. He's lucky I don't throw his sparking backside out onto the street."

She grabbed a nearly finished tea kettle and held it up for my inspection. "Just have a look at this!"

The kettle was a pretty thing, glowing copper with a neat runic sentence inscribed around the bottom. It stored additional heat from the fire or cooktop and released it back into the water over time, so the water would not cool too quickly. A common piece of artifice one might find in any shop.

But there was no rune to limit excess heat storage. And the releasing rune that allowed extra energy to leak safely back into the air was also missing.

My brows rose as I examined it. I knew enough artifice for simple projects, and that was only thanks to my studies and friendship with Delilah. But even I saw the seriousness of young Rolf's mistake.

"He built a bomb," I said, handing the pot back.

Delilah pulled an awl from her belt and destroyed the sentence with a few deliberate scratches, then tossed it in the slag pile to be melted down.

"Come on to the back," she said, lifting the gate.

We passed the apprentices, who kept their eyes on their work and habitually avoided the Boom Room, where all of the dangerous experiments took place. After watching that heavy door tumble across the street like a leaf in the wild, I didn't blame them. The Iron Rose had fewer accidents than any of her competitors, but one could never be too careful with artificery.

And Delilah was careful. She was also competent, stubborn, and one of the scariest people I knew, despite her dwarvish height.

She once forced me to make an Iron Promise by smearing my blood on the face of a hammer and swearing to tell her only the truth. That hammer now hung on the wall in a place of honor. It hadn't been used since, presumably so my head would be the first thing it crushed if I dishonored the metal by breaking my promise.

I eyed the tool as we entered the room and tried not to imagine the mess my head would make if I ever lied to Delilah Irons.

"You're here for the new gadgets?" she asked.

"Delilah, I am your friend and patron. Can I not visit simply to see how you are?"

She folded her arms and glared up at me, raising one cynical eyebrow.

"Fine," I said, "I am also here for gadgets. Anything new and fun?"

Her smirk said that's exactly what she expected. "There might be, but since I've got you here, we need to test a bit of artifice that's still in development."

My stomach tried to crawl away into my pelvis. The last time we tested a bit of artifice, I ended up dizzy for two days. "You can't test it on an apprentice?"

"I never took you for a coward, Lady St. James."

I sighed and shook my hands out to relieve the nervous energy. "Fine, so long as the potential side effects will not incapacitate me. I cannot afford to lie in bed right now, and I need to ask something of you."

"Fair enough," she said, clapping her hands and picking up a folded cloth that shook out into the most horrid piece of fashion imaginable.

Was it a coat with wide-legged trousers sewn into the bottom, or a pair of billowing overalls with sleeves? If the wearer stood still, it may be mistaken for a hideous dress.

"Percy and I have been working together on this," she explained, holding it out. "If we can get it right, it will be something like your coat, only more protective because each limb will be encased."

I stripped out of my skirt and petticoats and slid on the modified overalls. The legs were wide, much like a skirt, but the fitted bodice, sleeves, and wide lapels were distinctly coat-like. I hated it.

"Now, the purpose is to provide you with more protection and accommodate the rest of your gadgets. So, when it's finished, you'll have an updated version of your corset as well."

"You'd like me to run about fighting monsters in trousers? I've already flouted expectations, I suppose. Why not? How shall we be testing this new ensemble?"

"With fire," she said, a mischievous glint in her eye.

"I'm sorry. I don't believe I understood you."

"You most certainly did. Now stand in the empty corner and hold your arms out to the side."

I would tell her no, then turn and run. Her legs were too short to catch me. But when I opened my mouth, no sound came out. Delilah put her hands on her hips and raised a brow.

Before I could object, I stood against a wall with my arms spread as Delilah prepared to blow fire at my legs and stomach. She held the little device, a sparker made of flint and steel often used to start forges, with evident glee.

"Don't worry so much, you coward. It's been tested, just not with you in it."

I squeezed my eyes shut as I tried to sink into the overalls like a turtle into its shell, expecting every moment to be charred alive by my sadist of a best friend.

"Wait!"

I let out an explosive breath that was almost a laugh of relief. Fleur poked her head around the edge of the open door so that only her wide, canted eyes, flyaway red curls, and the tips of her elven ears were visible. She looked like a caterpillar poking its head out of a flower. Delilah's fiancée was one of my favorite people but, just now, I adored her.

"You haven't roasted Gwen yet, have you, luv?" she asked.

"I am still blessedly un-roasted, thanks to you," I said.

She pushed into the room carrying a folder and ink pen. "Good. I need a signature on a purchase order. If Delilah kills you before you sign it, we have to stop development on the secret project."

"Oh, by all means," I said, scrawling a signature on the line Fleur indicated with one delicate finger, "continue development after she fries me crispy."

She gave my arm a comforting pat. "Never fear. I'm sure it will be medium-rare at most."

"Don't get her hopes up," Delilah said as Fleur departed. Once the door was safely closed, she grinned at me. "Stand still, and try not to breathe."

"Not to bre–" I bit off the words, pinching my lips between my teeth as a gout of flame blossomed from the tip of the lighter and blew across my midsection. It felt like stuffing my torso into an oven. Tendrils of hair lifted up and away from my cheeks and neck in a blast of scalding wind. My feet even warmed through my boots and socks.

But my stomach and legs were blessedly cool.

I hesitated, then opened my right eye a slit once the heat disappeared.

"Did you feel any heat through the cloth?" Delilah asked, sounding as exhilarated as she looked.

"None."

"Ha!" She pumped one fist. "I told Percy it would work. Now peel that off so I can see the spell runes on the inside."

"Well," I said, handing her the cloth a moment later. "That was rather...exciting. Let's not do it again, anytime soon."

"At least you didn't die."

"There is that."

"Look at this," she said, patting the fabric like it was a favorite pet. "Nothing overloaded, not so much as a singed fiber."

I examined a lock of my hair. Several strands had curled up from the heat and crumbled beneath my fingertips. "I wish I could say the same for my hair."

"You've got enough to spare. The good news is, we can move forward with production."

"Lovely. Are we done trying to cook me for dinner?"

"We are. For now."

That sounded promising. "Good. What ingenious gadgets are ready for use? Preferably ones that don't require near-death experiences."

Gadgets in various stages of completion were displayed on a table along the back wall. Delilah plucked a familiar bracelet off a wooden stand and held it out.

"The Sightscreen!" I slipped the bracelet over my wrist. "That was a quick fix."

"Nothing quick about it. I made a duplicate because Percy keeps complaining about how often you destroy his lovely coats. Figured I had better be safe than sorry."

"It isn't my fault I keep getting attacked by monsters."

She grunted as if she didn't believe a word of it and pulled a gorgeous umbrella out of a wooden box. It was like the other umbrellas she crafted, with a raven's head handle and runes engraved in the shaft, but this one had a deep red canopy. Runic sentences were embroidered in gold down either side of the seams, and the threads glowed in the lamplight.

My fingers itched to touch it.

"This is the improved version of your umbrella," she said, clicking an invisible button on the shaft and pulling the blade free.

It was forged of silver and shone like liquid when she angled it toward the light. Familiar runes for strength and flexibility ran along the length of the blade, but several new symbols had been added.

"I started working on this when the monsters appeared," she said, turning to hand me the hilt. "Thought it might come in handy. It has all of the usual engravings, but I added a few new touches. See here?" She poked a curling symbol with one blunt finger. "This is from a spell to increase speed. Now, before you swing it around"—she held up one cautioning hand—"let me explain something. A mortal can only move so fast before losing the ability to predict the outcome of our actions. And our bodies can only handle so much force. If you move fast enough, you won't be able to react to changes in time to alter course or stop.

"The spell in the grimoire takes that into account; it affects the body and mind while it's active. But it's a complex spell, and replicating it through an object was too dangerous. We tried it, and I couldn't stand up for an hour afterward."

My eyes widened so far they hurt. Delilah learned a significant amount about magic over the last two years, but most of the magics we used, save for the spell on the Sightscreen, were relatively simple. This was impressive.

Then I realized what she had unintentionally given away. "Delilah, you tested it without—wait, what were you trying to cut?"

Embarrassment flamed in her cheeks. "Nothing important, that's not the point. The point is, the leftover energy not diverted to the canopy for a force blast goes into the sword. And that could be a significant amount. So, I put a limiting rune here." She pointed at a familiar symbol that was mostly right angles. "It will keep you from moving too fast. You need to know this because if this rune is damaged, don't use the sword. If you do, you'll end up stumbling around, disoriented. And that's if you don't throw your arm out."

I turned the blade so light slid across the runes. My swords were always engraved to limit damage, but not even artifice made metal impervious forever. Paying attention to scratches while fighting wouldn't be easy, but when had my life ever been easy?

"Noted," I said. "How long will the spell stay active?"

"If the umbrella is fully powered and the runes glow bright green, you'll have about 3 minutes. It's important to note that the sword must be disengaged from the umbrella for the spell to work.

Also, only the arm holding the sword will be faster, and not your whole body. You'll have to account for that with balance."

"So, challenging a werewolf to a footrace is not a good idea?"

Her brows lowered. "Please do not do that."

I snorted, both amused and insulted that my friends did not trust my common sense to help me avoid stupid endeavors. Which was, unfortunately, wise. I sheathed the sword and locked it in place before tucking the umbrella under my arm.

"Here are the rings you wanted," she said, holding out a small velvet bag. "They're all connected, so anyone wearing the ring can reach out to anyone else with an act of will."

"You made quick work of that."

"It would have taken much longer if we hadn't already bollocksed up those early communication devices."

"Failures are merely the preparatory steps toward success," I said philosophically.

"Oh, shut up."

I grinned and emptied the bag into my palm. Two small silver rings fell out, mirror images of the ring on my right forefinger...the ring Lia gave me in the Sunset Lands to help me escape. After returning to New London, I asked Delilah to study it using everything we'd learned about combining magic with artifice.

Unlike most of our other magical gadgets, which leaned hard on runic sentences to activate the magic, this one relied on the wearer's thoughts and will. There had been several memorable failures over the last six months, one involving overhearing a rather...private interaction.

After consulting Percy and Aris, who had no outward magic but understood enough of it for advice, Delilah replicated the telepathic rings. We could now communicate over vast distances.

She had carved delicate magical symbols inside the band to sit flush with the wearer's skin.

"I would still prefer a way to bind the ring to a specific wearer," I said, turning them over. "The way things stand, anyone who gets their hands on a ring can hear private conversations if they know who holds the other rings."

"Well, unless you know of a fae magician you can introduce me to, this is what you're going to get. And it was hard enough to manage this, if you'll remember."

"I am not criticizing your work," I reassured her with a hand on her shoulder. "Just wishing we had more knowledge. We discovered last night that a third of the murders in the city have been fae refugees."

Her brows rose. "That sounds unlikely, given the small number of them."

"In the extreme. But the names match my lists. And I've not contacted every refugee, so the numbers may be even higher."

"Is it possible the monsters are targeting them?"

"That's why I wish we knew more. It is us against all the monsters in New London, with no idea how they are getting into the city in such numbers, how they remain hidden, or what brought them here. We must address all this while trying to plan for an invasion we cannot predict..." My voice trailed off as the weight of the task settled on me. "I plan to ring Alix and Dr. Hesselius before the meeting, but they have their own problems to deal with. They may not be of much help."

Delilah chewed her lower lip, then straightened her shoulders and said, "Two things, Gwen. It's worth considering whether this influx of monsters has something to do with the legislation passing. The way I see it, the lords disappeared, Equal Representation passed, and then the monsters showed up. That's suspicious if you ask me. The opposition might have died down once the bill passed, but that doesn't mean they aren't trying to make us pay for it."

"Fair point. And the other?"

"I think it's time to press your sister for answers."

"Delilah—"

"No," she said, holding up a hand. "You have given her time and space. You've been understanding. But people are dying. If we are looking at a fae invasion, she is the best source of intelligence we have. She can put her slagging issues aside long enough to help us, whether she's angry at you or not."

"You don't understand what she's been through."

"Do you?"

"Only a bit. Just the edges, and believe me, that was enough. I will not traumatize her further."

It was Delilah's turn to press my arm in a comforting gesture. "I don't mean this to be insensitive, Gwen, though I know you might not believe that, coming from me. But, right now, her trauma isn't important. I know how much you loved your sister, but you've got to come to terms with the facts: that girl is gone. She's a woman now. She was a general. What she knows might be the difference between life and death. Not just for the fae in New London but for the whole city, if the fae armies invade. This danger is bigger than you or me...and bigger than her."

I tucked the sack into my pocket, ignoring her last comment, and said, "I have a new commission for you, a rush job. Can you handle it?"

She eyed me, weighing whether it was worth pursuing the issue, but decided it was not, at least for now. "I can push other projects back. What do you need?"

I explained my ideas and sketched out what was in my mind on a piece of drafting paper. She traced the lines with her fingers, asked questions, and finally said, "I don't know if either of these can be done, but if it is possible, I will make it happen. Do you have the alchemical recipes I'll need? Rolf is a shoddy artificer, but he's a genius alchemist."

I blinked. "Then why is he apprenticing here?"

"He wants to make his father proud," she said with a shrug. As if that wasn't what she had been doing for the last ten years. Then again, if I had a father like Benicio Irons, I would do my best to make him proud, too.

I fished the recipe from my pocket and handed it to her. "Thank you."

"That's what you pay me for. And Gwen? Think about what I've said about your sister, alright?"

I told Delilah to give my love to Fleur and left. I had to escape before I said something stupid. My heart pounded hard enough to hurt. For a long time, I sat in the auto, gripping the steering wheel until my knuckles threatened to break through my skin.

Delilah meant well, but she did not know what life was like for Lia in the Sunset Lands. How could she? Creatures of such cruel beauty, so skilled in manipulation, were too unbelievable to be real. Someone as strong and self-willed as Delilah would not understand how the fae made you want to give them everything, even your sanity.

If I chased Lia or pressured her, I would only lose her again.

But Delilah was right about one thing: the consequences of failure now, failure to protect the city from monsters or prepare for the fae invasion, were dire. People hid in their homes and whispered about killers on the streets. Passing the legislation for Equal Representation should have been a landmark for unity, but we were more suspicious of one another than ever.

After fighting so hard, they deserved to be safe, to tackle the mundane struggles of everyday life with the grit characteristic of New Londoners. They did not deserve to be confronted with supernatural dangers they were not equipped to face.

And yet...

I cranked the auto into gear and sped off down Artificer's Row, knowing in my heart that if the choice were between my sister and the city, I would let the city burn.

4

Domestic Bliss

ARIS

The explosion shook the door and made Sam hesitate halfway through throwing a right hook. Aris used the distraction to grab the boy's wrist, tug, and let his momentum take him off his feet. Sam stumbled forward and hit the mat in a roll.

At least the boy was good at falling. Of course, he did so often he should be, by now.

"Distractions may cost you your life, Sam. You must focus enough to notice when something changes, but not so much you falter."

"But," Sam said, wiping his hair out of his eyes and pointing at the door, "but there was—"

"I heard it. But if this were a proper fight and not merely a sparring match, you'd be injured or dead. You understand me?"

"Yes, but—well, look!"

Blue smoke trailed under the door, and coughing echoed in the hall outside. Aris inhaled, noted with some relief the scent was not alchemical, and strode toward the door.

When he jerked it open, Sally stood in the hall waving her arms and shouting, "It's fine! Everything is fine!"

Mrs. Chapman appeared a moment later, holding a white handkerchief over her nose and glaring like a hunting hawk. "God's breath, Miss Sally, if you do not stop blowing things up, we won't have a house left to sleep in. What have you done now?"

"It was a simple chemistry experiment," Sally said, coughing.

Sam stuck his head out the door, and said, "Your face is blue, Sal," then coughed as the plume of smoke billowed into the gymnasium.

"Enough of that, everyone out!" Mrs. Chapman said with an authoritative wave of her spindly arm. "Into the study, all of you, while we clean this mess up. Charlotte will bring in tea, but I don't want to see any of your faces until the smoke is clear. Am I understood? And that means you, too, Mr. Aris."

He slapped a hand over his heart. "But, my dear Mrs. Chapman. How am I to survive without seeing your radiant face, or hearing the dulcet tones of your gentle voice?"

Sam hid a snigger behind his hand.

"I'd prefer you didn't survive," she said with a terrible glare. "So, if that's all it takes, off to the study with you. All of you, now, I mean it."

No one dared interfere with the formidable housekeeper when she was in high dudgeon, so he, Sam, and Sally trooped down the long hall and filed into the study. Summer was too warm for a fire, but Aris found he missed the comfort of it crackling in the hearth.

The room was large, surrounded on two sides by floor-to-ceiling bookshelves that housed not only books but trinkets, antiques, and souvenirs of all kinds. Several plush chairs and couches sat in comfortable arrangements on the carpet, and Gwen's oak desk stood on the far side, covered in papers, books, notes, and the assorted impedimenta of her studies.

A morning paper lay unread on the table near the door. The headline read in bold black print: *Mystery Hero Saves Another Life*. Gwen was making headlines. Of course, the line below was a running list of victims' names separated into missing and dead. Unfortunately, the missing would be added to the list of dead once their bodies were found.

Vampires were much sneakier than werewolves.

"What were you making?" Sam asked as he plopped into a chair and mopped his sweaty forehead with a shirtsleeve.

"That is none of your concern," Sally replied, nose in the air.

"Suit yourself. But you'd better clean the blue soot off your face before Lady Gwen gets back, or you'll never hear the end of it."

Sally pulled a book from the shelf, curled into her favorite chair, and sniffed disdainfully. She was in a current fight for independence, often resulting in heated exchanges where Gwen tried to keep the girl safe, while Sally insisted she could take care of herself.

Neither of them was in the wrong. He'd tried to explain it once or twice, but they made it abundantly clear his opinion wasn't wanted. So, he pulled a handkerchief from his pocket and dropped it in Sally's lap as he sat at the chess table.

"Care for a game?" he asked the boy.

"You eager for another beating?"

"The way I see it, you deserve a bit of revenge after being trounced in the gym this morning."

"Yeah, well, if you'd move at human speed," the boy groused, settling into the chair opposite him, "it would be a different story."

Aris laughed. Sam and Sally knew who and what he was. It was impossible to keep the truth from them after he and Gwen returned from the Sunset Lands with Ophelia in tow. The children had grown used to strange things by then and accepted the truth rather easily. But Sam had a few requests in exchange for his silence; the most pressing of which was learning to fight.

The boy had never asked Gwen to teach him, despite her martial prowess, because the idea of throwing a punch at her made him nauseous. But he was more than happy to blacken Aris's eye any chance he got. Fortunately for Aris, Sam was at the age where his confidence outweighed his skills...or his brains.

"You think I beat you because of my speed?" Aris asked, moving his king's side pawn. "Why not a friendly wager, then? You win this round, and I promise to train you while only moving as slowly as a boring mortal."

Sam narrowed his eyes. He was smart enough not to make an unqualified bet with a faerie. He advanced his own pawn to block Aris's forward momentum, and asked, "What do you get if you win?"

"If I win," Aris said, as if thinking it over, "you owe me a favor." He pulled out his knight to threaten the pawn.

The boy snorted and flipped his blonde hair out of his eyes. "Nice try."

They were halfway through the game when the front door opened and Gwen sailed into the room. Her shoulders were tight, and while she smiled at the children, there were lines of strain around her eyes. Something hadn't gone quite to plan, then.

He glanced over his shoulder at Sally to see she had, in fact, cleaned the blue soot from her face and tried not to smile.

"Good morning, my loves," Gwen said as she pulled off her hat and gloves. "Do I smell..." She paused, took a deep breath, glanced at Sally, then said, "tea?"

Mr. Yates entered a moment later with the tea service. Apparently, Mrs. Chapman was still busy organizing the cleanup effort. Aris slid his bishop across the board and imagined giving Mrs. Chapman a hard time later. The old woman would be positively prickly and ready to take a strip out of his hide. He'd never enjoyed teasing anyone so much in his life, and he had no doubt the old woman secretly enjoyed every bit of it.

"Any new gadgets?" Sam asked as he stuffed a little sandwich into his mouth in one bite.

"None you can play with, Samuel," she said. "It took Delilah two weeks to fix the wheels the last time you took them out for a ride."

"She should have built in a brake."

Gwen snorted and brushed the hair off his forehead, which he shook back into place as soon as her head was turned.

She eyed the board. "Looks like another good clobbering."

"I thought the boy could use a win after getting thrashed during training this morning," Aris said.

Sam scowled at his magnanimous tone and advanced a knight, putting two of his pieces in danger. "You cheat."

"Yes, I do. But you know that, so you should account for it."

"You could just play fair."

"How dare you suggest such a thing."

Sally put down her book and leaned over to peer at the pieces. "Aris wouldn't be nearly so charming if he played fair. He's also going to lose his bishop if he doesn't retreat."

"Retreat?" Aris demanded. "My dear girl, I will advance or die."

"Why lose such a powerful piece for nothing? Your board position is terrible."

"It is the principle of the thing."

Sam captured the bishop, and the position put Aris's pawn chain in direct jeopardy. "Is your principle to lose? Because I'll have your king in three moves."

Aris examined the board, realization sinking in as he played out the next few exchanges in his mind. With a sigh, he tipped over the king, which rolled to the side to rest against the queen's skirts. "At least my king has a lovely consolation prize."

Gwen snorted and gave him an amused look as Sam sat back and cracked his knuckles. "I believe that's three in a row, old son."

"Don't rub it in."

"I'm definitely going to rub it in."

Aris leaned back and picked up his tea, glanced at the clock, and said, "Then I suppose I should mention that you are late for your riding lesson."

Sam bolted upright, eyes wide, then swore under his breath—which Gwen pretended not to hear—snatched another sandwich, kissed Gwen on the cheek, and disappeared out the door as he stuffed the bread and cucumber into his mouth.

"That boy," she said, taking the unoccupied seat, "is a whirlwind."

"Gwen?" Aris asked, eyeing her. "Is your hair burnt?"

"Yes. Delilah used me to test some fireproof fabric. I think she enjoyed herself overmuch."

"Perhaps not the best idea before your presentation this afternoon."

"Don't scold me, Aris, I am not in the mood. Sally, how has your morning been?"

Sally tried not to blush, but that wasn't what gave her away. The girl worked hard over the last three years to become a lady, fitted to her new station in life. And she loved Gwen desperately.

The result of the combination of study and earnest affection was that she lost much of the artifice she gained as a child on the streets who often had to lie or cheat to put food in her belly. Her honest face simply screamed she had done something dangerous.

Of course, she felt safe at home and didn't bother trying to hide her emotions. Aris would have to see what could do about that. Well-placed lies saved countless lives, and though he could not lie, himself, there was no one better at obfuscating the truth than the fae.

"I did a few experiments this morning, from *Alchemy to Chemistry* by Samir Abboud."

Gwen looked at her steadily. "I thought I smelled sulfur. Did you turn blue?"

This time Sally did blush.

"So did I, the first time I tried that one. And the next two times, after. I looked like a veritable blueberry. Are you waiting for the liquid to change color before you stir it?"

Sally opened her mouth, frowned, then closed her eyes and sighed. "No. You're not angry?"

"Sarah Elizabeth Dawes, when have I ever been angry at you for pursuing knowledge?"

"Well, you were not too thrilled about the potassium."

"That," Gwen said, raising a finger, "is because you might have burnt the house down. Experiments with potassium should only be done in the Boom Room at Delilah's shop. But you learned your lesson, so there is no need to repeat it."

Sally nodded and sighed. "I had better help clean up the mess. Mrs. Chapman won't like to touch the chemicals and beakers and such."

"A reasonable thing to do," Gwen agreed.

The girl replaced her book and headed for the door, glancing over her shoulder at the two of them before disappearing down the hallway.

"She did it on purpose," Gwen said with a sigh.

"What makes you say so?"

"She's angry with me, and I don't blame her. I am gone more often than home, so much of her education is falling to her tutor."

"I doubt the girl is so shallow as that."

"You have a different hypothesis, I assume?"

"I do. She wants your attention, Gwen, not your knowledge."

She fidgeted with her cup before dropping it back onto the saucer, where it clattered to the side. "Why do you let the boy win?" she asked.

"Why are you changing the subject?"

"Aris—"

"Because he needs it. The affair with the Cutthroat King made him question himself. He needs simple wins now and then, particularly over people more powerful than he."

"You do not consider that a sense of false confidence?"

"False confidence has a way of becoming real with time. If he believes it, he'll behave as if it's true. Soon, his behavior will make it so."

Gwen lifted the king and put him back on his square next to the queen. "I appreciate how much you care for the children," she said, her eyes downcast. "Sometimes I feel as if I am failing them. But I am not a mother and I never intended to be responsible for other people this way. I don't have the instincts for it. They deserve someone who—"

"Someone who cares for them? Will sacrifice for them? Is concerned for their well-being and tries to provide them with a full life? Someone who loves them?"

Gwen swallowed. "Someone who can make them the center of their world. That is what a mother does. And I cannot give it to them."

He slid out of his chair to kneel in front of hers, bringing them to eye level. Hers were rich, dark brown, like bitter chocolate, surrounded by the kind of long lashes most people only achieved through cosmetics.

"I know little of motherhood. I never knew my mother and my life has been devoid of caring female figures. But it strikes me that to make anyone the center of one's world is a bad idea. If you exist only for them, you cannot be a whole person. And a whole person is the only kind who has any business raising children."

"My mother–"

He knew where this line of thinking would lead her. Gwen wanted to establish herself as her own person, but she could not help idolizing the woman who raised her. Lady Evelyn would never be anything other than a saint, no matter how much her daughter tried to convince herself otherwise. Any comparison she raised between herself and her mother would end with Gwen being the loser.

So he cut her off and said, blithely, "Besides. The only person who should be at the center of your world—nay, your universe—is me."

"Does your arrogance know no bounds?"

"Not when I am trying to get your attention, my lady."

She shook her head at him, a gentle smile on her lips. "You are impossible, irritating, and infuriating."

"I am that," he agreed, leaning forward until their breath mingled; hers smelled like tea and lemon.

"What are you doing?" she demanded, but her voice was soft and her eyes strayed to his lips.

He leaned forward and said, against her mouth, "Being infuriating."

She did not resist when he kissed her, letting her bottom lip slide between his. With a little sound of pleasure, she leaned into him, opening her mouth, inviting his tongue. He tasted her, deepening the kiss, sliding a hand from her hip to her waist, and up to her breast.

She shivered and melted into him. Aris restrained himself with the will built over years of wanting her from a distance, of watching her, of realizing she would never touch him with anything more than the level of affection one might have for a pet.

But she wanted him now. And he could have her. He could brush the chessboard off the table, drop her on the surface, and bury himself inside her in a single thrust. She would do nothing but cry from the pleasure of it. She wanted to be distracted, comforted, to let pleasure drag her mind away.

He buried his hands in her hair and deepened the kiss for a final scorching moment. Her fingers curled around the lapels of his shirt, holding him close even as he leaned away. She watched him with heavy-lidded eyes, her pupils huge, her lips wet, flushed, and swollen from his kiss. He had never known a more beautiful woman, and he wanted her down to the depths of his soul if he still had one. He would abase himself for her sake: lie, cheat, even kill for her. He had already done so.

But she needed something else from him right now, and he knew her well enough to see it. If he forced her to confront her feelings for him, it would add yet another layer of difficulty to a situation she already felt ill-equipped to deal with. And he could wait. He'd waited this long.

But she expected him to tease her, to wake her up, to force her to live even when she wanted to withdraw from the stress of carrying so much on her shoulders.

So, Aris stood and gave her a wicked smile. Moon and stars, he loved it when she caught her breath. "Aren't you going to be late for your meeting?"

She blinked, then shot out of her chair, nearly plowing him over. "You rotten–if you were still a bird, I would pluck your tail feathers out one at a time."

"Gwen. What a thing to say. I am shocked at you. Shocked."

She snatched a pillow off the settee and threw it at his head. Instead of catching it, he allowed the pillow to hit him in the chest with an ineffectual *fwap*. One raised brow was enough to bring color to her cheeks.

She looked about for something more substantial to throw, sighed, and dug into her pocket. "Here," she said, holding out a silver ring. "You'll need one of these, as well."

He examined the small band, peering at the inside. It was a mirror of the one on her right hand, the one Ophelia had given her in the Sunset Lands. "A ring, and so soon? Very well, I accept."

"Oh shut up," she said, leaving the room. "I'm giving one to Tony, too."

That took the wind out of his proverbial sails. Tony Hardwicke, the paragon of blonde muscles and integrity, was beloved by everyone, including the children, who worshiped him almost as an idol.

Of all the people Gwen had ever cared for, he was the only one who might deserve her affection. And if she decided she wanted him, Aris would swallow his pain and step aside. He was used to being cast away, after all.

He sighed and slipped the ring onto his finger, where it fit as if it was made for him. It had, in fact. One more link in the complex chain shackling him to the woman he never intended to love and now could not live without.

With a sigh, he opened the window, shimmered into a raven, and leaped into the warm afternoon air.

5

Ulterior Motives

GWEN

Taking the auto would have been much more convenient, and faster, but in politics, perception mattered. If I arrived with goggle marks on my face, the uptight paragons of society I was about to meet with would write me off as the eccentric spinster they expected me to be.

But if I showed up properly attired and riding in the Wainwright coach with livery on the doors, I could slip past their guard and bring the weight of my eventual title to bear. And I needed their full attention and trust, or they would never believe me.

All of that was true, as far as it went. But I might have justified driving the auto, anyway, if my hands had not still been shaking from Aris's blasted kiss. I had rushed through my toilet trying not to think about his mouth, and gathered my notes while trying to forget the way his hands felt on my skin...all while failing miserably.

No one person should have so strong an effect on another. It simply wasn't fair.

I should kick him out of the house. He was a raven, after all. He could live in a tree quite comfortably.

Regaining some control over my mind took several more minutes of complaining and another thirty seconds of deep breathing. I could not afford to lose focus. Too much was at stake.

Once my nerves calmed, I closed my eyes and fixed Alix in my mind. I saw her raven hair, her crooked smile, the grace of her movements, and the way her eyes smoldered when she looked at Cyrus, her partner.

Then I said her full name in my mind.

A moment later, the ring that connected us grew warm.

Her voice appeared in my head. *Gwen? Is that you?*

Hello, Alix. How are you and Cyrus?

Her voice was amused. *We are...well enough. What do you need?*

We made a discovery last night and I wanted to consult you. So far, at least a third of the victims in New London have been fae refugees. And those are only the ones we know of.

That seems an unusually high number.

Exactly. Which leads me to wonder if vampires have preferences in their diet. Cyrus may correct me but, as far as I know, werewolves are indiscriminate in their prey so long as fear and adrenaline are present.

A moment of silence, and then, *Yes, werewolves will attack any mortal, regardless of smell or appearance. Vampires...it is certainly possible they have preferences. Human blood is richer, sweeter than the blood of goats or deer, for example. But I have never tasted fae*

*blood, nor have I consulted with other vampires or half-breeds, such
as myself. They tend to keep their distance, for obvious reasons.*

Alix had been hunting monsters for some three hundred years,
and though she specialized in werewolves, her half-vampire nature
meant she was equally suited to killing other creatures of the night.
It was irony of the highest level that she had fallen in love with a
werewolf.

Of course, Cyrus was a rather special case.

*Then vampires may be to blame for the high number of fae mor-
talities?* I pressed.

Possibly, yes.

Are you seeing anything similar in Paris?

*No. Monster reports are on the rise throughout the continent, but
they still avoid large cities. The few vampires who hunt in Paris
are very old, very powerful, and very careful. Not at all like the
indiscriminate killings you have reported in New London.*

*What could have drawn them here in such numbers, then? Why
are they behaving so out of character?*

If we knew that, she said, *we would be much closer to stopping
them. You remember the...incident in France?*

With your father?

*Yes. They were trying to make monsters more invulnerable, fo-
cusing on reducing the werewolf's sensitivity to silver, making them
more cooperative, and helping them retain more of their minds. They
nearly succeeded. I am not saying the same thing is happening in
New London, but there are similarities.*

I'll think on it, I promised. *Thank you. Give Cyrus my love.*

Alix chuckled and said, *I intend to.*

And then she was gone.

I had the uncomfortable feeling I interrupted them in an intimate moment and tried not to picture the two of them in an embrace. If children today knew that Little Red Riding Hood had fallen in love with the Big Bad Wolf, it would positively ruin the fairy tale and whatever moral platitude Perrault tried to communicate.

The carriage pulled to a stop, and I had to conceal my amused grin as Tony slid in opposite me. He closed the door and pounded on the roof for James to carry on. Since opening SPI, Tony could most often be seen in a waistcoat with rolled-up shirtsleeves and hair that had been mussed by a few passes of his hand in moments of stress. Now he was in a flawless lounge suit that fitted his wide shoulders like a glove, and his blonde hair was slicked back beneath a flat cap.

"Did you shave?" I asked, trying and failing to hide my amusement. "And is that pomade in your hair?"

"First impressions are important. Are you wearing perfume?"

I folded my arms and leaned back, eying him across the aisle. "Touché. Any news since last night?"

"Nothing. And the morning paper was blessedly free of new reports. You?"

"I just spoke with Alix, and she said it is possible vampires have a taste for fae blood. But she agreed that our monsters are acting out of character. Paris has not seen nearly the same level of activity."

"Then it is confined to England?"

"New London in particular, I think."

Tony raised a hand to run it through his hair, then paused and dropped it. "Then we need to know what is drawing them here and why they are behaving unnaturally."

"When I met Alix, she was hunting a man who was experimenting on werewolves, trying to make them resistant to silver and force them to cooperate and hunt in packs. We never found out why."

"You think something similar is happening here?"

"Who's to say? But I do find it oddly coincidental. And the fact that it is happening now, after we stole the faerie king's general and passed the Equality Act, is suspect."

Tony's eyes took on the faraway look that meant he was solving a puzzle, so I sat back and waited. My brain was full of questions I had no answers to, and there wasn't room for much else besides wondering how we were going to manage to convince several of the city's most powerful citizens that an invasion was imminent.

"I know you do not want to hear this," he said a moment later, "but Lord Rutledge is our only viable connection between events."

"It isn't that I disagree, but how can we prove it? We cannot find the man, and we have no reason to suspect his previous actions had any connection to the fae. He may have simply been trying to protect his power base."

"From what?"

That was a good question, but we had no time to explore it because James pulled the coach to a halt outside 43 Tromwell Lane, the building owned by the Triumphant Sisterhood. The coven had offered the building as neutral ground for the meeting, though I was not naïve enough to believe their motives purely altruistic.

There were likely listening holes, spells, or other ways for them to learn what transpired in the rooms they offered.

"My lady," James said as he handed me down.

"Thank you, James. You are well protected?"

His eyes flicked to the concealed carriage gun, and he nodded.

"Good man. Tony, shall we?"

He offered me his arm, and we climbed the stairs to the huge grey stone building with its white columns and oversized door. Patricia stood at the top of the stairs in her dark gown, as always, and greeted us with a nod.

She led us to a large marble room complete with a table and an electric chandelier hanging from the ceiling. The space was cold, clinical, and completely devoid of personality. It was as if the witches wanted to intimidate anyone who used it.

Hopefully, it did not backfire.

The only window in the room was a single, narrow leaded glass affair that sat squarely in the center of the far wall, and the only light that managed to pass through was hazy and diffuse. I cranked the lock open and slid the interior pane up, letting in a blast of air that stunk of horse manure and auto exhaust.

The first guest to arrive was a slender, dark-skinned elf with huge green eyes and a walk that looked more like floating. He sailed into the room in a maroon silk suit that was undoubtedly bespoke, and gave us a placid smile.

"You must be the honorable Mr. Lilyroot," Tony said as they shook hands.

"Indeed, I am. And you must be Mr. Hardwicke, the owner of SPI. The Artisan's Guild is very curious about your presentation, sir."

"Glad to hear it. This is Lady Gwen St. James," he said, gesturing to me.

Mr. Lilyroot took my hand in his long, elegant fingers, and brushed a kiss across my knuckles. "Ah, the future Duchess of Wainwright. I am at your service, my lady." He gestured to the room and then said, with mild distaste, "Interesting choice of venue. It is as cold as a morgue in here."

"It is a relief for me, sir, during such a hot summer," Tony said.

"That wasn't the kind of cold I was referring to, but your point is well taken."

Mr. Lilyroot was followed by Mr. Carbunkle, the head of the Artificer's Guild, Lord Eton, an influential member of the House of Lords, the Honorable Mr. Perez, an MP of great reputation, the Chief Editor of the Times, Mr. May, and several other representatives from important organizations throughout the city.

Last to arrive, and certainly least welcome, was Chief Inspector Mac Sweeney. He strolled into the room like a terrier, twitching his black scrub brush of a mustache and trying to decide which of the bigger dogs he could intimidate through sheer force of personality. We had argued about inviting the man but, at the end of the day, none of our proposals would be effective if Scotland Yard was not on board.

"Hardwicke," the CI said with an oily smile. "Congratulations on securing funding for your little agency."

Tony inclined his head the barest degree short of what might be considered respectful, but held his tongue, which was probably for the best. We spent months trying to wrangle these leaders of industry and public office into the same room, and if Tony chased them out before we could give our presentation, I would gleefully kill him. With a spoon.

Once everyone was seated, he positioned himself at the head of the table and said, "Honored guests, I first would like to thank you for coming. Your time is valuable, so I shall get directly to the point, though I ask you to hold your questions until the presentation is finished. We believe this is a matter of gravest import, but we will try to be quick. Lady St. James?"

I stood, heart thundering, and said, "We have reason to believe New London will be invaded sometime within the next year, if not sooner."

Shouting ensued, followed by questions and demands. Finally, Tony glared them into silence. It was a very good glare. "As I said, if you allow us to finish the presentation, you will find all of your questions answered."

"Everyone is aware of the string of unlikely circumstances that have plagued the city for the past few years," I said. "First, the kidnappings, followed by the riots, the disappearance of several prominent lords, and now monsters that are plaguing our streets and killing citizens under the cover of darkness. And we are only days short of the full moon."

They exchanged worried glances.

"This series of events is more than simply bad luck, however. We believe they have been orchestrated as a way to destabilize the city and, by extension, the Empire. To prepare us for invasion."

"By whom?" Mr. May demanded, slamming a hand on the table.

"It is in this that we ask your indulgence, because it will not be easy to hear," I said. "Tony?"

He stood, cleared his throat, and said the one thing that might entirely ruin his reputation as a respectable, logical man. "I have seen, firsthand on multiple occasions, incontrovertible proof that the fae are not only alive and well, but that they are actively seeking a way to bring large numbers through the wall that separates our world from the Sunset Lands."

Our guests sat a moment in silence, glancing at one another in disbelief. Mac Sweeney snorted, Mr. May's face turned red, and Mr. Perez said, "Do you truly mean to say that you have dragged us here, away from important work, to spout conspiratorial fairy tales, sir?"

"Aye, he has," Mac Sweeney said, shaking his head.

"Might as well say King Arthur has returned," Mr. May muttered.

"I recognize this is hard to believe," Tony said with laudable self-control. "But fae are not mere legends. They were separated from mortals by mutual accord after the Great War, but they are not gone. And they have found a way back."

"Where is your proof?"

"Incontrovertible, eh?"

"This is absolute rubbish and a waste of my time," said Admiral Norris before he stormed out of the room.

"Do any of you deny that our city is being plagued by monsters?" I demanded.

Mr. May rolled his eyes. "It may as likely be Jack the Ripper, or some copycat. We are not stupid, madame."

"We are not stupid, *my lady*," I reminded him in a sugary sweet voice. "And you challenge that assertion with every word that drips from your mouth, sir. How do you believe those monsters have come to exist, if not through magic?"

Mr. Lilyroot said, "Current research suggests there may be a germ or virus in werewolf saliva that is responsible for the change."

"Have you ever tried to capture a werewolf for study?" I asked.

"In short, my lady," Mr. May said, "magic is but a myth, and if it ever did exist, it has long since vanished. There are, no doubt, perfectly logical explanations for current events that do not involve mythological races."

Mr. Carbunkle, a dwarf of olive skin with a black beard that rested on the table and eyebrows that were positively looking for a fight, said, "It is an intimidation tactic by the electrical industry, nothing more. You humans bring monsters into the city, nighttime monsters, to make people afraid of the dark. You want them slavering for cheap electric lights on the streets so you can drive the artificers out of business!"

"That is ridiculous," Mr. Lilyroot said, standing up so he could scowl down at the dwarven man. "We both know this is a response to the Equality Act, to cause division between us just when we should be united."

"Blaming this on the humans is obfuscation of the worst kind, sir!" Mr. May shouted.

Fighting began in earnest, complete with finger-pointing, flying spittle, and arm waving. In all the hubbub, no one noticed the raven who flew through the window and perched on the back of Tony's chair.

"I cannot see that we have another option," he said, watching the meeting degenerate into a shouting match.

I swallowed the lump in my throat, told Aristotle, "This is entirely up to you," then folded my hands and took a few steps back.

Aristotle watched the madness, then unfurled his wings and stretched them to their full limit—which was impressive, to say the least—threw back his head, and croaked three times. Loudly. The combatants flinched as one and turned to see the bird making a display of himself.

"God's breath, how did that monster get in here? It is huge!" Mr. May said.

Aristotle shimmered, something like heat waves rising from hot pavement where the edges of his form blurred into indistinctness. A man stood in his place. A flawless black suit and white cravat with a raven's-head pin—complete with winking ruby eyes—made him appear as if he were returning from a formal affair.

He was tall, with ivory skin and black hair brushed back in waves that fell over his collar. Lean, elegant, absolutely aristocratic, he would have captured the attention of everyone in the room without effort. But it was his bearing and his eyes that really did the job: confident to the point of arrogance, with eyes black as coal.

The arguing men froze, mouths open, the way a rabbit might freeze at the sight of a hawk.

"Gentleman," he said, his resonant voice amused. "It has come to my attention that you do not believe I am real. Shall I give you a demonstration?"

"He's a witch!" Mr. Perez squeaked.

That broke the rest of them, and as a group, they retreated to the far side of the room. Aris jumped, shimmered, flew to the door, then regained his human form, blocking their retreat.

"Witchcraft is-is—" Mr. Perez stuttered, "out-outlawed in New London."

I rolled my eyes. "Does he truly look like a witch, sir? Do you see any warts?"

"Then it's you!" Mr. May pointed at me with eyes so wide the whites shone all round. "You've bewitched us!"

Mr. Carbunkle pulled a hammer from his belt, a long-bladed knife from his pocket, and squared off against Aris.

"Get behind me, lads," he told the other guests.

"I intend you no harm," Aris said, though I would have believed him no more than they did. He simply looked and sounded too dangerous.

"I don't think that is helping," I said.

For a moment, I considered asking him to overwhelm their senses, to calm their nerves and force them to listen. But I knew what it felt like to see Aris with no glamour. The power of his presence had been worse than overwhelming. I had been ready to do anything, to throw myself at him and beg for his attention, his touch, the pleasure of his smile.

If he were to do the same to these men, it would be akin to stealing their free will. I could not ask that of him. Perhaps when things were at their worst and there was no other hope, when protecting the people became more important than how we protected them, I might stoop to that.

But not yet.

So, I tried once more to bring them to their senses. "This man is not mortal, as you have guessed," I said. "He is a faerie, and changing shape is part of his nature. He is here today to convince you of the truth of our claims. If we do not join forces and prepare, we will be overrun when the faerie king invades."

They continued to back away, eyes wild, and only Mr. Carbunkle kept enough of his mind to say, "I don't know what you have drugged us with, lady, but we won't be taken in. Release us, or I will cut myself a hole to that door. See if I don't!"

Aris shrugged and said, "There isn't much more I can do, darling. Not without affecting their minds."

Dueling emotions fought on Tony's face; the desire to protect the city, and the knowledge that how we went about protecting it also mattered. He was tempted to ask Aris to do just that, but he could not force himself.

"No," he said, at last. "Let them go, if you will."

Aris feinted toward them, the men yelped, and he leaped into the air, laughing. The laugh turned into a caw that faded as Aris flew out the window and disappeared. They watched him go, then stood a moment in shock. Slowly, as if waking up from a dream, they turned toward one another, blinking.

"I think we have heard enough," Mr. Perez said, at last. "Lady St. James, as much as I respect your mother, I must admit that I do not appreciate having my time wasted in such a manner. Fairy nonsense, if you ask me."

"She has been pushing this narrative since her sister went missing, and she's clearly convinced Hardwicke, there, to believe her. I won't hazard a guess at her methods of influence, but that display of nonsense was more'n enough for me. Gentlemen," Mac Sweeney said, then turned and headed toward the door.

Tony's knuckles cracked as he clenched his fists, but there was nothing for us to do besides listen to ourselves being disparaged before they left the room, one at a time.

When the last guest closed the door, Tony let out an explosive breath and strode toward the open window, his neck red with fury. "How can those idiots be so blind?"

"They don't want to see, and I think it's fair to say Mac Sweeney has ulterior motives."

"So we just dragged our names and reputations through the dirt for nothing."

"My reputation was already in the dirt, my dear man," I said. "And Mac Sweeney will do his best to take you down, anyway, once he learns you are still hunting Lord Rutledge. We knew this was a long shot. When the invasion starts, at least they will know what it is. Perhaps that will make a difference."

"How are you so calm?" he demanded, turning angry eyes at me.

I shrugged. "I am a woman who has chosen not to let society dictate my life. No one has believed me about anything for years. My coping mechanisms are simply better than yours."

He rubbed both hands across his face, then said, tiredly, "They won't even remember Aris, will they?"

"No, not if he doesn't want them to."

"But they will remember thinking you are a witch."

I sighed. "Probably."

"The only way to convince them of the invasion will be irrefutable proof, and not the kind that scares them out of their minds when he transforms in front of them."

Tony eyed me for a moment, then strode toward me, grabbed my arm, and said, "We need to talk, and not here."

6

Hello, Goodbye

GWEN

"You're right," Tony said as we hurried down the stairs and into the warm breeze. He said something else, too, but it was carried away by the wind, perhaps the forerunner of a summer storm.

I waited till we were safely in the carriage to hold up one hand and ordered, "Repeat all of that."

"None of them could even pretend not to believe monsters are wreaking havoc on the city. Perhaps if we can prove this incursion is tied to the fae, they'll have no choice but to act."

I tapped on the roof with the handle of the umbrella, then sat back as James pulled the carriage into motion and regarded Tony. "And how do you propose we do that."

"Through Lord Rutledge."

"But we have no proof he is involved."

"Wasn't it you who claimed all of this was tied together?"

"Yes, but unless we can prove our suppositions, we cannot go after a member of the peerage, especially one protected by black-mailed members of Scotland Yard. Yes, he claimed responsibility for putting the Grimoire in Cassandra's hands, and for siccing the vampire on Lord Ashcroft, but we have no proof of either, besides his word. And if we focus on him to the exclusion of other possibilities, we may miss the true culprit entirely."

"Do you believe the monsters are tied to the fae invasion?"

"With my intuition, yes. But I must remain open to wherever the evidence leads."

Tony rubbed his hands together, his jaw muscle working. He wanted it to be Rutledge, and I could not blame him. I would love a good excuse to hunt the man down and drag him screaming before Parliament.

He said, "Then our first step is learning how the monsters are getting into the city, and why."

"I agree. But if we start investigating, we won't have the man-power to protect the city."

"Perhaps the best way to protect the city is to expose the truth."

A muffled shout came from the driver's seat and the carriage hit something that rocked us sideways, flinging us across our seats to slam together against the opposite door. Tony caught me around the ribcage with one hand and braced us with the other as the coach lurched back into balance.

"Pothole," James yelled. "Everyone okay?"

"Drive on," Tony hollered back, then braced his knees against the seat and levered us up. The motion pulled me against his chest, our noses nearly bumping. His breath caught, hitched, his eyes dropped to my mouth, and then...then he jerked backward and turned his face away.

Heart thundering, I regained my seat and brushed my hair out of my face, trying not to look at him. Of course, there wasn't much to look at inside a closed carriage, and if I scooted toward the window and pulled the curtains, that would be too obvious, so I absently spun the ring on my forefinger.

"Oh!" I said, realizing I'd forgotten. "This is for you."

After digging it out of my pocket, I dropped the silver ring on Tony's palm. He stared down at it, and his expression went through several shifts I could not trace.

"Delilah just finished them, so you can ring me when you have new information to share, or if you need anything. It should make us much more effective. But anyone who finds it can use it if they know your full name, so be careful not to lose it. Just call my full name in your mind, and I shall answer. If I can, of course. Or you can call Alix, Cyrus, or Aris. He has one, too. I need to have one made for Mama, but Lia is there so perhaps I should have her make some for the children, instead. Delilah, I mean."

After rambling like a nervous teenager, I stared down at my hands. What on earth was happening to me? Tony slid the ring on his forefinger, and a second later I heard him think my name.

Gwenevere Violet St. James.

His voice in my head was far more intimate than it should have been. *I hear you,* I replied.

He flinched, then shivered. *That was...rather unexpected.*

It takes a bit of getting used to, I agreed.

Tony took a deep breath, pulled off his hat, ran one hand through his hair, which came away covered in pomade that he wiped on his pant leg, and said, "Listen, Gwen. I've given you time. I know this situation has been awkward and so many things changed so quickly. But we cannot go on this way. If I can be nothing to you but a friend, I will accept that. But I cannot continue in the suspense of wondering if we could be something more."

He took my hands, his skin warm and soft. "I cannot keep watching you, and wanting you, and wondering if you will ever turn to me again with passion in your eyes."

Swallowing past the lump in my throat was impossible, so I didn't bother, just stared down at our joined hands. Tony was handsome, intelligent, generous, capable, gentle, caring, and honest. And, more than that, he was *whole*. I could extoll his virtues all day and not reach the end of them. Of all the people I had known, he was one of the best. He deserved happiness. He deserved someone good enough for him.

He deserved everything.

"Tony," said, running my thumbs across his knuckles. "You know that I love you."

"Then why do I sense a *but* at the end of that sentence?"

I took a deep breath. "Because there will always be a *but*. Nothing to do with me will ever be wrapped up in a neat bow. And you deserve more than that."

"Shouldn't that be for me to decide?"

"Not when you have such terrible taste in women. You simply cannot be trusted to make this decision for yourself."

His incredulous expression was adorable. But he didn't give up that easily. With a gentle tug, Tony pulled me forward, his eyes never leaving mine. He swallowed, took my face in his large hands, and kissed me. Gentle pressure coaxed me to respond, and the sweet desire in his embrace, the longing implicit in every movement, was enough to bring tears to my eyes.

But I felt no answering rush, no hunger, just warmth and comfort.

Being with Tony was like sitting next to a fire in winter. But it wasn't enough. I was not enough.

I pressed his lips once with mine, sealing them, and pulled back. He searched my face, hoping to see something he didn't find. When the hope in his eyes died, I felt the answering prick of tears behind my eyelids, and a little snap in my chest, as if the link of a chain had been broken.

The carriage jolted to a stop. Tony let go of my face, climbed out, then stopped and turned. "I didn't want you because you were perfect, Gwen. You were never the picture of a proper English wife, to me. I loved—I love you because you are irreverent, and infuriating, and challenging...and kind. And your broken pieces don't make you less worthy of love. I hope you find someone you are willing to accept it from."

Then he shut the door.

James snapped the reins and the carriage jolted into motion. Why had I never realized how loud the wheels were as they ground against the cobblestones? Despite the engraved springs meant to cushion the cabin, every bump and pebble vibrated up through my feet and hips like an earthquake.

I pulled at my tie and unbuttoned the neck of my blouse. It was unreasonably hot in the coach.

If I stayed in the bloody thing for another second, I was going to either melt or explode. Grabbing my umbrella, I pushed the latch and leaped, hitting the ground and rolling to a stop almost under the feet of a waiting horse.

"Gor blimey, woman! Wot in the 'ell are you on about?"

I ignored the irate wagoner, who glared down at me over the top of his bulbous nose, brushed the dirt off of my skirt, and made my way onto the sidewalk. Every now and then I surreptitiously fanned my skirts. How did people live in this city in the summer? I hoped Mr. Yates had the Heat Catch set up to drain the heat from the house because the muggy air was miserable.

A flock of pigeons burst into panicked flight, sending feathers floating down into my hair. Where was I? The lion statues, the fountain...Trafalgar Square? Wasn't I going home? My legs were tired, and the edge of the fountain seemed a nice place to rest them.

It was cooler near the fountain, and droplets of spray landed on my cheeks. Before long, my hair hung in bedraggled curls against my neck, itching like little crawling flies. Diffuse golden light cut across the square, dragging shadows out like knife blades on the pavement.

A deep, resonant voice broke through the mixed buzz of chatter, wagon wheels, and cooing pigeons. "Fancy seeing you here, my lady." I recognized that voice. "Fine afternoon to enjoy the ridiculous heat, is it not? And look at that, your cheeks are already sunburned. How charming."

Aris.

He strode toward me across the square, dark and lithe, a shadow come to life. The sight of him made the world condense, rushing back in on itself as if he were the gravity holding all things together.

"Where is your hat?"

I touched my head. Where was my hat? "I must have lost it when I jumped out of the carriage."

"Why did you jump out of the carriage?"

"It was too hot."

"Perfectly logical reason."

He knelt in front of me, filling my vision with the planes of his face and those eyes that bored into the dark places I tried to hide, making it impossible to look away.

"Did he hurt you?" he asked, his voice soft and flat.

"Yes, but...no. It was me. I hurt both of us."

It took him a moment to decide whether I was telling the truth, and a droplet from the fountain landed high on his cheek beneath his left eye. For a moment it hung there, then began trailing downward, like a tear. I wiped the droplet away, watching my thumb slide across his skin as if the digit belonged to someone else.

"Come along, darling," he said, taking my arm and levering me to my feet. "Let's go home."

I looked down at the toes of my boots peeping out from the hem of my skirt, and said, "My feet hurt."

The sky was on fire and glowed in every window when we stopped outside the townhouse. I absently paid the hansom driver and Aris guided me into the house with one hand on the small of my back.

"My lady," Mrs. Chapman said when she saw us enter the foyer, "I need your approval for—"

She looked at Aris and her voice died.

We did not stop to say hello to the children, or to look at the pile of mail Mr. Yates left on the entryway table. In fact, Aris did not stop pushing me until we stood in the center of my room before the windows that looked out over the street. The sun set behind the skyline, turning the buildings into black silhouettes that cast long shadows like fingers reaching toward me across the cobblestones.

I looked down to see Aris untying my boots. "What are you doing?"

"Building a bridge, obviously."

He did not stop with my boots. My jacket, vest, and skirt followed. Before long I stood in nothing but my chemise and the sky outside my window was blue-black.

"Come here."

Aris stood next to the bed, holding the covers open.

"I can't." Why couldn't I? Ah, yes. "I need to get ready to go out, and so do you. Where is my coat, was it washed?"

"You won't be going out tonight," he said, a note of command in his voice.

"Since when do you decide what I will and will not do?"

He dropped the covers and stalked toward me. My heart froze like a mouse frozen before a hunting cat.

"Since you will get yourself killed if you try to do anything dangerous tonight, and I won't allow it."

"Won't allow?" I demanded, a spark of flame kindling in my chest.

Aris reached me, lifted me off the ground until we were at eye level, and said, "Are your ears bothering you? Because I know I did not stutter."

"There is nothing wrong with my ears."

He turned me, like one might a child, and peered at my ears. "You appear to be correct. Your ears are perfect. How nice for you."

"Put me down."

"Very well."

He put me down on the bed, then slid in next to me, pulling the thick blankets up over the two of us. The heat sink had certainly done its job. The sheets were so cold that goosebumps broke out down my legs, but he wrapped an arm around my shoulder and pulled until I lay alongside him, my head on his chest. He wrapped both arms around me, one hand running up and down my back in lazy lines, the other smoothing my hair back from my forehead.

He was warm.

A low sound rumbled from his chest, familiar and comforting. He was purring, the human version of the sound he had used to make as Aristotle, my raven. My eyes filled with tears that spilled onto his chest.

"I hurt him," I whispered. "I always knew I would. And he said—he said he loved me."

Aris hesitated, his hand pausing for a heartbeat before he continued the motion. "He would be a fool not to."

"He didn't really love me. How could he? All he saw was the person I wanted him to see. And maybe the person he imagined me to be. But I warned him. I told him I would hurt him sooner or later."

My lungs were so tight I thought I might never take a deep breath again. We'd been existing in a liminal space for so long, separate but never quite separated. But the look in his eyes told me that was the final refusal. One can only hurt a person they love so many times before that love dies.

And how can one person love another unless they know them? Lia was the only one who had ever seen me at my worst, at my weakest, and loved me despite my faults. Though even she appeared to have grown weary of them. Tony had never even seen them, but that wasn't his fault. I was awfully good at hiding the worst of them. I ought to be. I had been practicing for a dozen years.

Aris kissed the top of my head but said nothing.

I fell asleep and dreamed about the people who might die tonight when I wasn't there to protect them.

Gwenevere Violet St. James.

I jerked awake, panting and covered in sweat. "What?"

Aris sat up next to me and put one hand on my back, then said, "It's alright, darling, it was just a nightmare," in the kind of voice people reserve for skittish horses.

I shoved my hair out of my face and blinked into the darkness. Had I heard a voice in my nightmare? It was difficult to separate my conscious thoughts from the visions of fire and blood, from the sound of remembered screaming.

Gwen? Are you there?

"No," I told Aris, catching my breath. "It wasn't a nightmare."

With a little concentration, I thought, *Tony?*

It's me. I need you. We've got a bit of a problem. Can you come? And maybe bring Aris, if he's around?

Bring Aris? They usually tried to avoid one another, if at all possible. If Tony wanted me to bring him, something serious must be happening. The clock read three a.m., and a gentle rain pattered against the window. I rubbed sleep out of my eyes and said inside my mind, *We will be there.*

We took the auto rather than waking James for the carriage, even though rain blew in above the short windshield. I was going to have to talk to Delilah about that. New London was no place for open conveyances, even in summer when surprise rain storms could ruin the loveliest of evenings. Every now and then a howl echoed off the stone, made more chilling for the hollow, directionless quality of it. Werewolves stalked the night, but at least they warned you in advance. I was certain other things lurked in the shadows, things that hunted—and killed—soundlessly.

"What a night to be out and about instead of warm in one's own bed," Aris said whimsically as he wiped rain from his eyes.

"You could have flown, instead," I reminded him.

"And miss all this?"

"Don't tell me you don't enjoy a bit of excitement. Besides, it was not your bed you were enjoying."

"Yours is so much softer. It smells better, too. And the view is simply beyond compare."

I let go of the wheel long enough to smack him in the chest, but he caught my wrist and kissed my palm. A little shiver of warmth shot up my arm at the caress, even through the kid driving gloves.

The humor was gone from his voice when he said, "Are you going to be all right, seeing him tonight?"

"I don't have much of a choice. My selfishness can only be humored for so long."

"It isn't selfish to care for yourself, Gwen. You are just as important as the people you—"

"I'd rather not talk about this right now if you don't mind."

"Fine. Just know that I will not ignore the matter forever."

"Why you think it is any of your business is beyond me."

"Because no one else in your life will tell you when you are being an obstinate ass."

Exactly who did he think he was? I hit the brakes just outside SPI, jammed the auto into park, and said through my teeth, "Remind me why I keep you around, again?"

"Because I'm handsome and charming?"

"And delusional?"

"And because I'm not scared of you," he said, seriously. "You cannot hurt me with your clever tongue or chase me away with your bad habits and violent tendencies, and deep down you know it. I have seen you at your worst, and I am still here."

Listening to him was like scraping a blade across an open wound. "The only reason you've seen any of that is because you let me think you were a raven for years. If you learned those things about me it is because you *lied*."

"And it is a good thing I did. You don't have to protect yourself around me, Gwen. If you need a punching bag, I will be that for you. If you need to fall apart, I will hold the pieces until you're ready to put yourself back together. But now that you know what I am, I will not sit back and let you hurt yourself without doing or saying something, whether you like it or not."

I wrenched the door open, flung it closed, and stomped to the other side of the auto, not stopping till our chests were nearly flush. My cheeks burned and my nostrils flared, but Aris stared down at me, unimpressed. The light from SPI's windows made his face look like a statue of an avenging angel, but I still wanted to punch him in the nose because I knew that he could, if he chose, strip me of the desire to do anything other than what he wanted from me.

I fought for too long to be the person I chose to be, and the idea of losing that autonomy was terrifying. All it would take to turn me into someone else was for Aris to lower the glamour that made him seem more human and less fae.

But this was Aris, my friend Aristotle who had saved my life several times, and I wanted to believe he would not violate me in that way. So, instead of reconfiguring his face, I said, "I am the only one who decides what I do with my life. My choices are my own. If you cannot accept that, you can leave."

"I would never try to take your free will. You have the right to act as you see fit. But so do I."

We glared at one another, the air between us crackling with energy that made my muscles tense for action. I was either going to punch him, slap him, or—

"If you two are quite finished," Tony's voice said from behind us, "I have a situation in here."

I released a deep breath, flexed my fingers to loosen the muscles that had cramped from clenching them so tightly, and fell back on Mama's training. As the future Duchess of Wainwright, I had been trained to have perfect self-control. When I chose to use it, anyway.

"I am at your disposal, Mr. Hardwicke," I said with cool politeness.

Tony eyed me, then Aris, his lips compressed into a thin line of distaste. "Are the two of you capable of behaving yourselves?"

"Never were two people more trustworthy," I assured him as I sailed by into the building.

Aris followed me and Tony closed the door behind us, locking it with a *snick* of the bolt. He wore only his trousers and a haphazardly tucked white shirt as if he'd rolled out of bed and tugged his clothes on in the dark.

"Follow me," he said, taking the stairs in long strides.

We followed him upward into the dark. The wood creaked underfoot, as if disturbing the building after nightfall was painful to its old bones. A long, narrow hall ran from the top of the stairs to the back of the building, with doors leading off to the left and right. A burning taper in an old brass sconce was the only source of fitful light.

"I know you can afford dwarven lanterns," I said. "Why waste money on candles?"

"We can talk about that later. They're in here."

"They?"

Tony stopped with his hand resting on the latch and ran a hand over his face. "They are quite frightened. I wasn't certain what else to do for them. Perhaps you will know better."

The door swung silently open to reveal seven people huddled near the back of the room. A fire burned in the hearth, there were blankets folded on a chair and a tea service on the table, but none of it had been touched.

When we were ten years old, Lia and I found a litter of kittens one of the barn cats hid in the hay loft. Their pupils had been huge in their wide eyes, their backs up and every hair on their spines raised. Until that moment, they had never seen a human, and each one of them was certain we were there to eat them.

These people looked like those kittens. Very slowly, I lowered my goggles. Through the hagstone, I saw past the glamour and caught my breath.

They were all faeries.

7

Gird Your Loins

GWEN

"They will not speak to me," Tony said in a low voice.

"How long have they been here?"

"The first knocked on my door late yesterday, but they have been steadily arriving through the night."

I pulled my goggles off and looked at each face. I had only visited three of these people. How did the rest know about the agency? I ran back through the countless nights of trying to warn the refugees, grasping at names.

"Mr. Hines, Miss Cho, Miss Buckley, it is a pleasure to see you again," I said as I stepped slowly into the room. "I am gratified you were able to find the agency. As I'm sure you are aware, this is Tony Hardwicke, the proprietor, and this is Aris Blackwing."

Someone whispered, "The Raven," in a voice filled with terror.

I ignored that because it was probably safer not to acknowledge that Aris had once been an assassin for the Obyrron, king of the fae, and plunged on. "All of us would like to help you however we can. If I may ask, why are you here?"

Miss Cho glanced at her companions, swallowed, and stepped forward. Her black braid hung over one shoulder, brushing against the cotton fabric of her night dress. Had she run from her house in the middle of the night?

"The wolves," she said at last.

"The werewolves?"

She nodded. "And worse things."

"Vampires?"

A visible shiver went through the lot of them and they cringed away from me. I thought that qualified as a yes. "Have you seen the vampires?"

They looked at one another, uncertain whether to answer.

"If you tell us, we might be able to stop them."

While they considered my statement, I passed my goggles backward to Aris.

"I did," one of them said. The crowd parted to reveal a faerie that wore the glamour of a hearty dwarvish woman with a belly like a beer keg and a close-cropped head of grey curls.

"What is your name?" Tony asked. I did not bother to tell him the faerie would never admit her true name.

She said, "You can call me Hilder."

"Thank you, Hilder. Can you tell us what it was you saw?"

"I's on me way back from the tavern, the Twisted Eel, it's called, when I got the feelin' summat was trailin' me. I ducked into the doorway of a butcher's shop and peered out the window. The butcher weren't too 'appy, I don't mind sayin'."

"What did you see?" Tony asked.

She raised her chin, as if daring the memory to frighten her, and said, "Tall and thin, 'e was. In a black frock coat and bowler 'at. But it were 'is face what scared me; pale skin, waxy like a candle stub, and eyes what burned. I looked away quick, 'fore 'e could catch me, but my skin went all over gooseflesh."

Someone moaned as if their lips could not hold the sound back.

"Did he have any other distinguishing characteristics?" Tony asked.

"I don't rightly know what's more distinguishin' than glowin' eyes, but..." She frowned, and her eyes took on a far-away look. "There were strange letters on 'is coat, jus 'ere." She pointed to her own collarbone, where the lapel would have been.

"Embroidered, or on a pin or broach?" Tony asked.

"Sewn on, looked like."

"Can you describe the strange letters?"

"A bit like an S, now I come to think on it. Only squished to one side."

Before Tony could ask another question, howling broke out. Unlike the howls from earlier in the night, these were loud and close. And there was more than one. The refugees let out a collective whimper of terror and took an involuntary step toward the warmth of the fire. Even the brave little Hilder shrank back against her comrades.

"They're terrified," Aris said in a voice meant only for Tony and me. "Let them rest if they can."

"Please do not worry," I said in my most calming voice. "You are safe here. We will not let anyone harm you while you are within these walls. There are blankets and pillows. Do try to rest."

I could not say if they heard me or not, but we left them to what comfort they could find and trooped back downstairs. Tony lit another lamp though the sun was already beginning to lighten the horizon, then sat on the corner of a desk with one hip and folded his arms over his chest.

"That was more than I could get out of them. They showed up here, one at a time, holding the pamphlets and staring at me with horror on their faces. It was the only thing I could think to do."

"It was probably the wisest decision. Aris," I said, "did you see them?"

"I did."

"None of them are powerful, or magic wielders, are they?"

He handed me the goggles and said, "Not one. In a fight with either monster, they would all have been killed, except perhaps the Hob."

"Hob?" Tony asked.

"Hobgoblin. Hilder. They've tough skin, they're quick and far stronger than they look. She might hold her own against a were-wolf long enough to escape, especially if she had training or a weapon. But Hobs are not Aos Sidhe, and she'd be ensnared by a vampire, though not quite as easily as you would."

Tony blanched. He had been ensnared by a vampire once and still had nightmares about it. It was not my favorite memory, ei-ther. Every now and then the memory of the vampire's bite—his kiss, he called it—would come upon me out of nowhere and make my knees weak with awful remembered pleasure. Tony had not been bitten but trapped inside his own head with no control over his body. Which was worse?

Aris knew exactly what had happened. He'd been there, after all, though in his raven form. That knowledge was a subtle weapon but unfair to use on Tony. He succumbed to the vampire as any mortal would have done.

I gave Aris a warning glare, then said, "And we are only three days from the first night of the full moon. No wonder they came here. They must be getting desperate."

Aris nodded. "Vampires cannot enter homes uninvited, and werewolves almost never pursue victims indoors, not when there is good hunting outside. They must have reason to believe their homes are not safe."

"We need to know what that reason is, then. And, at least now we have a kernel of where to look."

"The Twisted Eel and the man in the frock coat and bowler hat," Tony agreed. "If we follow him, perhaps we'll learn where the rest of the monsters are hiding, or at least why they are coming to the city. We can go later this morning."

"Gwen needs sleep," Aris said before I could answer. "She's had a difficult night. Noon will be early enough. And I don't think you should go."

This time Tony butted in before I could say anything. "Oh, you don't, eh? And just how much experience do *you* have running an investigation?"

"In human years? Longer than you have been alive."

That took Tony off guard long enough for me to say, "Tomorrow morning will be far too early to observe a vampire, in case anyone is interested."

Aris opened his mouth to respond but I turned on him and said, "Aris, kindly shut your mouth and don't speak for me when I am perfectly capable of speaking for myself."

He gave me a long-suffering look that said *my statement wasn't meant for you.*

Of course, it wasn't. He was trying to hurt Tony. That only made me angrier because I had to admit— "But I think he is right, Tony. Now that the faeries have come to you for shelter, you cannot leave them. At least, not until we have a better answer for protecting them."

For a moment he looked as if he wanted to argue, but it made too much sense. He settled back against the table with a sigh and shook his head. "Fine, you may be right. And we are going to need more help. I have only two office assistants with no training outside of paperwork and one investigator who is too old for dirty work."

"Then why hire him?" Aris asked.

"Because he is brilliant."

"Ah. I suppose muscles are not all that matters, then."

Tony did not precisely flex, but his shirt seemed stretched too tightly across his shoulders and biceps. Out of all of the men I knew, he was probably one of the most impressively made. His eyes only rested on me for a moment, but his voice was full of meaning when he said, "That depends upon who you ask."

I rolled my eyes hard enough to see my brain and said, "God's breath. How can two capable men be so absolutely childish."

Aris sniggered. "Says the woman who sleeps with a teddy bear."

"You leave Mr. Fuzzybum out of this."

"A teddy bear?" Tony asked. "Really?"

I picked up my umbrella and strode out of the room with massive dignity, calling over my shoulder, "I will see you tomorrow, Tony. Aris, you can find your own way home."

Their laughter followed me to the car as the sun began to lighten the ragged clouds.

Instead of driving home, I headed south. As the sun rose and cut downward through the buildings, the dwarven lamps lining the street flickered out, switching into light storage mode. When the sun set, all the sunlight stored in the lanterns would be released over the course of the night, keeping this part of the city safely lit till morning.

The wealthier parts of the city had broader streets, brighter lights, and better lines of sight, making it safer for the inhabitants at night when monsters stalked the city. Most of the terrified faeries hiding in Tony's building lived in the parts of the city with electric or gas lamps, where a majority of the deaths and disappearances had been recorded.

Still, I could not help thinking of Percy, and though he lived in a wealthier part of the city, I needed to know that he was safe. As a selkie, he had the same kind of innate magic as Aris, able to shift from humanoid to seal, but his gift was not enough to protect him from vampires or werewolves, no matter where he lived. And he was a gentle person, one who would not defend himself with the ferocity needed to stay alive.

By the time I reached the shop, his minions were already hard at work measuring silks, arranging window displays, and pinning fabric onto mannequins. The store was not strictly open so early, but as the patroness, I was not an average customer.

"Good morning, Lady St. James," Theris called, waving to me from the front counter as the bells on the door jingled behind me.

Theris was the only young woman in the shop and the only non-elf. She was the soul of efficiency and managed his books, appointments, and commissions with an ease far beyond her years. Like all of Percy's employees, she wore a sleek black suit, and her flaming red hair was pulled back in a bun.

"Good morning, Theris. Is Percy in the back?"

"Not yet, ma'am, he hasn't come down."

I grinned and winked at the girl, then turned up the stairway to the left, which led to Percy's apartment. His home wasn't much different than his shop, and far less neat. I picked my way past discarded bolts of cloth, stacks of boxes full of yards of lace and ribbon, and half-dressed mannequins. Sheaves of drawings were piled in every corner and left forgotten on table tops, and leftover fabric was draped on nearly every chair back.

It looked more like a wizard's tower than the home of the most sought-after fashion designer in New London. Beneath the mess, it was probably very posh, but no one would ever see it.

"Percy?" I called, peeking into a small drawing room.

"Gwen?" Percy's head peeked round the corner down the hall. He had not yet applied his glamour, so instead of a beautiful, angular, dark-skinned elf, I spied the rounded head, dark, speckled skin, and soft, doe-eyes of his selkie form. "What are you doing here?"

"I came to check on my favorite designer."

He disappeared, then reappeared a moment later wearing a plush dressing robe and carrying a cup of tea. He gave me a quick kiss on the cheek, and the downy fur on his face was like the brush of a soft blanket.

"I appreciate your concern, darling, but I am just fine, as you can see. The apprentices have taken to sleeping in the shop as we have so much work to do preparing for the season. Tea?"

"Yes, thank you."

I followed him into the drawing room and accepted my cup.

"Just push that to the side," Percy said, waving his hand at the silk crepe draped over the back of the armchair.

He sat across from me and smiled. "How are you? Has your jacket been holding up?"

"Of course, it has been doing beautifully. A bit warm for the summer," I said, "but still worthwhile."

"I promise to have summer variations ready for you next year, if our suit fails. Delilah said you tested it?"

"The overalls?"

He nodded, eyes bright with curiosity.

"Yes, we did. I do not mind saying it was one of the most uncomfortable experiences of my life."

"Then so far it withstands fire, blunt impacts, blades, and bullets. And all without exploding, I might add. Extraordinary. It is rather dowdy, but I have big plans for making it more fashionable,

I can assure you. You will be the best-dressed hero New London has ever seen."

"Hero? What a ridiculous bunch of tosh. It is far too early in the week for such nonsense, Percy. I will not be accepting any nonsense until Thursday, at the earliest."

"I promise to save all my nonsense for later. But what of you? You look tired."

"Tony woke me early this morning. The agency has been over-run by frightened faeries looking for a place to wait out the full moon. At least, that is what we assume. They aren't that interested in talking at the moment."

Percy frowned and swallowed a mouthful of tea. "I don't suppose they would be. Something must have happened to make them seek shelter outside their own homes."

"I agree. Which is why I wanted to see how you are. It turns out that fully a third of the victims so far have been fae."

"Really? That makes no sense. We cannot be a large population to begin with to account for such high numbers."

"I agree. Do you have any idea why faeries might be being targeted?"

After a moment of thought, Percy said, "I have never experienced anything like this. Most of the monsters had moved far beyond the cities by the time I made it through the wall. But with the apprentices here, I have felt safe, enough."

"Good. Make me a promise?"

His eyes narrowed. "What?"

"Don't go out after dark. At least, not until the full moon has passed."

"But the werewolves have been hunting despite the fool moon, we've heard the echoes of their howls."

"True, but that is by choice. The wolves are much more in control of themselves when they change by their own will. During the full moon cycle, however, they are completely consumed by the magic. I would take it as a personal favor if you stayed safely inside during the next week."

He pursed his lips, then sighed and said, "Very well, my dove. But only because you asked it of me. Do you have time to see my newest creations?"

"Unfortunately, I must get some rest before gallivanting off into the city this evening. Next time?"

"Only if you promise to bring Aristotle. I miss that feathered little fiend."

I nearly choked on my tea.

The house was already bustling with activity by the time I walked through the front door. Mr. Yates took my hat and gloves, then said in a low voice, "Prepare yourself, my lady. This morning has been exciting. I have managed to keep the peace, but only just."

"Who?"

"Sally and Mrs. Chapman."

I sighed. Poor Mrs. Chapman. "Thank you very much, Mr. Yates. When was the last time I gave you a raise?"

"Last month, my lady."

"That was good of me."

"Very, my lady."

I kissed him on the cheek, making the staid man blush furiously, and said, "How about a bonus this month?"

"My lady—" he began, trying to head me off.

"Mr. Yates?"

"Yes, ma'am?"

"Hush."

"Of course, ma'am."

The crash of a breaking plate echoed down the hall, followed by raised voices. Sam appeared with a muffin in one hand and an amused expression on his face.

"Good luck, my lady," he said, before taking the stairs two at a time.

"Gird your loins," Mr. Yates whispered.

Sally and Mrs. Chapman faced off across the dining table, Sally pale with anger and Mrs. Chapman dark with it. They looked like two members of the triune goddess, maiden and crone, preparing for battle.

"What has happened here?" I said in my most duchess-like voice.

"Miss Sally is having a fit," Mrs. Chapman declared, flinging an arm at the teenage girl as if her mere presence was proof.

"She refuses to unlock the door to the lab," Sally said.

"I told Miss Sally I would unlock the door once she returned from her lessons with Ms. Nevis, but she maintains she will not go."

"Sally, is this true?"

"Ms. Nevis is useless. She regurgitates the same lessons over and over, even though I know them by heart."

"Your current behavior would suggest her lessons on correct deportment have not set in," Mrs. Chapman said with a sniff.

Sally's cheeks flushed and her fingers closed around an empty glass. Bits of shattered plate already adorned the floor, so I said, "Thank you, Mrs. Chapman. I believe I can handle things from here. Please feel free to take the rest of the afternoon off, if it suits you."

"As if this household would not fall to pieces the moment I turned my back," Mrs. Chapman muttered to herself as she stalked down the hall.

Sally raised her chin defiantly and waited.

"Why haven't you told me you are unsatisfied with your tutor?"

"I have told you. You promised that *you* would teach me. And you said we would speak of my invitation from the Triumphant Sisterhood, but none of that has happened. Ever since you came back from the Sunset Lands you've barely noticed anything."

I flinched, stung. "That's not entirely fair, Sally. I have been focused on—"

"I know what you've been doing," she interrupted, sounding tired, and let go the glass. "I know. I just wish you would pay as much attention to what's happening at home as you do to everything else. Do you even know where Samuel goes during the day? Or that I worked my first real spell this week?"

A spear of pain pinned my heart to my ribcage in a single, white-hot thrust. "You what?"

Realizing what she had just said, Sally bit her lips together and stared at me with wide eyes.

"Do you have any idea how dangerous that was?"

She raised her chin. "I know what I'm doing."

"Where did you learn the spell? From the Grimoire?"

Her jaw locked. She wasn't going to tell me. I held my hands behind my back to keep them from shaking and asked, "What spell?"

"Just a simple one. To light a candle."

"Have you noticed any aches and pains? Any new marks on your skin?"

"Only a small headache afterward, and then it was gone. I'm fine."

God's breath, Sally was a witch. I pulled in a long, shaking breath to steady my nerves, and said, "Do you understand the danger of the path you have set your feet upon, Sarah Dawes?"

Rather than shrinking in fear, Sally's shoulders dropped and her chest lifted. "I am protecting Sammy and myself. We weren't poor because we were bad, or our parents were lazy. We were poor because we were ignorant. I promised myself that I was going to learn everything I could so that no matter what happened, Sammy and I would never go hungry again. Knowledge is power, and I'm going to get as much of it as I can."

"Do you truly believe I would abandon you and Sam? Or not make a provision for you?"

The defiance slowly drained from Sally's face, replaced by deep sadness and, even more painfully, resignation. "I will always be grateful that you took us in, and gave us home, and loved us. I know you did not *mean* to leave us last year...but you did. You left us. Just like our mama, just like our papa. I won't allow something like that to break us again. I'll be strong enough to stop it."

Every muscle in my body was frozen with pain. Sally bit her lip, looked as if she would speak, then closed her mouth and swallowed.

She touched my arm as she left.

I stood there for a long time, then wandered up to my room and undressed without paying attention. I kindled a fire, slipped my feet into my winter slippers despite the heat, and curled up in the armchair. The silver ring glowed in the firelight as I turned it round and round on my finger.

Emotions rolled inside me like a sea in storm, splashing over every part of me and making my stomach sick. I wanted to peel myself out of my skin and float away on a breeze.

I called out in the hollow spaces of my mind, *Ophelia Magnolia St. James.*

Nothing.

Please. Answer me. Lia, I need you.

Nothing.

The city is plagued by monsters, the faeries are hiding in Tony's apartment, and the children...I'm failing them. All of them. I thought I could do this, I thought I could hold on but...I also thought you would be here with me and I could stop feeling so alone. I can't do this by myself. I don't know what I'm doing, and I'm tired.

I miss you.

She did not answer.

8

Guest Rights

ARIS

fter leaving SPI, Aris flew around the city for a few hours to clear his mind. He scouted the waterfront around the Twisted Eel, stole a sandwich out of the hands of a grumpy-looking old dwarf who hit a few orphan boys with his cane, and spent an hour or so irritating pigeons, which always put him in a better mood.

The pudgy little birds really were ridiculous.

He even managed to make off with a pretty silver necklace, though he no longer had a nest to hide it in.

He returned to the townhouse just in time to see Gwen leaving it. Where was she going, and why was she walking? The woman had more than enough time to cool off from such a silly jest, but he could tell by the stiffness of her gait that something was still bothering her. Had there been problems at home? She turned toward the center of town and kept walking, now and then stopping to tilt her head, as if listening.

If he did not miss his guess, she sensed him watching her.

Gwen was not ready to come to terms with her parentage yet, but once she embraced it. she would benefit more from her natural intuition, strength, and speed. Several times he had been tempted to push the matter simply for her safety, but no one should be forced to confront a traumatic truth when they were not ready, and Gwen carried more trauma than most.

She stopped again, twisting to look behind her, then shaking her head and continuing on. Would the clever little ring work even in his raven form? He dodged a flight of pigeons, caught an updraft that let him float without effort, then concentrated and thought, *Gwenevere Violet St. James.*

Not so much as a flinch, but her voice echoed back to him in his mind. *Those are your eyes I feel, aren't they?*

Just watching over you from above, my lady.

I wish you would not call me that.

Why? That's what you are.

Because when you say it sounds too...possessive.

He did that on purpose, but she already knew that. So, he said, *Darling it is, then.*

She sent him the equivalent of a mental snort, then lifted her eyes to the sky. After a moment of searching, she saw him soaring above and to her left. He inclined his head, dropping his beak, and she shook hers.

You are impossible.

Of course, I am. Where are we going?

I am going to see the Cutthroat King.

How exciting. Why are we going there?

I am going because I have an idea, and he owes me a favor...unless I can get him to agree to an alliance.

This should be fun.

You are not invited.

It is a shame I am a faerie with no morals who does not give a damn about the rules and expectations of polite society. Whatever is to be done with me?

I can think of a few things, she thought back with an edge to her internal voice. He caught the barest hint of a mental image, only for an instant, but it left him with the impression of a feather duster.

Gwen held out her arm to hail a hansom as soon as she reached the busier part of town, then climbed into the cab and disappeared from view. Aris tucked his wings in and dove toward the cab, then flared them a the last second to slow his descent, landing on the bench next to Gwen with the delicacy of a dancer.

Neatly done, she thought to him. Emotions were not as easy to read in mental voices as they were in physical voices, but Gwen managed to add a wealth of sarcasm to hers.

He gave her an elaborate bird bow, extending one leg and flaring his wings as he dipped his head. She smiled but shook her head in resignation. *Impossible.*

He did not ask her what had happened, there would be time for that later. For now, he needed to know. *What are you hoping to get from the Cutthroat King?*

She explained her plan and he thought it over. *You might be right. He certainly has more resources at his disposal of the kind that will benefit us. But do you believe he will use them?*

There is only one way to find out, my feathered fiend.

Didn't you mean feathered friend?

Did I?

The cab pulled to a stop, and he hopped out to circle overhead while Gwen paid the driver. This part of town was older than Grosvenor Square, cramped with buildings and people, thick with the smells of industry, horse shit, and the rotten fish and refuse of the Thames.

Gwen wore her armored jacket and carried her umbrella despite the heat, but she clearly did not belong here and received the kind of sidelong glances that would have made most people nervous. Of course, Gwen was not most people, but they didn't know that.

Aris maintained his vigil from above, watching the other pedestrians as much as he watched her.

Suspicious type at your four o'clock, wearing suspenders and a flat cap, he thought. *He's trying too hard not to notice you while following your path. Take a few righthand turns.*

Is he our ticket? She asked after turning in a U shape around a block. Suspenders was still behind her and closing in.

Might be. Give it a try.

Gwen turned into a blind alley, waited, then spun and pressed the tip of her umbrella against the man's chest as soon as he followed her in. They exchanged words, and she pulled something from her pocket and handed it to him. Suspenders stared at his palm, then handed the object back and motioned for Gwen to follow him.

He led her down a maze of turns, away from the river and toward the East Side. Instead of the church, where the entrance to the underground lair had been, he stopped at an abandoned warehouse and knocked in a pattern: four, one, two.

Aris angled downward, spiraling out of the sky and landing on Gwen's shoulder before she could follow Suspenders through the door. She did not so much as flinch, but the doorman jerked backward and pulled a knife from his pocket.

"Oh, do calm down," Gwen said. "It is only a bird, and it has no idea how tough you are."

He sneered at her beneath brows that sheltered his eyes like windows beneath an overhung roof. "Show me the coin."

Gwen produced it, and he demanded, "Where'd you get your 'ands on that? No lady oughta have the smiling man."

"You can ask the king if you like," she said sweetly. "Or I could show you, myself, but I don't think you'd enjoy that very much."

Fear dawned on his brutish face, and not because Gwen was physically intimidating. She was no taller than the average woman, and certainly nothing for a street-tough to worry over. It was her voice that did it. She sounded as if the idea of proving to the wretch that she was valuable enough to carry the silver coin of those in service to the Cutthroat King, Lord of New London's Underworld, excited her.

What he heard in that sweet voice was that she would hurt him, and she would like doing it. Despite what most people believed about the average criminal, those who engaged in violence did so because their lives required it. Very few of them truly enjoyed cruelty, and Gwen sounded as if she were one of the few.

Aris knew better, but the doorman didn't.

His lady was a quite capable liar.

"Take her below," the doorman said, turning away.

The warehouse had a basement, but it wasn't just any old storage area. Cramped and low-ceilinged, dark and reeking of rotting things, it was merely an entrance to a series of tunnels that ran beneath. Suspenders led them through the honeycombs of openings, lit only by guttering torches, until they emerged into a cavern.

High ceilings arched above, almost like the nave of a cathedral, and dwarven lanterns hung at regular intervals. Carpets covered the stone floors, and chairs, benches, and tables of all shapes and sizes sat interspersed throughout the space. Some chairs were fine and upholstered in velvet, others tatty and worn as if they'd been stolen from an abandoned home.

Sitting on an engraved throne at the head of the room was a handsome man in black, wearing a crown of silver spoons. He might have stepped out of a seventeenth-century painting with his hose and tunic, but his eyes...those were the eyes of a practiced killer. Next to him sat a construct in the form of a clockwork dog, a mastiff to be precise, running on a mixture of Artifice and magic.

Be careful with this man, Gwen. He is dangerous. Terribly dangerous.

So are you.

He tightened his grip on her shoulder to emphasize his point and thought, *Yes, but I have scruples, thanks to you. He does not. He is more fae than man, and his moral code is more like King Obyrron's than yours or mine. Do not make any mistakes.*

He did not want to mention that if she were in real danger, he would kill every man and woman in this hovel, and do it without remorse. He'd rather not have her look at him like the ruthless killer he had been.

Have a little faith, Aris Blackwing, she thought back as she stopped and inclined her head just enough to be short of civility.

"Ahh, Lady St. James. I wondered how long it might be before you graced me with your presence, once more. And is that the Raven I see sitting so tamely on your shoulder? Come, Assassin of the King, do me the honor of appearing in your true form." He raised his hands to either side, and his wrists were covered with scars. "We are all friends here, after all."

Aris leaped from Gwen's shoulder and shimmered into his human form, complete with a flawless black suit. The King clapped his hands in delight. "I hoped we might meet. I have heard so much about you."

"Most of it is likely true," Aris said with a long-suffering sigh. "The bad parts, anyway."

"How delicious. Now, do tell me, lady, why have you brought a notorious assassin into my court? You do not have designs on my life, do you?"

Gwen smiled, and it was an expression Aris had never seen on her face; a smile like that could cut a man to ribbons from across the room. "My dear King, I do not require such as the Raven to kill *you*. No, I have come to propose a temporary alliance."

The mask of indifferent civility melted into a deadly serious expression. "Have you, indeed?"

"Indeed, I have."

"Speak on."

"I imagine the appearance of monsters in the city has been as bad for your business as it has been for ours."

"You know how I feel about locked doors and windows."

"So, I do. I have several leads that may expose how monsters are getting into the city, and why. And I also believe I may have a way to destroy them. All of them. But to make my plan work, I need manpower and eyes on the street."

"And here I sit with a city full of minions at my disposal."

"The first night of the full moon cycle is in two days, and the violence we have seen so far will be nothing compared to the damage of rampaging werewolves, particularly to those members of your court who rely on night work to fill their coffers."

That was a rather delicate way to insinuate that prostitutes would be in the most danger. Unfortunately, it was true. The nature of their work demanded they keep late hours, and anyone obliged to work the street was in more danger than most, even when monsters were not part of the equation.

Aris hoped they had the good sense to take a couple of nights off, but an empty belly was a demanding taskmaster.

The Cutthroat King ran a finger along his chin. "And if I loan you my minions, you believe you can prevent the abuse of my people as well as destroy the monsters plaguing the city? Forgive me but, are you not overestimating your capabilities?"

"What does it cost you if I am? You only stand to gain by this alliance."

With a smooth motion, the King was on his feet, stalking toward them with slow, graceful steps. Aris had already pegged the man as dangerous, and now it was clear that he was a predator. Without taking his eyes off the King, Aris slid in front of Gwen. A pair of iron knives appeared in his gloved hands, held low and casually.

"Control your pet, lady," the King said, amused. "I mean you no harm."

"Swear it," Aris demanded, his flat and dangerous.

The King held both arms out in a gesture of innocence, fingers open and palms up, but he did not stop walking. "I mean Lady Gwen no harm, Raven. I swear it."

"Do you extend us guest right?"

He froze. One corner of his mouth curled, but his eyes were cold. "Very well. I extend guest right to you both for so long as you remain in my presence."

As long as you remain in my presence. That was a dangerous qualifier, but Aris had already pushed his luck, so he nodded and sheathed the knives, then returned to his position at Gwen's side. The King circled them both, paying attention only to Gwen.

"Is this the armored coat I have heard so much about?" he asked, fingering a fold of the long skirt. Aris tightened his hands into fists to avoid batting the man's fingers away.

"Is answering that question a requirement for our alliance?" Gwen asked.

"It is. If I invest the time and effort of my people, then they cannot earn their wages or pay me a proper tribute. I must care for them from my own coffers. I want to know my investment will be well protected. And effective."

"You have seen my effectiveness, yourself. I believe your guards still carry the scars."

"How about a little demonstration? Just to—"

Gwen spun faster than Aris thought possible, catching the Cutthroat King's wrist in her left hand and kicking him in the chest with her right foot. He flew backward and caught himself in a crouch just as Gwen opened her umbrella. The runes along the shaft already glowed with stored energy that could be used like a battering ram.

Stay out of this, Gwen said in his mind, her voice disturbingly calm. *That construct will attack you if you touch him.*

Aris lowered his knives, the King smiled, and Gwen said, "Was that enough of a demonstration, or would you prefer we continue?"

Clever. She had acted before he clarified his request for a demonstration, and as his guest, he could not do her harm. By the King's smile, it was clear he knew what she had done, and approved of it. But she was still taking an awful chance.

"Consider me convinced," he said, standing. But his fingers left shallow gouges in the stone floor where he had planted his hand to stop his backward momentum. That display may have been more for Gwen's sake than his own.

"Are we agreed on this temporary alliance?"

"We are, if we can agree on terms and timeframe."

They spent a few moments hashing out explicit terms and the King resumed his throne. Once everything was agreed to, he leaned back and said, "Very well, ally. What do you want of me?"

"First, a question: are you or any of your vassals involved in smuggling monsters into the city?"

One pale hand slapped his chest where his heart should have been, and the King said, "You wound me, lady. Do you believe I would endanger my people so?"

"Answer the question."

"You already know the answer. I prefer my crime organized, neat, and by the books. Monsters only complicate things unnecessarily."

"Answer. The. Question."

This time his grin was honest and unrepentant. "No, neither I nor my vassals are involved in smuggling monsters into the city."

With that question answered, Gwen was free to push her true agenda. "I need your people to find a man, find but not approach. They can send a signal up for Aris. Three lights from a dwarven torch will be enough. He wears a dark frock coat with embroidery at the collar, a symbol that looks like this." She held up a drawing. "He was seen down by the Twisted Eel, wearing a bowler hat. Spot him, and signal for help."

"That can be arranged. What else?"

Gwen and the King made plans for tracking shipments, following suspicious individuals, and sharing information, but Aris ignored the verbal sparring—Gwen would fill him in, anyway—and focused on watching the King's eyes and his hands. He sounded relaxed and he appeared to be acting in good faith, but the muscles around his eyes were tense and now and then his fingers would twitch in a strange, stilted pattern, as if sending signals to someone watching.

Whether the King was acting from a sense of duty, self-preservation, or something else Aris could not guess at, he was involved in more than simply helping to remove monsters from the city. And he was nervous.

"If we are in agreement, Aris and I will be on our way," Gwen said.

Aris blinked and let his focus slide back to the conversation. The Cutthroat King sat up, then trained his flat eyes on Aris, staring without blinking, like a snake, or a shark.

Finally, he said, "And here I thought you had bestowed your favor upon the honorable erstwhile inspector, lady. But it appears you use your favor as purposefully as I use mine. Be careful with that one. Even I have heard rumors of his deeds."

"There is not a creature on earth I trust more," Gwen said, raising her chin. "And my favor has nothing to do with it."

Aris's chest squeezed in a not-quite-painful way.

"Are you so certain of that, lady? Perhaps you do not understand the power of your...affection. What about you?" he asked, turning his gaze upon Aris. "Does she speak for you, *pet*?" His voice caressed the last word as if it were a poisoned knife slid lovingly into a friend.

Aris laughed. "Has the mortal world filed the edge from your tongue that your insults cut so shallow? Yes, if the lady called, I would come to her heel like a happily trained hound. Perhaps one day you will be blessed enough to know what it is to trust someone blindly...but I doubt it."

The King did not move, not a muscle, but his bearing changed. He had been testing them, probing for weaknesses, and found a trap he did not expect. If Aris was right, and he was rarely wrong about matters such as this, that barb had found its way home and stung deeply.

"Do take care, as you leave," the King said in a low whisper. "It would be a shame if you got lost in the dark."

The trek back to the surface streets was strained and silent. Every sound marked a potential threat, and he'd stayed as close to Gwen as possible, close enough to smell her sweat through the thick jacket. But the King had nothing nefarious planned, and they exited the same building they'd come in by, blinking in the afternoon sun.

"Let us get out of here, quickly," Aris urged, and ushered Gwen down the crowded streets as fast as he could. She may have an armored jacket, but he was not so lucky.

"You realize there isn't anywhere we can go in this city outside of his influence?" Gwen said as they rounded a corner that spilled them onto Pennyworth Street.

"Then you took some awful chances back there."

"No more than you did."

"You kicked the man in the chest in his own home, Gwen."

She snorted. "He was expecting it, or he would not have allowed himself within striking distance. It is a game, you see. A conversation. A reminder that I know what he expects of me, but I will only be pushed so far. He wanted to know if I would back up my threats because he only respects strength."

"You are playing a dangerous game, then, my lady."

"I wish you would stop calling me that."

"I know."

She rolled her eyes, then waited patiently as he hailed a cab. Once they were inside, he asked, "Where shall we wait?"

She gave the driver instructions, then sat back and folded her arms across her chest. That wasn't right, it was less a posture of relaxation or anger, and more like she was protecting herself.

"What's wrong?" he asked.

"Did you mean that?"

"Mean what?"

"What you said about trusting me."

He hesitated, then cleared his throat and said nonchalantly, "Of course. You know I cannot lie. Did you?"

"What?"

"Did you mean what you said about trusting me, or did you only say that for the benefit of the King?"

She took a deep, shuddering breath, careful not to look at him, and said, "I did not realize I meant it when I said it, but I find that I do. Strangely enough."

"You don't sound happy about the prospect."

"I'm not."

"Why? Would you rather have discovered it was your *favors* that tied me to you?"

"Yes."

He barked out a painful laugh and shook his head. When he spoke, his voice was hard. "Very well, then, my lady. Consider me well and truly chained to your side because you were the best fuck of my life. Does that make you feel better?"

For a moment, hurt flashed in her eyes, and her long eyelashes fluttered closed to hide her expression from him. Dammit. He hadn't intended to hurt her, especially knowing how her fiancée had damaged her trust in men, and her father before that.

But then she snorted, and that snort turned into a giggle, and soon she was laughing so hard she held her sides as tears ran down her flushed cheeks.

"Oh, Aris," she said, wiping tears from her eyes. "Was I truly the best? Of your whole life? What a thing to admit."

He closed his eyes and rubbed his forehead with one weary hand. Living in the mortal world and speaking regularly with Gwen had ruined his ability to carefully phrase his words. With her, he had never felt the need to protect himself through faerie subtlety. At least, not until recently.

"I could not have said it if it wasn't the truth," he admitted with a sigh.

A moment later, her hand slid tentatively into his, and she leaned her head on his shoulder.

9

Fangs and Teeth

GWEN

*A*nthony Gawain Hardwicke, I thought.

I'm here, came the reply.

It was strange hearing Tony's voice echo through my mind while holding Aris's hand, but I did not allow myself to think too much about that. A girl could only deal with so many emotional upheavals before she went mad and did something unforgivable...like ravishing her faerie companion in the back booth of a seedy, dockside tavern that stunk of stale beer and vomit.

So, I allowed myself to enjoy the comfort of Aris's presence without guilt as I explained my interview with the Cutthroat King, our arrangement, and my plans for the evening.

Are you certain that's wise? Tony asked.

I think it is necessary if we want proof that will force the government to act to protect its citizens. With more eyes, we have a greater chance of finding evidence.

And a greater chance of more deaths.

I've told the King what protective measures to put in place so his people incur the least amount of danger possible.

But it isn't no danger.

No. This enterprise will certainly cost lives, one way or another.

There was a long mental silence punctuated by rowdy laughs from the front of the tavern as working men left their shifts and began letting off steam. Aris's thumb rubbed small circles on my palm. When I could no longer stand the silence I thought, *How are the refugees?*

Eating, which is an improvement. They're speaking to one another now, but still don't give me much to work with. The only time they leave that room is to use the facilities.

Small steps, I suppose. The sun is nearly set, I had better get started.

Be careful, then. And ring me if you need anything.

The mental connection fizzled into silence, replaced by an argument happening at the front of the tavern. A fight broke out, and it was stopped before any serious damage could be done, but our pints of untouched beer wobbled on the table as the crowd shifted to get a good look, their faces bright with interest.

"It's getting exciting in here," Aris said.

"And dark outside," I noted. "Old vampires who are strong enough may already be abroad."

"You are certain that bowler hat man is a vampire?"

"Yes, and so was Hilder. Not many creatures have glowing eyes."

"Vampires do not have glowing eyes."

"They most certainly do. At least they appear to, for those who can be enthralled."

"Does that not make you curious about why the vampire could not enthrall you?"

A shiver of panic ran down my spine, and I jerked my hand out of his to swallow half the contents of the pint. The beer was sour and hoppy, and my stomach churned when it hit, but the discomfort was better than answering that question.

"We had better get moving," I said as I stood.

Aris sighed and followed me through the throng, glaring at people over my shoulder who sidled out of the way as soon as they noticed his expression. We escaped the scent of sweat, grease, and sour beer only to be swamped by the heavy, rotten-fish-and-sewer stink of the Thames. The evening air wrapped around us like a wet blanket, sitting low and heavy as we left the watery light of the Twisted Eel for the dark corridors of the riverside.

Aris pulled me into a side street just out of view of the tavern, and said, "I'll be above, watching. One thought will bring me down to you."

I fastened the top buttons on my coat, despite the warmth, and said, "I will be ready."

He stared down at me and, for a moment, I was certain he would kiss me. My lips tingled at the very idea. But then he shimmered and was gone in a rustle of feathers. The man was a tease.

His voice floated into my mind, my full name almost like music when he said it.

I hear you, I thought to him.

I am aloft, Darling, with a splendid view of the waterfront.

Eww. I think I preferred it when you called me my lady.

You are such a fickle creature. How does 'Muffin' strike your fancy?

Only if I can call you 'Biscuit.'

Never mind, then.

I chuckled and lowered my wheels into place so they would be ready at a moment's notice, then set off at a casual walk down whatever street I was on, now and then raising my eyes to look for Aris. But the sky was nearly black, and Aris could only be seen randomly as a flicker of movement, quickly lost against the canopy of night.

I stopped to stare at the moon. It was so close to full, so round and lovely when the clouds passed by, like a pregnant woman glowing with promise. Only the fruit of this full moon would be bloodshed if we did not stop it.

Any luck? I asked, sometime later, when listening to the click of my heels on the cobbles became too monotonous to bear.

Patience, my dove, patience.

That is even worse. Never call me that, again. And patience, indeed. You have wings.

True, but I must flap them to keep myself aloft and, I don't mind telling you, it's murder on the arms. Besides, I'm not an owl. My night vision is only slightly better than yours.

That is disappointing.

My perfection only extends so far.

I turned right, heading back toward the river, having walked myself in a grid and not seen a thing.

Just how far does your perfection extend? Because you are terrible at choosing pet names.

That may be true, he said thoughtfully, *but I am very good at kissing.*

Even though he was not there to see it, my cheeks went up in flames. He was exceptionally good at it, but I would never admit that to him, so I thought, *Passable, certainly.*

Is that a challenge, my lady?

A little thrill ran from my breastbone to my knees. I was about to respond when he said, *Signal, Gwen. South of your position by two blocks. Don't rush, I'm following.*

I turned, locked my wheels in place, and leaned forward as I pulled my goggles from my pocket and slipped them on. The wheels were rubber, and much quieter than my boots on the cobbles, making me nearly silent.

Another signal, Aris thought. *The King's men are out in force tonight. You are on the right heading, keep moving south.*

I rolled past a cross street near a guttering lamp that stunk of scorched oil, heard a gasp, and someone whispered, "Did you see that?"

"See what?"

"I swear, I just seen a woman floating like a ghost."

"How much absinthe did you have, Jerry?"

Then the voices died away.

Turning east, Aris thought, *moving into the industrial district. Take the next left but maintain your speed.*

I took the corner slowly, checking for watching eyes before rolling into the shadow of a row of dilapidated apartment buildings that stared down at me with hollow, hungry eyes. I imagined the bowler hat man gliding along, secretive and menacing, with his glowing eyes and pale, waxy skin, and hoped he wasn't hunting.

Gwen, stop, Aris commanded.

I rocked back on my heels, cutting the forward momentum and rolling backward, farther into the shadows.

He's stopped outside an old refinery, one block up. If you roll slowly, you might not alert him, so long as the wind continues blowing west.

Leaning forward and breathing slowly, I crept through the darkness, watching as my shadow chased me across a pool of lamplight.

He's unlocking a chain looped round the front doors. The padlock is massive. He seems nervous, so go slowly.

I am going slowly, I thought in a whisper.

Gwen, he can't hear your thoughts.

Shut up.

The mouth of the street opened up to a four-way intersection, revealing the old refinery. It looked like a dead bug that rotted in the sun, nothing but a hunched carapace with broken legs sticking up into the sky. The figure standing before the wide double doors was barely visible thanks to the weak light of the closest street lamp, but the clink of rattling chains was loud in the darkness. I needed a better view, something I could use to identify him beyond his hat and coat.

I rolled backward, into the shadows, then skirted the closest building to the left, inching closer under the dark moon shadow of the building. He eased the chain out of the door handles one careful loop at a time, stopping every now and then to check for prying eyes. I rolled behind a low retaining wall that had, at one time, housed a flower bed, and crouched to watch. When he turned toward me, I froze. Lamplight carved his features into harsh, but familiar, lines.

I had seen this man before, but where?

His gaze skimmed past me, and my heart skipped a beat as he pulled the last loop of the chain free. With a mighty heave, both doors opened wide enough for a man to walk through, but bowler hat man did not enter.

What is he doing? I thought.

I can't tell. Wait a moment.

While bowler hat man looked over his shoulder, Aris shot down out of the sky and sailed into the building on silent wings, a shadow among shadows. No wonder he had been such an effective assassin. I waited and watched the strange man Hilder had described as a vampire, trying to place why he seemed so familiar.

He was unremarkable in height, average in build, and beneath that hat it was impossible to tell what color his hair was. I needed a closer look.

Shit. Gwen, get out of here, Aris thought, his mental voice tense.

What happened? What is it?

Werewolves. He's got them—ah!

Aris!

Run, damn you! he thought, and I had the flashing mental impression of slashing teeth a bare second before Aris blasted out of the building with three werewolves chasing him, snapping and slavering. They passed the man in the bowler hat as if he did not exist, and leaped after Aris's fleeing form.

He climbed into the sky with mighty pumps of his wings, high enough that they could not leap to catch him, but not high enough for them to lose sight of him. The idiot was trying to lure them away from me, but that wouldn't work for long because he did not drip the scent of fear into the air the way mortals did.

The sooner I got out of that square, the better. But the bowler hat man remained, watching the werewolves lope into the night. He turned to hook the padlock over the door handle, and the light caught his features just so...

God's breath, I thought. *It's the driver.*

What? Why aren't you gone?

The Marquis of Rutledge. Bowler hat man is his driver. That waxy-faced son-of-a-goat held a gun to my head, once. I've got to follow him.

Even you cannot face a vampire alone, Gwen. And if the werewolves circle back—

I have no intention of facing him, I thought, watching bowler hat man studiously clean his hands on a handkerchief he stuffed into his pocket and continue down the street with the walk of a man who thought his job was well done. *I'm only following him. He's the proof we need to tie all of this to Rutledge.*

We can't give anyone proof if you're dead.

Then I had better not die, eh?

The wolves are already scattering, Gwen. They're hunting.

We need Rutledge, Aris. Otherwise, we cannot put a stop to this.

The next time I heard his voice, it was resigned. *People are going to die.*

The sour beer I had hastily downed earlier threatened to climb back up my throat. Proof was how we saved the city. Proof was how we would catch Rutledge—who was certainly tied to this affair—and stop all the monsters. And proof was the only way we could force the government and people of this city to prepare for invasion.

But could I sacrifice whoever the werewolves would kill tonight for the proof I needed?

Come follow bowler hat man, I thought, angrily jerking a torch from my pocket and sending three blasts of light into the night sky to show him the location. *I'll stop the wolves.*

You cannot handle three werewolves on your own.

Do you want to get proof and stop Rutledge or—

I don't give a damn about Rutledge, or this stinking city! They can all go to the grave if it keeps you safe.

After a surprised pause that made my throat hurt, I said, *You don't mean that.*

Yes. I do.

Fine. I'm calling Tony. Now will you go?

...Yes, but I will be back, he promised.

I canted my wheels to the right, banking around a building, and leaned forward hard, picking up speed in the direction Aris led the wolves. Listening and watching the shadows while ringing Tony was difficult, but the wolves had already run far enough that I did not stumble upon them directly.

Anthony Gawain Hardwicke.

Gwen?

I need you. Come prepared for werewolves.

I'm on my way.

After giving Tony terse directions, I pulled the pistol from beneath my coat and held it in my right hand with the umbrella in my left.

A deep breath told me at least one of the werewolves was not far away. The musky scent of fur, rotting meat, and old blood perfumed the air: eau de monster. Leaning back even more, I slowed the wheels to a silent creep.

Darkness pressed in from every side, trying to smother me. This part of the city was still poorly lit with gas lamps. And though the moon was bright, the crooked buildings with their leaning second stories blocked the light, casting cutting shadows across the street.

Temporary wooden structures had been added, pell-mell, to the outsides of the buildings: awnings, stalls, and ramshackle shelters. These additions reminded me terribly of a man I'd seen in a Paris salon who resented encroaching age and tried to hold off the years by piling on every bit of tarnished finery he owned.

All of it crowded and hovered, stinking and dangerous, reaching out with bony fingers. People should not have to live this way. Jaw clenched, I avoided an open stairway that descended into a basement entrance, training my pistol on the gaping hole, expecting a monster to leap out of it.

But nothing moved.

Even people who normally slept on the street had managed to find shelter tonight. Which was a good thing, because a hulking shadow slunk across the street some fifty yards away with moonlight reflecting from hungry yellow eyes.

We had already learned that I did not create the kind of miasma of fear and adrenaline that drove werewolves to mindlessly hunt, but I did, at least, smell enough like prey that I was an option when other mortals were not about. And if I could sneak up downwind of the creature, I might get off a shot or two before it noticed me.

Crouched low, I leaned forward, avoiding random pieces of refuse, and rolled up the street. The wind was still coming from the west. I slowed before reaching the corner, double-checked the cross street, then looked behind myself for good measure. A pair of pale eyes stared back at me from the shadows.

I raised the pistol and fired once, twice, leaning hard backward so the momentum would drag me away from the werewolf that had been silently stalking me. The first bullet hit the monster just above its left eye, but that didn't stop the beast from snarling and leaping at me.

Its body did not yet realize its brain was dead. My momentum carried me away quickly enough to avoid the attack, and the beast hit the ground with my second bullet in its right shoulder. Its legs crumpled as it hit, sliding five feet before coming to a stop with blood leaking from one nostril. The monster would change back into a human, soon, but I did not have time to wait for that. The other werewolf was still close, and my first shot had been lucky.

Four more shots, and two werewolves left.

Gwen? I heard gunshots.

I'm fine, I thought back. I had forgotten Aris and I had left our rings open. *One down. Bowler hat man?*

Still walking. Tony?

On his way.

Be careful.

Good advice. I turned and leaned forward, hurrying down the cross street on the trail of the werewolf I had seen before being attacked. It had padded down one of the wider thoroughfares, which was odd because werewolves preferred stealth until they were close enough to frighten their victims into smelling like dinner.

Cyrus had described it as the mouthwatering rush of scents when one opens an oven to check on a roast or a baking pie. Apparently, that was how mortals smelled to werewolves when being hunted. We released the fear cocktail evolution primed us for and called them to us like ringing a dinner bell.

But if that was so, why had the wolf chosen one of the few streets that was wide enough to be open to the moonlight? Unless it already had a victim in mind. I thought Tony's full name and then blurted, *How close are you?*

Nearly there, his thought came back. *I thought I heard a gunshot, was that you?*

Yes. We might be dealing with smarter monsters than we thought. Can you come in from the north?

I'll have to do it on foot, my horse is getting spooked. I think she smells the wolves.

Hurry.

I had a terrible suspicion that the wolves were hunting me in concert with one another. I needed an open space, somewhere with room to move. Leaning to the left, I cut across the next intersection then turned and nearly toppled to the side as a feminine scream cut the air and made sympathetic goosebumps race up my arms.

I righted myself on the side of a building, scraping my arm along the stone before angling to the right, leaping an abandoned tin bucket, and rocking forward. Speeding down the street at blinding speed, I had just enough time to catch a glimpse of a woman lying on the ground, scooting away from the massive shape of a hunting wolf.

Leaning back, banking right, I circled toward the alley, wind whipping my hair across my face as I came round. I cut the wheels, landed hard on my feet, and ran the last few steps with my pistol raised over the tip of my open umbrella. But the werewolf had already heard me and was bounding down the alley into the dark.

I squeezed off one careful shot, then turned just in time to see the second werewolf before it plowed into me like a crazed bull. The impact took me off my feet, and I hit the building behind me with enough force to drive the air from my lungs and make me see stars.

Dimly, as if through cotton stuffed in my ears, I heard the woman scream. But there was nothing dim about the rancid stench of the werewolf who leaped atop my body, pinning my right arm with one forepaw before it bit my right shoulder with crushing force.

My bones ground painfully together beneath the pressure, but the miraculous jacket held. Waves of heat ran down my body as the embroidered runes absorbed and redistributed the force. The creature pinned my gun hand but, by some miracle, I had managed to hold onto the umbrella.

Gritting my teeth against the pain, I jammed the tip against the monster's ribs and squeezed the secondary trigger. The blast of force blew the wolf off of me, but also sent the umbrella spinning backward out of my hand. Gasping for breath, I raised the pistol, but my arm still shook from the impact.

With terrible grace and speed, the werewolf rolled to its feet and leaped to the side, causing my first shot to go wide, sending flakes of rock spinning into the air from the impact on the cobbles. The terrified woman was huddled against the opposite wall, and she moaned as the werewolf growled: a basso rumble I felt in my chest.

Two shots left, and the other silver bullets were tucked into an inner pocket. I wouldn't have time to reach them before the beast pulled my head off. But it wasn't interested in me, anymore. The trembling woman leaked so much fear into the air that the beast's head swung toward her like a hypnotized snake.

And she was far closer to the monster than I.

"Hey!" I shouted as I wobbled to my feet. "You stinking, rat-faced, piss-for-brains, piece of dung! Come on! Over here!"

It ignored me. I raised the pistol again, only a little steadier this time, and squeezed off another shot. The werewolf whined and tripped as the bullet hit it in the hindquarters, but that wasn't enough to kill it.

Another deep growl sounded from behind me and a shiver of fear raced like ice down my spine. I may not leak as many tasty chemicals, but my fear was real enough. I turned slowly to see another werewolf emerge from the shadows, its mouth open in a doggy grin that showed a row of stained, shining teeth as long as my thumbs.

My umbrella was three feet away, too far, and I only had one bullet left. Thanks to my coat I might withstand another attack, but the woman certainly would not. Gritting my teeth, I raised the pistol and fired again. Several things happened at once.

A shadow descended from the sky, changing shape halfway through its descent. I watched it happen through my goggles and was nearly blinded. The figure glowed with radiant light, like a falling star, and hit the werewolf in the ribs hard enough to slam the beast backward. It tumbled snout over tail.

The woman screamed, so I turned and ran, tossing my pistol aside. A grenade would kill us all, and my silver blade was still tucked safely into the shaft of my umbrella. The only thing I could reach quickly was a knife. Moonlight reflected off the blade as I took three running steps and leaped.

My shoulder screamed in pain as I landed on the werewolf and drove my knife down and down. The woman screamed, and the wolf reared back. I plunged the knife between its ribs and held on as it clamped its teeth in the skirt of my coat and pulled. It wrenched its head back and forth, spinning, trying to dislodge me. The wounds healed nearly as fast as I could make them.

I only had to hang on long enough for help, long enough to keep the woman alive. But the werewolf adjusted his bite, slammed us both into the side of the building, and flung me away like a discarded chew toy. I hit the street and rolled, stomach spinning and vision nearly black.

Three shots rang out, evenly spaced, neat as a pin. Then two more. I lifted my head to see Aris casually wrench the werewolf's head from its body as Tony turned and fired two more shots into the already limping beast I had attacked. Running feet. Crying. Blood on the pavement. My goggles were pulled from my head and my face was taken between a pair of hands.

"Gwen, look at me."

I forced my eyes to focus. "Aris?"

"Good girl."

Then the ground was gone. I blinked and saw Tony kneeling before the woman. Her foot hung at the wrong angle, and her leg was all over blood, but I thought she would live. I let my head fall against Aris's chest, and thought to him, *Bowler hat man?*

Moon and stars, Gwen. Yes, I tracked him. I'll tell you all about it after we get you taken care of.

I sighed, closed my eyes, and thought, *You may call me Darling, now, if you like.*

10

Enough for Me

ARIS

Running Gwen back to SPI was significantly easier, and faster, than disposing of the werewolf bodies. He held her tight against his chest so she would not jostle, but when she gasped in pain or sucked air in through her teeth, he wished he could kill the werewolf once or twice more.

He'd broken the beast's back when he shifted halfway through his dive and planted both feet in its ribs. Even a werewolf could not heal fast enough to recover from that in time to defend itself. The creature had been a woman when its body reverted back to a human form.

He tried not to think about that, or about the other people he had killed as a servant of King Obyrron.

He hadn't had much of a choice, then. At least, not until Ophelia St. James rose through the ranks and poached him. She had been as ruthless as the faerie king, but nowhere near as cruel or cold. He thought maybe he had loved her once, as an orphaned puppy loves the first kind hand to touch it.

But those times were long gone, and if he killed now, it was to protect. That truth was a small fire in his stomach as he carried Gwen against his chest, running at an easy lope, and turned toward SPI.

"We need the key," he told her.

Her lashes fluttered, but she did not open her eyes, just rifled through her pockets with one hand until holding aloft a key. Her knuckles were scraped and sticky with drying blood. Aris reminded himself that the culprit was already dead, and shifted Gwen so he could unlock the door with one hand.

SPI was far closer and safer than the townhouse. The last thing she would have wanted was to show up at home and run across a member of her household, who would be terrified to see her bruised and bloodied. Though, they certainly could have used a bit of Mrs. Chapman's tea.

The woman must have had a healer or wise woman in her family line, given her facility with healing herbs.

He sat Gwen in one of the chairs, locked the door, and lit several lamps. Then he opened the downstairs cupboard and pulled out a blanket. It wasn't cold, but Gwen was shivering, so he wrapped the wool around her and gathered medical supplies.

"Who was so stupid as to brick up the downstairs fireplace," he muttered, returning with an armful of cloth, plasters, water, and a tincture of iodine.

"There is a dwarven heater," Gwen said, one arm emerging from the blanket to point into Tony's office.

He retrieved the device, flipped the switch, and began peeling Gwen out of her clothes as the little piece of artifice pumped out stored heat at a steady pace. She said nothing, merely held out a limb at his request or lifted her hair when he removed a garment. Soon she was down to her blouse and skirt, with a pile of clothes and the wheels and outer corset sitting on a nearby chair.

She'd been bitten, he knew, and though her scalp bled, he had gotten a good look at that during the run. It wasn't serious. So he began unbuttoning her blouse, his heart pounding hard against his breastbone as he imagined torn flesh. She watched him with large, dark eyes, her long lashes unblinking.

He peeled the shirt back and winced. Her shoulder was deeply bruised and swollen, splotches of purple and red blossoming out from the edge of her collarbone to the smooth muscle above her breast.

"Can you move your arm?" he asked around the lump in his throat.

She took a deep breath, held it, then raised her arm to the side, stopping about halfway with a little noise of pain in the back of her throat. But after a moment, she tried rotating the limb, and given her range of motion, he didn't think anything was torn or broken.

"It looks like you might have escaped without serious injury," he said, looking through his supplies. But there was nothing there to help the bruise, not even any leeches to suck out the blood pooling beneath her skin. "The cut on your scalp is shallow, but I can have that cleaned quickly."

"My scalp?" she asked, then raised her good arm to her head, feeling through her thick hair until she winced and pulled her fingertips away, red with blood. "Ah. I see."

"We should have killed them together," he said with the iodine in one hand and a bit of gauze in the other. Her hair was thick and matted to her scalp. It took a moment to clear the wound so he could sanitize it.

"Then we would have lost bowler hat man."

"It would have been worth it," he said, pressing the iodine-soaked gauze against the wound.

She took a quick breath and froze, then said through tight lips, "If we can stop this invasion at the source, no more people will die or be maimed by those monsters. A few scrapes are worth that."

"Not to me," he muttered beneath his breath.

"Aris," she reached up and took his wrist, then pulled him around the chair so she could see his face. Her lips were white with pain, but her eyes were clear and warm, soft and dark as seal fur. "That's not true. You know it's not true. You care for people; I have seen it."

"Maybe I do, but not at your expense. Or Samuel, or Sally, or Mrs. Chapman. I would sacrifice this city and everyone in it a hundred times before I would let harm come to you. Any of you."

She stared at him for a long time, unblinking, as if he were a puzzle she could figure out. He wished her good luck because he still hadn't done it.

"And yet you go hunting with me, and you watch me put myself in danger night after night."

It took a moment to unclench his jaw, but when he did, he said, "Because that is what you wish. You want to be free, and I would never try to take that from you. Ever. I know what it feels like to lose your freedom."

That was true, but not quite right. There was more he could not say, but perhaps he could give her as much truth as he was allowed

After thinking about it for a moment, trying to put to words the complex welter of emotions he'd never bothered to name and avoided exploring, he said, "You are a sword, Gwen. Bright and sharp. You must do what you were made for. To ask anything else of you would be as disrespectful...maybe as sacrilegious as putting you in a corner to rust.

"But that does not mean I want to see you broken. So no, to me, your life is worth more than every life in this city. But your will is what makes you who you are, and to snuff that out would be worse than watching you die, because it would mean you would cease to be yourself. I'm not explaining this well at all," he said, surging to his feet and tossing the dirty gauze onto the table as he strode toward the front of the office and linked his fingers at the back of his neck.

Then he turned, strode back toward Gwen, and grabbed a triangle of cloth from the table. "Stay still," he told her and wrapped the cloth around her torso to form a sling. She smelled of sweat, blood, and lavender.

When he was done, he leaned back, crouching at her feet on his heels, his hands resting on her knees. She brushed the hair from his forehead with her fingertips, her touch light and gentle. "It must be very hard, then, to come with me."

He laughed once and shook his head. "I never knew fear until I knew you."

Her fingertips paused a moment, then resumed stroking from his forehead to the back of his skull, running through his hair, making tingles of pleasure shimmer down his spine. He fell to his knees and laid his head on her lap.

"Not even when you were an assassin?" she asked, her palm running across his forehead, soothing.

"I was never afraid then."

"Why?"

"I had nothing to lose."

"What about your life?"

"That was no loss. In some ways, to die would have been a relief."

Her hand paused again, this time laying upon his brow like a benediction.

"It would have been a loss to me," she said, her voice soft.

Aris wrapped his arms around her legs and held on as Gwen brushed her hand over his forehead, across his temple, over and over, in a motion both soothing and rhythmic enough to put him to sleep.

"My mother used to rub my head like this when I couldn't sleep, or when I was sick," she said.

"It must have been very nice."

"It was, though I don't think I ever appreciated it as much as she deserved. What did your mother do when you were sick?"

"I don't have a mother."

Another pause, this time longer, before the comforting touch continued. "What happened to her?"

"I killed her being born. Turns out I was an assassin from birth."

Her fingers tightened in his hair a moment, as if she could grab that memory and jerk it out of his head by the roots. But he had started speaking and found he didn't want to stop. "My father was the king's assassin. I think he had raped my mother. And when he pulled me from between her legs, he claimed me as the heir to his position. Training began when I was four years old. He was cruel, and I hated him, but...I still wanted him to love me. Sometimes I dreamed about sneaking into his room and slitting his throat. Other times I dreamed he would tell me he was proud of me, and hold me in his arms."

Gwen leaned down and rested her head on his upper back, her breath a warm spot on his shoulder blade. "How did you come to be so kind?" she asked with a note of awe in her voice.

He snorted. "I'm not."

"Liar."

"I cannot lie."

He felt her cheek tense in a smile. "You lie all the time," she said.

How he wished he could tell her everything, wished there were no secrets between himself and the one person who had ever proved to him that goodness existed, not just in the mortal realm or the faerie lands, but at all. And he could not. The magic kept the words from passing his lips.

She did not ask questions, as she normally would have. He would have answered them and told her that yes, faeries, even Aos Sidhe could die in childbirth. That being immortal did not save them from violence. And that faeries could love, something he had never believed possible.

She did not ask, so he kept his mouth shut and enjoyed the feel of her, the comfort of her presence, and fell asleep on her lap.

The bells rang, Aris sat up with a start, and a voice said in tones not meant to be overheard, "Well, isn't that a lovely scene."

Tony stood at the door outlined by the moon through the large plate windows. He shook his head, locked the door, and dropped the key into his pocket.

"Is she alright?" he asked.

Aris carefully extricated himself from Gwen's lap. She shifted, making a little sound of protest, and fell back to sleep with her head pillowed on her good arm as it rested on the closest table. "A cut on her scalp, sore ribs, and a shoulder joint she likely won't be able to move for a few days at least."

Tony stared down at Gwen, his heart in his eyes. Aris didn't know whether to feel jealousy, pity, or gratitude. He had saved Gwen's life more than once, and he loved her. How could Aris blame him for that? And he wasn't smart enough to know why Gwen had turned him away, at last. For that, at least, he could be thankful.

Aris sighed and stood, stretched his back, and asked, "The woman? How is she?"

"I found a doctor rather quickly. He thinks the foot might be saved."

"Really?"

"That's how it sounds. Any trouble getting rid of the bodies?"

"Not with the Thames nearby."

Tony shuddered and pulled off his hat. He was a good man, an honest man, one who would sacrifice himself and the people he loved for the greater good. Which was exactly why Gwen felt unworthy of him, even if she didn't realize it.

Tony sank down into a chair of his own with an explosive sigh and kicked his feet up on the back of another chair before rubbing his face with a broad hand. Exhaustion was written in every line of the man.

"Where were you?" he asked.

Aris stiffened. "Where was I when?"

"When the werewolves attacked Gwen. Where were you?"

"Following bowler hat man."

"Who?"

"Lord Rutledge's driver is a vampire who keeps werewolves locked in abandoned buildings and lets them out at night to kill people. Does that answer your question?"

"You are a grade-a pain in the arse, did you know that?"

"And you are a self-righteous prig. Does that make us even?"

Tony's fists clenched, then relaxed as he sat up. "Lord Rutledge's driver, you say?"

"Yes. And I tracked him to an absolutely ordinary house. He walked in as if he owned the place, and left. So I flew back to Gwen as fast as I could."

"From the look of it, you were just fast enough. I thought that one would kill her before I could shoot both of them."

They both looked at the sleeping woman, her brown curls spilling down over the back of the chair, the elegant and far too vulnerable line of her neck pale in the lamplight. A small, half-circle scar, barely raised, was visible at the junction of her neck and shoulder. More evidence of a time he'd nearly been too late.

"Now that we know Bowler Hat is involved with the monsters and he has a connection to Rutledge, we'll have to follow that lead to the end," Tony said. "You seem the most logical person to investigate."

"We will see if Gwen agrees when she wakes up."

Tony shifted his weight and considered Aris with the kind of speculative look wartime commanders use to assess the fitness of their troops. He had to control the urge to smirk.

"You do realize that Gwen is consulting for me in this?"

Aris shrugged.

"Is her permission so important that you cannot make decisions for yourself?"

He did not intend for his voice to sound so flat, so dangerous, but it came out that way. "She is the only reason I am here, human. And the reason I choose to control my instincts. Never forget that. Besides"—he turned to look at Gwen, and his voice softened—"This is her home, not mine. I'll protect it when and how she sees fit."

Tony looked down at his hands, his brow furrowed. "I appreciate your devotion to her—"

"Your gratitude means nothing to me."

"—but...you need a life of your own, and a purpose."

Aris wanted to laugh but didn't bother. Tony had parents, brothers, a connection to this city and its people, as well as a sense of duty that mattered to him. He had grown to manhood knowing he would have a life of his own someday.

But Aris had been brought up to be a tool, an instrument in the hands of his king, and then in that of his general. His life had never been his own. At least, until he forced his way through the rift, nearly died, and found a reason to care in the heart of that sleeping woman.

Tony might never understand it, but Gwen was reason enough for him, whether she knew it or not.

And now there was also Sam, and Sally, and Mrs. Chapman and Mr. Yates. A family he had never hoped to have. That, too, was because of Gwen. She sighed in her sleep and turned her head until he could see her dark lashes lying against her cheek.

"I have a purpose, Hardwicke," he said. "You had better get some sleep."

Light blazed in through the plate windows and turned the backs of his eyelids red. Aris blinked and rubbed a hand across his eyes. Was it past ten? He had fetched a pillow from Tony's room, since the man had fallen asleep in his chair, and turned himself into a bed for Gwen, leaning against the wall with her pillowed on his lap.

His neck ached terribly.

He should have just carried her upstairs but hadn't liked the idea of her in Tony's room. That had been a bit of foolish selfishness, but he didn't think she would have wanted to wake there, either, and the other rooms were still occupied by fae refugees.

"God's breath," Tony moaned, followed by the creak of chairs as he pushed to his feet. Did he realize he had adopted Gwen's favorite curse? "Remind me never to sleep in a blasted chair again. And to get a couch or two for the office."

"There's a piece of paper," Aris said. "Why don't you take a note?"

Tony glared at him through sleepy eyes and stalked off to the back room to make tea. Gwen yawned, rolled over, and blinked. He watched her pupils dilate, then narrow as she looked up at him and realized where they must be.

"Good morning, Darling," he said. Her nose wrinkled in dislike, so he reminded her, "You did give me permission last night."

"I rescind."

"Too late."

She began to raise her arm to rub her eyes but gasped in pain and froze. "Ow."

Aris levered her into a sitting position and put the pillow under her elbow to support the injured arm. "Here, let me look at it."

She didn't resist as he opened the neck of her blouse and pulled the collar down over her shoulder. Instead of looking for herself, she watched his face as he examined the bruising and swelling.

"We need to get some of Mrs. Chapman's tea into you," he said. She kissed him.

Moon and stars, her kiss made his entire body light up in a way he'd never experienced. Better than wine or sun or icy water. Her mouth was so soft and the taste of her, salty and sweet, was an aphrodisiac. His cock hardened in a rush that might have brought him to his knees if he hadn't already been kneeling.

In the past, Aris had lain with fae women when he was lonely. They were extraordinarily beautiful, graceful, skilled lovers. Most of them could have brought legions of mortal men to their knees. But nothing touched him more than Gwen's honest passion, her humor, the unaffected nature of her goodness. She drew him like the tide to the moon.

Gwen leaned back, gave him a sleepy, heavy-lidded smile, and said, "Good morning."

"Moon and Stars, Raven, I sent you here to protect my sister, not to tempt her into your bed."

Aris shot to his feet so fast that the wind of his movement blew papers off of a nearby table. Ophelia stood in the open door, the sun bright on her golden hair, her extraordinarily beautiful face twisted in disgust.

Gwen caught her breath, then said in a broken little voice, "Lia."

11

The General

GWEN

M y sister stood in the doorway looking like a wrathful goddess, and for a moment I could not force my brain to believe what my eyes saw. She was here. Lia had come. I'd heard her speak, heard her voice, and yet none of it felt real.

Aris stood frozen, Lia glowered, and my mouth popped open and closed like a landed fish.

"Explain yourself," she ordered.

Aris swallowed audibly, then replied, "Do I understand that you are no longer General of the Faerie Armies under King Obyrron?"

Her voice was cold. "Obviously not."

"Then, forgive me, but I am no longer obliged to follow your orders."

Lia's jaw clenched as if she would have liked to say something more but could not. "Will you please explain why you are kissing my sister," she said in an approximation of a polite tone that, nonetheless, carried a note of command.

"I will not."

"Have you forgotten your duty?"

"How could I possibly?"

"Because you are too clever for your own good and have clearly discovered loopholes I did not foresee."

I scrambled to my feet, winced as my shoulder throbbed with pain, and asked, "Why are you here?"

Lia gave up her staring match with Aris and said, her voice a little softer, "You asked me to come. I took the train. But if you've changed your mind—"

"No! No. Of course not. It's just...well, I have asked you several times."

She looked down and clasped her hands. "I could not."

Aris opened his mouth but I grabbed his arm to silence him and stepped forward.

"You are here now."

"Yes, well. You said you needed help, and from the sound of things, the sooner we get started the better. What on earth happened to your shoulder?"

My shoulder was still exposed, swollen, and splotchy with purple-black bruising and little red spots of burst vessels. "A werewolf bit me."

"For the love of..." She stepped forward to examine the wound. After a moment, color flooded her pale cheeks and she turned on Aris to snap, "And you let this happen?"

"Actually," I said, "he saved my life. Again. He and Tony are the only reason I'm not worse off. But we did save a woman's life and stop three werewolves, so I am quite lucky to get off with a mere bit of bruising."

"Three?"

Footsteps sounded on the wood floor, then stopped abruptly. Tony stood frozen holding a tray laden with tea things, his hair still tousled from sleep. An evening's beard growth darkened his jaw, and a look of thunderstruck awe settled on his face.

To be fair, Lia was extraordinary. Instead of dressing in the fashion of the time, she wore her blonde hair down in waves that reached her hips with only the sides pulled back from her face, and a dress that looked more like a medieval gown than a modern daydress. It was as if Rapunzel had walked out of a fairytale and into his office.

"Ah, Lady St. James," he said. "Welcome to SPI. I'll get another cup for tea, shall I?"

He set the tray on a table with a clatter and strode to the back room. Lia paid him no mind but frowned at my shoulder. "When did this happen?"

"Last night."

"And there was no one to tend it for you? Never mind, clearly there was not."

Tony reappeared with a cup and saucer, and the three of us awkwardly sat at the table while Lia strode around the room, eyeing stacks of paper, fingering the contents of folders, and glancing at signs on the walls. She slid gracefully into the chair opposite me and asked Tony, "What is it that you do here, Mr. Hardwicke?"

"Has your mother not told you?"

"She has told me what she asked of you when she financed the company. I would like to know what you *do*."

Tony took a sip of his tea, presumably to give himself a moment to think, and finally said, "We investigate supernatural and paranormal activity in New London."

"Why?"

Tony looked at me as if I should have answers, but I was still processing her presence and had no insight.

"To help people," he said, at last.

She considered him gravely, hazel eyes narrowed, lips pursed. "Very well then," she said, "I will work for you."

"Excuse me?"

"I'm sorry?"

"What?"

Lia weathered the barrage of questions in silence, waiting until each of us simply sat there, staring at her in mute confusion. She had the same expression on her face Mama often had when she knew the answer to a question and was merely waiting for others to figure it out on their own.

Had she truly only come here for a job?

"Gwen asked me to come here, and I need some way to pass the time. I assume there is a spare room upstairs?"

Tony nearly choked on his tea and grabbed a napkin to cover his coughing. "Here?" he sputtered, wiping drops of tea from the front of his shirt.

Giving Tony a moment to collect himself, I said, "That's ridiculous, Lia. You will come and stay with me in the family townhouse, of course."

"No, Gwen. I won't. That is your home, now, with a settled family life. I would not like to intrude. However, now that I am here, perhaps you can tell me how it is you think that I can help."

Lia was here, sitting across from me in the sunshine drinking tea as if she had never left, and yet everything was different. She was colder, autocratic, with all of Mama's aura of command but none of the warmth.

This was not the way I had pictured it when I imagined finally bringing her home. While Tony and Aris explained the situation, including Bowler Hat and his unlikely hideout, I tried to bury all the hopes I had cherished of what life would be like when Lia finally came home.

For months I had told myself to be patient, to give her space, and had somehow maintained the belief that eventually she would come around and we would be happy again. But the woman across the table was not the laughing girl I remembered. She was the stone-faced general who had ordered Aris whipped.

"...and that is about the shape of it," Tony finished, placing his teacup gently on the saucer.

"And they are up there now?" Lia said. "These faerie refugees?

"Yes."

"What exactly is it you think I can do for them?"

"Well," Tony said, hesitantly looking in my direction for support.

I hadn't any specific ideas when I'd cried to Lia for support over our ring connection. In truth, she had ignored me nearly every night since I had first tried to call her, and my request had been made with no expectation of her answering.

But now that she was here, I thought of a thing she could help with.

"We hoped you would convince them to stay at a house I secured some time ago. It is in a safer part of town where they can be protected more easily. So far, they have not been very receptive. Tony has an investigation to oversee, and he cannot look after them while trying to pin down Lord Rutledge."

Lia thought that over while running the tip of one finger around the lip of her teacup in slow circles. "Very well. What else do you need help with, Mr. Hardwicke?"

Tony's eyes were already wide with the same panicked expression I had often seen on the faces of anyone who found themselves on the commanding end of Mama's voice. But she didn't give him a chance to answer.

"Never mind, I am certain we will discover that as we go. As I am sure you know, I have honed particular skills in strategy, statecraft, and espionage. For now, there is something we can do for those people. Mr. Hardwicke, will you order enough carriages for our guests? Raven, come with me."

She stood, turned, and headed up the stairs with her green gown billowing behind her. Aris and Tony looked at one another, then resolutely began following orders. And what did she mean for me to do while she neatly took things in hand?

Gritting my teeth, I stood and followed them up the stairs, ignoring the pain in my shoulder and the growing frustration beginning to claw holes in my chest.

She had spent years as a general, second to the king, and was used to giving orders and taking command. It was probably second nature, by now. At least, that is what I reminded myself as I followed Aris up the stairs.

"This room?" she asked, pointing to the closed door at the top of the stair.

"Be kind, General," Aris said in a gentle voice. "They're frightened."

She ignored him, opened the door, and stepped inside. Sitting in small groups chatting or standing near the window, the faeries appeared to have grown more comfortable with the space, despite the fact that it was still far too small for seven people. Wait...I counted and realized two more had joined the ranks. Their heads snapped around and their eyes fixed on Lia.

Someone whispered, "The Raven," but that fearful voice was overshadowed by the few faeries who knew of my sister.

"It is the General."

"Moon and stars, no!"

"She has come to drag us back!"

"Silence," Lia said. Her voice was not unkind but it had the confident snap of authority. "Today you will be moving to a new house, a safer place where you will be protected so Mr. Hardwicke can focus on ending this threat to your lives. I give you my unqualified word that no harm will come to you through anyone in this building, and you will be protected with as much care as if you belonged to our own households."

The faeries looked from Lia to one another, cautious hope dawning in their eyes and on their faces. But it was not full-blown trust, not yet.

Lia said, "Furthermore, Lady St. James, the owner of the house, grants you full guest rights while you are under her roof."

This had the intended effect. Their shoulders drooped, their expressions lightened, and an overall spirit of enthusiasm bubbled up like a spring, making the whole room lighter. This was the reason Aris had demanded the status of guest while we negotiated with the Cutthroat King; a guest was to be cared for and protected, to eat at the host's table, and receive the protection even of the host's body, if necessary.

"We shall call for you when transportation has arrived. For the nonce, please prepare yourselves and whatever provisions you have at your disposal."

A bustle broke out among the faeries as they began tidying the room and preparing themselves. Lia backed quietly from the room, then descended the stairs without waiting for us. She had blown into the office, neatly taken control, and was now leading us by our noses like barely trained hounds.

"They will be ready when the carriages arrive, Mr. Hardwicke," Lia said before seating herself at the table and, with a snap of her fingers, conjuring a small green flame that sprung up around the base of the teapot. After a moment, she poured herself a steaming cup of tea and sipped it delicately.

"You retained your magic," Aris said, impressed.

Lia shook her head. "Only the vestiges of it. And it took me months to manage so small a flame as that. Mortal lands were not built for magic, as the Sunset Lands were. Everything is harder here."

Tony took advantage of the warm teapot to pour himself another cup, flicked his fingers at Aris, and said, "Then how is it he can flicker into a raven at the drop of a hat?"

"Flicker?" Aris asked, mildly.

"The Raven is a therianthrope. That is what he *is*, not merely something he can do."

"Like being born with green eyes?" Tony asked.

"Precisely."

"And how is that different from your magic?"

Lia thought about it for a moment, then said, "Can you do a backflip, Mr. Hardwicke?"

"A backflip? No, I don't believe I can."

"But you possess all the necessary anatomy, do you not?"

"I suppose so."

"And if you trained long enough, do you think you could manage one?"

He shrugged. "Perhaps."

"That is the difference. You cannot train yourself out of having blonde hair, or brown eyes, but you do possess the necessary requirements for a backflip if you have the patience to learn the technique for it. I have the necessary requirements for magic—faerie magic—but it is much easier to use in the Sunset Lands. I must train myself to use them here."

"I see," Tony said, in a tone that said he didn't quite see, but he was willing to accept the matter.

"How long till the carriages arrive?" I asked.

Modulating my tone to sound disinterested and polite, rather than irritated and hurt, took most of my impressive self-control.

Tony glanced at his watch. "A few more minutes, I think."

"Good. Ophelia, if you would?" I said, gesturing toward the back of the office.

She quickly disguised her surprise, then stood with all the grace of a queen and floated down the hall and toward the back room. I followed her with much less grace, gingerly avoiding jostling my shoulder, and heard Aris's voice in my head say, *Go easy, Darling*.

Do not *call me that,* I thought back, putting as much venom into my voice as possible.

Lia strode to the center of the crowded storage room, and, even surrounded by piles of boxes and papers, she looked icy and regal. I pulled the door closed with my uninjured arm and fought to control my temper.

"What are you doing?" I asked.

"What do you mean?"

"Why are you here?"

"I already answered that question. You asked me, if you'll recall."

"Oh, I recall. I also recall asking you—no, *begging* you—night after night for months to simply *speak* to me. I would have been grateful for a single word. And now you show up here as if you've been summoned for a job interview, ignore me, and order everyone about as if you are still the general of the king's army."

My voice steadily rose as heat suffused my face, but Lia met my anger with icy calm. "If you did not want me here, perhaps you should not have asked me to come."

"Of course, I want you here! But I don't understand this...this frigidity. I did not think you wantonly cruel and I do not understand why...this is not like you. None of it."

She raised her chin. "You do not know me, Gwen."

A pained laugh climbed up my throat using sharp claws. "Of course, I do. I know you better than anyone ever will. You are my sister, Ophelia Magnolia St. James, whether you regret that fact now or not."

An angry blush turned her pale cheeks red and splotchy. "You. Do. Not. Know. Me. I am not the girl who whispered her dreams in the dark and jumped into faerie rings. That girl died a long time ago."

"No, she—"

"She was beaten to death in the halls of the king," she interrupted savagely. "She spent years being abused, learning to lie, to cheat, to play politics better than immortal beings hundreds of years older than she. The day I killed my first faerie, the girl you remember as your sister died. I burned her in effigy, and the woman I cobbled together from her ashes *is* cold, Gwen; calculating, cautious, and cruel."

A tear spilled down my cheek, but I ignored it. "I don't believe you."

"No, you don't. Because you still think love conquers all. You are still wrapped up in storybook idealism, purposefully blind to the reality of the world because it is safer and it doesn't hurt as much."

How could she say these things? She could not be the cruel, cold person I saw, the person she proclaimed herself to be. "But you saved me."

"Yes," she spat, her face twisting in anger. "I saved you. At the expense of a decade of secrecy and sacrifice. Do you have any idea what it cost me to infiltrate Obyrron's court and gain his favor? To plan with Queen Titania, to recruit dissenters, to kill the opposition, to gain alliances and earn favors, all so that I could protect you and Mama and the rest of the mortal lands from domination by a creature as cruel and heartless as King Obyrron? I told you I could not come back, I told you to leave me, but you did not listen. You pulled me through the wall, anyway."

"I was trying to save your life!"

"No, you wanted to use me without any thought for what it might cost! You were trying to plug the hole in your chest because you thought I was a magic cure for your feelings of inadequacy. You were selfish, and you may have damned us all."

I stumbled backward as if she had hit me in the chest with a sledgehammer.

"You were so single-minded you never stopped to ask yourself what it might cost me," she said, her voice quavering. Her knees gave out and tears filled her eyes as she collapsed onto a pile of boxes.

"Everything tastes like ash," she whispered. "Everything is dull and ugly, and imperfect. My magic is gone, and all my hard work, for years, will amount to nothing. Without me to stop him, he will invade and destroy everything, even my memories. It would have been kinder to kill me."

My own legs threatened to give out as whatever remained of my life came crashing down on top of me. I remembered the perfection of the Sunset Lands, the unworldly beauty of the fae and the Aos Sidhe in particular, and the warning that if I ate faerie food, I would crave it for the rest of my life. I had willingly, and for my own benefit, dragged my sister from the most beautiful place I had ever imagined and trapped her in the mortal world, which was dull and lifeless by comparison.

And I had done it for myself. So I wouldn't be alone. I had allowed my own weakness to hurt the one person I had been desperately trying to save for nearly my entire life, and that weakness has caused her incalculable pain, pain I could not even guess at. No wonder she hated me now. But she had cared enough to save my life, once.

"You sent Aris to protect me?"

She nodded.

"And you put the geis on him so he would not be able to speak of your orders or his relationship to you?"

"Yes."

"Remove it."

She raised her head, her face tear-streaked and tired. "What?"

"Remove the geis."

"No. He will no longer be compelled to protect you if I do."

"Remove it. Now."

Lia stared at me for a long time, and whatever she saw in my face was convincing enough that she said, "I free the Raven from any oath he has made, and promise or favor he owes me."

The air crackled with something like static electricity, tingling along my skin and the ends of my hair. Lia sagged as if that act sapped whatever energy she had left. She looked like a broken doll left huddled on the dresser of an abandoned bedroom.

I turned to leave, dragging the hollow shells of my broken dreams behind me. When I reached the door she said, her voice quiet, "You never needed me, Gigi. This life you built for yourself, the people who love you, everything you have accomplished...you did all of it without me."

No, I had done it because of her. Stopping long enough to bite back a sob, I said over my shoulder, "I will always need my sister, Lia."

I opened the door and strode through the front office. I had to get out, get away, be anywhere other than here. Tony and Aris stood, concern in the tense lines on their faces. Aris reached out to stop me, but I caught his wrist and said, "Don't touch me."

The long muscles of his throat clenched in a painful swallow.

"You are free, Aris Blackwing," I said. "I made certain of it. No one controls you any longer. You can go and live your life as you see fit."

Pain pulled the corners of his mouth into a frown and drew his brows together, but he nodded.

I released his arm and left, letting the front door slam closed behind me.

12

Reflections

GWEN

S ally was practicing magic despite everything I taught her about the inherent danger of it. Aris had stayed by my side for years not because of any loyalty or love for me but because of an oath he could not break. The faeries would invade, unheeded, and destroy New London.

At least, they would destroy whatever was left after the werewolves and vampires had their way.

And Lia hated me.

God's breath, had I failed at every single thing I tried to do? And I thought myself so clever, seeing things other people missed and making plans to win the day, all whilst everything I built slowly rotted beneath me.

I barely saw the street, or the scandalized looks on the faces of pedestrians who saw my bare shoulder and hair hanging loose down my back. I was practically naked, as far as they were concerned, with not even a vest to cover my thin blouse. But I could not bring myself to care.

A shadow flashed across my face, blocking out the sun for an instant, then raced along the cobbles in front of me. Shading my eyes with one hand, I looked up to see a raven wheel overhead. The bird dipped its wings in acknowledgment, but I heard no voice inside my head. Aris had that much common courtesy, at least.

A line of carriages rumbled past me. If I did not hurry, the faeries would arrive at the house before I did. I made to lower my wheels, realized I wasn't wearing them, swore, and began jogging. Shooting pain radiated down my arm from shoulder to elbow with every step, so I held the arm tight against my chest as my feet flapped on the sidewalk.

By the time I reached the house, sweat ran down my temples and beaded on my upper lip, my shoulder burned and throbbed, and I couldn't catch my breath. But the carriages had all parked in a row, waiting, and Tony stood on the doorstep.

He said nothing and did not try to help me as I fumbled the key from the inner pocket of my skirt and unlocked the front door. I had not secured a butler, so it was up to Tony and I to ensure the rooms were prepared. Thankfully the place had come fully furnished.

We were short one bedroom, so Hilder and another woman elected to share, but they needed extra linens. I wrestled the blankets down with one arm, shut the door with my hip, and walked to their room.

Hilder was busy opening the window to clear the stale air, and the other woman sat on a chair near the bed with her bony arms wrapped around herself.

"These are for you," I said, and laid the cloth across her lap.

She reminded me of vines that had lived long into winter, spindly and dry, ready to crack with the slightest pressure but unwilling to give up. Her glamour was stupendous, even going so far as to make her eyes appear rheumy. She patted my hand with a gentle smile, then eyed my damaged shoulder, which I still had not bothered to disguise.

"That must hurt terribly," she said in the exact kind of voice I would have expected her to have: thin, dry, but warm.

"It has not been my favorite experience, but—well, I shall soldier on. What else is there to do?"

"What else, indeed. Sometimes all we can do is press on. But we don't have to do it alone." She held up both hands and said, "May I?"

I nodded, uncertain of what she intended but willing to let her do it. What could it hurt, at this point? She placed one hand on my chest just below the collarbone, and the other on the back side of my injured shoulder. Her touch was light and cool...cold, even. A shiver ran down my arm as the icy sensation sank into the joint, numbing the pain.

When the little faerie woman pulled her hands away, sweat beaded on her brow and she looked terribly tired.

"Don't move it too much," she said as I shifted my arm experimentally. "I haven't healed anything, only helped with the pain."

"You are kind," I said, pressing her hands and letting gratitude pour into my voice. "I hope you did not tire yourself, overmuch?"

"It is nothing a little nap won't fix. We are grateful for your help, even those who are afraid and cannot show it. We never expected to find kindness in mortal lands, only refuge. It is a great relief. Perhaps there need not always be enmity and fear between our peoples."

"I certainly hope not."

"If you don't mind," she said around a yawn, "I think I shall nap."

I left them to it and trudged down the stairs to the front door, feeling more exhausted than I had after a night of werewolf fighting. My bones wanted to sink into the earth. I imagined myself beneath a tree, growing moss.

"We are going to need someone to protect them, someone who does not reek of faerie blood. Many someones if we can get them." Aris leaned against the doorjamb with his arms folded, watching me with wary eyes. He'd neatly couched his argument in a way that prevented me from asking him to stay.

So, instead, I said, "Why are you still here? You are free from the geis and any other promises, agreements, or oaths to Ophelia. I made certain of it."

He lowered his eyes and his chest expanded in a deep breath. I knew him well enough to recognize the mixture of pleasure and pain in his body, on his face.

"If I were only here because of the geis," he said, "you would have been dead more than once. Or do you forget how good faeries are at obeying the letter of their oaths, rather than the spirit of them?"

"I have no desire for a companion with a misplaced sense of duty," I said, stepping past him and onto the porch.

He caught my good wrist and stopped me, knowing that the other was too injured for me to slap him the way I desperately wanted to.

"What about a companion who wants you so much they cannot breathe when you are near?"

"How can you—" I swallowed back the knot of pain in my throat and jerked my wrist from his grip. "How can you say that to me? No—don't answer. I'm not a fool, Aris. I saw the way you looked at my sister. You care for her. You stayed with me because she asked it of you, and that's...that's noble. But you are not bound to me or to this, anymore," I said, waving my hand at the house, the city, and everything else we'd been fighting for.

"How can *you* say that to *me*?" he asked in a vicious whisper, repeating my words with different emphasis, his eyes hot and only inches from mine. "You think you can chase me off as easily as you did Tony, is that it? You would rather wallow in self-pity than recognize—"

"I know your expressions," I snarled. "I saw the affection in your eyes, and I heard it in your voice. I know you had no choice in the matter, you were fulfilling a duty by staying with me, but I have freed you from that obligation. So go!"

"You little fool. Why would you try to convince yourself of this when you saw me whipped at her command and ordered about like a trained hound?"

"Do you deny your affection for her?"

"No. But it is the affection of a dog for the first hand that did not strike it," he said, his voice cold.

He leaned back, rolled his shoulders as he so often did in raven form, and seemed to settle back into his body. "Your sister fought for her place and overcame hardships I will not even speak of. I respect her greatly, and I do not blame her for the choices she made to survive. But she is also a tyrannical harridan unworthy of my love."

I slapped him, my good hand flying before I had a chance to think. "Don't you dare say such things about my sister."

"I could not have said it if it wasn't the truth."

"*Your* truth, you mean."

He raised one dark brow, waiting for me to catch the meaning of my own words. "Do you know why you insist on treating me like some human who can lie to you? Because that would make it easier for you to push me away. And if you cannot find a good enough reason, you will invent one, even something as ridiculous as that." He stepped close, the heat of his body bridging the gap between us. "But I am not going anywhere. You cannot chase me away because you are too hurt to believe you deserve love. Perhaps soon, you'll learn that."

Aris took two steps down the stairs, shimmered, and flew off. For some reason, the sight of him disappearing into the sky made my chest tighten and tears prick the backs of my eyelids. I wanted nothing more than to crawl into a hole and cry until I was too tired to feel anything...but I was *not* going to cry.

No matter how much my stomach hurt or my throat ached with unshed tears, important things needed doing, and there was a city of innocent people in danger with not enough heroes to protect them.

If the last year had taught me anything, it was that action was the best cure for pain.

I dug the silver coin from my pocket and stared at the emblem of the smiling man, a grotesque head with its throat cut pressed in silver.

Perhaps it was time to play this game an entirely different way.

Two burly men showed up to relieve Tony an hour later, to be spelled by another two at nightfall. The Cutthroat King was good to his word as an ally, and I needed to deliver on mine. I told him I would rid the city of monsters, and a plan had been slowly forming in my mind for the last two days.

Tomorrow was the first night of the full moon cycle, and while it would be a very bad night for the city, the night after, the true full moon, would be the worst.

I needed to work fast.

And while I did that, I had to track Bowler Hat back to Lord Rutledge and get the evidence we needed to expose the truth. I did not want to call on him, but I didn't have much choice. I spoke Aris's name in the hollows of my mind.

Yes?

Will you please investigate Bowler Hat's hideout? I'm going to see the witches. I think I've got a plan.

Is that wise?

They are part of this city and they claim to care for it. We will find out just how much.

Care to share your plan with me?

Not yet. Let me work out the details, first.

Gwen...

My heart stuttered, but I ignored it. *Yes?*

After a moment of tense silence, he said, *Be careful.*

I cut the connection and held out my good arm for a cab. It took a few tries to find one willing to carry me home, given my general state of dishabille and obvious injuries, but before another hour passed, I was being properly fussed over by Mrs. Chapman in the study.

"This is absolutely unacceptable, Lady Gwen, and I will not stand for it," she said, watching me drink down every drop of her medicinal tea. My shoulder was still cold with faerie magic, but Mrs. Chapman's healing herbs would bring down the soft tissue swelling and give me back a bit of my range of motion.

"My dear woman," I began, but she grabbed my face and forced me to look into her serious grey eyes. Her hair was pulled back in such a tight bun that it kept the skin on her forehead tight, making her strangely more intimidating than usual.

"No, you will not be talking yourself out of this one, girl. I want to know what is happening and I want to know, now, or I will send for your lady mother by telegraph. So help me, I will! You showing up at all hours of the night, bruised and injured, too thin, not eating..."

To my great surprise, tears gathered in her eyes, threatening to spill over, but she glowered them back into hiding.

"You will tell me, and you'll tell me now."

As her employer, I could order her to mind her business. But the good lady had been my nurse long before she'd been my housekeeper. She deserved to know the truth as much as anyone in the city. And the worry in her voice and eyes was irresistible to my bruised heart.

"Very well, Mrs. Chapman. If you will gather Mr. Yates and Charlotte, as well, I will tell you all three at once."

She stared into my eyes a moment longer to be certain I wasn't lying, then disappeared in a flourish of black skirts. Sam brushed past her on his way into the study, still sweating from a workout in the gym, and said, "Oh, is this tea?"

"Only if you want a bit of Mrs. Chapman's medicine."

He paused, then dropped his hand before he could wrap his fingers around the teapot handle. "Who needs—"

Then he saw me and his words puttered out. Judging by the look on Sam's face, I was as much of a mess as I assumed myself to be. Only, the look of shock and pity didn't last long. It was quickly replaced by fury I had never seen in his eyes. His jaw tightened, his fists clenched, and if I didn't know better, I would think the boy capable of murder.

"Who did this to you, my lady?" he asked.

"You have seen me injured before, Sam."

"Who did it? I'll beat them bloody, I swear it."

A response like that only came from genuine affection, and that hurt my chest almost as much as watching Aris fly away had done. "I believe you would, my dear. But even your new skills will not help you bloody a werewolf. Besides, the beast is already dead."

Sam's mouth popped open. He knew of my history with were-wolves, and he had been with me on more than one dangerous adventure, but for some reason, he hadn't expected this.

To distract him, I said, "Will you get Sally for me? There is something I must tell everyone, and I would rather not explain it more than once."

He continued staring for a moment, then shook his head like a dog shaking off water. "Sally isn't here, Lady Gwen. She's gone out for the afternoon."

My own hands clenched into fists. I suspected where she had gone, and as much as I wanted to be angry with her, that was my fault, too. Had I been home more, to teach and help her, perhaps she would not have felt so drawn there. But I could handle that later.

Mrs. Chapman entered the room with Mr. Yates on her heel. His calm, honest face was as placid as ever, but his eyes kindled to light when he saw me. I must make it a point to avoid the mirror, after this.

"I have some things to tell you, and they will not be easy to hear, but as I am a key part of it all, it is only fair for you to know so you might make choices that are best for yourselves. Please feel free to sit, if you'd like."

None of them moved, just stood and watched me patiently. So, I took a deep breath and explained everything—at least, everything that was mine to share. Mrs. Chapman sank into a chair halfway through. By the end, she was holding Mr. Yates's hand while her other was pressed to her chest.

"Miss Lia?" she asked, her voice choked. "My lady, is it true?"

"It is. But Miss Lia has been through much, so she may not choose to come here and see us. We must let her make the choices that are best for her, even if that means she chooses not to include us in her life. And that is the choice I give to you all now."

They looked at one another, questions in their eyes.

"The world has gotten infinitely more dangerous," I said. "And I am at the center of much of the danger. I think you have known for quite some time that my life is not safe, and now you know why. I intend to protect this city, and you all, by whatever means I have at my disposal, but life here will only get more dangerous. If you choose to stay with me, you will be in danger, as well. If you would prefer to leave, I will send you to the country, or to Wainwright, or wherever you'd like, with your full pensions plus a bonus."

For the first time in my life, I saw an expression on Mr. Yates's normally placid face that was plain and strong: disgusted offense. "I have no intention of going anywhere, my lady, and I am insulted that you should feel the need to offer it."

"Indeed," Mrs. Chapman said, standing and brushing out her skirts as if my offer had dirtied them. "Dinner is still at eight, my lady. And I expect you to be cleaned up by then. You are an absolute mess."

The two of them stormed out of the room, leaving Charlotte alone with Sam and me.

She fiddled with her fingers as she decided what to do. "I enjoy working for you very much, my lady. Perhaps...if the danger is as great as you say...perhaps I might work for the Her Grace for a few weeks? Just until the worst of things has blown over?"

I smiled at the girl. Her round cheeks were pink with shame, but I could not blame her in the least. "You support your mama as well, do you not, Charlotte?"

"Yes, ma'am."

"Very well. Head home while it is light, and get yourself and your mama ready to travel. James will take you to the train station. Ask Mr. Yates for your wages and a bonus before you go."

"Oh," she said, looking at her feet, "I could not take a bonus, my lady."

"Charlotte?"

"Yes, ma'am?"

"Hush."

"Yes, ma'am."

When they were gone, Sam said, "How can I help?"

I closed my eyes and pictured him, not as the tall, gangly young man he was now, with broad shoulders and long arms and a mop of messy blonde hair, but the small, snub-nosed boy sitting in my coach and glaring at me with jam smeared on his cheeks.

There was nothing I wanted less than to involve him and Sally in this affair. But this was his city, and his home, and had a right to defend it if he chose. Heart fluttering in terror, I reached into my pocket and pulled out the coin.

"I'll need a messenger," I said.

Sam's cheeks paled, but he clenched his jaw and took the coin with a nod.

"I will see if Delilah can make you a ring as well," I told him, then looked down at my hands, covered in silver rings; one for Lia, Tony, Aris, and Alix. Soon one for Sam. I had nearly killed myself last year freeing him from the clutches of the Cutthroat King, and now I was putting him back into the man's hands.

"Has Aris taught you how to use a knife?" I asked around the lump in my throat.

"Yes, ma'am," Sam said, then pulled a knife from somewhere in his trousers, did a complicated trick by flipping it around his fingers, and caught the hilt. At least he held the thing properly.

"No flourishes or fancy tricks, Sam. A knife is an ugly weapon, and if you have to use it be quick and quiet, and get away before it can be used against you. Efficiency is the key, not flash."

He nodded and pocketed the knife. "Where is Aris?"

"Miss him, do you?"

"No," he said in a tone of voice that told me he did, in fact, miss the older man and he did not want me to know it.

"He is off doing something dangerous of his own. And no, you cannot help him. For tonight, stay close to the house and protect Mr. Yates and Mrs. Chapman and your sister, when she comes home. Tomorrow will be a different story."

"Yes, ma'am."

Sam looked at my shoulder again and winced, then bent to kiss my cheek, and left me sitting in the study, alone, with a heavy heart but a lighter soul. They had chosen to stay, and they had chosen me. Somehow that made the rest more bearable, if more frightening.

I rocked to my feet and headed upstairs, calling for a plate of lunch on my way. After quickly breaking my fast and washing with a rag and basin of water, I twisted up my hair with one

hand—which was probably the most impressive feat I had managed all day—and wriggled into something suitable for a meeting.

I checked in with Tony, sent a note to Delilah by way of Sam
and James, and stared at myself in the mirror. Mrs. Chapman
was right; I was too thin, and pale. My eyes looked hollow and
my shoulder—though significantly less swollen thanks to Mrs.
Chapman—was misshapen beneath my clothes. I was certainly
not looking my best, but it would have to do.

I hoped the witches would understand because I was tired of
failing. For my plan to work, we needed their help.

13

Alliances

GWEN

Madame Matilda took three-quarters of an hour to meet me in the drawing room of the building on Tromwell Lane. Instead of her usual display of dignified elegance, she strode into the room with a frown and a stubborn set to her jaw, black curls bouncing on her shoulder.

She was a breathtaking woman, with olive skin and dark eyes surrounded by long lashes, but at that moment she looked rather intimidated as she glowered down at me with her lips pursed and her thick brows perched low over the bridge of her nose.

"I would like to make it very clear, Lady St. James, that neither I nor the rest of the Triumphant Sisterhood are at your beck and call. We have had a cordial relationship but I would encourage you not to presume upon our goodwill."

Her tone made me want to reply with a sarcastic comment, but insulting my hostess was not a good way to win her as an ally, especially not one as proud as Matilda. So, I swallowed my natural response and said, "Please forgive me, Madame Matilda, I meant no insult. But dire events are on the horizon, and I thought it only fair to warn you, and prudent to consult you."

She opened her mouth, clearly prepared for a snarky rejoinder, then blinked and narrowed her eyes at me. "That sounds...rather unlike you."

Charm and grace, Gwen, I told myself. "So it does. It is true, however. Might we speak?"

Matilda sat slowly, watching me with suspicious but interested eyes like one might watch a wild animal who has wandered too close. She pulled off her gloves with a few swift motions, then folded her hands in her lap and raised her brows.

Might as well get right to the point, and pray she would be understanding rather than hostile. And would not use the information against me. "When I was sixteen, my twin sister Lia was kidnapped by faeries. Last year I used a spell from the grimoire to retrieve her from the Sunset Lands, but when the spell broke apart, it pulled me through. Eventually, I succeeded in bringing her home, but I also learned that Obyrron, the fae king, plans to invade the mortal realm starting right here, in New London."

"You performed magic?" she demanded, dark eyes hard and shining like obsidian.

"Not quite. I used a different technique to activate the spell."

Matilda's expression said that she wanted to ask me a thousand other questions, but I had no intention of explaining the process Delilah and I had uncovered. At least, not yet. She must have seen that in my face because she nodded for me to continue.

"I tried to warn city officials on more than one occasion, culminating in the meeting you so generously hosted. Every attempt has been a failure. And I believe I know why."

"Because mortals are not prepared to acknowledge that they are not the rulers of reality?"

"That," I agreed, "and several powerful members of society have been colluding with the enemy and actively suppressing the information. Namely, the Marquis of Rutledge. He has been sabotaging the realm for years, including putting the grimoire in Cassandra's hands and setting a vampire upon Lord Ashcroft. We believe he is also behind the recent influx of monsters into the city."

My host thought a while in silence. Matilda was one of the cleverest women I had ever met. She had gotten the better of me on more than one occasion, which made coming to her for help rather distasteful.

She was also a witch with a large coven here in the city, meaning she was as much of an outlaw as I was, perhaps more so; I only broke societal norms, but the Triumphant Sisterhood broke the law that banned witches from the city.

If I could convince her, she would be as powerful an ally as the Cutthroat King, and I needed her coven for my plan to work at all.

"Do you have any proof he is behind it?" she asked, at last.

"Last night we spotted his driver releasing werewolves into the city, and tracked the man back to a nondescript house."

"That is not nearly enough, Lady Gwen, you know that. Especially if the conspiracy does not stop with Rutledge."

"We are still investigating. But I had hoped, with the combined social power and insight of the Sisterhood, you might have a bit more information."

"We are mere women," she said with venom dripping from every word. "What can we know about the inner workings of politics?" With a sigh, she settled herself and collected her thoughts. "You and I have chosen two different routes to power, Lady Gwen. You chose to work outside the system, and I within it. That is why secrecy is so vital to my organization. I have direct access to many in positions of power but, unfortunately, even I cannot open closed doors."

"But you can listen through them," I said.

She smiled. "That I can. But if anyone is discussing a clandestine alliance with the fae, they have not said so behind any doors I have listened through."

"Could you?"

"Not soon enough. Spells like that take time to craft, and they need a focus. We would have to know when and where a meeting was taking place, and even then, there is no guarantee we would hear anything worthwhile. And the full moon is only a day away."

So she had been thinking of the danger, as well. "Has the Sisterhood done anything? To protect the city, I mean?"

"I don't know that I can share that with you."

"What about an alliance, then? Only for as long as it takes to protect the city from these monsters and the fae invasion."

"No. We cannot leave anything so significant as an alliance open-ended."

"Three months?" That ought to be long enough.

Matilda leaned back and regarded me with penetrating eyes, one finger tapping as she thought. "You have something planned, don't you? Something you need the Sisterhood for."

Now or never, as they say. I explained my plan, both to capture Lord Rutledge and to expose the truth in a way that it could not be silenced or hushed up by those in power. When I finished, both her brows were raised and the toe of her boot tapped rapidly on the floor.

"Can the Sisterhood do something like that? If you agree to the alliance, that is?"

"Perhaps, but the toll it would take...for magic to work in a coven, all of our members must be fully committed to sharing the load, and to the consequences of their burden. So they must believe the goal is worthwhile. And with a spell as complex as this one, we would need every member to agree."

Human bodies were never meant to wield magic, one of the primary forces of existence. We were too frail. Channeling that energy had physical costs, which was why so many witches were identifiable by their broken and disfigured bodies. The Triumphant Sisterhood circumvented that cost by carefully choosing their spells for efficiency and sharing the burden of channeling the magic amongst many bodies. Less individual power, but less physical cost.

They were too clever to accept much danger, but that prudence also hampered them.

Which was why I brought a bargaining chip. "What if, as part of this alliance, I offered a focus?"

"It would have to be exceptionally powerful, and even then—"

I pulled the Eye from my bag. The faceted crystal was the size of my closed fist, and so heavy it was difficult to hold with one hand. Light gathered in its center, making it glow faintly, and the air around it practically hummed with energy.

Magical symbols were inscribed on one side in what I thought might be Mycenaean, across from a perfect jade iris on the other. I had accidentally stolen it from Lord Rutledge last year and used it to channel the magic needed to open the portal to the Sunset Lands.

Now it was the only thing I was certain could tempt Matilda into the alliance I wanted.

"Is that the Eye of the Graeae?" she asked in an awed whisper. "Never mind, of course it is. Goddess give me strength, where did you find it? Wait..." Her eyes flicked back and forth as she thought. "This is how you did it, how you opened the portal. And you used the Grimoire, did you not? I knew you would try, but I was hoping..."

With every word she leaned farther forward, her eyes fixed on the artifact straight out of legend. Perseus had stolen it from the daughters of Cetos to force them to tell him how to kill their sister, Medusa. I was now using it to force Matilda to help me protect the city.

"You were hoping I would try to use the spell myself, and fail, so you could draw me into the coven."

She shrugged. "It was worth a try. In any case, it was safer in your hands than in ours. The temptation of so many powerful spells is not a good way to maintain a healthy coven. But the Eye...you offer this as the price of our alliance?"

There was no disguising the hunger in her voice, despite her speech about protecting her coven from the danger of power.

"As allies, my resources are at your disposal."

She noticed the emphasis I put on the word *my*, and nodded, though not without disappointment. The limits on what her coven could accomplish would be pushed back unthinkably far if they did not have the concern of physical safety to contend with. I had no desire to remove those constraints. No one should have access to unlimited power.

"Very well," she said, folding her arms. "I must gain the approval of my coven, but I think we can proceed with the alliance, so long as you also agree to my terms."

I had been expecting this. Simple mutual benefit was never quite enough for Matilda. She always had something reserved, something to gain. "I am interested to hear them."

Gwenevere Violet St. James.

Aris. He was going to have to wait. I was too close to landing this alliance to break my concentration, now.

"We will assist in the ways we are able, including the spell you have mentioned, in return for access to the Eye with your approval. So long as you do not hinder our newest member from joining. Sarah, if you please?"

The door creaked open and Sally's pale face peeked around the corner. My ribcage tightened around my heart like a fist.

"Don't be afraid, dear," Matilda said.

Sally's face disappeared, then she walked through the door stiff as a board with her hands clenched into a knot at her stomach. Her eyes flew around the room like a bird searching for escape, willing to settle anywhere but on me.

"Sarah has asked to join the coven as an initiate," Matilda said. "She will learn from us how to properly and safely use her magic. At the end of her training, she will be obliged to become a contributing member of the coven for six years, after which time she can stay or go as she wishes."

"Before I respond, I have a question," I said, addressing Madame Matilda, but unable to drag my eyes away from the girl—no, the young woman—I had been raising for nearly three years. "Have you been actively recruiting Sally, or did she come to you of her free will?"

Sally's lips pressed together into a thin, white line, and her throat bobbed as she swallowed.

"Sarah came to us when she began to feel the awakening of her magic. I do hope you will not make her feel shame over her gift."

"Has she been properly warned about the dangers of practicing magic?"

"Of course."

Gwen, are you there?

Sally raised her chin and said, "You told us we should always learn the most about the things that are the most dangerous. I'm not stupid."

"No, you are not stupid. But you are—" I stopped, biting off the words that clambered up my throat before they could spill out and ruin everything. I wanted to say that she was young and impressionable, hungry to be her own person, to prove herself, and that would make her prone to mistakes, mistakes that could hurt her.

But those were the arguments my mother made before I left home, and I was too young to hear them. I only felt that she did not understand me, that she wanted to keep me at home as her little girl instead of letting me grow into the person I wanted to be.

If I said them to Sally now, when she stood before me with defiance in her eyes and desperation in her clenched fists, she would only believe herself even more alone. She would see the Sisterhood as the only people who understood and supported her. And she would believe that she was only valuable and accepted if she did as they told her.

For the very first time, though Sally was not my daughter by blood, I understood the pain my mother felt. Not because I had never worried over Sally, but because I had somehow believed that when she reached adulthood, my worries would cease. But they would never stop. So long as Sally was alive, I would be scared for her.

No amount of protection would remove that fear. It was not Sally's job to make me less afraid. It was her job to live the best life she was capable of. And mine to help her do it.

Dammit, Gwen, will you answer me?

"Is this what you want, Sally?" I asked.

"Yes."

"And you understand that this is a decision I cannot save you from, should you regret it?"

Her blue eyes flicked between Madame Matilda and me. "I won't regret it."

"Oh, yes you will," I said with an unwilling smile. "Sometimes you will think you have chosen the perfect path for yourself because everything is going well and you are improving and learning more each day. And other times, when your failure has cost more than you believed you were willing to bear, you will wish you had chosen anything else."

Sally bit her lip, thought a moment, then said, "Then I shall simply have to learn how to deal with my regret."

"Wise answer."

"So," she said as hope kindled in her eyes, "you won't...you won't try to stop me? You will give your permission?"

My brave girl, who had already endured more than people thrice her age, looked like a six-year-old who had been caught opening presents early, and desperately hoped they would not be taken away.

"Do you need my permission, Sally?"

With a raised chin, she shook her head, claiming her independence with a simple motion that she would feel the repercussions of for years to come. For the rest of her life, probably. The realization that she had carried a victory flashed in her eyes and her cheeks went pink with excitement and relief. She had done it.

But dread seemed to follow as her eyes widened and her bottom lip trembled. "Are you," she began, then swallowed and tried again. "Do you want me to—that is, should I find myself a place to..."

I stood and threw my arm around her. She stood stiff in the embrace for a shocked moment, then wrapped both her arms around my ribcage and squeezed. "My home is your home, Sally Dawes. Forever." Then I held her at arm's length by the shoulder and said in a voice meant only for her, "Your place in my heart is not earned by your being obedient, my darling. It is yours because of you. That will never change."

Tears filled her eyes but she blinked them back.

Gwen?

Not now, I thought, then said, aloud, "It was dreadfully unfair of you to set me up this way, however. Made it harder to say no. Well done."

She made a noise somewhere between a laugh and a sob, then wiped her eyes. "I wanted to give myself the best chance of success."

"Never change," I told her, touching her cheek with a fondness I did not try to hide.

She held my hand against her skin for a moment, and I let her hold on to the victory as long as possible before saying, "Will you give me a moment with Madame Matilda, please? We need to finalize some things, and then I'd like to take you home. There is something we must discuss, and Sam is waiting for you."

Sally had the good grace not to push her advantage, but said she'd wait for me on the stairs, and closed the door behind herself. I turned to Madame Matilda, and said, "Do we have an accord, then?"

She held out her hand and I took it. We shook, but I did not let go. She looked at our joined hands, and then at me, an uneasy question in her eyes.

If I wanted her dead, I could kill her now, before she had the time to gather any magic, and she knew it. I needed her to know it and understand it so this next part would be suitably intimidating.

"Sally is a special person," I said.

"I agree."

"So I hope you will understand this, and take it as seriously as I mean it. She came to you in good faith, and I expect her to be treated as such. If you hurt my girl, if you lie to her or deceive her, or cause her harm in any way, no magic will protect you from me."

Madame Matilda's chin jutted forward in an imitation of stubbornness, but there was fear in her eyes. "Sarah will be as safe here as she would be in your home," she said, at last, and there was a slight edge to her voice.

"I am glad we understand one another. If your word is good, you will find me a most loyal ally."

I held out the Eye of the Graeae, the ancient focus that would allow the Sisters to perform the magic so vital to exposing the truth about the fae, and said in formal, binding tones, "I entrust this artifact to you for the sole purpose of casting the projection spell we discussed. When the spell is complete, I expect to have the Eye returned within twenty-four hours having performed no additional magic. Any further uses of the Eye will be agreed upon between us in advance. If these terms are not met, our agreement will be null and void, and the full weight of any magic performed with the object will return on you threefold."

Her eyes widened as she accepted the orb and the air crackled with the subtle magic of a geis. If Lia could perform the binding magic of a sealed promise, then so could I. I may not be prepared to accept the full reality of my parentage yet, but that did not mean I would not take advantage of it if necessary.

Matilda behaved as if what had just occurred was nothing to remark upon, but held the Eye carefully against her chest. "We will begin preparations for the spell," she said, "and be prepared by tomorrow night."

"Will you need directions?"

"You may have Sarah bring them by. She has some paperwork to complete, in any case."

Gwen, if you don't answer me...we have a problem and I'm running out of time.

Are you safe? I asked.

For now. But we need to talk.

Can you meet me outside the Triumphant Sisterhood?

On my way.

I said a mostly cordial goodbye to Madame Matilda, my new three-month ally, and ushered Sally down the stairs, trying to imagine what Aris had found that made him pester me for half of an hour. He could handle nearly anything circumstance threw at him, which meant it must be something unusual. Which meant complications. Which meant my entire plan might be in jeopardy.

We pushed through the large double doors and squinted in the sunlight of a late afternoon that had settled on the city like a wet blanket. It was almost blinding, which was why I was so surprised to hear a deep voice say, "Lady Gwenevere St. James?"

I paused, tilted my head to block the sun with the brim of my hat, and saw two constables standing in front of my carriage with their thumbs tucked into their belts and their nightsticks on threatening display. Both of them wore oily smirks.

"We'd like to ask you a few questions, Lady."

14

Vampire House

ARIS

Buildings and streets flashed by as Aris pumped his wings, flying toward Gwen with all possible speed. His chest and shoulder muscles burned, but the pain wasn't enough to distract him from his thoughts. The house he had tracked Bowler Hat back to appeared inane enough, but the place was filled with the bodies of dead faeries.

The basement door, which should have held the housekeeper's room, pantry, and other functional areas of the house, was locked tight and bolted from the outside *and* the inside. If the old refinery held several werewolves, this house must clearly be hiding vampires. And he doubted it was the only one. But that didn't get them any closer to finding Rutledge.

Even in his raven form, the building had stunk of flesh rotting in the heat, and he was certain the stench was still in his feathers.

With a shudder of revulsion, he banked right, dodging a couple of swallows, and angled downward. Tromwell Lane opened beneath him, wider and straighter than the streets near that wretched house. It took him only a moment to spot Gwen's ridiculous hat and there, next to her, Sally's golden head. Two constables stood near them, too close for polite or comfortable conversation. In fact, they were crowding both women toward the street.

Aris flexed his clawed feet and dove, then pulled up short at the last minute, flaring his wings to a spectacular size, before landing on the edge of the carriage roof. He kept his wings spread and croaked menacingly, making both constables back up a pace, before folding his wings and glaring down at them.

"What's this, then?" one of the men said, edging away before turning suspicious eyes on Gwen.

"It appears to be a raven, Constable. Surely you have seen one before," Gwen replied.

She was angry. When Gwen was angry with him, her brown eyes lit up like banked coals that might burst into glorious flame at any moment. Now, her eyes were as hard and cold as frozen earth, and just as welcoming.

"It is rumored that you have a pet raven, lady. That wouldn't be your familiar, would it?"

"As I have already told you, gentlemen, I am no witch. And my raven disappeared many months ago, as I am sure you also know. Unfortunately, I do not control every bird in the city."

"So you said," the second guard—a man with a stubborn jaw and cleft chin—stepped closer, leaving less than a foot of space between himself and the ladies. Sally raised her chin bravely, but she was so nervous her lips were white. Gwen didn't move at all. She was as tall as the constable and stared him down with the cool pride of self-confidence. He was either too stupid or too arrogant to realize what danger he was in.

"But I have a feeling you're lying, Lady St. James. Just like you're lying about having nothing to do with the deaths in the city. Several eyewitnesses have seen a woman who matches your description running from the scene of the murders in the dead of night. A brunette woman in her early thirties wearing a long blue coat in the middle of summer."

Gwen tilted her head and lifted one aristocratic brow. "Good eyes your witnesses must have to judge the age of a woman from a distance in the dark."

A flash of uncertainty, followed by anger, rolled across the constable's features. He had expected to intimidate a woman, not have one stare down her nose at him as if he were out of his depth merely by speaking to her.

"If you'll just come down to Scotland Yard," the other said, stepping forward and trying to smooth over the situation, "we can take your statement and sort all this mess out, eh? Won't take more than an hour, I'm sure."

Gwen straightened, tightened her grip on her umbrella, and said, "I will do no such thing. Unless you are here to arrest me under the spurious claims of invisible witnesses, which I am certain my lawyer will get to the bottom of within minutes, I will be on my way. Now, kindly step aside."

The cleft chin sneered and thrust his jaw forward. "You'll watch who you're speaking to with that tone, lady or not. We represent the law, and you won't—"

Aris had enough. He leaped from his perch and sailed at the man, claws extended.

"What the hell!" Cleft-chin squealed as Aris hit his hat with both feet, knocking it from his head and beating him about the face and ears with his wings. "Ah! Get it off me!"

The second constable raised his hands thinking to shoo Aris away, but he gripped the constable's scalp like his favorite perch, tearing shallow furrows in his skin, then spread his wings and snapped at the extended fingers, which were jerked back with a muttered curse.

Before either of them could regain their wits, Aris jumped into the air, croaking, and began a series of strafing runs that ended with both men running down the street with their arms curled protectively over their heads.

After about a hundred yards of full sprinting, during which both of them screamed several times and drew amused looks from passersby, he let them go. But not without one more run that ended in messy white streaks on their uniforms.

"My, my," Gwen said to Sally when he returned. "The wildlife in this city has gotten quite out of hand, wouldn't you say?"

"Shocking," the girl agreed, then burst into laughter and reached up to run a hand down his chest. "You were spectacular, Aristotle."

He croaked and nibbled her fingers, which made her smile, then thought to Gwen, *It's bad. We need to talk.*

She nodded, then said to Sally, "Let's get you home."

Aris shifted to his human form and caught up to the carriage as it pulled to a stop in front of the townhouse. He'd stayed aloft for most of the trip, watching to see that Gwen was not followed.

Sally disappeared into the library and bent over the wretched grimoire with her brows knit together in concentration. He preferred to stay several feet away from the thing if possible. It leaked magical energy into the air the way the Thames leaked rotten fish smell in the summer.

Gwen waited a moment outside the door to watch the girl, then turned and climbed the stairs. He followed, growing more uncomfortable as she unlocked her bedroom door and left it open behind her.

"Why here?" he asked, feeling the weight of the privacy that would have been welcome before she'd tried to tear his heart out.

"You said it was bad, and while I have told everyone what the stakes are, that does not mean Sally or Sam need to be scared witless. You know them. They will not hesitate to eavesdrop."

Perhaps they should, he thought, seeing again the limp, decaying bodies discarded on the carpet in what he had begun to think of as the vampire house. Perhaps they should all be frightened.

He crossed to her bureau, pulled open a drawer, reached past the silky night things, and pulled out a hidden bottle of brandy before taking a long swig.

The liquid burned down the back of his throat, but not as forcefully as Gwen's dark eyes. She did not like being reminded that he knew her secrets, but he was more concerned about his nerves than her anger. Seeing others of his kind savaged and left rotting had bothered him more than he wanted to believe.

Faeries were immortal in the sense that they did not die by natural causes, such as old age or disease, which meant that—baring war and battles—the fae rarely saw death. Even then they were generally faster and stronger than their opponents, unless they were foolish.

Having his mortality shoved so viscerally in his face was discerning in the extreme, but to turn around and look at Gwen and Sally in their delicate mortal bodies made the short span of their lives all the more painful. He took another long swallow, then one more, and set the nearly empty bottle down on her bureau.

"Bowler Hat has turned that inconspicuous house into a vampire nest. I am assuming there are several because one vampire alone could not hold the blood of all of the dead faeries I found there. Unless it killed them purely for sport."

The color drained from Gwen's cheeks. "But, vampires only need to feed once every couple of weeks."

"Using that metric, there would be at least five vampires in that house, alone."

"God's breath. Did you see any signs of Bowler Hat?"

"None. But the basement door was locked from both sides."

"Can we burn it down?"

He raised both brows, but she continued before he could answer.

"Of course not, there would be too much danger to the surrounding houses. And even if you broke the door down, the two of us are not equipped to kill five vampires, especially if they are old ones who don't need to sleep during the day. Did you see any indication that this was the only nest in the city?"

"Impossible to tell. We would need to track Bowler Hat to the next location, and we don't have much time before the full moon. You cannot both protect the city and track the canary."

Gwen tapped her pursed lips as she stalked back and forth from the window to the bed, frowning. "Rutledge is trying to destabilize the city," she said, slowly. "So he needs to create fear, confusion, and distrust. The factions are already pointing fingers and assuming political espionage, and Scotland Yard is clearly compromised. That's it!" She snapped and turned to face him. "We call in Scotland Yard."

"And tell them there is a vampire nest in the city?"

"No, but we can report a sighting or the smell. I assume the bodies are not all...fresh?"

He shuddered. "No. But how can we guarantee they bring enough constables? Just one vampire would be enough to kill five men with relative ease."

"True. Perhaps a note?"

"A note?" he asked, incredulous.

"Yes," she said, picking up steam. "You were not here for the Whitechapel murders, but several notes were sent, supposedly from the killer, that turned Scotland Yard out in force. The furor was nearly as bad as it is now, except that nobody believed those murders to be politically motivated."

"Alright, a note. The constables show up, break down the door, and hopefully kill the vampires. And then we've lost our chance to find Bowler Hat. He certainly won't return to the house after Scotland Yard has been there."

"You're right. Dammit. We killed the werewolves from the refinery, so he can't have any reason to go back there. We should set out a watch, just in case but we cannot rely on it. Could you..." Her voice died away as she looked up at him for the first time since he drank her brandy. The warm glow of it was still deep in his gut and radiating outward.

"I know I said I would not ask you to do it, but if it were to save lives, would you be willing to use your, ah, *persuasive talents* on an inspector?"

A thrill of disgust ran from his neck down his spine and to the back of his knees. "I showed my true form, without a glamour of any kind, only once, and was to illustrate a point about your safety. You responded to me more completely than I've ever seen. You would have done anything I asked, allowed me to do anything I've ever dreamed of doing to you...if I was willing to take advantage of my power over your mind. Would you truly desire me to do that to another mortal? Do you remember how it felt?"

She shivered, both with fear and remembered pleasure, because she had enjoyed the experience, and perhaps even the idea of being a servant of his pleasure. And she had also hated it, hated the loss of control, and the feeling that her desires were not her own.

His longing for her in that moment was so strong it had been impossible to think clearly, and even then, he could not bring himself to take advantage of it. "For years I was subject to another will, incapable of making my own choices, and I will never overpower someone's mind again, even if I see the necessity of it, even for the greater good."

"I am sorry I asked," she said, her head down.

"It was only a request, and that with the intention to help people. But never ask it again, Gwen."

They locked eyes a moment, and he saw regret and pain there, but also resolve.

"I promise," she said.

"Very well. Then how are we going to track Bowler Hat and stop the vampires from ravaging the city and killing my people?"

The bedroom door sprang open without a knock, and Sally stood on the threshold with the open grimoire clutched against her chest, her cheeks flushed from excitement. "I think I've got something," she said, then noticed him standing in Gwen's room and flushed as red as a rose for an entirely different reason.

"Oh," she said, averting her eyes and backing away. "I'm sorry, I—"

"We are only talking, darling," Gwen said, gently. "But I'd like to hear what you found. We will be downstairs in a moment."

Sally fled without a response, and Gwen bit her lips together to hide her amusement. "There, see what you've done?"

"What I've done? You were the one who dragged me here, my lady."

Eyes sparkling with amusement, she opened her mouth—likely to tell him not to call her that—but stopped short. The humor faded from her eyes, replaced by something dark and cold. "I think I've got an idea, but let us wait until after Sally shares her discovery. I need a minute to flesh it out."

Aris didn't wait to be dismissed. He simply turned and left. Earlier he had told her that she could not chase him away, and that much was true, but a thousand tiny cuts could kill anything with enough time, and every one of them hurt.

But watching her eyes change while she looked at him hurt the most. He fled, and he didn't mind admitting it to himself.

When he reached the study, Sally was bent over the book and Sam stood next to her, their blonde heads pressed together in the golden light of the late afternoon. Mrs. Chapman had just delivered a tray of refreshments and was bustling out of the room when he caught her hand and stopped her dead in her tracks.

The woman was somewhere in her early sixties, long and lean as a stork with a nose to match, but she had a kind heart that made her indescribably beautiful to him. Her dodgy temper made her even more charming.

"Pardon me, Mrs. Chapman," he said with his best smile while holding her fingers delicately in one hand. "But has anyone told you that you look absolutely ravishing, today?"

Her thin lips pressed into an O of surprise, and a rush of embarrassed heat flamed in her cheeks.

"Mr. Aris," she said, pulling her fingers out of his and slapping him in the chest with a handkerchief. "That is...you are...well, I've never heard anything so—I'll thank you to keep your compliments to yourself. Ravishing, indeed," she muttered as she stormed out of the room.

"You've let a rake into the house, Lady Gwen, and mark my words he will be trouble," he heard her say as she stormed down the hall.

Gwen entered the room a moment later, biting her lips between her teeth to compress the smile threatening to take hold.
"What on earth did you do to Mrs. Chapman?"

"I merely gave her a compliment."

"Well, she was in high dudgeon but absolutely glowing, so I
suppose it must have worked."

"If you two are quite finished, I think I have something here
that will help."

Duly chastised, they crossed to the table to peer down at the
yellowed page of vellum covered in spidery script and carefully
laid out magical diagrams.

"I've seen this spell," Gwen said, "it is for finding lost items."

"Yes," Sally agreed, "but look at the way the symbols are
aligned."

Aris let his eyes wander over the symbols but tried to stand
as far back as possible to avoid the skin-crawling sensation of
magic polluting the air. No one else seemed to notice.

After a moment, Gwen said, "You must explain your
thoughts, Sally, because I have read this spell several times and
I fail to see how it will help in our present circumstances. We
haven't lost anything."

"But that's just it, the spell is not limited to objects. Here,
look." She pointed to the chant meant to accompany the spell.
"Look at the wording. I think we can substitute *that which* is
lost, for *he who* is lost."

"Changing the purpose of a spell is dangerous, Sally," Gwen
said, frowning. "The intent of the magic is inscribed in the fabric

of its foundation when the witch records it. Alterations can have unpredictable and dangerous consequences."

"No, look. Whoever recorded the spell writes that the intent is to locate the lost object of desire. A person can be an object. There is nothing in the intent about whether the object is alive."

Gwen folded her arms and stared for a long moment while the rest of them held their breaths.

"If you want my advice—" Aris began, but she held up a hand and said, "I don't."

He and Sam shared an exasperated glance but kept quiet.

"What is the power draw of this spell?" Gwen asked, at last.

"If I had to guess, I would say three witches could share the spell without any ill effects."

One hand pressed to her mouth, her toe tapping in impatience, Gwen thought while Sally held her breath. She did not want the girl to do magic, did not want her to put herself in danger, and was fighting an internal battle to either give in and let go, or place some restrictions on the activity.

At last, she asked, "Do you believe this will help us find the Marquis of Rutledge?"

Sally blew out an explosive breath and said, "Haven't I already said that?"

"And you are willing to accept the risks that come with it?"

"I am."

Gwen's throat flexed in a painful swallow, though her expression never changed. She said, "Very well. Approach Madame Matilda about it, then. I cannot help you with it."

Sally made that particular squealing noise unique to young women and threw herself into Gwen's arms. Gwen closed her eyes and pressed her cheek to Sally's head before the girl pulled away to grab a pen and paper.

"My sister," Sam mused aloud, "is a wicked witch. You know, that fits, really. I always thought—"

Sally threw a pencil at him without looking up. It bounced off his arm and clattered to the floor.

Sam pointed at her and said conversationally, "You see what I mean?"

Aris snickered, but Gwen ignored the byplay. "I need to prepare for tonight. I'll ring Tony. I think it will take all of us to pull this off. Let's meet at the agency in an hour."

Then she left the three of them in the study, with Sam and Aris staring after her.

"Is she okay?" Sam asked.

"To be honest, Samuel, I do not know."

"You're going to keep her safe?"

"I'm going to do my best."

"Do better. Protect her."

He looked down at the boy, who glared fiercely up at him, and said, "I promise."

15

The Council of Gwen

GWEN

Aris followed me from above, revealing himself with a flash of black feathers between rooftops, flickering at the edge of my vision. Despite still being angry with him, it was comforting to have him watch over me. Comfort was in short supply, and I was not too proud to take it where I could find it...especially since I was about to face Lia again.

The sun hung just above the rooftops when I reached SPI and maneuvered the auto between a carriage and a wagon laden with hay. Aris waited at the front door when I approached, and opened it for me with a flourish and bow suitable for the royal court, his eyes twinkling with mischief.

"If you *my lady* me, Aristotle, I swear by the three sisters I will gut you here on the sidewalk."

"Me?" he said, all over innocence. "I would never dream of it, my lady."

If both Lia and Tony had not been standing in the office, I would have slapped him. Of course, he would have caught my hand, but that was beside the point; it was a matter of principle. Instead, I entered the room on a wave of well-bred self-control.

The office always had an air of hectic bustle about it, and while it was never, dirty it wasn't precisely neat, either. That had changed. The desks and chairs were aligned in straight rows, papers were stacked, and the floor had been swept. Lia's influence, I imagined.

"Are those curtains in your office, Tony?" I asked.

"Ah, yes. They are. A vast improvement, I think. Gives me a bit of privacy."

"So," I said, pulling off my gloves and flopping them on the table. "You are scared of her already, are you?"

"He is no such thing," Lia said before Tony could defend himself.

I raised an eyebrow at him and he flushed but ignored me long enough to fetch refreshments from the back room. My sister had toned down the medieval flare in her wardrobe and now looked like a clerk or librarian, rather than a queen from a history book.

"So many shades of brown, Lia. You looked much better in green."

"My goal is not to be admired, but to be useful. You might try the same thing."

"Touché. I see you have not lost your edge."

She glared at me but sat at the table with the kind of neat precise movements that would have made Mrs. Chapman proud. I wandered into Tony's office to fetch the gear I left there, including my jacket, which was worse for the wear, and my wheels. I would need those tonight.

"How is your shoulder?" she asked.

"Usable, thanks to Mrs. Chapman's tea, though it still hurts like the devil."

"Mrs. Chapman? Is she still with you?"

"Oh yes, nothing can stop that formidable woman. She happily orders about everyone in my household, including Mr. Tall-Dark-and-Brooding, there."

Lia and Aris exchanged an uncomfortable glance but said nothing. I was beginning to think my decision to treat Lia like a friendly enemy might just be working when Tony reappeared with the tea.

"Seven cups?" Lia asked. "Who are we expecting?"

Tony looked down at his feet, then squared his shoulders and said, "I took the liberty of calling in reinforcements."

He answered Lia, but he was talking to me. What had he done?

The bell above the door jingled, and I smelled them before I saw them. Clean animal fur and spearmint. My eyes closed in relief for a heartbeat before I was plucked off my feet and spun into a hug.

"Don't squeeze her so hard, my love, you will break her before I get a chance to say hello."

That voice, rich and deep, sultry like summer honey, confirmed what my nose already told me. I hugged the big man back, ignoring the throbbing pain in my shoulder. He set me down a moment later, only for Alix to grab me by both shoulders and kiss my cheeks.

"I am so glad to see you," I told her, feeling a lightness in my chest.

"Of course, you are. Now, who are these interesting faces?"

I turned toward my companions and said, "Ophelia St. James, Aris Blackwing, these are my friends, Alix La Rouge and her husband, Cyrus. They are professional monster hunters."

Alix pushed her signature red hood back, revealing sharp features, olive skin, and long, glossy black hair. She was pale, but given her parentage that was to be expected.

Cyrus was a handsome, hulking brute of a man with a mane of blonde hair and a jaw like a cinder block. He also had a pair of the kindest green eyes I had ever seen. They were also, both of them, monsters.

Alix was a half-vampire, thanks to her father, and Cyrus was one of the last in a long line of true werewolves dating back to the days when druids offered their sons to the Moon Goddess for power and protection. And now that they were here, we might stand a chance.

Aris already knew them, or at least knew of them, but Lia stood to greet them with all the grace of a queen. "Pleased to meet you both," she said, coolly.

"Did I hear her name right?" Alix asked me, both eyebrows raised.

"Yes. This is my sister, Ophelia."

Alix swore under her breath but returned Lia's cordial nod. "And who is this fellow with the brooding face? He does not smell human."

Aris grinned, then shimmered into his raven form, croaked at her from the back of a chair, and performed an elegant bow, going so far as to extend his wings with a flourish. Alix blinked, but Cyrus threw his head back and laughed.

"Another therianthrope, eh? It will be nice not to be the only monster around. Well met, Aris Blackwing."

"Another?" Lia asked.

"Ah, yes. Cyrus is a werewolf. And Aris isn't quite the same kind of monster as you are, my friend. He is, in fact, a faerie."

Alix snapped her fingers. "I knew he smelled wrong. Well, we are all monsters here, aren't we? With one notable exception, Mr. Hardwicke. I hope you don't mind being the odd man out."

Tony's confusion was palpable as his eyes drifted to Lia and then to me. His expression practically screamed *there are three humans, here*, but he was wise enough not to ask what she meant.

Aris hopped off the chair and stretched into his human-like form, rolling his shoulders and giving me a wink. Then the doorbell rang, and we all flinched.

"Oh, don't look so surprised, the lot of you," Delilah said, waving us off impatiently. "This is my slagging city, too, and I have a right to help protect it. Care to get me a chair, Tony? Or two chairs, I suppose. Percy isn't far behind."

Delilah ignored my smile of welcome because she was wearing the business face she used to quickly establish herself as someone to be taken seriously. And she hadn't lied. Percy followed her moments later, tall and lean and elegant, wearing a perfectly tailored yellow suit that glowed against his dark skin. As far as everyone who saw him was concerned, Percy was an elf, pointy ears and all.

But he was, in fact, a selkie in a glamour. That was not my business to share, so I made introductions as quickly as possible while Tony expanded our seating arrangement and fetched more tea. Delilah sat on a dwarven chair made with longer than usual legs so that everyone's heads remained at an even level, except of course, for Cyrus, who was even taller than Aris.

We made a motley crew, the nine of us, with Tony the only proper human in the room. It was difficult to admit to myself, but given the company and our dangerous mission, coming to terms with my own questionable parentage, if only to myself, made it easier to contemplate what we were about to do.

Lia had clearly known that one of our parents was fae, though I had not bothered to ask her which. I wasn't certain I wanted to know. But sitting next to two monsters, a selkie, and an Aos Sidhe, admitting that I was a changeling wasn't so hard. It felt something like a key being fitted into a lock.

Rather than dwell on that fact, I pushed it away into the back of my mind to be confronted later, like a grenade that could either be used when needed, or explode if handled incorrectly, and focused on the companions who had gathered to protect New London.

"I will not bother to warn you of the danger we will face over the next two nights. You know that well enough. But we had better be clear about what faces us, and our goals for stopping it. Lia, I will need your help for this."

Lia's mouth popped open in surprise, but she recovered quickly and stood with her hands folded in front of her.

Ophelia Marigold St. James, I thought. *I know this will be hard for you, and I would not ask it except that lives are at stake. You thought your chance to stop King Obyrron ended when I pulled you through the rift in the wall, but that's not true. We can still stop him, with your help.*

Lia took a long, slow breath, and said, "My name is Ophelia St. James, and I have lived in the court of the faerie king, acting as his general. His intention is to invade the mortal realm and subjugate mortals to the whims of the fae. He believes this land was stolen from his people by the unlawful marriage of faeries and humans, and he intends to regain it by any means necessary.

"Over the last thousand years, the wall separating the Sunset Lands from the mortal world has grown weaker, and rifts that might have killed many faeries are now wide enough for even some stronger fae to squeeze through. More and more of them have fled the King's oppression, and his numbers dwindle.

"When I was kidnapped, he believed me the key to his invasion. As the first mortal captive in five hundred years, he used me to learn of our world so he could conquer and subdue it. His plan called for immediate invasion, but I told him of guns, warships, and armor, the skill of the dwarves and the cunning of the elves, and other advancements that made mortals stronger.

"Over time, I convinced him to weaken the mortals, first. To sew discord and fear. I told him this would make the mortals easier to conquer, but I thought to give myself more time to thwart him. In secret, I made alliances with Queen Titania and other powerful fae lords to plot the demise of King Obyrron.

"My goal was to stop him before the invasion. To end the threat before the king left the Sunset Lands.

"But I was returned to our world before my plans could see their end. And now there is no one left to manage the alliance and stop him from invading. I was deep in the king's council, and I know of his plans. I will answer whatever questions you have that might make it easier to stop this invasion or, if that fails, to defeat the fae."

Everyone stared at my sister with wide eyes and a few with undisguised suspicion. She confirmed everything I had suspected, but hearing it all from her lips made it much more real. If Obyrron had learned of her treachery, she would've been punished in ways I did not have the creativity, or cruelty, to imagine.

And if their espionage had failed? I preferred not to think of it, or to focus on my own part in removing the one person who was perfectly placed to stop the invasion.

"In this bid to weaken the mortals," Tony said, "the king looked for allies in the mortal world, didn't he?"

"He did. He found several and courted them over a span of years, promising them health, wealth, power. They are well-placed and influential."

"Do you know their names?"

"No. That is the one thing the king kept entirely to himself."

"How did he contact them?"

"Through a stone smuggled into the mortal world hundreds of years ago."

"What did this stone look like?" I asked.

"It is the size of my palm, polished into an orb, and the color of blood."

Not *the* eye, then, thank the stars.

"Then it is possible that our current unrest may be tied directly to the fae king?" Tony clarified.

"Yes, though the stone would be the only evidence."

Everyone considered that, but Delilah broke the silence. "Not meaning to be rude, but how can we trust a word you say? You were twice a traitor, once against the mortals, and once against the king who trusted you. Why should we believe you, now?"

Lia's cheeks flushed, but she knew Delilah was not the only one thinking such thoughts, so she said, "I have no reason to lie."

"How can we know that?" Delilah asked, waiving off the comment as nonsense. "I appreciate that you're related to our Gwen, but until there is a good reason to trust what you say, I'd prefer to operate as if you hadn't spoken."

"She's suffered more than you can comprehend in being here," Tony said, his voice stony and his expression hard.

"We've all suffered, Hardwicke," Delilah said. "She's not special for that. And suffering doesn't make anyone honest. Honesty is a choice, and we need to know if she's made it before we make plans based on her word."

Lia looked like she'd been struck, and I realized suddenly what Delilah was doing. She didn't distrust Ophelia; she was making a point for her sake. And for mine.

Aris said, "I can confirm the truth of what she's said."

I cleared my throat and said, "As can I."

Delilah looked back and forth between us, raised a brow at me to ask if the point had been made, then sat back and folded her muscled arms over her chest. "Very well, then, the faeries are out to get us. And you say they've managed to fill the city with monsters?"

"That is the entire point, and why we need proof," Tony said as Lia regained her seat, looking shaken. "Gwen and I brought the matter before Scotland Yard, the guilds, and even members of

Parliament. No one believed us, not even after seeing Aris turn into a bird."

"A bird?" Percy said, sounding intrigued. "What kind of bird do you turn into, sir?"

Aris chewed his lip and sent me a guilty, sideways glance.

"Ah," I said, rubbing my chin with one hand and trying to decide how to tell him that his favorite raven was a six-foot-two Sidhe who used to be an assassin when Aris cleared his throat and said, "A raven."

Percy's lips made an *O*, and then he said, "Wait..."

"Oh, come on, Percy, look at him," Delilah said, waving her hand. "Look at his eyes."

Realization made the tips of Percy's ears turn red, with anger or embarrassment I could not tell because his expression was frozen.

After a moment he said, "Aristotle?"

Aris bowed deeply. "At your service, good sir. So long as you continue to supply me with those dried berries I like."

Percy's eyes flashed to mine, an accusation on his lips.

I raised my hands and said, "I didn't know until recently either."

"As charming as this is," Alix said, "can we get to the point?"

Tony cleared his throat. "To convince the city officials to take the invasion seriously, we need incontrovertible proof that our current crisis is tied directly to the fae interfering, proof that cannot be hidden or destroyed or explained away.

"We recently discovered that several of the crises the city has faced over the past few years can be tied to one man, the Marquis of Rutledge. And last night we learned that his driver is releasing monsters into the city. As far as we can tell, he is our most likely connection to King Obyrron, but we have to prove it."

"Which leads us to my plan," I added.

Every eye turned my way, and I swallowed back a moment of misgiving. There was one part of my plan I was certain they would not agree with, so I stored it away, took a deep breath, and launched into my explanation.

As I spoke, their eyes grew wider, then narrowed in suspicion, and by the end of my speech I could not tell if they would support me, or tie me up and toss me into the back room. Aris glared at me, Delilah looked both amused and exasperated, and Percy like he might get sick.

"Will the faeries agree to it?" Alix asked. "Cyrus and I can handle, well, several werewolves each, I think. But werewolves and vampires both, and in large numbers? We will need help."

"They fled the Sunset Lands for safety," Lia said. "It would be madness for them to agree to this plan after risking so much."

"If New London falls, where will they go?" I asked. "They chose to make a home for themselves here, among us, and I mean to show them that we will protect them, just as we will protect one another. Because none of us will survive alone. And you might not like it, but you are our best hope of convincing them."

Lia stood slowly with her lips pressed into a thin white line, pushed in her chair, and walked upstairs. I made to follow her, but Tony took my arm and said, "I'll go. They need you here and...well, I'll go."

He took the stairs two at a time, and I watched him follow her wishing it was me. I wanted to be the one to comfort her, to put my arms around her and rest my forehead on hers. But she did not want me, and I had no choice but to accept it. For now.

"The sun has almost set," Cyrus said, turning to watch the last golden rays dance over the tops of the buildings, then wink out, leaving a lambent glow behind, soon to be chased away by growing shadows that would eat the city one bite at a time.

"We had better prepare, then," I said.

Delilah hopped down from her chair and strode to the front of the office, where a large canvas bag sat forgotten. "Don't sound so depressed," she said, hefting the bag onto one shoulder. "I've brought you all some toys to play with."

16

Bowler Hat

GWEN

We left the office separately, each with our own missions, and spread through New London like shadows. Aris was lost in the night sky above me but I still felt him there, the way one senses electricity in the next room. It was as if his very presence changed the shape of reality just enough to be noticeable, which was both comforting and irritating.

We covered ground quickly, he in the sky and I on my wheels, heading toward the vampire nest where he last saw Bowler Hat. Aris was high enough to spot any signals from the Cutthroat King's men.

No signs of life at Rutledge's townhouse, Tony thought across our ring connection. *We'll scout it out before entering.*

Don't forget that your Sightscreen only has about five minutes of protection, I reminded him. *Once the diamond has burned out, you'll be as visible as anyone else.*

Delilah has reminded me of that. Twice.

I'm not surprised.

Any sign of Bowler Hat?

Not yet.

A moment later, Alix's voice sounded in my head. *Werewolf scent on the air, strongest near Cheapside and Whitechapel. I expect we will spend most of the evening in this district.*

I nodded, though she could not see it. *Noted. There are likely to be more people abroad on that side of town, so be careful with your silver bullets. The light from the gas lamps is not as good as the dwarven lamps on this side of town, so—*

Gwen?

Yes?

I know how to do my job.

Right. I know that. Sorry.

Stop worrying and start paying attention.

Yes, ma'am.

Two of our teams were already in place. That only left Aris and I, and Lia and Percy. The refugees should be well protected by the men the King sent, but they needed more reasons to trust Lia if she was going to convince them to help us tomorrow night. I hoped Percy would serve as an ambassador in that respect.

Two flashes near the docks, Aris thought. *Bowler Hat has been spotted. Keep your current course, and I'll see if I can track him across the city.*

Every muscle in my body tensed in anticipation, even though our target was far south of my position. With only tonight left before the full moon cycle began, we could not afford to make mistakes.

My hands ran over my body, double-checking my tools: pistol, knives, Sightscreen, goggles, jacket, wheels, smoke grenades, dwarven torch, three slender wooden stakes strapped to the outside of my right thigh, and a handful of cayenne pepper. I was as ready as I could be, short of my shoulder.

Another signal. He's moving north, not stopping at the refinery.

He was heading for the nest, then. I leaned forward, pulling more speed from my wheels as I shot across streets and avoided pools of light, sticking to alleys and shadows. These streets were lit with electric lights rather than the gas lamps used in the Eastside, or the dwarven lamps on the Westside, and the hum was a constant background noise that formed the base of the nighttime harmony.

Only the streets were nearly empty, so the shouts, carriage wheels, and conversations were absent. People were smart enough to stay indoors, if they could, which made me wonder how the vampires had been able to attack faeries in the first place. Most people were safely behind thresholds at night. Those who had thresholds, anyway.

As I neared the street in question, I slowed and picked a hiding place; the deep shadows between two residences in the nearest square that gave me a clear view of the entrance. If Bowler Hat entered the street from the south, he'd have to walk through the puddle of light left by the lamps on the corner.

Sweat already beaded my upper lip and temples, making the curls there stick to my skin above the strap of my goggles. I would have loved to unbutton the wool coat, but I sat there in the muggy evening heat and stared across the street like a cat waiting outside a mouse hole.

Where are you? Aris asked.

Near the house, watching the entrance.

He'll be there in less than five minutes. I'm circling above, but I've already had to dodge two owls. As if there aren't enough rats in New London to keep them fed. Keep your eyes open.

I hunkered down, one hand on the butt of my pistol, and waited. Sooner than I would have expected, a shadow strode through the pool of light, which picked out the silhouette of a bowler hat and a long coat that brushed the man's ankles. His body was turned in the right direction for the light to shimmer off the embroidery on his lapel. Something about the shape struck me as familiar, but I ignored it and focused on the present.

Got him, I thought to Aris. *He's heading toward the house, now.*

Remember the plan. Don't engage the vampires. If they scent you, run. We'll follow Bowler Hat from here.

I know what to do.

In the silence of our joined minds, I had the fleeting impression of a dark pair of eyes rolling in exasperation.

Bowler Hat checked the street for activity, pulled a key from his pocket, and unlocked the door to disappear inside.

You left no trace? I thought to Aris, suddenly afraid that they would know he had been there.

I went in through the chimney and stayed in Raven form. They should smell nothing out of the ordinary.

I nodded to myself and waited.

Ten minutes later, give or take, the door opened and a sallow-faced woman appeared. She stood on the threshold in a tattered gown that would have been fashionable fifty years ago, took a deep breath, and smiled before gliding down the steps. A dark-skinned man exited behind her, wearing a cape so long the hem dragged on the ground, and flexed his fingers like a piano player. Two more vampires left the nest, each gaunt and hollow-cheeked, and beautiful the way a poisonous flower is beautiful.

They separated and glided off into the night, disappearing into the darkness as if they owned it.

Four vampires, I thought to Alix. *At least half a century old, spreading out from the house."*

One werewolf dead, she responded, *but it was close. He was very young, but exceptionally strong and nearly mad with hunger.*

Can you track the vampires?

Not as easily, but we will be watching.

Bowler Hat exited several minutes later, a placid expression on his waxy face as he strolled back down the street and headed north.

Wait a minute before following, Aris thought. *I'll guide you.*

I sat, listening to the echoes of his footsteps die away, wondering if the vampires I had not tried to stop would kill more people, tonight. The only vampire I had ever fought was very old, could move about in sunlight, and had killed four men in the space of a few breaths. I did not think these monsters were nearly as old, but four of them...

We're inside, Tony's mental voice floated into my head. *Rutledge appears to have maintained his service staff, but everyone is abed. We are searching, now.*

Start with his study. I saw several artifacts there through the windows.

I know how to do my job, Gwen.

Right. Sorry.

Gwenevere Violet St. James! Aris yelled inside my head.

I winced at the mental volume of his voice and thought back, *Yes, sorry. Tony was updating me.*

North on the cross street, two intersections west of your position.

A cold hand wrapped around my throat, stopping any thought I had of responding. It squeezed hard enough to cut off airflow. Blackness closed in at the edge of my vision.

Gwen?

"I thought I smelled something," the female vampire said, then leaned in close to run her nose along the side of my face as she inhaled. "Not a faerie, but not quite human either. Interesting."

Her accent was clean and precise, like the upper crust of American wealth. With no noticeable effort, she turned me to face her and gazed into my eyes. Stars began to swim across my vision, but I forced my hand to move slowly, so damnably slowly.

I had to avoid alarming her, even as she tried to enthrall me.

Letting my eyes take on a dazed look was not difficult as I strangled, but bringing the nose of the pistol level with her heart without struggling against her grip was the hardest thing I had ever done.

"What are you?" she asked, her head tilting to the side in a distinctly inhuman motion.

Gwen? Are you alright?

I pulled the trigger. My shoulder twinged with the recoil, but the impact pushed the vampire backward, and the shock made her release me long enough to drag in a deep, painful breath. As she stumbled backward I fired again, this time through her eye socket. She hit the ground like a falling log, but she would rise again within seconds.

Gwen!

Using my gun hand, I shoved my jacket aside, pulled a wooden stake from the sheath with my left hand, and fell onto her body, driving the stake down with all my strength. The tip hit a rib, sending a jolt of pain up to my shoulder, then slid off the bone, and sunk deep between the intercostal space above her left breast. Thank goodness she wore only an underbust corset, or the tip may never have made it through.

Her body spasmed like a bug that had been stepped on, and I scrambled off of her, panting.

I'm here. I'm fine, I thought.

Where are you? What happened?

Just killed a vampire.

Was that a gunshot? I told you not to engage!

I had little choice, I thought as I rolled back and away from the body, sickened.

Are you alright? Do you need me?

No, I'm fine. I'm coming.

After a tense moment, he thought, *Bowler Hat doesn't appear to have heard the shot, but you're going to have to hurry.*

By the time I turned away, the body had stopped twitching and started to deflate, muscles going slack and flat. Beneath her skin, the bones became so prominent that she looked almost like a starved dog, even through her clothes. I swallowed back bile and leaned hard into my wheels, putting as much distance between the gruesome corpse and myself as possible.

Three vampires, now, I thought to Alix, trying to take satisfaction in it and failing.

I sped through the streets, taking every turn Aris suggested, feeling the cobbles vibrate through the wheels and up my legs as the wind blew tangled curls away from my face. Instead of imagining the tip of the stake sliding into the vampire's body, I did my best to focus on my surroundings.

This part of town was not fashionable, but neither was it impoverished. The houses were farther apart, interspersed with businesses and warehouses. It was the rambling edge of Town where enterprising people built new neighborhoods and reformed old ones.

I passed gas street lamps, torches, a few small electric lights on the porches of sprawling houses, and finally slowed near the entrance to an officious-looking building in the Georgian style. Banks of dark windows stared down at me, even from the shadows.

Where is Bowler Hat? I thought to Aris.

He went inside, maybe two minutes ago. Wait for me. I'll ring you if I need you. Be prepared for whatever comes out that door. If it is Bowler Hat, follow him.

You can't go in there alone! Anything could be inside.

Gwen?

Don't say it.

Hush.

"This is getting tiresome," I growled to myself but crept closer to the building as Aris appeared at the door and slipped inside.

It appears to be a medical school, He said a few minutes later. *It is creepy as bloody hell in here. I don't think the building has been in use in the last five years. Everything is coated in dust. No, wait...moon and stars, it was an asylum. That's disturbing.*

What is?

You don't want to know.

I ground my teeth.

There is a lab, it appears to be in use, at least. Oh, fuck me.

What?

Shh.

We're inside your head, you don't need to whisper.

I need to think. Shut up. A moment later he said, *Bowler Hat is using the lab for something. He nearly saw me. I added a glamour but he stared in my direction for a long time before rolling down his sleeve. I think he is headed for the door. Be ready. I'm following.*

I crouched at the righthand end of the row of hedges, which were frightfully overgrown and lined either side of the steps leading to the building. Not daring to breathe, I waited as the front door swung open with a barely audible creak. Someone was keeping the hinges oiled.

Moonlight painted the scene in strokes of black, white, and grey, like an old woodcut postcard. Bowler Hat stood on the landing, staring off into the distance as if planning his next move. He took a deep breath, unbuttoned the front of his jacket, and pulled out a pistol.

"He's armed!" I screamed in my mind, standing to leap out of cover and draw his attention away from Aris, but I was too late.

He turned, faster than he had any right to move, and shot me in the chest. I had time to wonder how the hell he had seen me as the impact took me off my feet and planted me firmly in the arms of the overgrown hedge. Branches scraped the back of my neck and my scalp as I fought to breathe. Warmth spread out across the coat in a rush, starting at the center of impact and dissipating toward my wrists and ankles.

He bounded down the stairs and strolled toward me, holstering the pistol inside his jacket as he advanced. "I thought you might be following me, Lady St. James," he said. "Who else would be out shooting people in the dead of night during such dangerous times? I've been reading about your exploits in the papers, you know."

His voice was smooth and confident, as conversational as if we had just met in the park. He bent over me and tipped the brim of his hat back with one finger, peering at my face as I gasped for breath. "That looks like it was rather painful. Let's take a look, shall we?"

He reached for my chest, presumably to unbutton my jacket and look for an entrance wound, but he was ripped backward and flung off of his feet before his fingers settled on the wool. The bowler hat fluttered to the ground as its owner hit the street some ten feet away. The pistol bounced out of his hand when he hit and rolled several more feet. Aris stood over me, his face a mask of cold fury as his eyes locked on the bullet smashed flat against the wool on the right side of my chest.

Bowler Hat rolled to his feet with a sinuous motion, stopping himself with one hand, then standing and brushing the dirt off his britches. "That was rather rude," he said. "I don't even know your name."

When Aris turned toward him, it was like watching a hawk swivel its head toward prey; cold, calculated, and hungry. Bowler Hat recognized the violence inherent in the situation, and his placid expression changed. He crouched and sprung forward, leaping at least ten feet in a single bound, and threw himself at Aris with knives in his hands.

When had he retrieved those?

I tumbled out of the bush as Aris caught the man in mid leap, and ran for the discarded pistol. No human should have been able to put up anything like a fight when faced with Aris, but Bowler Hat was as scrappy as an angry alley cat, and they rolled across the ground in a tangle of limbs and knives.

Despite his unnatural strength and speed, the only reason Bowler Hat was still alive was that we needed a link to Rutledge. Aris spun them both, levered himself up, blocked one knife blow with enough force to break the man's forearm, and batted the other out of his hand. It spun through the air and buried itself point down in the dirt beneath the hedges.

Cooly, Aris took the unbroken arm in two hands and snapped it at the wrist. Bowler Hat screamed and tried to buck Aris off, but earned a sharp slap for his trouble. That open-handed blow would have been enough to knock out most men, but it only dazed Bowler Hat enough that his body went limp and he blinked drunkenly at the sky.

Aris stood, jerked the man to his feet, and dragged him back into the asylum. I retrieved the discarded knives and followed, making certain before I closed the door that no one was watching.

The inside of the building was lit by a few old dwarven lamps with red glass coverings. They weren't strong enough to light the huge antechamber properly, but they were bright enough to cast long, jagged shadows across tables, chairs, and pillars. In the lurid red light, the place looked like the processing room for hell after the demons had abandoned it.

Aris dropped Bowler Hat into a chair, pulled off his jacket, and used the fabric to secure him to the wood.

We have Bowler Hat, I thought to Tony after connecting our rings.

Can't talk, Tony said, his thought so soft it was hard to make out.

Are you alright? I asked, my heart thumping hard against my ribs.

Leave me alone, Gwen.

A flash of something, a dark hall, and a roving light, flittered across my imagination. Were they sneaking? Had they been discovered? A thousand fears opened their toothy mouths and sunk their fangs into the back of my neck.

But I could do nothing for them now, and I had to trust that with Tony's capabilities and Delilah's pure stubbornness, they would be okay. Because Bowler Hat was coming around and staring daggers at Aris.

In the red light, his face looked less human, like the mask a monster would sculpt to hide in the city. Sweat beaded on his forehead and ran down his cheeks in rivulets, and his lips were bloodless. Two badly broken wrists were nothing to wink at. Though the bastard shot me, so he did deserve it. That impact was going to leave a nasty bruise.

"Where is Rutledge," Aris asked. His voice was soft and completely free of inflection. Like a snake's voice might be.

By contrast, Bowler Hat's once congenial voice was now roughened by pain and resentment. "Who?"

Aris slapped him once, hard enough to snap his head to the side and pull his arms against the fabric tying them to the chair. The pressure against his broken bones caused him enough pain that his eyes rolled back in his head. With both hands placed on either side of his face, Aris held the man until he was lucid enough for eye contact.

"We know who you are, and who you work for. If you want to avoid more pain for the rest of your short life, you'll tell me where he is."

Bowler Hat's jaw worked for a moment as if he intended to speak, and then he spit in Aris' face. I flinched. Aris merely stood up, wiped the spittle off, and then reached down for the man's forearm.

"Don't," he pleaded, but Aris ignored him and ripped the fabric up the middle with a gentle tug. He positioned both hands on either side of the man's elbows.

"Wait!" I said, rushing forward despite feeling sickened by the entire situation.

Aris gave me a questioning glance, then released the trembling arm. I plucked one of the old lamps off of a table and held it over Bowler Hat's body. There, at the junction of his forearm and elbow, were a series of neat, circular injection marks.

"Get off me," Bowler Hat growled, his meekness gone, but I ignored him and peeled back the shirtsleeve on the other side. Matching injection marks marred his cool skin. Cool skin? He should have been flushed with pain because he was not going into shock.

"What have you done?" I asked, bewildered as fear and dread made my stomach sink.

He only sneered at me.

"Which room did you say was in use?" I asked Aris.

He told me, and I took the stairs at a run, saying over my shoulder, "Find Rutledge, I'll be back."

Inky darkness pressed in on me like grasping hands, and the throat-closing stink of old sweat and mildew permeated every surface. I tried not to retch as I turned into the second to last room on the third floor and skidded to a stop. A wooden table sat near a window in the moonlight on the far side of the room, its surface stained with marks that were nearly black in the moonlight.

Near the center of the table on each side were a set of steel restraints. Deep scratch marks marred the wood where the restraints fastened to the table.

I approached the sickening tableau and read what signs I could see: a trash can of discarded syringes, the stained and scratched table, bloody rags in wrinkled lumps on the floor. Putting that together with everything else painted a horrifying picture in my mind.

I backed away slowly as my stomach threatened to revolt, and bumped into a wheeled cart with a tray of half-full vials on the top. Very carefully, I picked one up and passed it beneath my nose.

"Aris!" I screamed as I sprinted from the room and down the hallway, taking the stairs two and three at a time. When I reached the bottom floor, I was just in time to see Aris fly backward twenty feet and hit a pillar, cracking his skull against the corner as Bowler Hat exploded in a bloom of fire that enveloped the front of the room.

17

Proof of Life

ARIS

Heat washed over him, scalding his exposed skin in a searing blast. Fire followed his gasp of pain down into his lungs, heating the air inside like an oven. He tried to turn away from the pain but his body didn't respond. Had Gwen called his name, or was that the sound of his brain sizzling, cooking inside his skull like a slab of beef on a skillet?

Was he dying?

His mind pulled away from the pain and attempted to escape the possibility of death by unlocking a door in a dark corner of his psyche and running headlong through it.

His father's face was handsome and stern but without emotion, as he bent over Aris to haul him to his feet.

"What have I told you about rolling when you hit the ground? Falling that way will give you broken bones. Move with the force of

the blow so it can dissipate instead of rebounding into your body. Now, try again."

But that wasn't much less painful than the heat, so another door opened.

He stood behind his father on the grass, watching other children play, pounding down the field while swinging ash sticks in the last hurling match of the season.

After the winning goal, a mother picked her son up off the field and swung him through the air. Both of their faces were shining with victory.

"Watch them, lad, and soak it in, for this is all you shall ever have of that life. Your job is to kill so these might continue in ease and safety. Tis a noble task."

But it felt more like standing in the shade while everyone else enjoyed the sunlight. After his first kill, when he stood over the body with blood on his hands and his stomach in his throat, he wondered if he might feel the sunlight.

But his father only said, "Clean your blade."

His mind retreated farther, running through door after door in a desperate search for a memory without pain.

He stood on a branch, staring down at the dark-haired young woman he'd been sent to protect. She sat in the crook of a mossy tree with a book in her lap. Dirt smudged the soles of her bare feet, and a crown of flowers graced her brow.

"I thought he would make me feel whole again, but all he did was prove that you are the only person who will ever love me without reservation. I tried to be everything Mama wanted," she said, *running her fingers across the spine of the book.* *"But she was happy with a girl who didn't exist. She loved the pretend version of me. And he loved the title and the money. And everyone else? They love the entertainment of the strange girl who does and says inexplicable things. At least they did. Now they love the gossip."*

Slipping to the ground, she left the book sitting on a low branch and removed the flower crown. She laid it on a patch of dirt and moss in the sunlight. *"I won't be back to read to you for a long time. I don't know how long, only that I can't stay here. But I promise I will never stop looking for a way to bring you home."*

He hopped down to the branch and leaned over the book to read the cover. The Collected Works of Aristotle.

"Hello? And who are you?"

She watched him with an amused expression, a gentle smile hiding in one corner of her mouth despite the tears spilling down her cheeks. Sunlight burnished her hair to the color of rich earth, and her eyes were warm and sad and edged by long lashes.

"You like to read, do you, pretty bird?"

His job was protecting her, not making friends. He should maintain his distance, fly away, and watch from afar. But she pulled something from a pocket and held it out to him on her palm.

"Here's a bit of bread if you want it. It's leftover from my lunch but I swear I didn't bite this part. Just don't nip me, okay? I'll break down and cry if you do, and I have had quite enough of that for one day. But I will not hurt you. I promise."

Edging toward him slowly, she raised her palm high enough that he could catch the bread without much effort. It sat perfectly still on her skin, waiting for him to reach forward.

"Aris? Oh, God's breath, these burns...Come on."

Dull pain scraped along his back, making his tender skin tingle with little shocks of electricity. His feet thumped once, twice, three times on something hard. Throbbing pain made his head swim, but the heat was blessedly gone and his lungs no longer burned.

"No. Aris, wake up. Please—please, stay with me. I know I said you were free but I lied. Damn you, Aris, stay!"

He dragged in a deep breath and a surge of life ran down his limbs.

"That's it!" she said as his shoulders shook violently. "Stop being so blasted over dramatic, you wretched crow. It wasn't that bad. Wake up!"

One beat at a time, the throbbing in his head subsided until he could, at last, think clearly. They were outside, not in the creepy asylum. The memory of what happened came hurtling back. Bowler Hat had arched his back and raised his hips enough to pull something from his trouser pocket, something he squeezed until it broke.

Aris had turned round to look up the stairs, worried about Gwen and what was taking her so long. The mistake blew him off his feet. There had been fire. And Gwen. He blinked his eyes open and saw her face swimming above him, orange in the firelight. Soot was smudged across her cheek and some of the hair near her temple was singed. Tears stood out in her eyes, obvious even in the flickering light.

"I'm not a crow," he croaked.

The tears fell. "So, you say, but you certainly sound like one."

She pulled him up by his shoulders and wrapped her arms around him, pressing her lips to his in a desperate kiss. It hurt, but he held her and tasted the salt on her lips. Gwen was crying in earnest now, shaking against his chest and sobbing between kisses.

A siren sounded in a long undulating wail that joined the crackling of the fire as it spread. She pulled him to his feet and they stared for a moment as flames escaped the broken windows and licked up the sides of the building, destroying any evidence left within.

"Come on," she urged, pulling on his arm. "We've got to leave before the fire brigade appears."

They stumbled away from the burning building, hiding in shadows and flattening themselves against buildings as spectators emerged from their houses to enjoy the conflagration.

It took nearly fifteen minutes, but they found themselves safely hidden several blocks away. They took shelter behind a screen of vines that grew up along what was left of a brick wall. Whatever building used to occupy the spot was long gone, and the front garden capitalized on the opportunity to grow, turning the crumbled walls into a strange, sheltered garden of sorts.

Gwen took hold of his face, staring into his eyes. "Your pupils are behaving properly. How does your skin feel?"

"I'm fine, Darling."

"Answer the question."

"Gwenevere," he said, catching her hands, "I am a faerie. My body heals quickly, remember?"

She ignored him and turned his face to catch the moonlight. "Your skin was so blistered," she said in a quavering voice. "Even your mouth and your eyelids. I thought"—a shuddering breath—"I thought you were dead. You hit that pillar hard enough to break every bone in your body. I was sure you left me."

"Look at me, Gwen."

Her lids fluttered up, lashes beaded with leftover tears that caught the moonlight like stars.

"I will never leave you. Never. Could I say it if it wasn't true?"

A little sound of pain escaped her lips, and she threw herself into his arms and kissed him, again. This was not the ecstatic kiss of relief she gave him upon realizing he was alive. This kiss was hungry, selfish, and desperate. She pulled at him, her tongue invited him in, her body pressed urgently against his from breast to knees.

Gwen may not have been able to accept the truth of his place in her life and may not have been able to forgive him for the deception he played a part in...but she needed him.

If he was dead, her need would have dragged him from the grave. Aris could no more turn away from Gwen than he could stop his heart from beating. After all, he'd been eating from the palm of her hand since the moment he met her.

A low, deep sound of answering need rolled out of his chest as he wrapped his arms around her and turned, pinning her between himself and the wall. She squirmed delightfully against him and bit his neck hard enough to make him draw in a sharp breath.

There were too many clothes between them and weapons strapped to every limb—moon and stars he wanted to feel her skin and suck her breast into his mouth, to tease her nipple with tongue and teeth until she cried out—but her mouth was hot and demanding and her hand trailed down his torso to press against his crotch through his trousers.

He had not touched her this way since their imprisonment in the Sunset Lands, and need was a monster inside him, raging to life after months of being tightly controlled.

"Please," she whispered against his lips.

He slid his hands beneath her jacket, bunching the fabric at her waist, but she was wearing trousers. Instead of tearing the fabric down the middle as he longed to do, he unbuckled the belt, unfastened the waistband, and slid the canvas over her hips.

Moon and stars, she was so soft, her skin flushed with heat, and the smooth curves of her hips and ass fit into his hands like she'd been carved by the gods for him alone. He squeezed, dragging her hips against him and trapping her hands as they fumbled with his trousers.

Gwen caught his lower lip between her teeth and tugged, stilling his movements long enough to slide her hand through his open fly and stroke the length of him. He buried his face in her shoulder and rolled his hips against her hand, increasing the pressure as she stroked him once more before pulling him free.

With agonizing slowness, he slid his hand to the front of her thigh and ran his thumb up the center of her, parting her lower lips and dragging the wet warmth of her response up the cleft until he could circle the knot of her pleasure. She was slick and hot, and her hips rocked with instinctive need against his hand.

"Aris," she whispered, pulling on him. "Please. I need you."

Hearing her moan his name, even in a whisper, sent a shiver from his neck to his knees. He released her, sunk his fingers into her hips, and lifted her off the ground. The trousers kept her legs trapped, but she opened her knees as far as she could and guided him home with one hand.

"Gods," he choked, as the heat of her body swallowed and cradled him, welcoming him home. He pinned her body and rolled his hips in one long thrust, positioned so his flesh slid against the center of her pleasure as his cock sank in deep. "Gwen. I've never wanted anything in my life the way I want you."

With a low, hungry sound, she fisted her hands in his hair and kissed him, trusting him to hold her as they writhed against one another with mindless desperation.

"Harder," she breathed, releasing his head with one hand and grabbing the fabric of his trousers to pull him against her.

That command broke something in him, released some animal hiding beneath his skin. Aris drew back and thrust his hips forward hard enough to make her cry out. Someone might hear her and investigate. With whatever was left of his common sense, he covered her mouth with one hand, supported her weight with the other, and drove into her over and over with bruising force. She only pulled harder.

"Tell me you want me," he growled against her ear. "Say it."

Her body was tight, thrumming with energy, her legs shaking with every thrust.

"Say it," he repeated.

"Yes," she groaned against his palm.

He replaced his hand with his mouth, kissing her while he drove forward, swallowing her cries as she bucked against him. Shivering on the edge of release, he kept the rhythm steady until she broke, her body tightening like a bent bowstring, then snapping from the pressure.

Only then did he let go and follow her over the edge, warmth spreading from his groin, his cock throbbing as his entire body clenched, and then...and then...everything shimmered into a pool of heavy, warm pleasure that made his head spin and his knees weak.

He stayed locked inside her that way for a long time, their chests heaving, listening to the siren in the distance. Before he freed her, Aris lowered his head and captured her mouth in a kiss that promised everything and held nothing back.

One slender hand cupped his face as she kissed him with slow, sensual sweeps of her tongue. When he pulled away, her cheeks were flushed in the moonlight, her lips swollen from kissing him, her pupils wide with pleasure and soft with some tender emotion he was too scared to name.

"I thought you were gone," she said.

"So did I, for a moment."

"I still have not forgiven you, you know."

"I know."

Her grip tightened, and she said, "But I...you must promise me something."

"Anything."

"I need you to live forever, alright?"

An unwilling laugh rumbled in his chest.

"I mean it. When I thought I lost you—"

"I promise," he said. "But only forever until you're gone. There's no point after that."

Tears welled in her eyes, and she opened her mouth to say something but stiffened as if she'd been shocked.

He released her, letting her slide off his softened flesh. "Gwen? Are you alright?"

She held up one hand, her eyes going far away. Her cheeks flamed in embarrassment and she pressed her lips together as if holding back a curse. In moments like those, Aris was particularly glad faerie eyesight was so keen. Gwen blushing was a sight worth seeing. But she didn't seem to be enjoying whatever was happening, because she shook her head and closed her eyes.

After a moment she opened them, cleared her throat, and said, "I...may have forgotten to close the ring connection between Alix and me."

For a moment, that statement made no sense. But then it did, and he had to bite his own lips together to keep from laughing. Poor Alix.

"I think I would very much like to know what she heard," he said.

"No. You do not. And we need to go."

Just like that, she was all business again, fastening her britches and pulling her coat back into place as if that intense moment had never happened.

Once Aris made sure he was also neatly arranged, he followed Gwen from the ruins of the building and back toward the center of New London. Every now and then a howl floated toward them through the night. The buildings grew taller, the streets narrower, and New London swallowed them up once again.

"Did Bowler Hat let slip anything about Rutledge?" she asked.

"Unfortunately, no. I might have cracked him with a bit more time, but when I turned away, he managed to slip something out of his pocket. That's when everything went to hell."

"Yes, that was why I came running. He had a form of dynamite, a kind of alchemical corollary. There were tubes of nitroglycerine upstairs, and a few other chemicals that I didn't recognize the smell of right away."

"You saw the table, then."

"Yes. And I think I know what they were doing with it."

"I am all ears."

"You noticed the injection marks on Bowler Hat's arms? I think he was injecting himself with discreet doses of vampire blood."

"Isn't that how vampires are made?"

"From what I understand, the victim must be drained, first, and given a significant amount of the parent blood, enough that the parent blood is the dominant blood in their system."

"How is it replaced before the victim dies?"

"Vampires do not exactly share their methods for creation, so no one knows. But Bowler Hat was stronger and faster than any mere human has a right to be, and his skin was that of a corpse. And he healed himself well enough to retrieve that vial of alchemical dynamite."

Aris remembered the exact moment he turned to see the man grinning maniacally as he squeezed the vial in his fist. "He won't be doing any more injecting. His chest blew open when he detonated that vial."

Gwen glanced up at him with concern on her face, but she said, "If he was doing it, there is an even chance others have been, as well. And if he is dead, so is our only link to Rutledge. Come on, we've got to hurry. Meet me at the townhouse. I've got a feeling we are going to need Mrs. Chapman."

She flicked the wheels down, leaned into them, and sped off toward Grosvenor Square. Aris leaped, shimmered, and pumped his wings, carrying himself up and up, and followed her flickering form through the streets. He watched for monsters in the shadows, spotted a few dead bodies, and guided her around them.

Every time she teased him or said something sarcastic in return for his instructions, gratitude washed over him. If she had been standing next to Bowler Hat when the vial exploded, nothing could have brought her back.

Instead, she wheeled through town beneath him, sending witty repartee through their ring connection, not knowing that a few streets away a werewolf was devouring the body of her country-man.

They reached the townhouse in decent condition and found the study already filled. Delilah reclined in a chair by the fire with a cup of tea in one hand and a bandage across one leg at the knee. Fleur, her wife, stood behind her with one elegant hand possessively on her shoulder.

Tony had a series of deep scratches up one forearm that bled through his shirtsleeves, and Sam sported the beginnings of an impressive black eye.

Ophelia stood at the window with her golden hair in a waterfall down her back, arms wrapped around herself as she stared out the window, and Percy slept on the chaise with a blanket around his shoulders.

"Where are Alix and the big man?" Delilah asked.

"They'll continue to hunt until they cannot find more were-wolves," Gwen said, yawning.

"What happened to you?" Tony asked, his eyes flashing from Gwen's soot-smeared face to Aris's shirt, which hung from his chest in burned tatters.

"Alchemical dynamite," she said, tiredly. "Bowler Hat blew himself up rather than answering our questions."

Ophelia turned to stare, her eyes worried as they catalogued her sister's injuries. At least, until she noticed him watching her, and then her expression flattened into immobility.

Sam handed Gwen a cup of tea and passed a second one to Aris. "Looks like you had a rough night," the boy said, gesturing to the gaping holes in his shirt.

Aris grinned and flicked a finger at the blossoming black eye. "You don't look so chipper, yourself. Make a pass at the wrong person?"

"Got a bit too froggy with one of the King's men. But I won that fight."

"Did you?"

Sam nodded, his chest puffing up a bit.

Aris extended a hand. "Well done, boy."

They clinked tea cups, gently, in congratulations. Mrs. Chapman's tea, a secret mixture of her own he was certain included willow bark among the long list of herbs, not only smelled medicinal but tasted like it, too. It was not bad, precisely, but it wasn't comforting the way a good cup of chai was.

He did not need the tea, but he drank it, anyway, in solidarity with all the weak and injured mortals. Gwen saw his expression and raised a brow. He winked at her. She blushed, and her expression sobered.

Like a man preparing to walk the plank, she swallowed the rest of her tea, set the cup down, and took a preparatory breath.

"We failed tonight," she said, catching everyone's attention, even Percy, who sat up and blinked like an owl. "Bowler Hat was our surest connection to Lord Rutledge. We had him, but we failed."

She explained the circumstances, as well as her guesses about what had been happening at the asylum. He watched the faces in the room, noting the dismay, but also the respect and admiration. He doubted she saw it, and if she did, he doubted she believed it, but that woman was surrounded by people who loved her.

If only he could make her accept it.

But just now, swamped with guilt for feeling as if she failed, she wouldn't see clearly at all.

"That was my fault," Aris said. "I was watching the man, and I should have seen him move. He couldn't have pressed the blasting cap if I hadn't taken my eyes off him."

Eyes swiveled to him, giving Gwen a moment of reprieve.

"We didn't find the stone, either," Tony said. "It was probably too much to hope that Rutledge left something so valuable in his home after disappearing. But we did find something else."

Delilah shifted to one hip, pulled a folded sheaf of papers from her pocket, and held it up for inspection. "That worthless piece of scrap has been bribing the other missing lords."

Gwen took the papers and scanned them, one at a time. "This helps, but it isn't enough. And tonight was our last chance. I heard more howls in the city tonight than I've heard in the last three weeks, and tomorrow will be worse. There are at least three more vampires roaming the streets, if Alix and Cyrus have not killed them."

"Perhaps there will be no one to let them out of their crypts, now that Bowler Hat is dead," Percy said.

"We can hope," Gwen replied. "But I don't know what else we can do."

"We can kill the slagging monsters," Delilah said. "That will have to be enough."

Ophelia turned around. "But it will not convince anyone that the faeries intend to invade. And when they do, when they pour out upon this city like the breaking tide, the outcome will be far worse than a few roaming monsters."

"You have a better suggestion?" Delilah asked, raising her chin.

Everyone stared at each other, silent, as Mr. Yates entered and began handing out trays of food. If there was nothing else to be done, at least they could protect the city a bit longer. They ate with their heads downcast, either thinking or feeling sorry for themselves.

"I've got it!" Sally burst into the room with the grimoire pressed to her chest, her youthful face haggard from effort and lack of sleep, but panting with excitement. "I've got it. I worked out the spell. I can find him."

18

Good Advice

GWEN

The first response to spring to my lips was *let someone else do it, Sally*. But I clamped my jaw shut until the risk of blurting it out passed. There were bags beneath her eyes, and lines around her mouth, but Sally's face shone with victory.

If I took this moment from her and stole this chance for her to contribute, she would not forgive me. Instead, she would go to Madame Matilda for guidance and comfort, and while the woman was certainly clever and capable, she did not love Sally.

So, I took a moment to swallow my desire to protect her, and said, "What do you need?"

"Two more witches, I think, and an object that belonged to him. I can make it work with something he's touched, but it won't be as strong a connection."

"Those ought to do it, then," Delilah said, pointing to the papers I still held.

"How soon do you think you can work the spell?" I asked.

Sally yawned and rubbed her face. "How long have we got?"

"Until sundown, but that will be cutting it close. Sooner is best."

After glancing at the clock, which read 3:30 AM, she said, "I think we can do it after breakfast. If I can sleep, I had better. The words are starting to blur when I read them. And the others will be ready by then."

"Good. We all need rest if we want to survive the night."

Mrs. Chapman entered the study with an armload of linens and announced that rooms were ready for anyone who needed sleep. She did an admirable job of not staring at Lia, but her eyes flicked in my sister's direction more than once.

Good-hearted woman, she was trying to give her one-time charge a bit of space, but I wondered if it would not have been better for her to order Lia about as she did when we were young.

Mrs. Chapman bundled everyone off, one or two at a time, until only Ophelia, Aris, and I remained in the study.

"You need sleep, too," Aris said, brushing my hair back.

"I will. But I'd like to talk to my sister for a moment if you don't mind."

He nodded, but his eyes were concerned, and his gaze was warm on my back even as he left the room. It was difficult not to think of his touch, his mouth, the stolen moments of desire, and the feeling of being wanted, needed...*loved*.

Those few moments of fearing him dead felt as if the world had been stripped away, and I stood naked before the cruel censure of every eye in it. Never again would I hear amusement color his voice, watch the softness in his eyes as he looked at the children...k now that despite everything the world threw at me, I was not alone.

But I had not forgiven him for years of lies, and while I sheltered an ember of hope deep in my chest, I would not kindle it until we had a proper discussion. Relieved lovemaking in the shadows was one thing and could be written off as mere mutual comfort. But the commitment of a relationship? That was something else.

There was nothing to be done about it for the present, in any case.

So, I pushed all of that out of my mind and focused on the first person I had ever loved more than myself. I did not count Mama, because loving her was inevitable, like breathing. Lia was another matter.

She stood by the window, still as the statue on which Aris loved to perch, proud and cold as marble. But the stillness of her body was not arrogance. It was fear. Fear radiated off her in sickening waves, from her white knuckles to her wide eyes and tense shoulders. She hid it well, behind a mask of reserve.

I mistook it, just as she intended me to. The years we spent separated and changed us both in unexpected ways. But maybe if I paid more attention to who she *was* instead of who I wanted her to be...

"What happened to your face?" she asked.

"The explosion. I wasn't close enough to be hurt but I had to wade through fire to drag Aris out a window."

"A window?"

"Don't sound so disbelieving. The explosion made the front door impassable, but the impact blew several windows out and they were relatively low to the ground."

"You could have been killed."

I shrugged.

"You should not take chances like that, Gwen. It's foolish."

"Loving someone enough to take a chance is never foolish, Lia."

She shivered as if a cold draft blew across the back of her neck. "It is if it makes you weak or ineffective. If you died, who would have protected this city? There is more at stake than your feelings."

I wanted to ask her if this was the argument she had with herself when I stumbled into the Sunset Lands and back into her life: save me or protect the plans she worked so many years to accomplish. Leaving me to my fate in the court would have been more moral, according to her estimation. She would have saved far more lives that way.

Instead, I asked, "Any luck with your visit to the faeries?"

Nonplussed by my change of subject, it took Lia a moment to gather her thoughts. She chose a chair, sat on the edge of the cushion, and admitted, "I had less influence than I would have liked. They were terribly afraid. But Hilder was rather convincing."

"Hilder?"

"Yes. She cleverly realized that, if faeries do invade, mortal races will have cause to be suspicious of *all* fae. But if the faeries help us now, before it is needed, they can position themselves as allies at the least."

I nodded. "Clever, indeed. Though I cannot promise mortals will not be suspicious, either way. Or even dangerous. People are unpredictable when threatened."

"True. But they have their glamour to fall back on, and their magic, should they need it. And we have promised to protect them. I shall be ready to lead them out of the city, once everything is over. In the interim, they will be safer at Wainwright."

"Perhaps we should give them the option and leave it to them to decide. Most of them have built lives and businesses here. They may not wish to abandon it all."

"They already abandoned their homes once, Gwen."

"Running for your life is not the same as abandonment."

"Is it not?"

We stared at one another, and I could have sworn the temperature rose by a couple of degrees.

"The Sunset Lands were never their home to begin with, merely a construct meant to keep us separated. Technically, faeries belong to this world as much as you or I do."

Her face twisted in revulsion, or anger, I could not tell which. "They have no right to this land," she said in a whisper. "They lost their claim when they slaughtered and enslaved mortals."

"The refugees had nothing to do with that."

"Didn't they? Do you know? Have you asked them where they were when the war broke?"

I had not. In fact, I hadn't any idea how long they had been alive. There was a more than fair chance that at least some of the refugees we protected had, in fact, been alive then.

Had Hilder killed mortals?

"A thousand years is a long time to hold a grudge, Lia," I said, my voice tired.

"Yes, it is. And I know exactly what a grudge of that sort can do. Obyrron sees mortals as lesser life forms to be exploited, and it galls him that they were able to exile him from a world he considers his property.

"He wants mortals subjugated, but he *hates* Titania. He wants her dead and to break her before she dies. He has been nursing his hatred for millennia. It has driven him mad, like some sort of creeping fungus that ate him from the inside.

"And if you believe none of those faeries hold the same grudges, you are a fool."

Unable to look away from the fire reflected in her hazel eyes, I asked, "If this is how you feel about them, why are you willing to help them?"

Her jaw clenched, then released. "Because it is the right thing to do. Because they defected. Because I know the pain of being separated from your home and forced to build a life for yourself in a place that does not *see* you."

A fist of grief tightened around my throat. I knew what happened to my sister in a general way, but hearing the pain in her voice made the reality of it hit me like a wave.

"Lia," I said, but my voice died.

"That's enough for the night, girls," Mrs. Chapman announced as she strode into the room with a cloth over one shoulder and resolution in her eyes. "Off to bed, both of you. No arguments now."

She stopped to stare us both down, then rolled her eyes heavenward when neither of us moved. "It's as if they think I speak only to hear my own voice. Out, the both of you! Now!"

Lia and I exchanged an amused glance and allowed ourselves to be shooed up the stairs.

By the time I pushed open my bedroom door, I was so tired my bones were heavy. My back throbbed from where I'd landed during the blast, faint ringing still buzzed in my left ear, and my eyelids were competing to see which was more affected by gravity.

All I wanted to do was collapse into my bed. But Alix sat on the edge in the dark, her hands folded in her lap, pale window light turning her amber eyes into lambent jewels. Concern for her and Cyrus flamed in my chest, but embarrassment smothered it. Her expression told me all I needed to know about why she visited me.

"Hello," I said, dropping my jacket onto the chair. "How are you?"

"Worried," she said, sounding like a governess and not someone who just spent several hours fighting monsters on the streets.

"Oh?"

She made a scoffing noise. "Don't play dumb with me, Gwen. It does not suit you."

I took my time sliding my shoes off and folding my corset so I could fight back a blush and control my emotions. "I apologize for the oversight and leaving our connection open. I am willing to forget the incident happened if you are. I would imagine it was as unpleasant for you as it now is for me."

"It would have been less unpleasant if I was not in the middle of killing a werewolf, but that isn't the problem. I do not like to see my friend suffering."

The memory of Aris's mouth made my lips tingle. "That isn't what I was doing."

"Isn't it?" Alix stood and forced me to look at her. She was several inches taller than me, and while she did not have Delilah's intimidating bluster or Mama's autocratic authority, she had a dangerous gravitas that was impossible to ignore. Only a fool would not take her seriously. I bit my lips and stopped fiddling with my clothes.

"You are one of the smartest and most capable people I know," she said, her voice soft. "So, I cannot understand why you are so intent on pushing away your chances for happiness."

Her words were a knife in the guts. "I am doing no such thing."

"You think I do not recognize the signs? I see how thin you are. I feel the tension in the air around you every time that man is in your presence. I can smell it, Gwen."

Damn her half-vampiric senses. "Yes," I said, stalking away and gritting my teeth. "I find him attractive. Who wouldn't? I thought the explosion killed him and I was relieved to find him alive. It was sex, nothing more."

"People only interested in sex do not think the kind of thoughts I heard in your mind."

I spun on her, my face hot with anger. "What you heard was a mere moment of passion."

"You are devoted to him, and he to you."

"Devotion?" I spat. "He spent years with me because he was *trapped*, Alix. He had no choice in the matter. It was not even obligation tying him to me, it was chains of magic. I cannot afford to indulge my emotions, not for someone I cannot trust. We can enjoy one another, but nothing more."

"Oh, my friend, you are a fool."

I drew myself up and squared my shoulders. "I do not appreciate your tone, madame."

"No," she laughed, "I don't suppose you do. But you will listen to it, nonetheless."

No, I would not. I was tired, sore, and had enough emotional turmoil to deal with. I did not need this. I turned to leave.

"Did you know I wanted to kill Cyrus?"

That froze me before my hand settled on the door knob. "You nearly killed yourself trying to save his life," I said without turning.

"Ah, well, you met us after I had already fallen in love with him. But before that? I wanted him dead. He is a werewolf, after all. A monster not to be trusted. I took him hostage and planned to turn him over to the Sisters of St. Christoph for experimentation."

I turned, unable to ignore the truth of her words. Early morning light limned her slender form, making her glow like a saint of some forgotten religion. And while Alix was aggressively beautiful, her expression was tender, almost beatific at the mere mention of her husband.

Rarely had I seen two people who shared a love like Alix and Cyrus. The idea of her wanting to hurt him was unthinkable.

Then again... "You told me werewolves were responsible for the death of your grandmother," I said. "I can understand it would be hard to trust one, after pain like that."

"It was hard enough," she agreed, "but that was not the source of the true problem. I hated Cyrus not because he was a monster, but because *I* was one."

I rocked back on my heels. Alix had protected mortals for more than three hundred years. She was the furthest thing from a monster I could imagine. "Why would you believe such a thing of yourself?"

"I murdered my grandmother. I killed hundreds of werewolves without ever stopping to wonder whether they were monsters by choice, or by a cruel whim of fate. I hated werewolves because it was easier than hating myself. If I did monstrous deeds, it was their fault."

And along came Cyrus, a decent, gentle, warm-hearted man who flew in the face of everything she believed to be true. Falling in love with him must have been distinctly painful.

She nodded as if she read my mind. "He made me see myself truly for the first time, and want things I believed I did not have a right to desire. God's breath, I was cruel to him. I did my best to chase him away so I would not be forced to face who I was."

"I see," I said. My bones decided they were done trying to keep me upright, and I collapsed onto the bed.

"Good, because this is tiring. Gwen, listen to me." She knelt in front of me and took my hands. "You must learn to let people in. Tony is a good man, maybe one of the best. But I knew he was not for you. He is far too...what is the word? Stodgy?"

I snorted a half-pained laugh. I used that word to describe him on more than one occasion. But she was right. Tony was far too good a man for the likes of me. While he may be slowly loosening his strict ideals, he was the absolute soul of true propriety and kindness. I did not want to admit that if he saw the darker parts of me, he would be horrified.

"But this one?" she said, gesturing toward my door as if Aris stood on the other side. "He is your match. Yet you push him away, just like you pushed Tony away. You keep him at arm's length, and Sally, and the boy, because then you can love them safely without risking your heart. But love requires risk to mean anything. And despite what you believe of yourself"—she squeezed my hands—"you deserve happiness."

"I am happy."

She said *no, you are not* merely by raising a single brow.

"You have done nothing that disqualifies you from deserving happiness. But you will never have it if you are more concerned with protecting yourself than accepting it. I know this better than anyone, and Cyrus almost died to prove it to me.

"I lived a half-life for hundreds of years, Gwen. That is time I spent in pain, time I will never recover." She stood, brushed off the knees of her trousers, and touched my cheek. "But you are smarter than me. You will not make my mistakes."

Alix left me with clenched fists and tears that would not fall. She was wrong, of course. If I did not share everything, it was to keep them safe, not keep them out. My insides were full of broken pieces and sharp edges that would hurt the people I cared about.

And how was I to trust Aris when he spent the last ten years lying to me? Granted, it was not his choice, but that was part of the problem. Lia had wrapped her concern for me about his neck like a chain.

He was free for the first time in a decade. I could not steal that from him.

I sprang to my feet with a pounding heart, realization electrifying my limbs. Before consciously making the decision, I pushed my way into Lia's room.

"Gwen?" she asked, sitting up and blinking into the dark.

"Why did you send Aris to me?"

"What?"

"You heard me. Why?"

The covers rustled. "I thought you might be in danger."

"Why?"

Lia did not so much as shift position in the long silence that stretched between us. Stalking to the bed and shaking her by the shoulders was tempting, but I managed to stay put and fight down my impatience.

A small green flame rose from the tip of her forefinger. She considered the fire, expression still as green light bathed her face. "Obyrron kept me because of the magic. And you and I share the same blood. When I gained enough political power to discover what his plans were, I knew he would find you, too, someday. I could not let them do to you what they did to me."

There wasn't enough air in my lungs to properly speak, but I forced the words out, anyway. "Why didn't you let him tell me?"

She looked up and the fire died, leaving us in darkness. Did she know how different my life would have been had I known she was alive somewhere and thinking of me?

"Because I knew you would try to find me. You would never have any peace. I did not want that life for you."

"Peace?" I laughed. "What peace?"

I turned and left without closing the door, then flopped onto my bed, threw a forearm over my face, and fell asleep in an instant.

19

Sally Casts a Spell

GWEN

Monsieur cursed happily in French as dishes left the kitchen for the busiest breakfast the townhouse had seen in ages. Everyone ate with single-minded determination, so the only sound in the dining room was scraping silverware and clinking glasses.

Alix and Cyrus stumbled downstairs mid-meal looking surprisingly well-rested. Cyrus demolished more food than half of the gathering combined, but after the exertion of their long night, he earned it.

Once Mrs. Chapman cleared the breakfast things, everyone shook hands and left to see to the tasks that would prepare us for the evening. Sally stood by the door vibrating with impatience as she waited for Aris and me.

"Stay clear of the workstations," I told Sam as he followed Delilah out the door. "And bring the rings as quickly as you can. No stopping on the way back for sweets, or James will tell me."

Sam reached into his pocket and produced a napkin-wrapped scone pilfered from the kitchen. He must have snagged it while Monsieur's back was turned.

"I've already got a plan for that," he said, then kissed my cheek and playfully tugged one of Sally's curls. She slapped at him, but he danced aside and stuck his tongue out as he hopped into the carriage with Delilah, Fleur, and Percy.

"That one," Aris said, "will be trouble."

I snorted. "He's been trouble since the moment he set foot in the house."

"Have I been trouble, my lady?" Sally asked with a hint of mischief in her voice.

I titled my head and considered her, letting my brows draw down in confusion. "I'm sorry, who are you?"

Sally snorted and skipped down the stairs to the auto.

The lighthearted banter was something of a smoke screen for the heaviness in my chest. Almost everyone I cared about would risk their lives and livelihood tonight, and that was enough pressure to make breakfast curdle in my stomach.

To top it all off, my skin prickled with the awareness of Aris's presence.

Alix's words from last night sounded in my mind. *You keep him at arm's length, and Sally, and the boy, because you can love them without risking anything. But love requires risk to mean anything. And despite what you believe of yourself, you deserve happiness.*

Was I keeping everyone just far enough away from my heart to keep my walls intact?

My experience with Tony, and how careful I'd been to never let him see me at my worst, said yes. But Aris? I never had the chance to hide from him. He saw every weakness and vice from the beginning.

Did I love him? Of course, I did, in a general way. He was my longest, closest friend, even if our relationship was mind-bogglingly complicated.

But...did I *love* him?

"I think we're ready, my lady," Sally said.

I blinked and forced myself to focus. Hopefully, there would be time to ask myself such questions later.

If we survived.

The three of us piled into the auto and trundled across town to the building on Tromwell Lane. I parked in the stable at the back, where Patricia waited in her standard black dress to escort us to the spell room.

Unlike the sitting room in which I normally met Madame Matilda, the spell room was large, square, and empty aside from a small collection of magical instruments. No fire had been lit in the hearth, and despite the summer heat already smothering the city, it was cold. Was that a result of spells laid on the place, or simply the marble?

Two women waited inside, chatting quietly as we entered. One I recognized as Lady Chatsworth, the witch whose housekeeper I rescued the year before: a pale-skinned woman with a pretty face and impeccable bearing. The other was shorter and softer of frame, with dark red-brown skin, round cheeks, and large, serious eyes.

Sally rushed forward to greet them, taking both their hands and holding their fingertips to her forehead in a gesture of respect. Was that a formal greeting among witches?

"Lady Chatsworth," I said, with a polite nod. "May I present Aris Blackwing?"

She replied with a perfunctory, "It's a pleasure, sir," though her cheeks flushed and she had a hard time keeping her eyes off his face.

Through the rings, I thought to him, *Try not to fluster the women, we need them to concentrate.*

I'll thicken up my glamour, shall I? The corner of his mouth curled in a smirk.

Lady Chatsworth blinked a few times, cleared her throat, and said, "And may I present Lady Patel."

"Lady Patel," I said, trying to mask my surprise while not frightening her with my enthusiasm. "Your experiments with alchemical chloroform have been most illuminating."

"You have read them?" she asked, smiling in a way that made her dark cheeks glow. "I am so pleased."

"I always make it a point to read about chloroform on Wednesdays, and no Wednesday is complete without a summary of your experiments."

"That was pushing the irreverence a bit far," Sally said over her shoulder.

"I did overdo it, didn't I? You must forgive me, Lady Patel. I am trying not to overwhelm you with my excitement at meeting such a renowned scientist. Aris?"

"Yes, my lady?"

"Next time, pinch me before I make myself ridiculous."

"Of course, my lady."

Neither Lady Chatsworth nor Lady Patel knew how to respond, so they said nothing and exchanged sidelong glances. Sally rescued the moment by opening the grimoire and explaining the process to her...I supposed they must now be called her sisters, though just thinking of their relationship to one another made me frown.

Try not to show your dislike on your face, if you can help it, Aris thought.

I don't dislike them.

Tell that to your face. We need them to concentrate, remember? If I can hide my extreme good looks, you can hide your illogical dislike.

I forced my expression into something neutral while the women pulled tools from the canvas bag in the corner. Salt, chalk, several bundles of dried herbs, and a silver bowl. Patricia left and returned with a pitcher of water, and set it on the floor while the women went about drawing a circle, first with the chalk, and then with salt.

Sally crouched and drew several symbols on the floor around the inside of the circle, then connected them with straight lines using a piece of string as a guide while Lady Patel held the opposite end taut at each symbol.

Not all spells required symbols and diagrams but, in general, the more precise the request, the more precautions it required. And finding lost things was a finicky bit of magic. Without very clear guides to control it, the magic may get distracted, like a dog chasing a pixie.

After they marked the lines, Sally placed the shallow silver bowl in the center of the circle. Lady Patel filled it with water from the pitcher and dropped in torn corners of the papers Delilah stole from Rutledge's townhouse.

Finally, bundles of dried herbs were placed at equidistant points around the bowl.

The three witches stood equally spaced between the dried herbs and joined hands. Their expressions were peaceful, and they stood unmoving as their breathing fell into sync. Aris and I both stopped breathing for fear of distracting them. When Sally opened her eyes, they were clear and unfocused, as if she were looking inward.

She recited the spell once, clearly, and when the second recitation began, the other two joined in. I say she recited it, but it sounded more like singing as she stressed certain words, her voice rising and falling in a strange melody. The language was similar to Russian, but the accent seemed off, and I could not translate it.

The herbs sparked and fire sprang up in each bundle before dying down to a smolder that sent trails of white smoke dancing in the air. Each woman leaned forward and took a deep breath, pulling smoke into their lungs, then continued the recitation. They swayed like trees in the wind, and their hair rose from their shoulders and floated next to their heads in a phantom breeze.

In time with the change, the smoke began to swirl in a lazy circle between the bowl on the floor and the women joined hands. The river of smoke undulated in time to the chanting. It was hypnotic.

Sally stopped speaking, leaving the recitation to the other two, and a milky film passed over her eyes, like a second eyelid. My stomach flip-flopped.

"I see a large man," she said in a hollow voice. "Barrel-chested, with the hands of a sportsman and a white mustache. He is...he is sitting in a leather chair with a large stone in his hands. His eyes are closed."

That was an apt description of Lord Rutledge.

"What is in the room?" I asked.

"A table, chairs, a bookshelf, a decanter of whiskey."

"Are there any windows?"

Her brows creased. She was sweating and breathing as if she were jogging instead of standing still. "Yes, two windows."

"What do you see outside the windows?"

Sally swayed backward as if she would fall, but her sisters held her fast despite her pale cheeks and bloodless lips. My heart thudded hard against my breastbone, and I clenched my fists to stop myself from walking forward and dragging my girl out of the circle.

Aris took my hand and squeezed.

"Buildings," she said between panting breaths. "Tall spires. It looks like Westminster. The river is there. And a barge."

"What shape are the windows?" Aris asked.

"Ahh," Sally groaned, her hands tightening on her sisters. "Square with—with rounded tops."

The spell broke, the smoke swirled straight up into the air and dissipated, and Sally collapsed. Aris left the room, and his running footfalls echoed back as I waited for the witches to break the circle.

Tell me she's alright, he thought.

I crouched at the edge of the circle. Lady Patel dragged the toe of her slipper through the salt, and I reached out for Sally before they could stop me, pulling her limp body into my lap. Her cheek was cold, but her heartbeat thumped against my fingertips as I pressed them to her neck below her jaw.

"She will be well," Lady Chatsworth said, kneeling beside me to brush the damp curls from Sally's forehead. "Most witches react this way to their first strong casting. She held the vision incredibly, however. Sarah will be a strong witch if she studies."

"There will be no lasting effects?" I asked, my voice quavering with worry.

"No. This spell was meant for a single, experienced witch, but she was right to split the burden. She is wise for one so young."

"Sally?" I asked, brushing my fingers against her cheeks. "Sally, can you hear me?"

After a moment her lashes fluttered and she took a long, deep breath.

"Don't ever do that to me again," I said.

Her voice was weak but amused. "Consider that payback for the tea you drank in Chatsworth."

I laughed, but it was a strangled sound. That tea had brought on visions that helped me solve the mystery of the missing housekeeper, but it had also scared Sally likely as much as she had just frightened me.

"Fair play, one point for you."

She smiled.

I've got him, Aris said inside my head. *The bastard never left town.*

She is awake, I thought back, then said, "Sally?"

Her eyes fluttered open and focused on me.

"You did it. Aris found him."

She smiled and burst into tears.

Madame Matilda opened the door and floated into the room wearing a simple white gown that made her look a bit like a milkmaid who was a secret priestess. "Patricia tells me the spell was successful. Well done, sisters."

Sally clambered to her feet despite my protestations, hurriedly wiping tears from her cheeks. She was pale, but she held Madame Matilda's fingers to her forehead. "Yes, ma'am. And Aris found him."

My relief at salvaging our plan to save the city was only slightly less than my relief that Sally would be alright. Madame Matilda examined the girl's eyes, her lips, and the palms of her hands with professional interest, proclaiming her clear of danger.

"Go and cleanse yourself," she told Sally. "You know where the tools are."

Sally gave a neat little curtsy, sent a shy look my way, and hurried out of the room. We watched her go.

Matilda smiled. "She has great promise, your Sarah. I have rarely met anyone so hungry or dedicated."

"That is because you were born wealthy," I said.

"Pardon me?"

"Are any of the witches in your coven poor?"

Matilda blinked. "No."

"Were any of them born in poverty?"

"No, as a matter of fact, they were not."

"Sally was. And she lived in poverty alone with her brother after her father abandoned them, caring for them both first by stealing, and then by taking a job as a laundress. Thanks to Cassandra, she is now independently wealthy, but Sally swore never to be at the mercy of circumstance, again."

Matilda stared at the empty doorway. "I see."

"Do you?" I fixed the woman with a glare that could have set fire to stone. "Then handle her with care, and do not let her hunger for self-sufficiency turn into a craving for power. If she is as strong as you seem to think..." I let the implication speak for itself. Madame Matilda was smart enough to come to her own conclusions. A powerful witch without self-restraint could be catastrophic.

After a moment, she said, "We have experimented with the Eye and tested the spell. We shall be ready to perform it tonight at your signal. I would like to keep Sarah with me, so she might observe."

I tried not to sound grudging or irritated at her constant use of Sally's full name. After all, she had committed her coven to helping me save the city. So, with great generosity of spirit, I said, "Very well."

"There were far fewer deaths last night, according to this morning's paper. Of course, there was also a burned-down medical school with several charred bodies inside. Was that your doing?"

Several? There should only have been one, though we had not thoroughly checked the place. "In a manner of speaking."

"Holding up your end of the bargain already? Well, you may be assured we will hold up ours. However"—she turned toward me—"Are you certain you wish to accept the consequences of the task we are about to undertake?"

So, she understood the situation and my intentions better even than my companions. Then again, I had long known this woman to be formidable. That was what made her such a valuable, and dangerous, ally.

"It is the only way to ensure this cannot be brushed under the rug or explained away. They will have no choice but to listen, and every paper in the city will write everything that happens, including all of the salacious details."

"Is it wise to take such a risk? You have become something of a savior to this city, though they are not aware of it. What are the papers calling you? The Shadow Woman?"

"Moon and stars, they're not saying that, are they?"

"I read it just this morning."

"How dreadfully unimaginative."

"It does not signify, I suppose. What matters is that you are one of the few people trying to protect this city, and if you are...indisposed..."

"That was an elegant way to phrase it."

"Who will keep them safe?"

"You will," I said. "And Aris, and Tony, and Sally, and Delilah and the rest."

"You are taking an awful risk, Lady St. James."

"Aren't we all?"

She stared solemnly at me, so I winked at her, turned, and left.

We've found him, I thought to Tony as I settled in behind the steering wheel of the auto.

His mental voice was tight with excitement when he thought back, *Where?*

Across the river from Westminster in a set of rather fine rented apartments, if Aris's description is accurate.

He never even left town? That arrogant son of a—damn, we were searching in all the wrong places. How he managed to outmaneuver the Cutthroat King is a mystery. When are we taking him?

Aris is reconnoitering the building as we speak.

We'll need a plan and secure transport. Given who we intend to deliver him to, I don't think he will be inclined to go quietly. Shall we meet here to prepare?

Yes, but you've just given me a marvelous idea. I'll be there shortly.

I left the auto behind and hurried back into the building. Lady Patel nearly ran me down as she rounded the corner on her own way out.

"Oh, Lady St. James," she huffed, pressing one hand to her bosom. "I am sorry, I did not see you."

"Lady Patel," I replied, smiling. "I have a favor to ask you."

20

Cherry Tart

GWEN

After settling matters with Lady Patel, I wove the auto through the crowded streets at an unreasonable pace and pulled to a screeching halt in front of the townhouse full of faerie refugees. A burly man sat on the doorstep picking his teeth and watching me with suspicious eyes.

"Lady," he said. It was *not* a greeting.

I dipped my chin and replied, "Taciturn guard."

He grunted and let me pass. As soon as I stepped foot in the house, a second guard blocked my path to the drawing room and faced me, eying me up and down, folding a pair of muscular arms thicker than my legs.

"I need transport," I told her, "for a guest the King has been expecting."

"When?"

I calculated our timing along with moonrise and sunset, and said, "Eight o'clock," before giving her the address and instructions.

She chewed something unsavory kept tucked between her teeth and her cheek, then nodded and said around the lump, "Alright. I'll be back."

Faeries gathered on the stairs and emerged from doorways, staring at me with curious apprehension.

"Is anyone willing to answer a few questions for me? I do not mean to make you uncomfortable, but your safety and the safety of the city are at stake."

They swallowed, or fidgeted and looked at one another. I reminded myself these people were not sihde, like Aris, who could rip a werewolf's head from its body. They were of a gentler nature and had fled persecution and violence, not gone looking for it.

But a man stepped forward at last and bobbed his head. He was ambiguity personified, the prototypical clay from which every other—more interesting looking—person could be built; neither tall nor short, thin nor thick, not terribly masculine or noticeably feminine.

His features were symmetrical and easily dismissed. His hair was a nondescript shade of brown, and so were his eyes. He would have melted into any crowd without being noticed. Which was likely his purpose in choosing such a glamour.

"Thank you, Mr. Hines," I said.

"I'll do what I can to help, ma'am."

"I very much appreciate that. Let us sit."

He followed me into the drawing room and slid into a chair, staring at me with uncertain eyes of a middling, dull brown, not dark enough to be striking or light enough to be unique.

"Mr. Hines. How much control do you have over your glamour?"

His eyes widened. He had not been expecting such a question. "In what way?"

"Can you change your glamour to look like someone else? Like me, perhaps?"

"No, ma'am. Well," he grimaced, "not quite. That is, I could make my glamour resemble you, in a general way."

"Please, explain."

A thoughtful frown twisted his face into the only interesting expression he likely made. "To create a convincing glamour, I must know everything, down to the last detail, and picture it in my mind; which way your hair grows, how your mouth curls when you smile. It gets easier with practice. But mimicking a real person? I would require weeks of practice to do it well."

"What can you do in a short time? Can you make yourself resemble me closely enough that someone might mistake you for me in the dark, or at a distance?"

"I might, yes."

"How marvelous. Do all fae possess this capability?"

"Some find it easier than others."

"Do you?"

He concentrated for a moment, then blurred. It was like watching someone's reflection in window glass as they passed through the streets behind you. The clean lines of his form fuzzed and softened, and then I was sitting across from myself. Or, rather, I was sitting across from a reflection of me seen in a dirty mirror, caught only in passing.

He'd gotten the height, body type, hair, and eye color, and my general shape correct, but no one who knew me would be fooled. It was the kind of reproduction where someone might say, *you look a great deal like a friend of mine!*

"Extraordinary, Mr. Hines," I said. "Would you be willing to do this, to double as someone else, for a short time tonight? You will not be in any danger."

He fuzzed again, retaking the bland masculine form he wore while living in New London, and picked at his fingernails while the toe of his shoe drummed on the carpet. "I suppose I could."

"That is good of you. Now, one final question: what do you know of the Cutthroat King?"

All the nervous energy drained from his body, and he went as still as a hare hiding from hounds. He trapped his fingers beneath the outsides of his thighs and took a shaky breath. "He came through the rift only to be captured by a mortal man who kept him hostage in iron chains for years. Then he escaped and became the Cutthroat King. He's the most dangerous man—faerie—in New London."

"Can I ask how you learned this?"

He looked at his knees. "I would rather not say if you don't mind, ma'am."

Which meant either Mr. Hines had dealings with the King in the past, or he had worked for him, or both. I was inclined to believe the latter, so I hazarded a guess. "Did he help secure your butcher's shop?"

Mr. Hines swallowed hard and averted his eyes. How else was a refugee in a strange land to make a safe living for themselves with no connections and no capital? A fuller picture painted itself in my mind and fitted into my plans like a missing puzzle piece.

"Thank you very much, Mr Hines."

Looking up, he caught my eye and blushed. With a simple *thank you*, I put myself in his favor. If he needed something, I would be bound to help. Magic did not compel me as it would have a faerie, but my knowledge of the custom told him I would see it through, regardless. He released a deep breath, and his shoulders relaxed.

"Now," I said, rubbing my hands together. "Here is what I need you to do."

I pushed open the door of Supernatural and Paranormal Investigations at two o'clock in the afternoon and dropped a paper box onto a table with a flourish.

"Fear not, I have come bearing gifts," I announced to the room.

People appeared from every corner of the office, lifting their noses to scent the air. With expressions of curious pleasure on their faces, Tony, his two assistants, and even Lia floated toward the heavenly scent leaking through the paper.

I opened the bag and pulled out steaming pastries of every description, from flaky meat pies to sweet danishes and chocolate croissants. Tony's employees snatched them up with alacrity and before long the sound of contented munching filled the air.

A cherry tart sat a bit to one side, and I watched Lia from the corner of my eye to see if she would choose it from the smorgasbord of delicacies.

She did. Cherry was still her favorite. That small victory meant not everything about my sister had changed. Perhaps there was still a way back for us if I could survive this evening...and everything coming afterward.

Around a mouthful of meat pie, Tony said, "You're in a good mood. What happened?"

"I have an idea of how to get our hands on Rutledge without causing a scene."

"Really?"

I explained my plan and his brows rose until there was a smile on his face, as well.

"Why does this make me nervous?" Lia asked, gesturing between the two of us and frowning like a mother who had just caught her toddlers whispering in a corner.

We only continued to grin.

We spent the rest of the afternoon in preparation, coordinating through our rings, and gathering supplies.

"The timeline will be dangerously tight," I told Tony. "So you must be prepared with the secondary plan."

"I don't like that plan, Gwen."

"Do you have a better one?"

"No," he grumbled.

Lia came in from the back and laid a map out on the table, smoothing the wrinkles with her palms and holding the edges down with paperweights.

"I have marked out the route in red," she said, tracing the ink with her fingertip starting at Tromwell and winding through the city, focusing on the East Side and ending at Trafalgar Square. "The faeries will be positioned here and here, so you must enter the square from this side."

I visualized the path in my mind and nodded. "Very well."

"I will be here," Tony said, pointing to the steeple at the corner of the square. "Cyrus and Alix will come in from the opposite side. You'll need to send the signal from here for greatest effect." He pointed to the exact center, between the two fountains.

"If Delilah's gadget works," Lia said, hands on her hips.

"She has not failed, yet," I said.

"The entire plan hinges on this single point of failure. If it is defective, it will destroy everything. From a strategic standpoint—"

"But we don't have the time for anything else unless we let the monsters terrorize the city for another month until the next full moon. Who knows whether the fae will invade by then?"

"You will be overwhelmed if this fails," she said, slapping her palm on the table. "You asked me to help, and I am here, helping, so listen to me. The likelihood of you accomplishing this unscathed is zero. Zero, Gwen. And the chance of getting out of this...this *trap* alive, is only slightly higher.

"And the likelihood of everything happening in concert is astronomical. You are taking too many risks without a large enough margin of success."

I had plans I could not speak aloud because if I admitted what I was doing, they would go out of their way to stop me, which would be terribly inconvenient. Of course, there was a better-than-average chance my secondary plan would also backfire, but she did not need to know that, either.

"Do you have an answer, Lia? Can you fix this, use your strategic mind, and make us infallible?"

"No!" She said, pushing the map and paperweights off the table with a crash. "But almost anything would be better than this madness. You must agree with me." She turned to Tony, her eyes imploring, but he only stared helplessly at her.

"Moon and stars, you, too?"

"It is the closest answer we have," he said with a shrug.

"Don't behave as if you have not run your own share of dangerous plans," I said.

She glared at me. "Those were only dangerous to me, you great, cotton-headed idiot! And I spent years ensuring it would work, years wasted as soon as you pulled me through the rift."

"Lovely, here we are again," I said, throwing my hands in the air and stalking away as my temper, and my good mood deserted me. "Holding a grudge is not going to help any of us—"

"I am not holding a grudge! I am trying to stop you from being—"

"Ladies," Tony tried to interject, but our voices reached the level of screech owls and we ignored him.

"I am not incompetent or selfish," I said, stabbing a finger at the ground. "And you cannot use your anger at me for wanting to save my sister as a shield to—"

"I did not need to be saved!"

"Ladies!" Tony bellowed and stepped between us, both arms raised as if to ward off an imminent attack, which was likely given that Lia's fingertips were glowing with green fire. Only then did I realize the three of us were alone. Tony's assistants disappeared during our row.

He narrowed his eyes at my sister and said, "Ophelia, take a walk to calm your nerves. I would rather you did not burn the office."

She glanced down at her hands, surprised to see them burning, and shook her fingers to put out the fire.

He turned his gaze on me and said, "Gwen, if you don't mind," and stalked into the back room, which was quickly turning into the most-used room of the building.

Lia stormed out the front door with her fists curled at her side, and I followed Tony down the short hall, closing the door behind us. He stood with his arms folded, the muscles in his exposed forearms tense, and glowered at me. I was about to be scolded, and familiar pain tightened my throat.

We were alone, a fact that would have tempted my self-control mere months ago, but now the pain felt...sad. Nostalgic. A cut from the broken shard of a mirror reflecting life as it might have been.

Tony shook his head and said, "For one of the most intelligent people I have ever known, you are short on wits."

My mouth popped open in surprise. This was not the kind of scolding I expected. "Excuse me?"

"Your_sister_is_scared," he said each word slowly as if I were too dull to catch his meaning. "She is not attacking your intelligence, she is afraid you will be hurt."

"That is not what happened in there," I said, pointing at the door. "She has questioned my judgment more than once and insinuated I am selfish for not considering—"

He grabbed my shoulders and shook me once, hard enough to shut me up and make me stare at him in disbelief. "She came here because of you. Because you asked her. She sent that damnable raven here and kept him trapped by magic to protect you. She also freed him because you asked her to. She joined this crazy alliance and hasn't slept in days because she is trying to bring back enough of her magic to help *you*. How can you be so myopic as to miss it?"

"Myopic. Good word."

"Gwen," he said in a warning growl.

"I'm sorry. I am…" I sighed and wriggled free of his grasp, trying to pull my emotions in order. "I cannot see it. When she looks at me or speaks to me, all I can see is the sister I lost and the woman who took her place, a woman I don't recognize. I should not resent her for it but I cannot seem to help myself."

He raised my chin with one finger until I stared up into a pair of kind brown eyes. "Have you thought about getting to know the woman she became?"

"When I try, she pushes me out."

"Because she's scared."

"She told me the person I loved was dead, Tony."

"Because she is afraid you will not be able to love the person she has become. You want the girl you knew, but she grew into someone else, a person of necessity, not choice. And every time you remind her of what she lost you make the divide between you deeper. It is not her job to make loving her easier or more comfortable, Gwen. And it isn't yours, either."

I dropped my chin and stared down at my feet, feeling strangely vulnerable. He was right. How had he seen so much when I missed it all? Myopic, indeed.

"She's mad at me," I said in a small, hurt voice.

"She has a right to be. But mad doesn't last forever. She's an adult, she will learn to cope. But she cannot forgive you unless you ask her to."

I stared at the silver rings adorning my fingers. Every ring represented a person I loved; and realized the truth with startling, painful clarity. "What if she doesn't, Tony? What if she doesn't forgive me? What if *I* became someone *she* cannot love?"

"You won't know unless you try."

"But what if she can't?"

"You won't be any worse off than you are now," he said.

True. But I may not recover from the disappointment and rejection. Aris barely held my broken pieces together the last time.

He flipped the familiar silver franc across the back of his knuckles as he stared into the middle distance, his voice thoughtful and far away. "You have to let her love you, because you believe yourself worthy of it and because she chooses to. Not because she is obliged by your blood or the kind things you've done for her, but because you are yourself."

When he looked up, the naked honesty in his eyes told me exactly what the last six months had cost him. Tony was not referring only to Lia and me. My heart expanded until my lungs hurt and breathing became impossible. I wormed my way into his arms and squeezed, enjoying the warmth and comfort of his presence as his strong arms wrapped around me.

But if I accepted the comfort of knowing he loved me despite the way I hurt him, I must also accept the pain of grieving whatever we might have become to one another. If I was less broken. If I was someone else. If he was, perhaps, a little less perfect.

"How did you become so wise?" I asked.

"Pain."

"Tony, I—I'm so sorry."

He kissed the top of my head, and said, "Me, too. But I don't regret it. Not a moment of it, Gwen."

"I love you, you know."

"I know. I love you, too."

The doorbell rang and we both flinched, separating ourselves and smoothing our clothes before emerging from the back room. Lia stood near the front of the office, not looking any less angry, and staring at the two of us like we had been caught in a compromising situation.

Which, of course, we had...if either us cared or had anything to lose.

But our embrace had been a kind of farewell; an apology and reconciliation rolled into one. There was no passion in it. That would never exist between us again, not with Aris running around in the world being damnably irresistible despite my better judgment and all common sense.

But I had no time to think about relationships. The sun was lowering and before long, Aris, Tony, and I would put our lives in jeopardy, again, while Lia protected whoever she could.

Of course, that was what she had always done. Lia was a protector. She watched over me when we were children, placed herself between Obyrron and the mortal world, and stood watch over the displaced faeries. Now, she was trying to protect me, again, in the only way she knew how.

Tony was right. I missed it. She stood at the front of the room, defiant...and alone.

And I had left her that way six months ago; dragged her back from the Sunset Lands and abandoned her to nurse my own pain while she mourned everything she lost. Soon, I would abandon her, again.

Grief, hope, and fear clutched my heart with invisible fingers, but I strode to the front of the room, ignoring the look of surprise on Lia's face, and pulled her into an embrace. She stiffened as if she would back away, but I held on. She smelled like lilacs and cherry Danish.

"Gwen," she began, but I only squeezed harder and said, "Shut up and hug me."

And she did.

She hugged me back, and I closed my eyes, and we were both sixteen, sitting beneath an oak tree making plans about our future. My entire life played itself in reverse, unfolding from the moment I hugged her until the moment I lost her.

We would never be those girls again, but maybe we could be something new...if I survived the night.

I held her at arm's length by her shoulders and said, "I love you. No, shut up. *I love you*. Don't say anything, you'll ruin it."

An unwilling smile tugged at one corner of her mouth, but she didn't speak. A simple hug hadn't fixed anything, of course, but it felt so much better than no hug, at all.

The doorbell jingled and Sam walked in with Delilah and Fleur at his side, carrying a wooden box between them.

"They're done," Delilah said as they plunked the box onto the floor. "Though I don't mind telling you it was a slagging pain in my arse. They're nowhere near the quality my shop produces, but they'll have to do."

Tension stole over the room as everyone realized how close we stood to the precipice. Once the plan was in motion, there was no going back.

"I need to send a message, Sam," I said as I buttoned my coat. "It's time."

21

Special Delivery

GWEN

C hief Inspector Mac Sweeney strode down the sidewalk, heels striking the pavement with confidence and echoing off the surrounding buildings. The last vestiges of daylight bathed the street in a reddish glow, turning his pale skin orange.

A fashionable hat sat on his dark hair at a jaunty angle, casting shadows across his face that made his confrontational expression more severe.

A delivery cart rumbled to a stop at a nearby building, the driver wearing a floppy hat that hid his face and made the trail of his pipe smoke curl up over the brim like a wizard. An auto buzzed around the stopped horses, honking as it passed.

Mac Sweeney noticed none of it. His eyes were fixed on the unremarkable bank of flats lining the path on the river side of the street.

Where is Rutledge? I thought to Aris.

Somewhere in the front of the house. He left the sitting room about an hour ago and hasn't come back to this side of the house, since.

Is the stone still there?

Sitting on the table, ripe for the picking.

Care to pick it?

It would be a pleasure, my lady.

I smiled and watched from cover as Mac Sweeney approached the door. As soon as he knocked, I pressed the button on my Sightscreen to activate the spell and slid from between two parked carriages.

On my way in, I thought to Tony.

The back doors of the delivery cart opened and a burly dwarf began unloading boxes, stacking them on the sidewalk in a row. He did not see me as I passed, but neither did anyone else. The spell engraved on my bracelet made me about as noticeable as mud smeared on the cobbles.

If, by chance, someone saw through my camouflage and tried to work out who I was, the magic would give them a nasty headache, followed by dizzy spells. Not conducive to remembering faces.

With a fitful flicker, the sun retreated behind the tops of the buildings, turning the street into a flat, grey landscape with looming shadows reaching out of every corner. It was just dark enough for human eyes to struggle to recognize details.

I picked up my pace as Mac Sweeney knocked on the door with three sharp raps.

When it opened, a voice said, "You ain't supposed to be here," in the kind of whisper people regularly mistook for private, but only made listening ears more interested.

For a moment, I thought Mac Sweeney wouldn't reply, but after a tense few breaths, he drew himself up and said, "We have a problem. I need to see him. Now."

"But I ain't supposed—"

"You will open this door. Unless, of course, you'd like to explain to your boss why half of Scotland Yard is on his doorstep and you did not warn him."

I sidled up behind Mac Sweeney and got a good look at the guard. He was no more than a street tough, but his fists were the size of hams and his head was as blocky as a pound of concrete. If he decided to take Mac Sweeney's attitude personally, I may have to step in.

Mac Sweeney, however, was notorious for not realizing his comparative size, so he puffed out his chest and raised his chin, displaying the one intimidating element of his person: his mustache.

It was thicker than a scrub brush and bristled at the hired thug like an angry dog. I slid to one side and angled myself to fit between the thug and the doorframe, inching sideways into the foyer.

The fit was tight and I pulled in a silent breath, trying to flatten myself against the wall and take up as little space as possible. But my coat was thick wool and with all of the other accoutrements I wore... the fabric covering my bust brushed his arm.

I froze.

He shivered and looked at his elbow with furrowed brows, perhaps expecting to find a bug crawling across his shirt sleeve. Seeing nothing, he shrugged and continued glowering at Mac Sweeney.

Barely daring to breathe, I edged further into the hall one quiet step at a time, pulling the chloroform from my pocket with one hand and readying the handkerchief in the other.

"Alright," he said, at last, "but stay here, by the door. He won't want anyone coming inside."

"If you don't want trouble, you'll go and retrieve him. Now!"

The small man looked like a terrier about to jump up and bite a Great Dane, and the performance intimidated the thug about as well as it would have the dog. He left Mac Sweeney standing near the door and hurried into the flat. I tucked the alchemical chloroform away and followed.

I'm inside, I thought to Tony, then repeated the message to Aris.

I cannot get out through the window, Aris thought back. *The rock is heavier than it looks and too slick to carry with my claws. I'll have to bring it out the front.*

Wait till Rutledge is clear.

I have done this sort of thing before, he thought back, dryly.

Then you should know better than to distract me, you irritating corvid.

His mental voice disappeared in an insulted huff, and I smiled as I crept behind the thug. He turned into a room and I flattened myself against the opposite wall.

"Mac Sweeney is here," he said without preamble.

Chair legs scooted across a wood floor. "What? Why on earth is that little rat of a man here? He should know better than to compromise our position."

That was Rutledge. He always sounded as if his lips and cheeks were curtains flapping in the wind of his breath, too lazy to get out of the way of his words.

"He didn't say, but he demanded to see you. He's standing in the entrance."

After a moment of silence, Rutledge said, "Very well. Grab a pistol, as insurance."

He charged out of the room like a bull, brushing by me like I was so much furniture, while the thug headed off in the other direction.

Thug on the loose, I thought to Aris. *He's after a gun. I'm following Rutledge to the door.*

I hear him.

Rutledge was a big, barrel-chested man in his late fifties or early sixties, with a white walrus mustache that would have given Mac Sweeney's face hair a run for its money, a heavy paunch, and the bulbous red nose of a wine drinker.

Despite that, he was in excellent condition—as I knew from our confrontation last winter—and tall enough that my next maneuver would be tricky. He turned the corner toward the entrance, saw the much smaller man, and stopped cold.

"What? Who are you? What is the meaning of this?"

Here we go, I thought to Aris as I pulled the chloroform and handkerchief from my pocket.

"Malcom!" Rutledge shouted, turned in my direction to glare down the hallway, staring past me and toward Malcolm, who popped around the corner with a gun in one hand and a frown of confusion on his blocky face. "Who is this?"

Malcom's face went white as Rutledge turned back to Mac Sweeney to demand, "Why are you impersonating the Chief Inspector?"

There was murder in his eyes. I could wait no longer. I leaped onto his back, catching him around the neck with one hand and pressing the chloroform-soaked cloth over his nose and mouth with the other.

He tried to shout, then flung himself backward in wild panic. We crashed into the wall and his substantial weight smashed the air out of my lungs. The back of my head smacked the wood and stars floated across my vision. But it didn't take long for the chloroform to drain the fight out of him.

He wobbled as his body went limp and we crashed to the floor like a pair of felled trees. Malcom came running down the hallway, his heavy features arranged in something resembling shock.

Aris emerged from a doorway and punched him in the side of the head with cool precision. Malcom hit the carpet, bounced, and lay with his face pressed into the fibers, snoring.

"Neatly done," I panted, trying to wrench my arm out from beneath Rutledge's big body. The motion pressed the button on my Sightscreen, and Aris located me with a glance.

"Practice," he said with a self-deprecating shrug.

The pocket of his coat bulged with what I assumed was the communication stone, and it bumped against his leg as he hurried toward me and lifted the unconscious lord by his armpits.

"Can you support him that way?" I asked, brushing off my coat and replacing the stoppered bottle. I held the soaked cloth as far from my face as possible.

Aris gave me an offended glance, ducked under one of Rutledge's limp arms, and positioned himself as if he were helping a sick man walk. Hopefully, anyone who chanced to see the two of them would only think a drunk man was being escorted home. I was still too wobbly from striking my head to be of much use.

"Can you help him?" I asked Mac Sweeney.

The little man had lost his bluster after Rutledge passed out, and gave a nervous nod. He ducked under the other arm and took as much weight as he could bear. The two of them guided the unconscious man into the twilight gloom, behind the boxes stacked conveniently by the delivery crew.

I slid out behind them, closing the door and keeping my body hidden behind the three men as much as possible. The cart doors hung ajar as the dwarf stacked the last box, creating a screen between us and the business side of the street. Aris and Mac Sweeney hefted Rutledge inside, ducking to drag his limp body after them.

I handed Aris the chloroform and said, "Keep this rag far away from your face, but use it to put Rutledge under if he wakes," then swung up onto the bench next to the silent driver.

He grunted, waited for the dwarvish man to pound on the side of the cart from his position at the rear, and snapped the reins against the mule's flanks.

"We have less than two hours before moonrise," I told him. "Let's see how quickly we can make it across town."

That went better than we could have hoped, Aris thought.

It isn't wise to say such things, I warned him.

Why not?

Because you're tempting fate, and she likes a challenge.

He gave me the mental equivalent of a snort. *That's ridiculous, Gwen.*

A gunshot cracked behind us and a chunk of wood blew off the back corner of the cart mere inches from the dwarf's head. He swore and swung to the other side as the driver flicked the reins again, hard.

I twisted around to see Malcom standing outside the flat with the heel of one hand pressed to the side of his head. The pistol we neglected to take was leveled at the fleeing cart.

I castigated myself for overlooking something so stupid and thought to Aris, with a note of acid in my mental voice, *See? You've ruined it.*

Was that a gunshot?

Malcolm attacked a passing rider and jerked the man out of his saddle by the front of his shirt.

It was. Hold on back there. I think our situation is about to get a bit more exciting.

Malcolm dragged himself into the saddle and kicked the horse into a full gallop, while the dwarf swung himself onto the roof and pulled a false panel off the top. He chucked it into the street behind us, where it splintered into several pieces and made the horse shy away and rear up.

Malcolm stuck to the saddle like a burr, and he was after us again within seconds. The only bullets I had were silver, and I would need every one of them tonight, so my pistols were useless. As I searched for something else to fight with, my dwarvish companion hunched over the opening in the roof and hauled out a heavy leather sack.

As he tried to work open the bindings, Malcom fired again. The driver's hat tumbled from his head and floated to the street behind us to be trampled beneath the hooves of the charging horse. Tony's blonde hair glowed in the deepening dark, but no red stained his locks.

"Are you alright?" I shouted over the commotion.

"Fine. Hang on!"

The coach took a hard left turn, coming off two wheels. The dwarf flattened himself like a spider, while I ducked, grabbed the rail with one hand, and Tony's sleeve with the other. Our wheels reconnected with a jarring crash, making several rolling thumps sound from the storage car as Aris and Mac Sweeney lost their footing.

"Lachlan?" Tony shouted.

The dwarfish man yelled, "Here!" from his stomach.

Wind whipped my hair into my face as I turned. The horse pulled behind and to the right of us as Malcolm reached for the rail. Lachlan kicked the outstretched wrist, making Malcom draw back with a curse, before raising his pistol and sighting on the dwarf.

Panicked, I grabbed whatever was in my pocket and hurled it in his face. The wind caught the handful of cayenne pepper and disbursed it into a cloud that got into his eyes, nose, and mouth. His shot went wide, but barely.

He coughed and let go the reins to wipe at his face. The horse began to fall back.

"Well," I said, "that was rather clever of me."

Lachlan looked over his shoulder in surprise, then barked a laugh and went back to work on his bag. But Malcom wasn't done.

The henchman blindly kicked the horse back into motion while wiping tears and snot from his face with the back of his gun hand. He was certainly earning his pay this evening.

I searched for a weapon that would not damage any pedestrians or nearby structures, fighting to see past my flying hair while Malcolm pulled alongside the coach again. The dwarf yanked open the bag with a shouted, "Ha!" and threw a handful of something on the ground in front of the horse.

The animal tossed its head and screamed, crow hopping to the side and crashing into a cart before it fell in a tangle of flying legs. The poor beast. My throat closed up with pity, but I pushed the hair out of my face long enough to see the struggling animal and the bystanders who rushed to its aid.

"What was that?" I asked.

Holding up a handful of twisted bits of iron, Lachlan said with pride, "Caltrops!"

Both practical and devious. I should have expected nothing less from one of the Cutthroat King's minions. I did not expect to see a bloody hand reach up over the edge of the cart roof, catch the dwarf by the leg, and drag him over the side, screaming.

Without thinking, I threw myself after him, managing to catch his wrist before he tumbled over the edge. But Lachlan was off balance and heavy with muscle. The front wheel bumped over a large stone, and his tenuous equilibrium shifted. He slid backward and his body weight dragged me across the roof to the edge.

I flung my foot desperately toward the hole in the roof and hooked my ankle on the edge. We stopped just as my elbows bent over the corner. Lachlan hung between the churning wheels, his eyes wide with fright as he fought for a foothold, his boots sliding against the polished wood paneling.

My fingers went numb beneath his panicked grip as cobbles flew beneath us at an astounding speed.

"'Hold on!" Tony shouted, and the mules dragged us into a left-hand turn that gave Malcolm the leverage he needed to haul himself onto the roof. He rose to his knees, his eyes bloodshot and swollen, tears leaving streaks in the dirt on his red cheeks. With a sneer, he pulled the pistol from the belt of his trousers.

"Take this, you bitch," he snarled at me and thumbed back the hammer.

The dwarven man's weight and iron grip kept me locked flat against the roof, and I hadn't the strength to pull him up. My coat should be enough to protect me...unless he aimed for my head. Which he did.

The cart jostled to the side, the gun went off, and splinters exploded less than six inches from my face, sending a line of burning pain from my cheekbone to my temple. Aris suddenly loomed out of the hole in the ceiling, grabbed Malcom's ankle, and yanked.

His feet flew out from under him and he toppled off the edge, his wide eyes and reaching fingers disappearing into the dark. The rear wheel rocked up and Malcom screamed. The cart tipped, and the wheel hit the cobbles and snapped, wrenching the iron band into a twisted mess and making the vehicle list dangerously to one side.

I tried not to imagine the blocky-headed henchman as the rear wheel rolled up and over him. Aris grabbed me around the waist and hauled me backward, far enough that Lachlan was able to gain a handhold. He scrambled onto the driver's seat, his face white, and held on with both hands as Tony snapped the reins.

Slowly, Aris lowered me into the cart where the unconscious body of Lord Rutledge lay next to the traumatized Mr. Hines. The fae man had released his glamour of Chief Inspector Mac Sweeney during our flight. His pale face was nothing but a thumbprint in the darkness, the lack of mustache making his identity clear.

"Mr. Hines," I said over the rolling growl of our three remaining wheels. "Are you quite well?"

"I'll do, ma'am," came the weak reply.

Several minutes later the cart slowed, and minutes after that, it stopped. Tony opened the doors and the dim light of the stables backlit his broad-shouldered form. Aris hopped lightly to the floor, then reached up to lift me down as Tony grabbed Rutledge by the shirtfront and dragged him across the wood.

Aris took my arm, pulled back my sleeve, and examined the bruise already forming in the vague shape of a hand print.

"Lachlan has quite a grip," I said.

He turned my wrist over, noting the curving marks of fingers, and ran the pad of his thumb gently along the bruise. Then he lifted it to his lips and kissed the sensitive skin, making a shiver run up my arm and down my spine. It had been a long time since anyone kissed an injury better, and it made warmth uncurl in my belly.

Then he pushed my matted hair back and examined the scratches on the side of my face, his dark brows low over his eyes.

"Remind me to have a word with Mr. Malcom, later," he said.

"I think he might be dead."

"It shouldn't be hard to find his body."

I snorted, but his expression was deadly serious. "Aris, that is—that's ridiculous."

He shrugged, then slid under Lord Rutledge's free arm as Tony lugged him from the cart. The man had a purple lump on his forehead and muttered incoherently as Tony fought to keep him upright.

Mr. Hines crawled out of the cart, looking like he never wanted to ride in another vehicle ever again, and edged away into the shadows to stand alone.

"Lady Gwen?"

I turned to find Lady Patel, Sally, and several other witches descending upon us. They formed up like a detachment of guards and escorted out of the stable behind the building on Tromwell Lane, and through a cellar door at the back.

"How did the chloroform work?" Lady Patel asked as we followed the train of witches into the basement.

"Within seconds," I said, "as your research suggested."

"That's the alchemical additives," she said. "Doctors don't like to use anything related to Alchemy, the fools. Imagine how quickly we could relieve pain, or prepare someone for emergency surgery. Most patients suffer for at least a quarter of an hour before traditional ether takes proper effect."

We chatted about chemicals as we descended into the belly of the building, pretending we were not party to a highly illegal—and terrible—kidnapping. But Scotland Yard could not be trusted to handle the affair, and Lord Rutledge had proved himself capable of ruthless cruelty and violence.

His voice grew stronger and more coherent the deeper we strode into the dark. Aris bound his hands and feet while in the cart, so he could only take small steps, and he fell several times, slowing the procession.

"That was clever thinking," I congratulated him.

He shrugged one shoulder and said, "I do what I can."

At last, we reached a room that was equal parts cave and cathedral. Stone arches supported a high barrel ceiling and torch rings gleamed dully from the wall next to us, suggesting the building was far older than the Georgian architecture on the upper level.

Slate floor tiles had been set in concentric circles leading to the center of the room, where a large, ornate iron chandelier cast a single pool of light over a wooden chair. They forced Lord Rutledge into it and bound his hands and feet to the arms and legs with rope. They left him sitting alone in the single point of light as the rest of us retreated into the shadows.

He searched the dark with blurry eyes and demanded, "What is the meaning of this? Release me at once. I am Lord Herbert Cornelius Mayflower, the Marquis of Rutledge, and if you do not set me free this instant, I will bring the full might of the metropolitan police down on your heads!"

The familiar voice that floated out of the darkness sounded like the lazy caress of a knife. Smooth, cold, sharp, and delighted. "Oh, I don't think you will be doing any such thing."

Rutledge stiffened, making his mustache quiver. "Who's there."

"You know who it is, don't you, my pet? That is why your hands are shaking and your flabby cheeks are so pale. You thought I could only harm you in your dreams."

Rutledge jerked back and forth, his head swiveling like an owl as he tried to see everywhere at once, but the voice in the shadows seemed to come from nowhere. "Where are you?"

"You thought, when you left me to die, that you were rid of me. But you should have known better when you consigned me to the shadows, my pet. You should have known..."

The Cutthroat King emerged from the shadows behind Rutledge, walking like a hunting cat, his entire body alive with energy, but his voice was terribly soft when he crouched behind the white-haired man and said, "...monsters only grow stronger in the dark."

Rutledge jerked and screamed, fighting against his bonds until his wrists bled.

"We are going to have a marvelous evening, you and I," The King said as he backed away.

A sliver of dread embedded itself in the back of my neck, making me wonder if I made the right choice in leaving the questioning of Lord Rutledge to a man who was not exactly sane. But Tony made a deal, and they seemed to have a score to settle between them.

Rutledge's fear was real. There was likely no one else who could draw truthful answers from him as easily as the King. And the witches were here to oversee things as they prepared the spell, so they would keep everything in order.

At least, I hoped they would, or I had made a terrible mistake.

22

The Chase Begins

GWEN

W e left Lord Rutledge guarded by several of the King's men and met the King himself in the hall.

"This ends Tony's commitment to you," I said.

He inclined his dark head. "So it does. And now begins the enjoyable part of *our* association. Unless" —he stepped forward and ran his fingertips down my cheek, lifting away a bit of blood from the scratches the splintered wood had given me during our chase— "you would like to engage in other pleasurable activities."

The Cutthroat King was a handsome man, perhaps more than handsome. But his eyes were flat and cold, and being touched by him was like being brushed by the wind blowing through a graveyard.

"The only pleasurable thing you will do for me is keep your commitment to our alliance."

He raised his hand again, as if to touch my face, and said, "But it doesn't have to be the only thing. I could—"

Aris was there in less time than it took to blink, slamming the King against the stone wall of the passage. He pressed his forearm across the King's windpipe and the tip of a silver knife to the soft flesh beneath his jaw.

The King smiled, as if he'd been waiting for that reaction, and said, "This could be fun, too, Raven. No need for jealousy."

Aris responded in a conversational tone that sounded more threatening than anger could have. "If the woman says no, she means it. If you try to convince her when she doesn't want convincing, I will let her watch while I cut your eyes out and eat them."

"My, my," the King said, lifting his free hand to lick my blood from his fingertips. He made a pleasurable little purring sound. "Possessive, are we?"

"Unfortunately," I told Aris, trying to control my tone, "we don't have time to stay and chat. And the King has a job to do. I'm certain he will remember your warning."

"I will," he assured us. "I remember everything."

Aris said, "What you remember is your business. So long as you keep your word, and keep your hands to yourself, you won't become mine."

The King raised his hands in an amused show of peace, and Aris released him slowly, leaving a shallow cut on the side of his neck. The man did not seem to notice.

"I await your signal, Lady Gwen," he called as we retreated down the hallway.

"One day," Aris said as we emerged into the night air, "you should let me kill that creature."

I shivered, remembering the look on his face when he tasted my blood, and the hungry light in his eyes when he'd spoken to Rutledge. The Cutthroat King was a deeply unsettling man. "You know, I just might. By the by...please *never* call me pet."

"On that, we are agreed."

Sally waited for us in the carriage house with her hands clasped tightly in front of her, and threw her arms around me as soon as we neared. I squeezed her tightly and closed my eyes. She, at least, would be far safer than the rest of us.

"You have your ring?" I asked.

"Sam delivered it earlier."

"And you will be watching for the signal?"

"Yes, ma'am."

"Good girl."

She let me go, gave me a brave smile, and then, surprisingly, stepped into Aris's arms. "Protect her," she said against his chest.

"With my life."

"And maybe try not to get yourself killed, either."

He laughed and tugged on a lock of her hair in an echo of Sam's affectionate teasing. "I will do my best."

We waited till Sally disappeared into the building, then looked at one another with apprehension. Every muscle in my body thrummed with adrenaline, but I was hesitant to move. I had done many dangerous things in my life, but taking on a city full of werewolves and vampires ranked at the absolute top.

"Are you ready?" I asked.

"Not yet."

"What could you—"

Aris pulled me into his arms and crushed my lips in a scorching kiss that turned my insides to pudding and my brain into a jiggling pile of mush. His arms, arms that both protected and cherished, slid around my back.

And I almost lost him more than once. Aris put himself in danger for my sake more times than I could count. When I looked back over my adult life, over the adventures and dangers, he was the one constant. And though I'd only known him as a man for a little over six months, I was more deeply connected to him than anyone else in my life.

He lied to me for years. And yet our relationship was, perhaps, the only honest relationship I'd ever had. And tonight I stood to lose it.

As if sensing my emotion, Aris tightened his arms and deepened the kiss, stealing my breath—my soul—with every sweep of his tongue. The hungry noises he made in the back of his throat caused goosebumps to run up my arms.

When he let me go, I wobbled and had to steady myself by grasping his arms. Whatever happened tonight, I could not lose him. He brushed curls off my forehead, his dark eyes glowing.

"There," he said with a self-satisfied smirk. "Now I'm ready."

With that, he reached into his pocket and pulled out one of Delilah's gadgets. The brass box was carefully engraved with runic symbols and fitted with two clasps on the back. Aris flipped the delicate latch to open the top, then handed the device to me as he pulled a silver knife out of its sheath and rolled up his sleeve.

I bit my lips together as he drew the blade across his forearm. Blood welled and poured into the box in a steady stream until his wound began to heal.

"Will that be enough?" he asked as he rolled his sleeve over the angry red line of healing skin.

"It will have to be."

He clipped the device onto his shirt and depressed the small button on the side. The box whirred to life, and the air around us filled with the coppery-sweet scent of Aris's blood. I stepped back, swallowing convulsively until the smell wasn't strong enough to make my stomach threaten violence.

"Your turn," he said.

I pulled the small brass necklace from beneath my blouse. It was shaped like a cylinder wrapped in brass cords and engraved with runes and magical symbols. Instead of a button, there was a little clasp on top that I flicked open. It released the lid of the cylinder, which I turned inside out and refastened to the top in its inverted position.

We hadn't had time to test any of the gadgets, and it grew warm in my hand, but I could not tell if it was working. I looked up to ask Aris and froze. His pupils had dilated until nearly his entire eye, iris and sclera, were black. His normal expression of laconic amusement was gone, and he looked uncomfortably like the Cutthroat King. His eyes were fixed on me with a predatory intensity that made my skin crawl.

"I take it the device is working," I said, trying and failing to sound nonchalant.

"Oh, yes," Aris said, his voice terribly seductive and hungry. "I smell the fear, like a fine wine."

He closed his eyes, inhaled deeply, and shuddered, clenching both hands into fists and making his jaw muscle stand out against his skin. When he opened his eyes, he was more or less himself again. Either that, or he had altered his glamour for my comfort.

"When we start," he said, "stay behind me. If I see you running, I may not be able to control myself. At least"—he took another deep breath—"not until I can get used to the scent. She concentrated the fear, somehow. Every damned werewolf in New London is going to be snapping at your heels, Gwen."

I tried to smile. "That was the idea, dear man. A girl can't have too much attention, after all, and never let it be said that Delilah Irons is a slouch at her job. Shall we go hunting?"

My attempt at humor seemed to settle him. "I would say after you, but that probably isn't safe, so—" He turned and jogged into the night, turning right on Tromwell to follow the route Lia laid out on our map.

The path was designed to spread the scent of fear and faerie blood to the widest possible area in the most densely populated parts of the city, while still giving us plenty of room to maneuver. And once the monsters took the bait, we would need it.

I took a steadying breath, locked my wheels in place, and leaned forward, rolling over the curb and hitting the street at about the same pace as a jog. With a few careful adjustments, I advanced until I was just far enough behind Aris that he should not be able to smell the fear bubbling out of the necklace.

We've begun, I thought to Tony.

I'm in position, he thought back. *Be careful, Gwen.*

You, too.

Then I disconnected my thought from that ring, followed Aris around a corner, and thought to Delilah, *Gadgets one and two are working beautifully.*

Hammer and tongs, hearing your voice in my head is uncomfortable, she thought back. *And of course, they're working. They were simpler to construct than I thought. I'm most worried about the last one, though. If that one misfires, you'll be in trouble.*

I have complete faith in your craftsmanship.

Of course, you do. There was a moment of silence, and then, *Gwen?*

Yes?

Be careful.

Yes, ma'am.

I gave myself a moment, then thought, *Ophelia Magnolia St. James.*

I'm here.

We've started. Everything has gone to plan so far.

Don't get overconfident, she warned.

There is nothing less likely. Are you ready?

Yes. This prototype Percy made is rather extraordinary.

He is something of a genius, but don't tell him I told you that.

The St. James sisters, keeping egos in check since...moon and stars, when were we born?

Her mental voice was full of trepidation, which made her attempted humor all the more endearing. *Stay safe, Lia, and get out of there if it looks like we will be overrun.*

I would say the same to you, but I doubt you will listen.

A howl echoed off the low ceiling of clouds that had been slowly building since just before sunset. Aris leaped the curb and cut between two buildings, and I followed, using my knees to absorb the shock of the landing. *I wouldn't mind you saying it, anyway.*

...Stay safe, Gigi.

My eyes filled with tears, but I dashed them away and felt once more for my gear, making certain everything was in its place with a quick sweep of my hands. Another howl, this one closer, and hungry.

"It's beginning," Aris said, over his shoulder.

"I'm ready."

He angled us toward Whitechapel and shifted from a jog to a long-legged run when we hit the broad main street. He could run at that pace for hours, but when the vampires joined the hunt, he would have to sprint to keep ahead of them. Which, guessing from the shadow that flashed across an adjoining alley to our right, they were beginning to do.

The chase was on.

For a while, it was enough just to run. Buildings flashed by in a grey and black blur, and the sound of pursuing monsters grew until I could not stop myself from glancing over my shoulder. Two werewolves ran behind me, digging at the street with their claws and snapping if one strayed too close to the other. Foam flecked their lips and spittle hung in flapping strings from their open mouths. Their eyes were devoid of anything resembling thought as they chased me.

The idea of turning on my Sightscreen and hiding somewhere was almost overwhelming, but if the beasts could not
see me, I couldn't lead them into our trap. So, I dragged my
attention back to the darkened street in front of me and leaned
harder into my wheels.

Several citizens were crossing the road in front of us, walking
in a stumbling gaggle and singing off-key. Breath of god, they'd
be slaughtered. Before I could shout at them, Aris bellowed,
"Get inside! Now!"

At Aris's shout, they froze beneath the street lamp and stood
staring as we barreled toward them. If they didn't get out of the
street, they would be easy prey, and we would not have the time
to stop and protect them.

I stuffed my hand inside my pocket, pulled a smoke grenade,
and hurled it at them as we passed. The smoke plumed out in an
instant, covering the four of them in a green haze. I screamed,
hoping I sounded terrified enough to keep the werewolves'
attention, and looked over my shoulder.

Two wolves burst from the smoke, having gained at least a
foot of ground. The vial of fear Delilah created was doing its
job, but it was hard to be grateful for that when another werewolf, bigger than the rest, careened out of an alley. It swerved
in front of the other two to take the lead. Its teeth were as long
as my thumb, its muzzle already stained with blood, and it was
gaining on me one leap at a time.

We need to speed up, I thought to Aris.

A pair of shadows hurtled across the tops of the buildings to our right, and two more flashed through the alley on the left side. That made four vampires and three werewolves.

Good thinking, he replied.

Before we could increase our speed, two huge monsters leaped into the road ahead of Aris, skidding on the cobbles as they corrected course and aimed their huge heads at us. They were too close to Aris; he would have no time to avoid them. I drew my pistol as the first werewolf leaped, jaws open and slavering.

Aris leaped, too, but he shimmered in midair and swerved left in his raven form, spinning below the leaping wolf and just out of reach of the second as it snapped at him, teeth clacking together inches short of his tail feathers.

I leaned hard to the left, bending my knees and shifting my whole body to drag me away from the leaping wolf as I sighted on the second and pulled the trigger. We were close enough that my aim was good. The werewolf crumpled mid-stride, going down in a rolling ball of fur and fangs.

I jumped, tucked both knees into my chest, and floated through the cooling air for a full second and a half as the tumbling wolf passed beneath me. A heartbeat later I hit the ground and a shockwave ran up both legs, making me wobble dangerously close to a street lamp. I leaned away at the last second and heard a *whoosh* as the pole passed within a foot of my face.

The leap had cost me; the wolves were close enough now to smell their sour breath. It was too easy to imagine their fangs sinking into the back of my legs. I had a chile grenade in my pocket, and my fingers itched to smash it on the road behind me.

The crystalized capsaicin would blind the werewolves and damage their noses, giving me precious moments to escape. But the beasts could not track me afterward, not until the chemical wore away.

Lights kindled in windows, and heads poked out of doors as we passed. If I left the werewolves behind us now, innocent civilians would be forced to deal with them on their own. We were gaining the attention we needed. That had to be worth the risk.

I ground my teeth together and steeled myself as Aris changed back into his human form and hit the ground running, gazing over his shoulder long enough to check that I was still behind him. He was grinning.

You are enjoying this, aren't you? I thought.

It is rather exhilarating.

Masochist.

Now there's an idea...

Save it for later. We need more speed.

Do you have much more in those wheels?

As much as you have in your legs.

See if you can keep up, then, Darling.

Aris leaned forward and bolted, his long legs eating ground as he pulled away from me and into the part of town lit by electric street lamps.

"Show off," I said, leaning harder into the wheels.

The warmth of friction spread across my ankles and the sole of my foot where the balance bar connected one side of the foot rig to the other. Werewolves growled and barked as I pulled away from them.

Buildings, lamps, and cross streets came at me in a blur. Reacting on instinct, I leaned and shifted, navigating behind Aris like a bird in a murmuration, silently grateful for the expertise I earned from all the time spent patrolling these streets.

Shoreditch flew past, growing our monster following as more New Londoners appeared to investigate the noise. The blood and fear cocktail proved more potent than I expected, and several fights broke out between the wolves as more joined the chase. They careened into one another and left a trail of blood and damaged body parts in our wake.

My legs burned and the skirt of my coat blew behind me like a flag, nearly getting caught more than once by the swifter wolves. Delilah's ugly overalls would have been a welcome replacement for my coat just then.

Aris turned onto Cheapside and a vampire leaped from the corner of a building, catching him by the front of his shirt. They tumbled to the side, hitting the street like a wrecking ball and plowing through the door of the opposite building.

"Aris!" I screamed as I rushed past the wreckage, too fast to stop or even to turn.

The werewolves did not seem to notice, simply plowed on with wild eyes and slavering jaws. How could I get to Aris with more than ten monsters less than twenty feet behind me?

Heart hammering against my chest, I took the next righthand turn and barreled down the narrow street, dodging a broken box and leaping a heap of rags lying strewn about the cobbles. It wasn't until I cleared the bundle that I realized it was not discarded rags, but a savaged body, torn to bloody pieces and left lying in the street.

Two wolves stopped to inspect the remains, but I only heard echoes of the fight. I rounded the next corner and circled back toward the building Aris and the vampire plowed into.

What on earth are you doing?

I flinched, nearly careened into the corner of a butcher's shop, and jerked myself back on track.

Aris?

Of course, Darling. You didn't think a single young vampire would get the best of me, did you? Be with you in a moment.

Nearly sobbing with relief, I pulled myself together and followed the next part of Lia's route, blasting out of Cheapside and onto Temple Avenue. A shadow flickered past on my right, and before I could blink, Aris was running next to me.

Did we lose the vampires? I asked.

Only for a moment. They should be back on track in seconds, he thought, flicking his arm and spattering droplets of fresh blood on the side of the building to our right.

You're bitten!

Yes, well, I had to distract him long enough to rip his heart out. Watch out.

I slid around a pothole and crouched, pulling all the speed I could manage from my wheels as we closed in on Scotland Yard. This was part of the plan I had revealed to no one. I slid my hand inside my jacket between the buttons and retrieved one of my real grenades.

Time to wake up the constables and thin the pack a bit.

As we neared the large grey building, I pulled the pin and began counting. *One, two, three, four...*I dropped the grenade. It made a metallic plink as it bounced, and I slowed just enough to position myself behind Aris, giving him the shelter of my coat.

Five, six… The explosion was followed by animal cries of pain and surprise. The impact wave pushed me forward as a piece of shrapnel hit my shoulder, bounced off the magical coat, and sailed into the dark.

What have you done? Aris thought.

Added a bit of insurance to our plan.

Dammit, Gwen.

Scold me later. There's a vampire to your right, and I don't think he wants to wait for supper.

Aris glanced to his right, where a dark figure emerged from the shadows, keeping pace as we flew past Scotland Yard toward Westminster Bridge. The clock tower glowered down at us from the end of the road.

Aris pulled something small and bright from one of his pockets and casually flicked it at the vampire. The metal object caught the light of the full moon and glowed for a split second before burying itself in the vampire's chest. He fell into a tumbling roll and was caught by the fastest of the werewolves, who closed its massive jaws over the vampire's head and shook it like a rag doll.

I cut the turn onto Bridge Street but my speed was too great and my wheels lost traction, skipping across the asphalt as I fought to maintain control. My leg muscles cramped as I pressed hard into the turn. Unyielding stone flew past, inches from my face as I nearly collided with the wall outside Westminster.

My wheels regained traction as I rounded the building and wobbled onto Parliament Street with Aris beside me and a horde of beasts at our heels. Their claws raked the ground as they took the turn with far more agility and gained another few feet, closing the gap and whining with excitement.

We're coming in, and we have friends with us, I thought to Tony.

Trafalgar Square lay directly ahead at the end of the street, where Tony and the others waited to ambush the monsters. But three clever werewolves had taken the alley between Whitehall Gardens and cut us off, forming a wall of two-inch-long teeth between us and our reinforcements.

"Three-headed son of a lame mule!" I growled, pulling out my pistol and a silver knife.

This was going to hurt.

23

Pursuit

ARIS

They were moving too fast to stop or change direction. Werewolves were both in front of and behind them. And though Gwen might not be able to see them, there were at least six vampires leaping from the rooftops and racing along in the shadows. If they stumbled now, they would both be dead before reaching the end of the street.

Gwen pulled weapons from the holsters strapped to her jacket, but she would not have time to put the wolves down before they reached the point of no return. And the monsters were closing in.

He needed to do something stupid, and he would have to wait until the werewolves were close enough not to react in time.

"Don't shoot," he said.

She blurted, "What?" in a voice several octaves too high.

"Hang on, and try not to squirm too much."

"Aris!"

The werewolves were almost upon them, close enough that he could see the whites of their madly rolling eyes and lamplight glinting off strings of slobber. He dashed behind Gwen, wrapped both arms around her middle, and leaped.

His muscles coiled and released like loaded springs, sending the two of them sailing over the surprised heads of the werewolves as Gwen screamed. The beasts tried to catch his feet, rearing up on their hind legs and snapping, but he was out of their reach before they had a chance to catch a dangling limb.

They crashed to the ground ten feet beyond the wolves. The impact buckled his knees, but he maintained his footing long enough for Gwen's wheels to gain traction on the asphalt and drag her down the road.

He rolled to absorb the rest of the impact. The rough surface of the road scraped along his leg, hip, and arm, tearing the jacket and pulling off a layer of skin with the fabric. Werewolves collided, setting off several vicious fights and giving the vampires time to attack.

One dashed from the shadow of a building on his left, flying at him so fast it was hard to track. She grabbed the lapels of his jacket as she sprinted past, twisting his torso to the side and hauling him off the ground.

She made to drag him into the darkness, but a second vampire landed on her chest from the roof of the building behind him like a dropped piano.

"Aris!"

Gwen's voice rang through the street like a bell as a werewolf caught hold of his leg, the teeth sinking through his calf with a hot knife of pain. The wolf shook him, wrenching him away from the second vampire and whipping him back and forth with powerful twists of its neck and shoulders. The back of his head bounced off the street with flashes of white light.

Apparently, the vampire was not happy about the treatment of his dinner and leaped onto the werewolf's face with fingers curled into claws. A blast of force took the vampire in the back, catapulting him into the werewolf and sending them both rolling into the other monsters.

"Fly!" Gwen screamed.

Good thinking.

He rolled away from another set of gnashing teeth, shimmered, and hobbled a moment while trying to leap on one good leg. The report of a gunshot echoed off the buildings and a werewolf whined in pain, giving him a moment to launch himself into the air.

His wings beat hard enough to make his chest muscles burn as he rose like a comet. Below him, Gwen caught an attacking vampire with the open canopy of her umbrella, fending off claws and teeth as it shoved her backward. The werewolves turned, noticing Gwen's distraction, and attacked.

Aris banked and dove, tucking his wings in tight against his body and stretching out his claws. He hit the vampire square in the face, damaging both of the monster's eyes as the creature screamed in fury and pain.

Go! he thought to Gwen, but she had already taken advantage of his distraction and leaned hard into her wheels. She shot down the last leg of the street like a bullet from a gun, narrowly missing the teeth of the closest wolf.

He wheeled to follow her, watching from above as a tide of monsters closed in.

Get ready, he thought to Tony. *We have at least ten werewolves and six vampires—that I've seen. There are probably more in hiding.*

Mother protect us, Tony thought back.

Aris wasn't sure who the mother was, but he would take any help they could get. A single vampire was bad enough, but six? It was a miracle the two of them made it this far. He suspected the only reason they weren't dead was that the vampires didn't want to share a meal.

He flexed his foot, which hurt but had healed enough to be functional, and watched Gwen near the intersection across from Trafalgar Square.

They're less than fifty feet behind you, he told her.

She jumped the curb, wobbled, and crashed, throwing her arms up over her head and rolling to a stop just short of the midpoint between the two fountains. The necklace smashed between her shoulder and the ground, and the liquid fear Delilah alchemized from sweat and oil spread on the paving stones and stained Gwen's coat.

A great howl rose from the werewolves as their prey went down at last and the scent of fear blossomed in the air. It was as good as ringing a dinner bell. Aris dove, shimmered, and hit the ground in front of her, blocking her prone body from the oncoming rush.

The blood on his pant leg and in the little device on his back made him an irresistible target for the vampires, who darted between shadows like wraiths, careful to avoid the pools of sunlight beneath dwarven lamps.

After them came the tide of snapping, slavering werewolves with gleaming teeth and madness in their eyes.

"Gwen," he said, as the wolves closed in.

"Don't bother me."

Twenty feet until impact. "Gwen!"

She stepped out from behind him holding a gadget that looked like a glass ball wrapped with bands of embossed brass. A single rune engraved on the surface of a button stood out from the top. Gwen pressed it, bent down, and flung the ball as high into the air as her arm allowed.

Monsters crossed the street into the square.

The little ball hung suspended some fifty feet in the air and spun in place.

Gunfire erupted from the tower, rolling like thunder. Werewolves stumbled, yelping in pain.

The brass rings around the magic ball spun like a gyroscope, faster and faster, until light burst from the center.

An enormous wolf, half again as big as any of the monsters that followed them, came barreling from the shadows to their right and made a fifteen-foot leap to land in front of Gwen and himself.

The beast threw its head back and roared a challenge that shook the stone fountains and made the ground tremble. A red-cloaked figure appeared next to him with dual pistols shining like silver in the glow.

Cyrus and Alix had joined the fight.

All around them, vampires seethed in the shadows, suddenly confronted with more enemies than they wanted to deal with. Unlike the wolves, vampires knew they didn't need to fight for food. All they had to do was wait to engage until it suited them.

In the sky above, the spinning ball grew brighter.

Before the vampires could cry off, faeries stepped out of hiding. Hob goblins, sprites, brownies, dryads, even a leprechaun. Without their glamour, they seemed to throw the natural world into chaos, as if their presence warped reality in some way.

And each one of them had a dripping cut on their forearm.

The sweet copper scent of faerie blood spread like an invisible cloud, and the vampires halted. Their desire for the taste of rare prey overwhelmed their need for self-protection, and they rushed from the shadows with hungry, glowing eyes, skirting the pools of lamplight as they blurred into sight.

Alix and Cyrus attacked, the faeries raised guns and opened fire, and Tony began picking off targets from the clock tower with precision timing. The vampires rushed in, faces twisted in lines of desperate, mad hunger. Aris spun, putting his body between Gwen and the monsters. The ball whirred so fast he could hear it spinning.

It looked like a miniature sun, but the light didn't reach them.

"It's not working," he told Gwen in a voice tense with stress. He wanted her out of here, out of danger. If Delilah's gadget failed, they were all dead, despite Gwen's backup plans.

A frisson of electricity ran through the air making the hairs on his forearms stand up.

"Alix!" Gwen shouted. "Get down!"

The half-vampire woman covered herself with her cloak as the ball exploded into furious, incandescent light that blazed across the sky like a lightning strike. It filled the square with three days' worth of stored sunlight in a single burst.

Gwen bent over and shaded her eyes with her arm as vampires screamed in pain.

The high-pitched shrieks scraped at the bleeding edge of hearing, tearing at his eardrums until he covered them with the heels of both hands. Chunks of flesh and skin, blackened by the blast, fell off their bones in smoking gobbets that hit the ground with a *splat.* The rest of their bodies followed, collapsing like empty balloons, leaving three vampires behind.

The older vampires, those strong enough to endure the sun, did not melt, but their skin burned and blistered before they could shield themselves. Delilah's miniature sun worked, momentarily blinding the werewolves, as well.

This was the only chance the faeries had to retreat to their firing positions.

"Stations!" Aris shouted.

The faeries broke from cover and fled with all the speed they could manage. Hilder, running in her bowlegged hobgoblin form, guided her compatriots into the light of surrounding street lamps. The vampires were in too much pain to follow, which meant it was his turn to attack.

He grabbed Gwen by the front of her coat and kissed her hard, then pulled out his knives and sprinted toward the closest vampire. She heard him coming and spun to meet him despite the pain.

Blisters punctuated her skin like angry red eyes, but the accelerated healing of vampire magic had already begun. She had enough self-control to ignore the pain long enough to fight back.

Vampires did not have claws or fangs, but their strength and speed were greater even than the werewolves', and the open-handed blow she swung might have taken off his head if he were a human. He leaned back, away from fingers curved into claws. Her hand passed inches from his face.

Spinning beneath the second blow, he dragged the silver knife across the underside of her outstretched arm, severing the muscles and tendons. She screamed as the arm fell useless, but the vampire was old enough to be a skilled fighter.

She aimed a kick at his knee. Were he any slower, she would have crippled him. But he was Aos Sidhe, not some mere sprite. He spun into her guard, swinging the knife with his left hand, and the tip sunk into the base of her skull with a meaty crunch.

She was not dead, but her body hung limp from the knife blade, which severed her spine and brain stem. The monster would heal, even from so severe a wound. So, he jerked the knife out, gripped her head with both hands, planted a foot in her back, and kicked.

The sound was horrible, but he ignored the wet, tearing crunch and flung the head as far from the body as possible, rendering the vampire helpless for the remainder of the fight. She would need to be staked or burned afterward.

A werewolf tumbled past him and crashed into the fountain. It collapsed to the ground in a pile of debris and a cloud of rock dust with its head twisted the wrong way round. The faeries continued to shoot at every available target. But the vampires began running around the perimeter of the square, beyond the reach of lamplight, making accurate shots nearly impossible.

Alix, Cyrus, and Gwen were being overrun, and when the scent of fear finally faded from Gwen's coat, the monsters would attack the faeries. Sunlight released from dwarvish lamps would do nothing to stop *them*.

More spectators joined the growing throng, thanks to the grenade Gwen dropped outside Scotland Yard. Lights flickered in windows as citizens gathered in the street and at intersections around the square. They were nothing more than dark figures in the gloom, but their scent made them potential targets for the monsters.

If the witches didn't cast the spell soon, more people were going to die.

Aris assessed the situation in less than a second and determined the next course of action: stop the vampires before they picked the faeries off one at a time. It was only the faeries that stopped the vampires from joining the attack on Gwen, Alix, and Cyrus.

A street lamp gave a metallic screech as a vampire launched himself six feet in the air, struck the brittle cast iron at the thinnest point, and rode it to the ground. The lamp crashed into the paving stones and died with a flicker and a small pop of expended energy.

Vampires ran cackling toward the next light. If he couldn't stop them, the spectators would not be able to see proof of the infestation, and the faeries would be defenseless.

Though it had been hardly three seconds since he killed the last vampire, the fight was devolving. Gwen's revolver barked, Tony's rifle shots echoed off the buildings, and Alix sailed through the air, landing in a crouch before rushing back into the fray. They needed some breathing room.

He drove through the knot of fighting werewolves, dropping his shoulder and plowing into one beast. It careened into the others, making three werewolves tumble out of the fight with surprised yelps.

Sprinting to the other side of the square, he charged the vampires before they could attack the next lamp post. They scattered like a flock of pigeons when he drew near, then swarmed back in from every angle, hands ripping and mouths open in hissing screams.

Aris kicked one in the chest, sending it flying backward to smash into the plinth of a statue. The spectators released a collective gasp as he flung bodies off himself with vicious abandon. But the vampires were too strong, and he was outnumbered.

A female vampire slid behind him and grabbed his head, fingers tightening in his hair as she lowered her mouth to his neck with a hungry growl. The back of her head exploded before she could bite down.

The report of a gunshot followed.

Aris thought, *Thanks for that,* as he twisted free and ripped off a vampire's arm, using the limb to club another vampire in the face.

After a moment, Tony replied, *Don't mention it.*

It was an impressive shot.

I missed.

I'll rib you about that later.

If you live that long. Behind you.

Aris swung the arm around and clubbed another vampire with it, making the creature topple backward. He sprang into the air, having scattered the vampires. It should give him a moment to help against the werewolves, to make sure Gwen was still safe.

But when he turned, she was nowhere to be seen.

24

The Battle of Trafalgar

GWEN

Being attacked by several angry, desperately hungry werewolves is something like being in the center of a toothy tornado: fur and fangs, blows and bites from every side with nowhere to turn. I was out of bullets, and my umbrella had been knocked out of my grasp earlier. It lay on the ground several feet away.

Alix and Cyrus were a veritable whirlwind of destruction, but with five werewolves still fighting there was no way not to suffer injury. Luckily for me, my coat took the worst of the impacts and saved me from death more than once.

Of course, it was also absorbing great amounts of force, and it would not last much longer before it overloaded.

I wasn't certain which was a worse possibility: being mauled by a werewolf or blowing myself up inside a very expensive coat. What I needed was a way out to regroup. So, I did what any sensible, well-brought-up woman would do: I fainted.

Well, I pretended to faint. I dropped below the level of the main fight and hit the button on my Sightscreen, letting Alix and Cyrus deal with the situation long enough to roll out of the fracas and retrieve the umbrella.

"Get down!" I yelled.

My friends immediately dropped, and I let loose all the energy the umbrella stored while fending off the last attack. The blast pushed me backward, scraping the toes of my boots on the paving stones, but it blew a hole through the center of the fighting wolves, letting me see Aris running toward me.

But he could not see me, which meant his panicked gaze was directed at something else.

I dropped to my knees as he leaped with the grace of a jungle cat, sailed over my head, and crashed into the vampire that had been behind me, the two of them rolling over and over as they fought for the dominant position.

Vampires surround the faeries on the opposite side of the square. They were saved from becoming food only by the dwarven torches they pointed at any monster who got too close. But they would not hold that defense for long, not against older vampires who only had to overcome pain, and not certain death, to reach the rare blood just inside the light.

There were not enough of us to win this fight. Where was Scotland Yard? They should have...of course. Mac Sweeney was making them wait for us to wipe out as many of the monsters as possible before he risked the lives of constables. Or, until the monsters killed us.

I should have known.

The first vampire risked attacking the faeries, and it wouldn't take long for him to jerk one of them out of the circle of light and into the dark. I sprinted toward them, pulling the hidden blade from the umbrella shaft as I ran.

Hilder caught the vampire by both arms as it attacked, her bowed legs braced against the impact. She bore down, barely holding it back, as the two faeries nearest her turned their torches on the vampire. The beams of light hit him full in the face.

He screamed and I yelled, "No!" but I was too late.

As soon as they removed their lights from the protective perimeter, an opening of darkness allowed the second vampire to charge in. She was so fast the leprechaun did not have time to adjust aim, simply went down screaming as the vampire dragged her into the shadows beyond the street lamp, leaving the scent of burning flesh behind.

Without bothering to slow, I swung the blade in a cross-body arc that hit the vampire between his neck and shoulder. And completely forgot about the speed spell Delilah inscribed on the blade. The silver sword cleaved through his torso like a scythe through wheat, splitting the creature in twain.

It also jerked me into an unbalanced spin that was impossible to control. I hit the ground in a loose-jointed roll, gasping as throbbing pain shot down my arm from my previously injured shoulder and sent my sword skidding away. A wave of giddiness rushed over me as the Sightscreen failed, and I realized, with dawning horror, that I'd fallen outside the circle of light.

The vampires couldn't resist such an easy target.

People like to tell stories about staking vampires, making it sound as if a stake is all one needs to become a certified vampire slayer. In truth, most people never even get close enough to employ the weapon. Vampires are far too fast for that.

We had given the faeries stakes without much expectation they would have a chance to use them. After all, if a vampire gets close enough for a stake to be useful, they are also close enough to overpower their victim...if they have not already enthralled them. The best advice when dealing with vampires is to stay safely indoors.

Of course, we did not have that option, and the closest vampire that was not dining on a faerie meal decided I would do instead. Fingers curled around the lapels of my coat and dragged me into the shadows with such speed my stomach dropped as if I were falling.

My arms flailed instinctively, fingers scraping against the paving stones as I fought to stay within the square where I had half a chance of survival. But I was nowhere near strong enough to fight back, and I had no weapons that could...

I shoved my hand into a pocket, pulled out another grenade, held my breath, and hurled it at the feet of my attacker. The reaction was instantaneous. Vampire senses are dozens of times more sensitive than that of humans, and the chili grenade exploded in a cloud of burning particles that filled the creature's eyes, nose, and mouth.

It screamed in a sound like tearing metal, coughed, and clawed at its face. I scrambled backward, trying not to breathe and ignoring the burning on my skin as trace amounts of capsaicin burned my hands and cheeks.

The vampire spun toward the sound of my panicked flight, restorative tears running down its unnatural face, and sprang at me. Luckily its aim was off, or it would have crushed my chest when it landed. I rolled and pushed myself to my feet, and my fingers brushed the familiar hilt of my umbrella.

Hands like crushing vices locked around my waist and spun me backward. I did not have time to set my feet or prepare for whatever speed was still stored in the runes, but I swung the sword anyway. The silver blurred, catching traces of lamplight. Searing pain shot up my arm. And the vampire's head fell, thumping against my chest before hitting the ground with a sick smack.

I stumbled backward and wiped the blood from my face with my free hand, too shaken to pay much attention to the way my hands shook or the horror of what just happened. This fight wasn't over.

"Those of you who can and are willing, go and help fight the werewolves," I told the faeries in a shaking voice as I reentered the lighted square.

They watched me with wide eyes and slack mouths, as if I were as frightening as the monsters we fought.

Perhaps I was.

Hilder, who had pale green skin and long pointed ears when she wasn't wearing a glamour, said, "I'll go. Can't have you mortals taking more risks for my hide than I'm willing to," before trotting toward Alix and Cyrus, who were down to three werewolves.

I'm out of bullets, Tony thought to me. *And I see more shadows moving in the moonlight. They're on top of the buildings. We're outnumbered, Gwen, it's time for reinforcements.*

I searched the square for Aris. He was still fighting the vampire, the two of them grappling like a pair of octopuses. Another vampire lurked in the shadows, draining the body of the leprechaun it had dragged off, and more were closing in.

The witches had either abandoned us or lost control of their spell.

Fear welled up inside me like a black geyser, true fear that turned my guts to water and made my hands shake. I did not want this. Not after fighting so hard to bring her home and keep her safe.

Gwen! Tony thought. *It's time for the backup plan or those vampires will attack and you will all die!*

The werewolves lifted their heads, scenting my vulnerability, and abandoned the fight. Cyrus leaped after them, catching one by the tail in his massive jaws and flinging it backward over his shoulder with a yelp of surprise.

Alix plowed into the second, digging her knives into its chest and holding on like a jockey. But the third came on.

I had no choice.

We need you, I thought.

Less than a second later, green fire erupted from the shadows at the head of the square, illuminating a beautiful woman with her head thrown back and her arms extended. Fire rose from her lifted hands and bathed her face with an eerie light.

Lia stood like a beacon, making even the ugly overalls look like the garment of a queen. More fire rose, not just from her hands, but from the tips of her floating hair. It wreathed her, swirled around her body like a living thing, brighter than any lamp.

My sister made herself a prime target.

The crowd gathered along the streets and intersections gasped as the green light bloomed. A few cries of *witch* punctuated the fighting.

Lia screamed and thrust her hands up to the sky.

One by one, spots of green fire caught on the rooftops like enormous candles, one, two, three. Screeches of pain followed a moment later, echoing from building to building.

The vampires were burning.

And the werewolf was almost upon me. I raised the blade but my shoulder was too damaged. The point wavered and fell.

Hilder leaped between the werewolf and me, and the sky erupted with an undulating display of light.

The werewolf plowed into Hilder and the two of them went down, her arms wrapped around its neck. They skidded another ten feet, snarling and biting. I tore my eyes away from Lia's green fire and threw myself at the monster.

Hilder clung to its head like a burr stuck to dog fur, and every time it tried to turn and bite me, she sunk her own teeth into its neck with a vicious growl.

I switched hands and lunged, plunging the long, slender blade between the monster's ribs with my left hand. The silver sunk home again and again until the beast went limp, leaving the hob trapped beneath hundreds of pounds of suffocating fur.

I grabbed handfuls of fur and pushed, but the werewolf was too big, and I was too injured to move it. I turned to the faeries and cried, "Help me!"

They rushed from the protective circle of light to lift and push the massive body off the hobgoblin who had bravely thrown herself into danger. She gasped, her mouth stained with blood and fur, and coughed as she rolled away from the corpse, arms wrapped around her chest.

The faeries dragged her back into the light, and I staggered in a clumsy turn to see Aris pull his fist from the heaving chest of the vampire. His arm was covered in blood past the wrist, and he clutched a blackened bit of flesh.

Its heart.

Cyrus shifted to his human form and lifted Alix's limp body off the ground. Her long hair hung undone over his arm, matted with blood. Two faeries I had not noticed lay in pieces between the fountains. They must have rushed into the fight at some point.

The green candle vampires on the rooftops continued to burn and scream, and Lia collapsed in a puddle, her light extinguished.

Lia! I called to Tony in my mind.

I've got her, he thought back

Above us, something like the northern lights appeared, colors undulating along the bottom of the low clouds in muted shades that slowly coalesced. The light show distracted the crowd long enough for Tony to escape the tower. He picked up Lia's limp body and ran toward the opposite end of the square.

Percy appeared out of the dark as if he stepped through an invisible curtain, waving his arms. He guided Tony toward him, and he and Lia disappeared, followed by the faeries, with Cyrus in the rear, carrying Alix.

Once everyone was accounted for, Percy met my eye.

His voice in my head said, *Come on, Gwen. That's everyone. The diamonds are almost spent.*

I shook my head.

His brows dropped in confusion, then realization froze his features.

No.

Take them home, Percy. Make sure they're safe. Take care of them. You don't have time to argue.

He glared at me as if determined to rush in and drag me out. *This isn't right, Gwen. I can't let you do this.*

You cannot stop me, my darling. You've saved our lives more than once, tonight. That is enough. Protect them one more time. Please.

He knew I was right. With a last anguished look, he turned and ran back toward our secret project.

The auto was as large as a cart and inscribed with the same spell as a Sightscreen, only amplified several times. It was bloody expensive and required both Fleur and Delilah to operate, but it was worth it.

They pulled away, bouncing over the curb and rumbling into the darkness, carrying away almost everyone I loved. Tony shoved his head out the window, staring back at me with grief-stricken eyes before the spell activated and they faded from sight.

I sighed as relief weakened my limbs. No one in the crowd noticed a strange vehicle warping the night air because a picture had appeared in the sky. The lights twisted and shimmered together, like a moving painting. They gasped and flinched away from the vision coming into focus beneath the clouds.

A man sat tied to a chair in a dark room, a single light illuminating his head and shoulders. A shadowy figure circled him beyond the reach of the light.

"Release me, you monster, or I will have you hunted to the ends of the earth!" the bound figure said.

The words echoed through the square as if piped through a dwarven loudspeaker, and this time several members of the assembled crowd screamed and covered their ears.

"Now, now, Lord Rutledge," the dark figure in the vision said. "You are not in any condition to make such threats. As I told you, all you must do is answer my questions, and I will release you."

"You lie!"

"You know better. I cannot lie. No faerie can."

The gasps and murmurings of the crowd reminded me of sitting in a packed theatre on opening night when no one knew what to expect from the newest play.

My legs gave up trying to support me, and I collapsed to the ground before Aris could catch me. I did not see or hear him approach, but I leaned against his solid form and let his presence comfort me the way it always had.

He was alive. He was safe. We were alright. At least, for now.

"You'll find some way out of it, you always do," Rutledge said.

The picture looked almost as if it had been projected onto running water, constantly shifting just enough to be noticeable, so when the Cutthroat King slipped up behind Lord Rutledge and lay both arms over his shoulders, cheek to cheek in an intimate embrace, the knife that dangled from one hand appeared to wobble dangerously close to the Lord's round stomach.

"So suspicious," the King chided.

He scraped the tip of the knife over Rutledge's belly, making one of the buttons on his waistcoat pop off. Rutledge squealed and jerked, likely because the King cut his belly as well as the button.

"Don't," he begged.

"Calm down, pet. I shall give you my word. Answer my questions, and I will release you."

"Swear it."

"I swear it," the King said in the placating voice a mother might use with a distraught toddler.

Rutledge shook with fear and relief. He knew faeries could not lie. His head bowed and his shoulders, which had been squared and defiant before, drooped. "Ask your questions."

Here it was. My throat tightened in anticipation as I sat between injured faeries, dead werewolves who were slowly shifting back into their mortal forms, and the pieces of vampires we had destroyed. This was what we needed, and the square was full of an audience who had seen and heard it all.

"How long have you been working with the faerie King to help him invade mortal lands?" the King asked.

"Close to ten years, I suppose."

"That long?" Aris muttered.

"What did you do on his behalf?" the King asked.

"I helped elect certain people and placed them in positions of power. I made deals with the vampires on his behalf."

"Then it was you who helped the monsters enter New London?"

"You knew it was me. Stop wasting my time."

"Your time belongs to me right now, Rutledge," the King said in a low, dangerous voice. "Answer the question."

He sounded sullen when he said, "Yes, it was me."

"How?"

"On the river, of course. By night."

"Clever man. But tell me truly: how could you betray all mortals in favor of their long enemy?"

"Quite easily."

"But why? Why side with the invaders?"

Rutledge snorted. "Power, you fool, why else? Don't act as if you don't understand. You've cultivated power yourself."

"But don't you care about your people?"

"What a stupid question. Why would I? There will always be more of them, new coopers to replace the old, new washerwomen, and farmers and…oh whatever else they do. One dies and another springs up to take its place, like rats, or fungus. They'll die and be forgotten, easy as trampling a flower."

"Then you only care about power?"

"Power is the only thing any sensible man cares about because it is the only way he can order his own life as he sees fit, free of control by other men."

"Have any other members of Parliament helped you in these schemes?"

The crowd muttered angrily, surging back and forth like waves threatening to overtake the rocks.

"You think I could have done all this on my own?"

"Where there is a will, they say there is a way," the Cutthroat King said. "When will King Obyrron invade mortal lands?"

"He hasn't told me that, only commissioned me to prepare the way."

"And what do you get, in return?"

"Power," Rutledge said, his voice tired. "What else?"

"Just one more question, before I release you."

"Ask it, damn you, and be done."

"How many innocent lives have been taken by your collusion with the faerie king?"

Rutledge snorted and tried to shrug but winced. He was covered in bruises and shallow cuts, so he must have held on a long time before breaking. "Who knows, man. Hundreds? Thousands? What does it matter? Now keep your word, and release me."

"Very well, Lord Rutledge. I am a faerie of my word, after all." The King knelt in front of his captive and began cutting the ropes that bound his feet. He was almost gentle as he released the man, cutting the last rope around his wrists, then touching his face with delicate fingers. Rutledge shrank away like a turtle retreating into its shell.

"I have kept my word," the Cutthroat king whispered. "I have released you."

"Yes...now—now let me go."

The King lifted his leg and sat astride Rutledge's lap, wrapping his fingers around the man's jaw almost like a lover. "Oh, that was not part of the bargain, my lord," he said in a voice dark as velvet.

"Help!" Rutledge squealed, trying to buck the smaller man off, but the King wrapped his legs around Rutledge's hips and rode him to the ground as they struggled, knocking the chair aside as it clattered out of view.

"You remember what games we used to play, my lord?" the King asked as his knife blade caught the light.

"No!"

"Now it is your turn. And *my* turn."

"By the gods, no!"

The vision began to dissipate, but not before the King made the first gruesome cut. I turned away, and Aris held my face against his chest as the sound of screaming and vomiting echoed through the square.

"Are they safe?" I asked into his torn shirt.

"Tony says they're clear. Fleur picked everyone up. You didn't tell me Delilah has an entire auto fitted with Sightscreens."

"It was terribly expensive. Any word on Alix and Lia?"

"Nothing yet."

My heart rattled against my ribcage but I could only sit and shake. We had done it. The people of the city saw the truth. Now it was time to pay the piper and hope they would do something with it.

Gwen, Tony thought, *are you out? Are you safe?*

I pushed myself to my feet despite my body's protests and began unbuckling my wheels.

"I need you to take these," I said, handing them to Aris.

"What? Why?"

The goggles were next, followed by the rest of my explosives, one by one creating a pile in Aris's arms. "Take these home, and hide whatever else may be incriminating. Hide everything someplace no one will find it."

Alarm made his eyes bright, and he started looking for places to drop my gear. I touched his cheek, and said, "Protect our family, Aris. Please."

The *clomp* of running boots grew louder as the constables began to clear the square, much to the dismay of the watching crowd. His gaze flicked to the hubbub, and then back to me as realization sank in.

"This is why you dropped that grenade outside Scotland Yard," he said.

"They can still brush this under the rug if they are willing to sacrifice enough. I must make certain that doesn't happen."

His jaw tightened. Through clenched teeth, he said, "Is this what you want?"

"It is what must be done."

The constables began trying to disperse the crowd, shouldering in and forcing them back and away from the gruesome sight of blood and mangled bodies. But the people had already seen enough to make them angry, and they would not allow themselves to be ushered off without answers.

"It's a conspiracy!" someone shouted.

"They're lying to us!"

"Disperse peacefully," an authoritative voice ordered, "and no one will be hurt. Go home, where it's safe."

"We are not safe, sir, not even in our homes!"

"Didn't you see that? He admitted everything! They're killing us for power."

"They was faeries, I seen 'em with my own eyes. Oi, don't push me, I got rights!"

That had done it. The crowd began to struggle as the constables joined ranks and forced them back. One or two broke free and ran into the square, pointing and screaming, "It's a werewolf! See!"

"Look there she is! The witch!"

I sighed and forced a smile. "This is how it begins. But it ends with nowhere for Rutledge's co-conspirators to hide."

Aris leaned down and pressed his forehead against mine. He was close and warm, and nothing sounded better than running away with him somewhere quiet and peaceful.

"Don't let them take your ring," he said. "Swallow it, if you have to. Contact me the moment anything seems suspicious. If they are willing to sacrifice an entire city, they will have no qualms about killing you to shut you up."

"They won't kill me," I said, hoping it was true. "Not when they can turn me into the villain."

"Promise me, Gwen. Or I will take you out of here this instant, consequences be damned. This city, hell the entire island, can go to the devil."

I kissed him...maybe for the last time, reveling in the softness of his lips and the sweetness of his mouth, the way he held me as if I might disappear as soon as he let go.

Finally, I said, "I promise. Now, hide. Or at least fix your glamour. And protect our family. Promise me."

Indecision twisted the lines of his face, making his jaw muscle flex as he fought the urge to scoop me up and flee the square. God's breath, the thought was tempting. But one thing Aris had always done, no matter how much he disagreed, was respect my right to choose my own path.

His Adam's apple bobbed before he pressed his forehead to mine one last time and said, "I promise."

The air sizzled between us with the electric current of a magical bond springing to life.

"You! Miss! Don't move!"

"That will be the constables," I sighed, then winked at Aris and turned to face the Metropolitan Police as they stalked toward me with nightsticks out and handcuffs shining in the moonlight.

25

Come Quietly

GWEN

Over the course of the last three or so years, I had many novel experiences, but I never thought to add getting arrested in a public square to the list. They dragged me through Trafalgar Square by both arms while constables tried either to protect me from the rioting crowd or to stop them from absconding with me.

"She was fighting the beasts, I saw her!" someone shouted.

But for every protest of my innocence, there was an accusation of "Witch!" to balance the scales.

I was too tired and worried about Lia and Alix to pay much attention as they dragged me down the darkened street toward Scotland Yard. The imposing building frowned down at us as they hauled me through the front doors and into the well-lighted room.

I sat on a hard wooden chair for an indeterminate amount of time, seeing Lia collapse in my memory over and over again, hoping at every moment to hear a familiar voice in my head telling me that the people I loved were recovering.

I had not wanted Lia dragged into defending the square, especially not when her magic was so much harder to access outside the Sunset Lands. But it had been her choice, and not mine.

God's breath, how would I explain it to Mama?

"Lady St. James," sneered a Scottish brogue in a manner entirely too familiar. "Why am I not surprised that you were the ring leader of this entire affair? Bring her."

Mac Sweeney motioned to the constables who had been guarding me. They lifted me off the chair by my arms and escorted me down the hall, up the stairs, and into Mac Sweeney's office. He fussed about getting himself seated, waited for me to take the opposite seat, and flicked his fingers at the constables. They closed the door behind themselves and left me alone with the most aggressive mustache in New London.

"I wish I could say I was pleased to see you again, Chief Inspector. But I would rather not be forced to endure your company. Ever."

Mac Sweeney had not expected me to insult him to his face. Likely, most people who sat in this chair had either been cowed by threats or were too afraid to speak their minds. I was too tired to feel either emotion.

He sat in silence for a moment, black brows raised, then cleared his throat and said, "You may think you are too wealthy or too important to bear the consequences of what you've done, lady, but I am here to tell you that the law is no respecter of—"

I rolled my eyes and interrupted, "Oh do shut up. Or, if you must speak, do not treat me like a fool and get to the point. You cannot intimidate me with the law—which you are only passingly acquainted with—and I can defeat you in fisticuffs with very little effort, so you cannot intimidate me with brute force. Say what needs to be said, and see me to my cell. There's a good lad."

As I spoke, his face reddened progressively, until his neck and his cheeks were the color of boiled lobster. If he became too angry, would his mustache begin to steam? I watched, enthralled, to see if it would happen.

Mac Sweeney stood, trembling with suppressed fury, and barked, "Higgins! Rodriguez! Get in here."

My guards reappeared.

"Bind this woman."

"Sir?"

"Do as I say, man!"

After securing my wrists, Higgins and Rodriguez left again, giving me worried glances over their shoulders. They knew what was about to happen, and neither of them had the stones to try and stop it.

I raised my brows but did not try to hide the amusement in my voice. "Do I make you so nervous, Inspector?"

He stalked around the table, drew back his arm, and slapped me with all the force in his slender body. My head rocked to the side and little white stars danced at the edge of my vision. It didn't hurt, yet. There was only the pressure and numbness of force. But the blow would begin burning and stinging shortly.

"You have destroyed years of work," he snarled in my face, grabbing my chin and forcing me to look at him. "And you are responsible for the murder of a peer of the Realm. Not only that, you have practiced witchcraft inside the city walls, and drawn in the monsters that have murdered so many innocent lives."

"I didn't—" I said through numb lips, but he did not let me finish.

"It doesn't matter, does it? That's what everyone will believe by the time we are finished. Tomorrow's headlines will read that a witch was apprehended. The *infamous* Lady St. James. We will tear your entire life apart for evidence, and manufacture what we cannot find. But you've made that easy, haven't you? With all of your occult nonsense."

"You are the one who protected Rutledge and the others," I accused. "You are as responsible as they are."

"And who will believe that? It will be the word of a Chief Inspector with a spotless record against that of a crackpot heiress who studies alchemy and thinks faeries kidnapped her sister."

"They will learn the truth. I swear it."

He threw his head back and laughed. It was a nasty sound. "Who will tell them? You? The witch?"

"If I must."

"Oh, that is rich. No, Lady St. James. You will take the fall for this entire affair, and those of us who are preparing for the new world will continue our work. You've done nothing but remove yourself from the playing field, and quite neatly if I might add."

"Are you going to keep talking? Because I'm rather tired."

Mac Sweeney had built up a good head of steam, and he was thoroughly impressed with himself, so his inability to cow or threaten me into submission stung his pride. Jaw clenched, he slapped me again.

"Really, Inspector, you should learn to control your temper. For someone with as much to lose as you have, you—"

His hand flew.

But I had not been idle while he gloated. The untied rope lay in my lap, leaving me free to catch his wrist, lean back, and kick him in the gut. The chair rolled backward and I tucked the rail beneath the door handle for a bit of privacy. The small man was bent double with both hands wrapped around his stomach as he gasped for air.

My ears were ringing with the force of the blows, and my cheek had begun to properly sting, but my vision was clear and my reflexes hadn't abandoned me. I was going to jail, whether I punched the inspector or not. I arranged it that way. So, I might as well earn the trip.

"You colluded with the enemy, Inspector," I said. "You sold out the Realm and betrayed every oath you've taken. There are consequences for such things, and I am one of them."

I jerked him upright by the front of his shirt and headbutted him in the nose. A good headbutt is a surprisingly effective tool. The crown of the forehead is a rather thick bit of bone, but the nose is a fragile thing.

Mac Sweeney's nose flattened against my head and began bleeding immediately. He crumpled, hands over his face, and made a high-pitched wheezing noise.

"Oh, don't be such a baby, Inspector," I said. "Do bear up. After all, that was not nearly as bad as what you have coming."

He looked up at me from the floor, blood covering the bottom of his face, his eyes already blackening and full of fear. The door handle creaked, then rattled.

I leaned in to leave him with a parting blow before they hauled me away. "Oh yes, I have not told you that part, yet. Do you see the raven standing on the window sill? The one watching you with glowing eyes?"

His gaze flicked to the raven, then back to me, wide with fear.

"His name is Aris, and he's rather protective. He watched you strike me twice, and I don't think he appreciated it. I wouldn't go to sleep alone if I were you."

The door banged open, sending the chair rolling, and the guards rushed in to find me standing over the sobbing body of their bloody inspector. They looked from him to me, likely noting that my left eye was swelling shut, but I was the one standing.

"You are welcome," I said magnanimously, sure that one or both of them had fantasized about hitting the man at least once. "Now, I would really appreciate going to prison, if you don't mind. I'm rather tired."

———— 〰 ————

Holloway looked more like a medieval castle than a prison, and sat brooding at the juncture of two streets. The intake took far longer than I expected, having never been to prison. By the time I was processed, forcibly cleaned with soap that stung my skin, given my uniform, and marched to my cell, I was so tired I passed out as soon as I fell onto the small cot.

I stood at the edge of the stairs, shaking. Below us people danced and laughed, spinning and smiling, as if there was nothing better in the world than a ball. But the idea of parading myself while pretending to be one of them made my throat close up. As soon as they saw me, they would know I didn't belong. They'd sneer and turn up their noses.

Lia grabbed my cold hands and shook them. "Gigi, it's just a little dance, don't be so silly."

"I can't do this," I said.

"Of course you can. It's not so hard. Just—"

I pulled my hands out of hers and held them against my sick stomach. "I'm not like you! I can't just be confident and smile and say something clever to make everyone laugh. I'll sick up all over the floor and everyone will see it, and I'll never be able to show my face in public again!"

"Then I'll sick up, too. All over Lady De Guerre's gaudy shoes. Have you seen them? Look." She pointed over the rafter and down to the floor below, where a pair of ribboned chartreuse shoes peeked out beneath the hem of a purple gown. "Those are a crime against fashion and deserve to be destroyed."

A desperate little laugh escaped my white lips. The vision of Lia getting sick on those loud shoes, to the horror of all the guests, was too ridiculous for solemnity.

"There, you see?" she said, chucking me under the chin. "It can't be that bad. Besides, if you mess up it's not the end of the world. We're only fifteen, we have plenty of time for dancing."

"Easy for you to say. You're beautiful and funny and confident. Everyone will be dying to dance with you."

"Gigi—"

"Oh shut up, Lia. I have a mirror."

"Look at me," she ordered, sounding so much like Mama that I obeyed without thinking.

"Anyone who cannot recognize your value does not deserve your concern."

"You are my sister," I said tiredly. "You have to think that."

She frowned, snapped her fingers, and said, "I have an idea. You pretend to be me, and I will pretend I am you. I'll be proper and intelligent and mysterious, and you'll be loud and gregarious."

"What?"

"If you think it's so much easier for me, just do the things you think I would do. And I'll do the same."

"I don't think I can."

"If you don't"—she leaned in— "I'll tell Tommy Rowe you chickened out."

My eyes widened. "Don't you dare."

"I swear I will."

I clenched my fists till they hurt, and imagined myself as Lia, with her confidence and humor, imagined people smiling at me, glad of my company. "Fine. You win, I'll try."

"Of course, I win." She grinned, taking my arm in hers and leading me down the stairs. "I always win."

"Don't rub it in."

"What fun is winning if you cannot brag about it?"

The first part of the evening went swimmingly, and I got a small glimpse of what it must be like to be my vivacious sister, with her admirers and sunny smile. She caught my eye from across the room and winked at me. I began to believe I could do this.

Until Reggie Upworth, the seventeen-year-old heir of the Roth estate, spilled a glass of punch on my dress.

"I am dreadfully sorry." He sneered. "I didn't see you there."

Through trembling lips, I whispered, "You did that on purpose."

"It was an honest mistake. If you'd try to be a bit less mousy, maybe you wouldn't be so invisible."

His cronies cackled and followed him to the other side of the room.

Lia found me later, hiding in the pantry.

"I've been looking for you everywhere! What are you doing in here?"

She coaxed the truth from me between sobs, and her face flushed with anger.

"That little rat," she growled, then turned and stormed from the pantry.

"Lia, wait!"

I chased after her, but it was no good. She stomped across the room, past groups of laughing guests, every eye turning to follow her until she stopped directly in front of Reggie and the other boys.

"Well look what we have here," he said. "The beautiful sister. I'd be happy to dance if you—"

Lia punched him in the nose.

He staggered back, hands pressed to his face, eyes wide with shock.

"*Ophelia!*" *Mama's voice rang like the bells of doom, but Lia ignored her.*

"*If you so much as look at my sister again, I'll won't just bloody your nose, I'll break it.*"

Mama appeared, grabbed Lia by the arm, and dragged her away, making apologies. I followed them up the stairs, my face hot with embarrassment and pride. Hours later, after a good scolding, we lay in the dark, curled up in Lia's bed.

"*How does your hand feel?*" *I whispered.*

"*It throbs every now and again.*"

"*I didn't know you could throw a punch.*"

She giggled. "*Neither did I. I've never been so mad!*"

"*You were brilliant.*"

"*Mama didn't think so.*"

"*What does she know?*"

"*That we won't be allowed to the next party, that's what.*"

I wrapped my arms around her. "*Thank you.*"

"*It was worth it. Sisters protect each other. Besides, did you see the look on his face?*"

We laughed until tears ran down our cheeks and wetted the pillows.

After our hilarity wore down, I said, "*You should not always have to defend me. It's not fair.*"

"*And you should not always have to write my lessons,*" *she replied,* "*but you do.*"

"*Miss Morris will never let you hear the end of it if I don't. What does it matter if you don't conjugate Latin verbs?*"

"Look, we are stronger together, see? That's why we're twins. We compliment. What's mine is yours, and what's yours is mine. You take my humor any time you need it, and I'll take your brains when I need them."

"I'd like to keep my brains inside my skull, thanks."

"You have too many, it's selfish not to share."

We fell asleep with our arms around one another, two very different people sharing one beating heart.

⚜

"Wake up!" The voice was followed by a sharp bang on my door.

My whole body stiffened as if an electric pulse ran up from the soles of my feet. For a moment I had no idea where I was, why I was so sore, or why I could not see out of my left eye.

The cell door opened, and a woman in a badly fitting uniform placed a tin plate of food on the floor.

"Breakfast," she said, then closed the door behind herself and locked it with a clang that echoed through the room for a long time.

Ah, yes. Prison.

The floor was cold through my stockings despite it being summer, and a beam of light from my small window created a square of warmth on the floor. I limped gingerly toward the plate, picked it up, and sat in the square of warmth, letting the sun heat my back as I slurped up the watery porridge.

My teeth had cut sores into my cheek when Mac Sweeney slapped me, so my mouth was too tender for the rough bread.

I left the plate on the floor, climbed beneath the thin wool blanket, and went back to sleep.

Gwenevere Violet St. James, a voice in my head called.

I sat up from a dead sleep, gasped, and pressed the heel of my hand against my forehead to keep my brain from spilling out as my pulse pounded in my skull.

Yes? I thought back, eyes squinted shut as the throbbing heart-beat ebbed away.

Are you alright?

I'll be better when this headache goes away and I can see out of my left eye.

It was a moment before Tony replied, but he sounded hesitant and unsure. *Are you badly hurt?*

Nothing that a few days won't cure. I swallowed, prepared myself to hear an answer that might break me, and thought, *How is my sister?*

Still unconscious, but alive.

Who is seeing to her?

Mrs. Chapman, of course. She could not be stopped. And Aris has not left her side, except to see to the children.

I laughed, closed my eyes, and dropped my head into my hands. *Has she given a prognosis?*

Exhaustion. At least, that is what Aris says, and Mrs. Chapman doesn't disagree. One of the faerie women looked at her, a delicate older lady. She said Ophelia used too much of her magic too fast. Her heartbeat is strong, her breathing regular, and she has no fever or other signs of injury.

When I saw her fall—

I know. Seeing her this way...is more difficult than I would have expected. I had not realized what a strong presence she had until it was gone.

Don't speak of her as if she's dead!

I'm sorry. Gwen, I'm sorry. That isn't what I meant.

I took a shaky breath. *I know. Forgive me, my nerves are a bit shot.*

The scratchy blanket bunched between my fingers, and I focused on taking deep breaths. Lia was alive, and if Aris and Mrs. Chapman were with her, she would recover, I was certain of it. *How are you?*

Unscathed. Sam and Sally are tired, but well. Delilah and Fleur have been bossing everyone around since picking us up in the auto, and Percy has been watching over the refugees.

How is Alix?

Intimidating.

I hid my laugh in the blankets, feeling as if the world were lifting off my shoulders one update at a time. *She does heal quickly.*

One would never know she had been injured. And I think Cyrus might challenge even Monsieur's skills. He's eaten as much as three people.

He is a rather large man. I suppose it takes quite a bit of food to keep him.

How are you? Really?

I did not want to answer that question. My friends likely resented me for making this decision without consulting them, and adding suffering to the list of things they worried about felt unkind.

But if I was going to heed Alix's advice and let the people I loved know the real me, it had to start sometime. *Tired. Sore. Scared. Not looking forward to life in Holloway or the terrible food. My cell is cold, my blanket scratches, and I've been told they will put me to work in the laundry.*

...Oh.

You did ask.

I suppose I did. I am surprised they did not take your rings.

They would have. All except one, which they believe to be my wedding ring.

Then how...

I swallowed them.

God's breath, Gwen.

The exasperation in his mental voice made me laugh aloud. *We will need to communicate if we are to make it through this. Especially if the invasion begins while I am stuck in here. How do the headlines look?*

A strange vision in the clouds, dead monsters, rioting in the streets, and a witch.

That would be me. Any mention of the invasion?

Yes, but they glossed it over with words like alleged, and speculation. The irritation in his mental voice made me picture his jaw clenching.

It looks like we still have work to do.

So it seems. Gwen?

Yes?

What did you do to CI Mac Sweeney?

I head-butted him. He deserved it.

That is all?

Yes. Why?

Because that was the other headline. He was found in his home this morning, dead.

A sliver of dread settled in my stomach. Dead? *I only bloodied his nose, I promise. Well, I may have broken it but he was alive when they dragged me out of the room.*

Ah.

You will update me regularly?

Of course. Take care of yourself in there.

I will do my best.

The feeling of his presence disappeared and I was suddenly alone again, far more alone than I had been before waking with his voice in my head. But I had to remind myself that our plan—my plan—worked; we saved lives and exposed the truth.

The more we learned about the patterns of the monsters, the more I realized the ways in which they adapted to our city. The faerie deaths were mostly in the poorer quarters because those lamps were either gas or electric. It was the sunlight-bearing lamps of the dwarves that kept the wealthier parts of the city safe from vampires.

But one thing remained a mystery: how had Bowler Hat trapped any vampire long enough to transfuse their blood? And was it a forceful transaction, or a cooperative one? Who taught him to do such things, and was it an isolated experiment, or were there more mortals walking the streets with vampire blood in their veins?

No matter the answers to those questions, there was one thing I did know: the people I loved were safe and whole. And if the faeries did invade New London, my family would be there, standing next to me for the fight.

26

Jailbird

ARIS

The moon rose above the jagged skyline of New London, her pale face smiling down on the quiet city. But Aris waited. Windows filled with lamplight and made the summer night seem warm and inviting, but still Aris waited. When the streets were empty and a blanket of quiet sleep lay over the landscape, he opened his wings and dropped from the nearby church tower to sail down through the cooling air.

Now that the monsters had either been killed or fled, the sense of unease that permeated the city was gone. It was as if a mother had soothed her child back to sleep after a nightmare. He watched a barn owl take silent flight from a nearby ledge and pluck a rat from the shadows beneath Holloway Prison.

Good hunting, brother.

Without as much quiet or stealth as the owl, he flared his wings to slow his descent and landed on the window ledge. Gwen lay on her cot below, one eye mostly swollen shut, her hair in a tangled mess on her pillow. A deep surge of satisfaction welled up, and he wished he could kill the Chief Inspector all over again for daring to strike her.

It had been the first time in ages that killing brought him any kind of pleasure, but watching the man strike Gwen as she sat bound made wrath burn away every other thought in his head.

Of course, she handled the situation quite neatly, but she was more tenderhearted than he, and some things needed to be dealt with in a more...permanent way.

Holloway, a women's prison famous for confining suffragettes, was cleaner and more humane than the average penal institution. Each cell appeared to have a small window that opened to let in light and fresh air, which made things much easier. And Gwen left the window open a crack.

Clever girl.

He pushed the window frame with his beak and edged inside to sail down to the cot. Landing at the foot of the bed, he walked along her body until he stood just beneath her elbow, wormed his way into her arms, and purred.

Normal ravens did something similar, but he noticed early that the sound seemed to soothe her, so he altered it to be a bit more like the purr of a cat. In her sleep, she made a little contented noise and pulled him closer.

She was very warm.

With a minor effort of will, he shifted back to his human form, leaving Gwen tucked alongside his body with her arm around his neck. Even in the moonlight, the bruising around her swollen eye was apparent. But she was still so beautiful it made his heart ache. He gently kissed the little birthmark high on her cheekbone. How many times had he wanted to do that?

Her breathing deepened and relaxed. She smiled in her sleep. There was not much room on the small cot, and before long, he was stiff and uncomfortable, but he would not have moved for all the gold in both worlds.

It wasn't long ago he had seen her swarmed by werewolves, and the only thing keeping her alive had been that blessed coat. He reminded himself to give Percy his personal thanks one more time. But she was alive, and as safe as possible, given her goals.

As much as he wanted to whisk her away, drag her to some safe, hidden location where danger could never touch her again, he would not. He respected her too much to force his will upon her. More than that, he trusted her. If she believed this must be done, he would see that it happened.

Gwen's nose tickled his neck. He tried to edge back, to give her more room, but her arm tightened, holding him still.

"I thought I smelled you," she mumbled in a sleepy voice that was far too sexy for a battered, tired woman.

"What do I smell like?"

"Grass," she said, nuzzling closer and running the tip of her nose up the column of his neck, sending pleasurable little shivers across his skin. "And wind."

"Wind, eh?"

"Don't ask me to explain it," she said as she burrowed in closer, till there wasn't enough space for air between them, and sighed contentedly.

He brushed his hand across her forehead, carefully sliding the hair from her face. "Very well. I wanted you to know that your sister is awake. Or, rather, she has woken, and she appears to be fine, merely tired."

"You could have told me through our rings."

"Not if I wanted to hold you while I said it."

"Mmm, true."

"You should sleep."

"Can't. Not with you here distracting me."

"Shall I go?"

Her lips pressed against his neck in a decided manner that made his cock harden in a painful rush.

"No," she said. "Distract me some more."

"You are injured, Gwen."

"Aris?"

"Yes?"

"Shut up."

"Yes, Darling."

He would never cease to be amazed by the wonder of her passion, the miracle of her body, the ecstatic joy of being inside her, and the sound of her voice as she whispered his name.

They moved together with slow, lazy strokes, deep and quiet and rhythmic, and she opened for him with eager rocking hips and a hot mouth.

So far, their lovemaking had been hurried, primitive, almost desperate. Not this time.

A little cry of pleasure escaped her lips, her eyes fluttering closed as she surrendered herself to pure sensation.

"That's right, Darling. Feel me. Take me. Because I mean to claim you, Gwen." Thrust. "I'm going to take you from the inside." Thrust. "And make you mine, body and soul." Thrust. "I will not stop until you swear it."

He played her body like an instrument, with fingers, tongue, and teeth, making her cry in the most delicious mortal music.

"Tell me," he whispered. "Say you are mine."

She arched her back and moaned, "Yes. Yours."

It was a simple declaration, yet a thrill ran through his body and lodged in whatever was left of his heart. He would have loved her from afar if that was all he could do. But she chose him, chose *them*, despite everything they'd been through.

He deserved none of her, but he wanted, anyway.

Wanted her silliness and humor, her burning passion, the way her eyes softened when she looked at the children, and the little curl of her hidden smile when Mrs. Chapman complained.

He even wanted her temper, her flashing eyes and clenched fists, and the way her sense of justice made her throw herself into problems with abandon until she solved them.

Whatever bits of herself she was willing to give into his care, he would cherish and protect them.

She held his face between hands that were scraped and bruised. She wrapped her legs around his waist, rocked her hips up, and squeezed, pulling him into her body so tightly that he groaned and nearly came from the pleasure of it.

"Now, tell me," she ordered, rocking against him again.

"Three gods," he groaned, turning his head to kiss her palm. "Whatever is good in me has been yours for years, Gwen. Yes."

She made a pleased little noise and pulled his face down to kiss him, her mouth sweet and hungry.

"That's not good enough," she said after their kiss. "I want all of it. What came before, and after. Every part of you, even the parts you want to hide."

His spine stiffened and he stilled. "There are parts of me...you don't know what you are asking. Those—there is nothing but weakness, pain, anger," he said, trying to make her understand.

She ignored him and rolled her hips again, turning his legs to jelly as pleasure built in the base of his spine.

"All of you," she whispered, "or none. Your darkness doesn't scare me, Aris Blackwing."

"It scares me," he admitted, dropping his forehead against hers. "It scares me, Gwen."

She hooked her leg around his and, in an impressive display of acrobatics, rolled them both over without falling off the cot. He lay on the flat of his back, looking up at the most perfect woman he had ever known as she sat astride his hips like a goddess.

Moonlight glowed on her skin and the pink tips of her breasts, and love glowed in her eyes.

"I am learning that love does not exist by halves," she told him, seating herself and pressing his palm over her heart. "I want you, darkness and all. And I will give you all of me, all of my weaknesses and fears." She rocked her hips, making his eyes roll back in his head. "And my hopes and my dreams."

His free hand slid to her hip and tightened, following the rocking motion as she slid over his sensitive flesh. Her head fell back and all of that glorious hair made a waterfall down her back, resting cool against his thighs. Breathing in short gasps, she rode him and held his wrist so her heart beat against his palm.

His fear could not compete with her passion or her trust, and his body was losing the fight, tightening until he thought he would either break or die.

"All of it," he groaned as her pace quickened, catching him up in a torrent of pleasure that threatened to overwhelm his sanity. "All of me, Gwen."

Passion and victory filled her voice when she ordered, "Come with me."

And like any good and faithful lover, he obeyed.

They led Gwen out of the prison by her handcuffs and lifted her up into the transport vehicle. Her face had healed quickly thanks to Mrs. Chapman's tea, which he smuggled in over several flights. She looked as calm as could be expected of someone on their way to a trial for treason.

Lord Rutledge's powerful partners, whoever they were, had pushed this to trial as fast as the law allowed, and not only because they wanted it out of the way. The public had gathered outside Parliament in a heaving throng, both to protest the innocence of the woman who had been protecting them night after night, but also to call for her hanging.

The divide between the innocent and guilty parties was as wide as any political disagreement could be, and several fights had already broken out on the streets. Her supporters had gone so far as to protest outside Holloway Prison. Now that she was being delivered to trial, they lined the streets and placed themselves between Gwen and the counter-protesters who wanted to drag her off and hang her.

He wouldn't let that happen.

Just say the word, Darling, and I will take you and escape, he thought.

This trial must proceed. It is the only way to stop everything from being swept under the rug before it's too late.

It would help if we knew when it would be too late. Or who the co-conspirators were.

The prison car bumped down the road, followed by protestors who pushed in from every side and had to be kept back by the accompanying constables.

Delivering Rutledge to the King was not the most strategically sound option, but Tony made an agreement and I did not have time to figure a way out of it. Perhaps we should pin the King down badger more information out of him.

Why do I get the feeling he would enjoy that?

Because the man is a master manipulator, she thought back. *I do not think we have even scratched the surface of his mind.*

The vehicle turned a corner and Aris wheeled after it, staying high enough to watch proceedings.

A crowd is blocking the road, he told her.

They are a feisty bunch.

Stay inside and try not to let them see you through the windows, he said, sinking down to get a closer look at the faces of the protestors. They shouted, thrusting their fists into the air and pushing back as the constables formed up and created a blockade to allow the car to pass.

You've emptied the house of anything incriminating? she asked.

Of course.

And the children are safe?

As safe as I can make them. I can send them to the country if you'd like.

No, they'd only sneak back. I'll ask Delilah and Percy to make the children coats or shirts or something protective. Although I suppose Sally will have ways to protect herself now beyond clothing.

And Sam is far more capable than you believe, he reminded her.

I know. I do know. It is simply difficult to accept. He is so young.

Age is relative for people like Sam and Sally. But you can do nothing about that, now. Focus on the interview. We can sort out everything else later.

True enough. Very well. Are we close?

Yes, he said, watching the horses turn into the Westminster gate. *A few minutes will see you inside. I will change and be there in a glamour, just in case.*

What did I ever do to deserve you, my raven?

He faltered for a moment, losing speed and altitude, then righted himself and caught the next available updraft as the iron gates closed behind the carriage. She was safely inside.

You were kind, he said. *And truly, deeply, imperfectly good.*

That you can say that despite knowing me so well proves you are blinded by love, she thought, amused.

No, my Darling. Love is the only reason I see clearly.

Her mental voice sounded whimsical and tender. ...*you love me, Aris?*

Haven't I been telling you that every day for years?

Now that I think of it, I suppose you have.

The horses pulled the car to a stop, and the constables dismounted.

Do you know something? she thought as they began unchanging the doors. *For years, I thought no one would ever love me the way Lia did because no one else would ever see my imperfections and still find me worthwhile. At least, no one who did not want my title and money more than they wanted me. I could not stand to let anyone that close because I knew, deep down, they would be disappointed.*

I know.

But you did not even give me a chance to hide. You have always seen me, haven't you?

He remembered finding her in the forest so many years ago. She'd been a magical creature; something rarer and more moving than any faerie he'd ever seen. He remembered her saving the children, sacrificing herself, her safety, her happiness over and over.

He tasted again her hunger for connection, felt the heat of her tears when she held him while she cried. Saw the look of contentment in her dark eyes when she helped someone in secret.

Always, he said.

Aris?

Yes, my lady?

I love you, too. Very much.

His heart swelled in his chest until it felt like his delicate ribcage might snap.

I know that, too, he thought back as they handed Gwen out of the back double doors.

I'm sorry it took me so long to realize it. I did not want to admit it, but when I look back over the course of my life, you have been the only person who never left or judged my imperfections. Honestly, you know far too much of me, and that...

He held his breath.

It scares me. I think I may still fail. Learning to be vulnerable without fear may take some time.

I will wait, Gwen. A hundred lifetimes, if that is what you need.

She looked up and spotted him in the sky. Her cheeks were pink, stray hairs blew across her face, and she was smiling. How could she be the most beautiful thing he had ever seen, despite being towed about in chains?

Her face twisted in shock and pain. She fell before the echo of the gunshot made the spectators duck. The sound ricocheted off the buildings like the crack of doom as the world melted into chaos.

The constables caught her body and turned to shield her, dragging her behind the protection of the car as they shouted for help.

A high-pitched noise rang in his ears, starting off quiet but getting louder and louder until his brain vibrated with the pressure of it. A red stain grew on her chest while men tore open her blouse and pressed their hands against the wound.

The sound grew until he could not hear anything else, and a red film covered the world. Darkness crept out of the hole in his chest and swallowed up every stray bit of emotion.

With the ease of long practice, his mind slipped back into the cold, detached armor that let him murder enemies of the fae king for years without remorse. The monster he kept hidden in the back of his mind woke and rattled its chains, demanding to know who fired the shot.

He angled his wings and examined the crowd. They were in a full riot now, pressing toward the gates, throwing bricks, shoes, and anything else they could reach.

Bodies surged forward in a tidal wave...except for one. One dark, recognizable hat moved through the crowd in the opposite direction.

Aris did not bother wondering how the man was still alive after the explosion, he simply tucked his wings and dove. He could already feel the man's blood warm on his talons, hear the wet ripping sound as flesh parted, smell the rancid, sour stench of exposed bowels. A bolt of anticipation electrified his limbs.

He would savor every pained cry he wrung from those bloodless lips as the bastard explained why he killed Gwen.

Bowler Hat stopped on the edge of the street between two buildings, turned, and searched the sky. He saw Aris plummeting toward him, smiled, and tipped his hat. Ah, it was a trap, then. Aris followed him into the alley, anyway. Bowler Hat had no idea who was truly following him. The man may have been polluted with vampire blood, making him inhumanly fast, but he was still not fast enough to outrun flight.

Aris climbed higher, waited for his moment—a long, straight alley—then dove again. He shimmered, but not into the human-appearing form Gwen and the children were familiar with. No, this was who Aris really was: this darkness, this *monster*. This was who Lia and King knew as the Raven.

Who he pretended not to be so he could earn Gwen's love.

Four-inch-long claws hit Bowler Hat in the back full force and bore him to the ground. They plowed into the cobbles hard enough to break bones, bouncing off the stone until fetching up hard against the brick building at the end of the lane. Aris trapped the man's wrists before he reached for a weapon.

He spun the body until he was sitting on Bowler Hat's chest, then broke both of the man's arms at the elbow, twisting until they lay at opposing angles. He screamed, a sharp counterpoint to the ringing in Aris's ears.

"You will tell me who you work for and why you killed my...why you killed her. If you do, I will end this quickly. Not fast enough for you, I would imagine, but it is a concession I am willing to make." He leaned down until the scent of the man's fear filled his nostrils, and said in the low, growling voice of the Raven, "If you do not, I will make it slow, and I will enjoy it."

"I am not afraid of you, faerie," Bowler Hat sneered through the pain. He probably thought he would live long enough to heal. Fool.

Aris leaned down and said, with one clawed thumb, put out the man's right eye. "You should be."

The man screamed a high-pitched wail that was certain to bring spectators, so he had little time to finish. He flared his enormous wings to hide himself and held the man's face between his monstrous hands to position his left thumb over the remaining eye.

"You can still speak with no eyes. After this, I will tear off your arms and watch you bleed out. Who do you work for?"

Aris?

Her voice wrenched his mind away from the monster and back to the dirty cobbles of New London. A shockwave of pain rocked him. *Gwen?*

Who knew being shot—would hurt so much? God's breath, Aris...I'm...

Her mental voice faded away. He had no time to finish this job properly. He would simply tear the man's head off and be done with it.

But BowlerHat managed another smile and said in a voice weak with pain, "Long live the king."

Aris twisted his arms, ignoring the wet crunch, and left the head lying next to the body. He ripped the embroidery off the man's lapel, stuffed it into his pocket, and leaped into the sky.

He shifted, tucking the monster safely away, and beat his raven's wings furiously until he was out of breath and every muscle hurt.

Gwen was still alive, and she needed him.

THE END

To read the free epilogue, follow the author on Ream or subscribe for exclusive content at https://reamstories.com/nic olemckeon

27

Also By

OTHER TITLES BY THIS AUTHOR INCLUDE

SERIES: The Gwen St. James Affair

Vanished

Eccentric social outcast Lady Gwenevere St. James knows many secret things: magic, alchemy, artifice, and even the truth about the long-forgotten faeries. But she does not know why common criminals are using rare and dangerous magic to kidnap orphans from the streets of New London.

After rescuing one young girl, Gwen vows to save the rest, no matter the cost. But the handsome Inspector of Scotland Yard is also investigating the case, and he thinks Gwen knows far too much about the kidnappings to be innocent.

To save the children, Gwen must dodge the Inspector, bully a coven of witches, and outsmart her marriage-minded Mama, all while managing a wily young pickpocket and a headstrong raven. But an unexpected secret hides at the center of the mystery, one that will force her to confront the most painful event from her past, and possibly sacrifice her future.

Moonstruck

Gwenevere St. James may be a lady, but she's never been interested in playing by the rules. Instead of ingratiating herself into high society, she spent a decade searching the world and studying the occult for a way to find her lost twin sister.

So when a coven of witches offers her a missing person's case in return for a book of spells guaranteed to locate her twin at last, Gwen cannot refuse, even if it means doing something she swore she would never do: attend a country party for the wealthy elite.

But the case is far more complicated and dangerous than she expected. Villagers whisper of ghostly riders in the night, and an unknown monster hunts the nearby forest, putting everyone in danger.

As people go missing and innocent bystanders die, Gwen must make a choice: how many lives will she risk for the thing she wants most?

Spellbound

After years of searching, Lady Gwen finally has a chance to find her missing sister and heal her wounded heart. All she must do is work a dangerous spell that punches a hole through the wall separating the mortal world from the Sunset Lands.

Before Gwen can decipher the spell, she discovers her youngest ward, Sam, is tangled up with the murderous leader of New London's criminal underground. With no other options, she makes a thieve's bargain: Sam's freedom in exchange for a high-profile burglary.

But honoring her word has unintended consequences and exposes a conspiracy that endangers everyone she cares about. With a corrupt system on one side and the Cutthroat King on the other, Gwen must walk a knife's edge to get out alive.

Can she protect her new family and bring her sister home, or will the bargain cost more than she can pay?

SERIES: The Eververse Chronicles

The Founding Trilogy

The Laws of Founding

Legends and fairytales aren't all they're cracked up to be; especially when they're trying to kill you.

Since losing her father, Allie Chapter has stumbled through life, using friends, books, and alcohol to numb the pain. When she wakes up in the wrong world and gets kidnapped by supernatural forces, everything changes. Allie learns she is a Walker, blessed–or cursed–with the power to travel between different versions of Earth.

Allie must rely on Ronan, her devastatingly handsome mentor, to guide her through magical worlds she's only dreamed of, and teach her the Laws that govern all Walkers–Laws she must not break at any cost.

But a failed assassination attempt turns her dream into a nightmare. The Eververse is full of danger, and whoever wants her dead may also be behind her father's accident. As she searches for answers, Allie must decide what makes breaking the Laws worthwhile: love, or revenge?

But when she learns she is a Walker, one of the rare few with the ability to travel between different versions of Earth, an entirely new problem arises: can she master her powers fast enough to figure out why someone wants her dead?

The Founding Lie

The monsters we face aren't always the ones we expect.

As the newest member of the interdimensional police force, it's Allie Chapter's responsibility to find out who is stealing magical weapons and bring them to justice before war breaks out.

She's certain the thief is Goll MacMorna, the man who still haunts her nightmares, and she intends to prove it...no matter the cost.

She will either free herself from her nightmares or discover the real monster is the one in the mirror.

The Founding War

"Necessity knows no cruelty. She only makes demands, and we answer as seems best to us."

Allie Chapter went from aimless college student to interdimensional cop in less than a year. Now she's an outlaw, hunted by both sides of an oncoming war that threatens to destroy the Eververse. As her newly discovered magic grows in strength, Allie realizes she might be the only one who can stop the war and save countless innocent lives from obliteration. But her allies have betrayed her, and powers too large to comprehend are manipulating the battlefield, hoping to use her gifts for their own purposes. With no one left to trust, Allie must rely on her wits and her conscience to make the ultimate decision: sacrifice her future–and maybe her life–for the greater good, or save the people she loves and let the Eververse fall.

Acknowledgements

A special thank you to Katherine Roberts, Teralyn Davis, Sandy Eichner, and Marie Wikle. Your support has meant so much to me, and I cannot thank you enough! This journey can often be a lonely one, and walking this road is so much easier and more fulfilling with fellow travelers at my side.

And to my amazing editor, Abbie Lynn Smith: I love you to pieces.

www.ingramcontent.com/pod-product-compliance
Lightning Source LLC
Chambersburg PA
CBHW031059030726
47496CB00002BA/293